P9-BZZ-589

THE SECOND ASSISTANT

THE SECOND ASSISTANT

A Tale from the Bottom of the Hollywood Ladder

CLARE NAYLOR

AND

MIMI HARE

VIKING

VIKING
Published by the Penguin Group
Penguin Group (USA) Inc., 375 Hudson Street, New York, New York 10014, U.S.A.
Penguin Books Ltd, 80 Strand, London WC2R 0RL, England
Penguin Books Australia Ltd, 250 Camberwell Road, Camberwell, Victoria 3124, Australia
Penguin Books Canada Ltd, 10 Alcorn Avenue, Toronto, Ontario, Canada M4V 3B2
Penguin Books India (P) Ltd, 11 Community Centre, Panchsheel Park, New Delhi – 110 017, India
Penguin Books (NZ), Cnr Airborne and Rosedale Roads, Albany, Auckland 1310, New Zealand
Penguin Books (South Africa) (Pty) Ltd, 24 Sturdee Avenue, Rosebank, Johannesburg 2196, South Africa

Penguin Books Ltd, Registered Offices: 80 Strand, London WC2R 0RL, England

First published in 2004 by Viking Penguin, a member of Penguin Group (USA) Inc.

10 9 8 7 6 5 4 3 2 1

LIBRARY OF CONGRESS CATALOGING-IN-PUBLICATION DATA
Naylor, Clare, 1971–
The second assistant : a tale from the bottom of the Hollywood ladder / Clare Naylor and Mimi Hare.
p. cm.
ISBN 0-670-03307-3
1. Hollywood (Los Angeles, Calif.)—Fiction. 2. Motion picture industry—Fiction. 3. Theatrical agents—Fiction. 4. Young women—Fiction. I. Hare, Mimi. II. Title.
PS3614.A95S43 2004
823'.914—dc22 2003066586

This book is printed on acid-free paper. ♾

Printed in the United States of America • Designed by Nancy Resnick

To our parents

THE SECOND ASSISTANT

PROLOGUE

If you close your eyes, you will hear the tap-tap of an actress's Christian Louboutin scarlet soles as she trips lightly across the marble floor of the atrium, having just inked the deal of her life. If you open them, you will see, flooding through the vast windows, a light so brilliant that you will reach into your purse for your sunglasses and then quickly shove them back when you realize that they are this season's Gucci. Not next season's. Unless you are employed as an assistant to Cameron Diaz, in which case she'll have tossed you her free pair across the room as she rummaged through the piles of goodies that every PR on the planet has sent in the desperate hope of getting some face cream or ugly jeans associated with her.

Then, when your eyes are accustomed to the light, you'll realize that you are in the hallowed portals of The Agency, arguably the most important place in Hollywood. You will see the Jackson Pollocks on the wall in front of you, which are bigger than your entire apartment, and you will sit on the same leather sofa that Tom Cruise once slipped nervously around on when Top Gun was just a glint in his accountant's eye. And if you choose to stay, if you decide to take their offer of a job as second assistant to the hottest young agent in Hollywood, your life will never be the same again.

At least that's how it was for me.

Stand inside the mirrored elevator and the lingering scent of Must de Cartier barely masks the more potent whiff of serious money. Aside from the obviously stratospheric paychecks negotiated by The Agency, I would say that a fair amount of that wealth lies in shoes. And I just don't mean the actress's kitten heels.

There are also the Manolos that, elsewhere in this building, are kicked off under desks, nervously jiggled on the end of thrice-weekly-pedicured toes during meetings, or, heaven forbid, scuffed at the end of a pair of glorious, glossy, kneeling legs in the name of career advancement as their owner blows her boss exactly the way he likes it. Or, with a nod to sexual equality, the boss's shoes as she blows her handsome young assistant. Though in my experience the latter is a much less likely fate for a pair of Manolos.

And then there are the men's shoes. If you come from anywhere other than Milan or Hollywood, it won't have occurred to you that men die for Prada, too. But in this town they do. And Gucci. They especially drool for anything that comes from Europe and is hand-made. If you're ever at dinner with Hollywood Man and are at a loss for conversation, I'd suggest you start with his shoes. There will always be a story behind them. And it will save you discussing his issues with intimacy. Which might put you off your foie gras three ways. A Spago specialty that nothing should be allowed to spoil.

The parking lot of The Agency is another place where rare and beautiful things are to be unearthed, should you wish to risk both carbon-monoxide asphyxiation and the valets. Valets, as far as I'm concerned, are the most intimidating people in this whole town. Perhaps it's because I own a racing-green Honda Civic, but the thing I crave most, apart from world peace and the secret phone number for reservations at the Ivy, is the approval of one particular valet at the Peninsula. As I arrived for my first-ever business lunch, he looked at me as if I were something unpleasant that he'd just stepped in with bare feet. The day I rock up there in a car that makes him toss my keys jauntily in the air and smile as he settles into the driver's seat to park it is the day I can retire from this business. It's not that I'm as shallow as a puddle, you understand, only that when in Rome you don't want to feel like the fat tourist who just dropped a gelato down his Chicago Bulls sweatshirt.

Anyway, I'll save that for therapy. Back to the parking lot. It's a subterranean affair, probably not dissimilar to the lower regions of hell, and it houses some of the most desirable automobiles on the face of God's earth. All in black. In Hollywood black is always the new black. Even hearts, like Seven Series BMWs, rarely come in any other color. Now, I'm not good with cars, so I can't regale you with a list of names sexy enough to pitch any man's tent, but I will tell you that in this parking lot there are prancing horses and checkered black-and-yellow shields and silver peace-style insignia galore. There are also hubcaps beautiful enough to persuade almost any man in this building to sell his grandmother down the river at a discounted price. But that's pretty much the job description of an agent anyway.

And as for secrets: The walls of The Agency have heard stories that would make an avaricious journalist rich beyond the dreams of Rupert Murdoch. The phones burn with firsthand news of who's doing what, to whom, taking what, wearing whom, or not. And the discreet shoulders of The Agency staffers take their secrets to the grave. Unless a publishing deal comes along first. Though usually this means renouncing summers with the Spielies in the Hamptons, so discretion invariably remains the order of the day.

Welcome, then, to Hollywood's premier talent agency, whose clients include everyone you've never met even though you know who they're sleeping with; to an industry where anything goes, as long as it's dysfunctional; in a town where the only indigenous species are cactus and coyote. Whatever else flourishes here is by definition a freak of nature. Welcome, in other words, to my world.

1

All you need to start an asylum is an empty room and the right kind of people.

—Eugene Pallette as Alexander Bullock
My Man Godfrey

"Your job will be to separate the white thumbtacks from the colored ones. Be sure to throw the colored ones away. They must leave the building. If they don't, then *you* will. The president, Daniel Rosen, likes only white thumbtacks at The Agency. Also, should you ever serve him a drink, he has just four ice cubes in his Diet Coke. If you put in more, he will throw the surplus ice cubes at you. If you put in three, he'll throw the entire drink at you."

This was honestly my first task in Hollywood. And I know it's not normal. I knew then that it wasn't normal. But as anyone who's ever been involved in an abusive relationship will tell you, it's a process of erosion. It's not as though the guy just thumps you in the face on your first date. Oh, no, it's a more subtle, undermining, mind-fuck of a process than that. It starts with the little things that you let slide because they hardly seem worth making a fuss over. But somehow it culminates with you believing that black is white, right is wrong, and eventually your entire universe is topsy-turvy, ass over tits, and the lunatics have taken over the asylum.

My abusive relationship with Hollywood started not with a kiss but a thumbtack. There are other things that I know are not normal but, since I became involved with Hollywood, I now cease to bat an eyelid at. They are:

1. Men who wear mascara in between eyelash dyes.
2. The sign in the bathroom of my office that says "Smoking and Vomiting Prohibited."
3. Kabala water that retails at $126 a bottle.
4. Men who take you to the Beverly Hills Gun Club on a first date.
5. Women who take fertility drugs even though they don't have a boyfriend.
6. Promises Rehabilitation Centre in Malibu, which runs an Equine-Assisted Therapy Program for recovering addicts because "horses have no agenda or ego and respond to contact rather than titles, status or celebrity." (www.promisesmalibu.com. I kid you not.)
7. Men who ask you not to sue them after they kiss you.
8. Actors. Of both sexes.

"Okay, that shouldn't take me too long." I smiled and sat down at my desk, keen to make a good impression by the efficient sorting of the thumbtacks. It was my first day at The Agency. My first day as second assistant to Scott Wagner, Hollywood agent extraordinaire. And even though a career in Hollywood hadn't always been my life ambition, I was determined to put my heart and soul into it. Perhaps stay a few years, see some of my favorite novels turned into lavish, Academy Award–winning movies, and then return to the East Coast with a like-minded husband and a suntan.

I was born and, bar the occasional summer vacation in Europe and Florida, had spent my entire life in Rockville, Maryland, a suburb of Washington, D.C. As far as I remember, I'd always planned on doing something vaguely worthwhile with my life. At four I was going to be an astronaut. Then the *Challenger* shuttle blew up, and I began to dream of a more earthbound career in medicine. I became an expert with a plastic stethoscope, and every member of my family received the lifesaving Kool-Aid vaccination. But the genes will out, and as my parents had always been involved in government and served in soup kitchens every Thanksgiving, I eventually followed the yellow-brick path of least resistance into politics.

I graduated summa cum laude from Georgetown. Double major: economics and political science. And then, after a seemingly endless round of interviews, was offered a job with Congressman Edmunds. I loved politics. I loved being part of a team. I would happily stay in the office past midnight photocopying flyers, I pumped helium into balloons, I fetched coffee, I avidly read everything from the *Washington Post* to the *Nation,* and I looked forward to the day I would be able to go to work on a public-waste bill or launch a petition on behalf of refugees. I didn't have time for a meaningful relationship, and I'd never had my hair highlighted.

But when Congressman Edmunds's campaign collapsed because of dubious fund-raising practices, I found myself out on a limb. I didn't want to take an internship and would rather have eaten my mother in a pie than accept the vacancy I'd been promised working for a Republican senator with a pending murder charge. Though with crippling student loans, my options seemed bleak. That was until I discovered the dog-eared business card of Daniel Rosen in my jacket pocket. He had pressed it on me at a fund-raiser a few weeks before. Had I known then that this onetime member of the Young Turks, the Hollywood band of hell-raising superagents, now president of The Agency, was the nearest thing to the Second Coming in Los Angeles, I might have behaved differently. But as with all things Hollywood, at that time I had no clue. All I knew was that this man had offered me a job, and I was desperate enough to follow up on the offer.

Daniel Rosen had stood by a tray of chicken satay and pensively stroked his Hermès tie as he tried to convince me that my political aptitude would be an asset in the entertainment industry. He said that Hollywood was always in need of bright young minds, and while he didn't exactly promise that I'd be running a studio within a year, he did hint that I might soon be influencing the morals and minds of the entire planet. Political power was nothing compared to Hollywood power, he informed me. After all, how many Democrats can get as many butts in seats as the new Vin Diesel movie can, huh? How many world leaders can make $104 million in a weekend? I smiled politely and was about to shake his hand and tell him thanks but no thanks when he spied Kevin Spacey by the poached salmon, so I never actually got the chance.

Which was about the only stroke of luck I'd had that month. When I eventually called, his assistant had set me up with an interview with the head of Human Resources at The Agency. In preparation I had gone to Blockbuster and rented every movie that I've ever been castigated for not having seen, from *Taxi Driver* to *The Godfather,* and *Antz* for good measure. Then I'd maxed out my credit card and flown to Los Angeles. Even though my interviewer never asked me about movies—only my typing speed and whether I had a history of mental illness—I was hired.

Back in Rockville I packed my suitcase for the migration and read an unauthorized biography of Steven Spielberg. I ignored my dad's chuckle as he handed me a giant canister of bear mace and told me that when God made America, all the loose marbles had rolled down to Los Angeles.

Now, on my first day at work, as I sucked my bleeding fingers, I received news of my next task.

"When you're done with the thumbtacks I'll run through a call sheet with you."

"Great." I smiled my newly minted new-girl smile. My insouciance was touching. Little did I know that for the next six months of my life, this seemingly innocuous list of names and telephone numbers would prove more puzzling to me than Antonio Gramsci's theories on hegemony and cause me more sleepless nights than the threat of nuclear war ever had.

The person navigating me through this foreign, and dangerous, terrain was Lara Brooks. She had cropped red hair, a black pantsuit, and an expression on her face that perpetually resembled that of a nun forced to give a blow job. As Scott's assistant, she was my immediate boss. But just as she was about to regale me with the intricacies of the call sheet, we were interrupted by a gothically thin, poker-haired woman who emerged from behind a glass door,

"Where's Scott?" she snapped.

"He's in Switzerland getting his blood swapped with Keith Richards's 'cause his is cleaner." Lara replied, deadpan.

"No, seriously." The woman didn't appear to be in the mood for frivolity. Ever.

"Marketing meeting at Dreamworks."

"Asshole." The woman vanished back behind a closed door and silence settled over the room.

"So what's Scott actually like?" I asked. Because I'd been interviewed by someone in Human Resources, I had never actually met my new boss. I imagined him as quite suave, quietly intelligent, and softly spoken. But with edge. I wasn't naïve enough to imagine that any agent in the entertainment industry would be a complete pussycat. But neither was I prepared for Lara's eviscerating character analysis.

"Scott is an undereducated, in-over-his-head, coke-snorting, X-taking, Vicodin-popping junkie. He has platinum memberships to every strip club in L.A. and dresses like a gas-station attendant. My job is to keep him solvent and out of rehab."

"I see."

"Your job is to support me in that role. That is why you went to college, isn't it?"

"Er . . ." I stammered, unsure of exactly what I was supposed to say here.

"Well, I'm assuming it's always been your ambition to nursemaid a guy who in any other town but here would be asking, 'Would you like me to supersize that shake for you?' Am I right?" I caught a sarcastic glint in her green eyes and laughed. Lara wasn't a bitch, she just hated everyone and everything in Hollywood without discrimination. But at least she had a sense of humor. Black, naturally.

"Don't worry." She looked me bang in the eye. "Therapy's included in the health-care package."

As it turned out, I didn't have to wait as long as I'd anticipated to meet my new boss. Seconds later the office door crashed open, and a man of medium height, wearing combat pants and a khaki sweater that wouldn't have looked out of place on a teenage skateboarder, marched toward the desk where Lara and I were working.

"Lara?" His voice reverberated off the office walls. His black, spiky hair looked young, but the lines around his slightly bloodshot eyes hinted that Lara's brutal assessment hadn't been too far wide of the mark. He was probably a well-partied thirty-four years old.

"Scott?" she replied, without a hint of submissiveness or even trepidation. If someone had yelled my name out like that, I'd have buckled at the knees. Lara merely looked bored.

"Wassup." This was spoken as an order, not a question.

"Messages." Lara held out a limp arm, and Scott took his call sheet.

"Yup." He strode by, heading for the heavy maple door of what I assumed was his office, though it had no name on it, only a Lakers sticker.

"And this is Elizabeth, your new second assistant."

"Sure." Scott seemed not to notice me and scanned the sheets of paper in his hand before pausing dramatically. "Ashton called?"

"He's on location in Hawaii."

"Get him on for me." Scott ignored the fact that I was now standing up, awaiting my formal introduction to him. Ready to curtsy if necessary. Hell, ready to let blood if necessary.

"I'll try." Lara shrugged without much optimism. "Oh, and hey, Scott?" He looked up at her quizzically as she motioned to me. "This is Elizabeth."

"Oh, sure, sure." Suddenly a light switched on in his brain, and the full wattage of his gaze fell upon me. I smiled politely and held out my hand to meet his enthusiastic shake. "Elizabeth. It is. Great. To meet you."

"Oh, you, too, Mr. Wagner. You, too. Well, I'll just be here if you need me. . . ."

"So where are you from, Elizabeth?" Scott asked as I anticipated golden days ahead, basking in the warmth of my new boss's appreciation and admiration, not to mention the tutelage of one of the most famous agents in town. He was a good-looking, young, cool guy. This was going to be a fun job. Cocktails, premieres, movie stars . . . well, didn't Ashton have to be *that* Ashton?

"Rockville, Maryland. It's a suburb of D.C., actually. I worked for Senator Edmunds for a year until his campaign—"

"Wow, you worked in politics?"

"Yes, I did."

"Incredible. You must be one smart chiquita."

"Well, I'm not sure about that, but I'll certainly try my best and—"

But suddenly the light went out. Scott had looked down. Only for about .003 of a second but nonetheless it was enough. He was gone.

"Reese called?" He was scowling at his call sheet. I was as distant a memory as his first day at kindergarten. "Why in hell's name didn't you tell me before now? Jesus Christ, Lara. Reese called and you didn't tell me?"

"You told me not to put any calls through."

"It was Reese, for fuck's sake."

"You said tell everyone you were in the elevator."

"Christ, Lara." Scott stomped into his office and collapsed behind his desk. "Get her for me now. *Now.*"

And that was that. In actual fact that was probably the longest conversation I ever had with Scott. Another distinguishing feature of the inhabitants of Hollywood is that their attention spans are no longer than a very fast, witty pitch for a movie. Which is about two and a half minutes. And that is only if the pitch has million-plus legs. Anything under that price tag and you lose them at hello.

2

I'd hate to take a bite of you. You're a cookie full of arsenic.

—Burt Lancaster as J. J. Hunsecker
The Sweet Smell of Success

My floor at The Agency resembled a battery hen factory; it consisted of about twenty neat little squares of desk. Each one featured:

- An assistant in his/her early twenties, clad in regulation black with a face that would probably crack if it smiled. Though nobody had ever tested this theory.
- An iMAC. Bright, white, luscious, and triffidlike, with a screensaver featuring a life-affirming statement in a foreign or ancient language—i.e., *Plus est en vous* or *Carpe diem.* Most assistants had been to NYU film school or majored in literature at an Ivy League college, and this was their only opportunity to exhibit their $100K education.
- A can of some diet soft drink.
- A framed poster hailing a piece-of-genius movie, the likes of which hasn't been made for at least fifty years, often starring Jack Lemmon or Audrey Hepburn.
- A blister pack of Advil or, for the more hard core, a silver Tiffany pillbox containing Valium.

All of these details were virtually obscured by vertiginous piles of scripts bound with glossy black endpapers bearing the legend THE AGENCY, in gold letters. These were stacked up on every available surface, every square of carpet tile, and often in the hands of an overburdened, buckling teenage intern on the way to the copy room. Each had a title in wonky black felt-tip lettering scribbled on the spine. Nobody had ever heard of any of these movies. In time I learned that unless Julia Roberts fell in love with one of them, nobody ever would.

It was late Friday afternoon of my very first week, and I had just put a call from the president of Universal Studios through to the mailroom instead of to Scott. Thankfully Scott didn't notice, because he was watching the trailer for one of his client's new movies in his office and laughing uproariously.

"Hey, you guys, get in here. Check this out," he yelled. His door was open, so Lara and I took off our phone headsets and shuffled into his office. We perched on the arms of his leather sofa.

"Isn't it the fucking best?" Scott hit the play button on his remote control and spun around delightedly in his chair. Lara and I watched the trailer.

It wasn't the best. It was the worst. But it starred one of Scott's biggest clients, who had just been on the diet of the century. She actually looked great on the multiplex-size plasma screen on his office wall. Though when she'd walked into the office a couple of days ago, trailing her stylist and half a dozen Barneys bags, you could see the bones on her shoulders through her sweater, and her face was covered in all those little blond hairs that anorexics sprout.

"Joined the 'rexy files." Lara had rolled her eyes heavenward.

"But she looks like a total rock star," Talitha, another of the assistants had sighed enviously.

Scott rewound the tape and paused it at a part where the actress was doing push-ups in a tank top.

"Great, huh?" he marveled again but didn't really pay much attention when I said, "Yeah, I think it looks like a lot of fun. I'm sure it'll do great box office. She's so bankable." I'd been reading what were popularly known as "the trades"—those movie-industry rags *Variety* and the *Hollywood Reporter*—that land on every single desk in this town each morning of the week and detail Hollywood's every breath, from photos of heavy hitters at premieres to domestic box-office profits. Consequently I had picked up moviespeak almost as quickly as I'd mastered the art of wearing black.

"Look at her rack." Scott slapped his thigh. "Lara, go get her on for me." I followed Lara back out toward our desks. Though just as I was about to sit down and update the call sheet, my phone rang.

"Is this Elizabeth?" A woman's voice inquired.

"Speaking."

"This is Victoria."

"Victoria?" Who the hell was Victoria? Was she the new Angelina or Uma, who required no last name, and I hadn't yet read about her in the trades?

"Elizabeth, I've been watching you." Oh, hey, I thought, my first stalker. But typical—it's a woman.

"You have?"

"I'd like you to come into my office."

"Okay, well . . ."

"Preferably now." And she hung up.

I sat at my desk for a moment and looked around me for clues. All the other assistants had their heads down, bent as if at prayer. Lara was listening in on a call as Scott told the shrunken actress how *fucking* fabulous her movie looked. One of the millions of things I still had to get used to in this job was the listening in on phone conversations. It betrayed all my polite instincts, and I was usually so embarrassed that I forgot I was supposed to be making notes of script titles, actors' names, restaurant details, and the like, so that Scott could read *Hustler* and pick his nose safe in the knowledge that he didn't have to remember a thing.

Lara was chewing her pen and smiling to herself as she eavesdropped. Scott had his feet up on the desk and was watching MTV as he chatted to the actress. But nowhere could I see a Victoria. I leaned over to ask Talitha, whose desk was next to mine.

"Hey, Talitha, am I supposed to know who Victoria is?"

"Victoria?"

"Yeah, she just called me up and asked me to go into her office, only I have no clue who she is or where her office is."

"That figures."

"It does?" I wondered which part figured, Victoria's calling or clueless me.

"Victoria's office is over there." She pointed to the door across the corridor where the poker-haired woman had emerged from on my first day.

"Oh, her." I stood up and smoothed down the wrinkles in my pants. "Okay. Thanks."

"You won't be thanking me later. That's for sure," Talitha said ominously.

"Elizabeth, take a seat." The woman smiled, revealing a row of small, even teeth behind her thin lips. She was wearing Saint Laurent, but it might as well have been Talbots it was so creased and baggy.

"Thanks." I sat down on the very, very edge of an armchair and glanced surreptitiously around her office. The sparse furnishings were rendered even less friendly by a series of miserable nudes that graced the walls.

"Lucien Freud. I love him," she informed me as she poured herself a glass of prune juice.

"Want some?" she proffered.

"I'm fine, thanks." Anxiety was all the laxative I needed right now. "They're . . . very impressive, your pictures."

"I don't like anything too colorful. Except perhaps for my little friends." It was then that I clocked a trophy cabinet filled with Barbie dolls. Summer Vacation Barbie. Winter Gala Barbie. Olympic Games Barbie. There was more nylon hair on those shelves than on Ben Affleck's head. (If the rumors were to be believed, and Lara had it on good authority from an assistant at Disney that his tresses were faux as faux can be.)

"Ooh, you collect Barbies?" I displayed my teeth, but it could hardly be considered a smile.

"They keep me sane," Victoria informed me, oblivious to the irony of this comment. "So how do you like your new job?"

"Oh, it's great," I replied enthusiastically.

"I see. Then you're happy to just answer phones and fetch coffee for the rest of your life, are you?"

"Well, no. I mean, I'll use my time here to learn the basics of what I'm sure will be a fascinating career," I fudged quickly.

"Oh, so you think that you're too good for us? You'll be on to the bigger, better deal as soon as you can?" she spat witheringly. She was clearly bipolar. Or merely a good old-fashioned lunatic.

"I'm . . . well . . . I'd like to . . ."

"So do you want to learn or not?" Victoria snapped.

"I'd love to learn." She couldn't argue with that. Could she?

"What's your favorite movie?"

"La Dolce Vita." I lied because I couldn't tell her it was *Meet the Parents*.

"Pinnacle of your ambition?"

"To see *Crime and Punishment* made into a movie."

"Starring?"

"John Malkovich." Again untrue. It was Jude Law.

Victoria paused for a moment, looked at my shoes, and took another sip of prune juice.

"I'd like to take you under my wing and teach you what I know. I've been in this business many years now, and you can learn from me."

"Thank you so much, Victoria. I'm honored."

"Great. Well, you'd better get back to your desk. I'll clear this all with Scott, but I'm sure it'll be fine. It's a wonderful opportunity. See it as a fast track to success." She folded her hands together, and I took this as my cue to leave.

"Oh, and by the way, there's a 'Barbies of the Seventies' auction at Sotheby's on Monday. I'd like you to go along and bid on a few pieces for me. I have a ten-thirty with Nic, or I'd go myself."

"Sure. Sounds fun."

"Good. I'll let you have the catalog later. Oh, and I have some dry cleaning that I'll need picked up this afternoon. Here's the ticket. Hollyway Cleaners. It's just off Santa Monica, shouldn't take you more than twenty minutes if you go at lunchtime." She handed me a blue ticket.

"Right, okay. Well, thanks again, Victoria." I edged my way backward across the room and out the door, my smile petrified on my face. When I closed the door behind me, I saw the twenty faces of the assistants stare up at me. And then hastily look down again. Burying themselves in their call sheets.

The only person who didn't look down was Lara. Instead she motioned me over to her desk.

"Did Victoria ask if she could mentor you?" she asked, frowning.

"Yeah, she seems . . . well, she seems nice. Enough."

"Elizabeth, what are you doing after work?"

"Nothing. Actually, I'm going to look at a couple of apartments. I haven't found anywhere to live yet, and I'm still staying out in the Valley with my aunt, but—"

"We need to talk. I'll take you for a cocktail and explain a few things to you. Okay?"

"Okay," I agreed, an uneasy feeling settling in the pit of my stomach. "Thanks."

Words that I have never liked very much: *We need to talk.*

My first Hollywood cocktail was in the Polo Lounge of the Beverly Hills Hotel. The peaceful palm-tree wallpaper and lowered voices softened by the tinkling piano music relaxed my frayed nerves. My afternoon had been further pissed upon from a great height because Victoria's dry cleaning had turned out not to have been hand-finished and Scott had left his stash in the bathroom at the Standard last night and asked me to go retrieve it while he underwent cold turkey on his office sofa. Lara had plied him with black coffee while I dashed to the bar and scrambled among condom wrappers on the floor of the men's room hunting for the remnants of an eight ball. It had turned up behind a dusty, God-only-knew-what-covered pipe leading to the urinals. And I was supposed to be thrilled.

I sipped my cocktail as Lara leaned back in her chair and ran her fingers through her shiny red hair. Out of the office, and in Seven jeans instead of her terrifyingly tailored jacket and a pen in her hand, she had the cool, edgy look of a top model. In fact, she looked pretty gorgeous, and at least three men in the room were circling our table and staring at her as though she were the proverbial long drink of water. One was really cute, too. He looked like Johnny Depp at twenty-six. But Lara seemed oblivious.

"This is a really fucked-up town," she began. "And the way I look at it is this: Who needs lovers in Hollywood when your friends will fuck you at the drop of a hat?"

"It can't be *that* bad, can it?" I smiled, thinking she was joking.

"No, it's much worse. I like you, Elizabeth. I think you're smart and you're probably a good person."

I shrugged my shoulders in a self-deprecating way.

"Which is why there are a few things you need to know."

"In that case, fire away." I took a large sip of my drink to disguise the fact that I wasn't altogether sure whether I wanted to hear what she had to say.

Lara cracked her knuckles and began. "The thing about this town is that it's a very insular place, and nobody gives a shit about anybody else. Armageddon could be looming on the horizon, and people here would just assume it was smog. Don't for a second think that anyone cares about global warming, world hunger, human-rights violations, or Third World debt." Lara skewered her cocktail onion very efficiently.

"I didn't really expect them to, though," I said. "I mean, it's entertainment, right? It's supposed to be fun."

"Oh, sure, superficiality isn't so much a condition as a requirement," Lara answered.

"Do you really hate it that much?" I asked, shocked by her vitriol.

"Yeah, I really do."

"Then why do you stay? I mean, surely there are a hundred other jobs you can do."

"I want to be a writer. This is a great place for contacts and learning what it takes. Though I'd never tell anybody at The Agency that, okay?"

"Sure."

"So Victoria wants to mentor you?"

"She said so. Does she say that to all the new girls?" I tried to make light of what seemed like my preferential treatment.

"No, but it's generally the kiss of death when she does."

"I see." I ordered another drink. "What is her position, by the way? Roughly."

"She's an agent. They keep her because she's got a couple of AAA-list clients who are really loyal to her."

"So she's powerful?"

"-Ish," Lara conceded. "But she's not a player or a partner. Scott is a partner. He's powerful."

"I see." I nodded.

"But don't worry too much about Victoria. She's just a very psychotic lady who's worked in this town for too long and doesn't get laid enough." Lara looked intently at me. "I'll keep an eye out for you. She won't mess with me."

"That's really kind of you." I nodded gratefully. If I only made it to my first paycheck at this rate, I'd be ecstatic.

"But there are some things that you have to take my advice on, Elizabeth." She was deadly serious. "And if you don't, you might as well leave this town now. Do not pass go, do not collect two hundred dollars."

"Okay," I nodded.

"I'm not kidding," she warned.

"I'm listening," I assured her.

"Always read the trades, and never date anybody in the business."

"That's it?" I asked. Thinking that if this were the case I was already Sherry Lansing manqué. Bring on my first Jil Sander suit.

"Yeah, but it's not as easy as it sounds. Which is why there are a few caveats. At least where the dating is concerned." Lara crossed her legs and rested her elbows on the table and told me The Rules of Sex and Dating in Hollywood, as stipulated by Lara Brooks. They were pretty much as follows:

1. Never sleep with your boss unless you have a good sexual-harassment lawyer on retainer.
2. If you're sleeping your way up the ladder, remember it's the ugly men who are the cruelest.
3. Be prepared to tell all the details of your sexual exploits to as many people as possible as soon after the event as possible. Because his version will be ten times worse.
4. Never give stock tips, script secrets, or movie ideas to your lover. He *will* steal them.
5. AA, NA, and SA are all good places to meet movie stars, producers, and directors if access is proving to be a problem.
6. In all reality, if you need to have sex, do it with the pool boy or craft-services guy on a movie set. You'll save yourself a lot of heartache.

As I waited for the valet to bring my car around I said good-bye to Lara. She pressed a business card into my hand and told me to call her friend Charlie, who had a lead on a studio apartment in Venice.

"I've got to rush to dinner," she said as our cars arrived.

"Anyone exciting?" I asked, thinking of the great dating possibilities that must be available in this town to someone as beautiful and cool as Lara. Even outside the business—barring producers and actors and studio heads and directors, et al.—there must be some very cute, eligible guys around.

"Ugh, yeah right." She rolled her eyes sarcastically. "I've got the date of the fucking decade."

"Oh, well, it might be fun, you never know. See you Monday."

"Later." She waved and pulled away. I watched the small man in the car behind Lara's struggle to climb up into his enormous SUV. Cars in L.A. were disproportionately huge and obviously symbolized power, ego, penis size, or zip code. I just couldn't quite work out which. I only knew that if I were his wife, I'd buy him crampons and a rope for Christmas to make the ascent easier. Then I got into my own car and followed Lara down the driveway from the hotel, wondering whether I'd be able to afford to drive a shiny, brand-new Range Rover like hers when I made it to first assistant.

3

I'm hard to get. All you have to do is ask.

—Lauren Bacall as Marie Browning
To Have and Have Not

The apartment in Venice that Lara's friend Charlie looked after turned out to be perfect for me. Granted it was only one room, with a kitchen somewhere to the left and a bathroom without a door to the right, but if you shoved your head out the window and twisted your shoulders, it had a view of the ocean. It also had the Spanish hardwood floors that I'd dreamed about since I got this job. And it was *almost* affordable on my pittance of a salary if I was prepared to eat out only one night every two weeks and do my own manicures. I was thrilled and immediately began moving my suitcases and boxes of books and the two pairs of shoes I owned over from the Valley.

The building was also inhabited by about a million other young people—assistants, gonnabe actors, scriptwriters, and an Ashtanga teacher in the room next door to me.

"Focus on the soft space between your anus and your sex organs," she was telling somebody in her room. I could hear this because we shared an air vent.

"That's harder than you think," a male voice came back.

"You'll get the hang of it," she assured him.

Once I'd unpacked most of my stuff, I realized that I was ravenously hungry. I grabbed my purse and the Dostoyevsky novel I one day planned to see adapted to the big screen and set out in pursuit of food.

I figured that I could at least afford a bagel or a bowl of pasta in some el cheapo café by the beach. I walked beneath the palm trees, past the basketball courts, the iron men of Venice crunching as if their lives depended on it, and at least a hundred cute, Rollerblading girls who could have been on a casting call for a Tampax commercial. I was about to take off my sandals and walk barefoot on the sand when I literally saw stars. Not, you understand, the Hollywood variety. Not a Brad or Jen in sight. No, I saw the sucker-punch kind of stars. I collapsed to the ground, and when I came to, a man with the bluest eyes and most handsome face I'd seen outside the Calvin Klein billboard that reigned over Sunset Boulevard was looking down at me, very, very concerned.

"It's okay, man, she's coming around," I heard him say.

"Thank fuck for that," another voice lolled in the background. "I'll get back to the game, then. You can take care of her. Just make sure she doesn't sue. It'd suck if we had to stop playing down here."

"Hey, are you with us? Can you hear me?" he asked me. I realized that my head was in this man's lap.

"I'm . . . sure . . . I'm just fine. . . ." As the seconds passed, I also noticed that I was lying on the gross, dog-pee asphalt, so I struggled to get up.

"Honey, I think you should just lie still for a few seconds."

I may have been unconscious, but I could tell that he was checking out my body. Giving my exposed legs the once-over. I made a lame attempt to pull my skirt down past my knees.

"I'm Jake, by the way. I was playing hockey with my buddies, and the puck hit you on the head," he informed me.

"I'm Lizzie."

"Well, Lizzie, I'm gonna help you up and take you to where you live so we can make sure you're okay." He smiled.

"Sure." I was aware of a stabbing pain in the side of my head and raised my hand to it, wondering if there was blood.

"It's not bleeding. Just kinda red," Jake reassured me. "Now, on three, I'm gonna stand you up. One. Two. Three."

He held my hand and pulled me to my feet. I managed a few woozy steps. As we passed the hockey court, a group of thuggy-looking frat boys began whooping delightedly.

"My buddies," he announced proudly.

I concentrated on putting one foot in front of the other. He had his arm through mine, guiding me like an old lady. I think that Jake was planning to take me to my apartment, jettison me off on a concerned girlfriend, and leave with a clear conscience to resume his hockey game. Unfortunately, when he saw that I didn't so much as have a sofa, let alone a girlfriend, he seemed to change his mind.

"Oh, no, I can't leave you here," he said as he surveyed my bare, minuscule room. "Jesus, this is like Raskolnikov's room!" He laughed.

"You've read *Crime and Punishment*?" I looked at him with new wonder. I was about to wave my novel in his face triumphantly, but then I realized that I must have left it back on the dog pee.

"Sure. You think everyone in California's a dumb-ass?" He laughed again.

"I have no clue. I'm new in town."

"Would never have guessed." He looked around the apartment for some sign of life or hope and, finding none, extracted his car keys from his pocket. "Which is why you're coming with me. Oh, and for the record. I *am* the only smart guy in this town." He laughed once more as he slammed the door on my room.

Two minutes later and common sense was a distant memory. I was in his Porsche, zipping up the Pacific Coast Highway with the wind blowing the parts of my hair that weren't plastered down with the Neosporin he'd borrowed from the Ashtanga teacher, whose name turned out to be Alexa and whose ability to sniff out a single man in a crisis was as finely honed as her pert little butt. Not that I cared about Alexa. Or anything. Jake could have been planning to strip me naked to star in a porno for all I knew. In fact, Jake could have done anything he wanted with me that day, because he was the best-looking man I'd seen in my entire life. He looked like a movie star. But tall.

"Where are we going, by the way?" I yelled to be heard over the thudding bass of "Still" by Dr. Dre.

"My place. I just think that we'd best keep you under observation." He kept looking at my legs, as if he'd hit them with a hockey puck, too, and was searching for bruises.

"I don't want to be any trouble," I mumbled. Not meaning it even slightly.

And that's how I came to spend one of the most blissful afternoons

I can remember. He drove me out to his house in Malibu. It was literally on the beach. You could jump off his deck and land in the sand. And he kept me under observation. Together Jake and I drank Coke and watched some of the World Series. We took a walk on the beach, he ordered takeout from Nobu, and every so often he'd touch the side of my head to make sure my brains weren't spilling out. We talked about everything from books to politics, but it was only later that I realized we hadn't discussed what either of us did for a living. I think possibly because I assumed from his perfect looks and seriously beautiful home that he was a very successful actor whom I'd never heard of. This was entirely possible since I barely ever went to the movies. So I simply didn't ask for fear of embarrassment and exposure.

When it finally got dark and the air out on the deck became damp, after we finished the last drops of red wine in our glasses he turned to me.

"So, hot stuff, I guess that you're not gonna die, then?"

"It doesn't look that way. Which is bad luck for you, 'cause it means you have to drive me home." I shrugged. Meaning, "You could ask me to stay, though." Clearly he wasn't fluent in Shrug.

"Oh, that's no problem. The traffic's not too bad at this time of night." He stood up and, offering me a hand, pulled me to my feet. And then, thank Christ—otherwise I'd have thought he was gay or I was too unattractive for words—he kissed me. If I hadn't gotten a hint of action in those movie-cliché surroundings—moon over the ocean, Trotanoy Pomerol '75 flowing in our veins, me with my fragile concussed pallor, and he with large hands—I would have had to go back to politics and grow my leg hair in preparation for a life of same-sex crushes and chastity. Instead the waves crashed and I didn't kick my empty wineglass over and it was a great, fabulous, spectacular kiss that made me forget my own name. Hurray for Hollywood, I thought. Not giving a flying fuck if this was *The Truman Show II* and I was the star.

"Morning." I walked into the office on Monday.

"Hey," Lara managed as she typed an e-mail. She was *le dernier cri* in her third new Marc Jacobs dress in a week. From whence? I wondered. As did everyone else in the office, judging by the looks on their faces. But who cared? Thanks to Winona, shoplifting your clothes had become almost as cool as knitting them yourself. "How was the apartment?" she asked.

"Oh, great. I took it."

"Cool. It's a great deal." She barely looked up.

"Yeah, though it's not like I spent much time there this weekend."

"Oh, well." Lara was back in work headspace, but I was desperate to tell somebody about my amazing day.

"I was up in Malibu at some guy's house," I persisted. And that got them. Not Lara, but the other assistants in my office, Talitha and Courtney.

Until this moment my fellow assistants had been almost entirely uninterested in me. They'd looked me up and down on my first day and pretty much ignored me since. Talitha had brown, sloe eyes and long, blond mermaid hair. Her midriff was permanently exposed in an array of jewel-colored, mind-blowingly expensive hippie clothes. She was the exception that proved the black-clad Hollywood rule. She was also staggeringly ignorant of anything that happened outside the Los Angeles city limits. Except for dating, and then she was interested, conversant, and very, very prepared to travel. Apparently her parents were both prestigious Hollywood writers, but you'd never have known it, and her only ambition seemed to be to have a romantic life as colorful as her Schiaparelli-pink skirt. Her boss was a permanently absent woman called Gigi whose back I'd only ever glimpsed being trailed by a small wheelie suitcase out of the door. She was always on location with some actress or other in London or Zagreb or Sydney. I did see her face once, though, when I went into her office to find a copy of a script that Victoria asked me to read. There, on her wall, above a long-dead plant was a six-by-four framed black-and-white studio photograph of the elusive Gigi laughing her surgically lifted ass off, her hair blowing gently in the wind machine with a bewildered Labrador trying his hardest to look frolicsome for the camera and his hysterical owner. Rumor had it that Gigi only took on clients who looked like her, with oversize lips, undersize nose, and parched blond locks. Or perhaps she had grown to look like her clients over the years. Nobody really remembered how the cloning had begun, but I'd stake my life that being a fly on the wall at a Christmas party for Gigi's client list would be a wild, freakish thing.

Still, it was perfect for Talitha to be a latchkey assistant because she was resourceful enough to spend her days on Friendster in search of her ideal studio executive.

Courtney, on the other hand, was sly, opportunistic, and deeply plain. Her appearance was only just saved from being irredeemably dull by a flock of freckles across her nose. For her, gossip was currency, and I imagined that it was not coincidence but evolution that was responsible for her long, twitching ears, which poked out through her flat, brown curtain of hair. She didn't miss a trick in the office, and I knew that somewhere she kept an extensive filing system documenting everyone's mistakes and shortcomings that she would not hesitate to use against them in a court of law or watercooler debate. She would slander, insinuate, and eye-roll her way to the top of the tree, and then she'd sit there for the next twenty years filing her nails and bitching about what everyone else was wearing. Whenever Courtney was around, I tried to make myself invisible to escape her hypercritical eye.

But when I mentioned my Malibu weekend to my fellow assistants, they were instantly like a pair of irresistible kittens purring all over me. And though I suddenly remembered Lara's lecture about not dating anyone in the business and realized that she might be furious with me if Jake did turn out to be an actor, there was no getting out of it. They were hooked.

"You were?"

"Yeah."

"Whose place?"

"Oh, some guy."

"Really? Who?"

"His name was Jake."

"Jake what?"

"You know, I don't really remember."

"You don't remember?"

"No."

"What did he drive?"

"Some little Porsche sport thing."

"What did his last name begin with? Think about it."

"I don't know. He didn't say."

"Weintraub? Thompson?"

"I don't think so."

"Was he cute?"

"Really cute."

"Cute like how? Like cheesy actor cute or rich and sexy cute?"

"Um, handsome. But smart."

"What does he do?"

"Well, I'm not entirely sure. But he was just so nice."

"You don't know what he does?"

"I didn't ask."

"What was his house like?"

"Nice. Cozy."

"Small?"

"Well, not huge but—"

"Where, exactly?"

"Carbon Beach, I think."

"On the beach? Or across the PCH?"

"Right on the beach."

"Wow."

Unfortunately, our stimulating chat was interrupted. The previously scarce Daniel Rosen, *El Presidente,* chose that moment to appear in the office doorway. Actually, he didn't arrive completely unannounced. He was preceded a few moments before by Aaron, a young assistant from across the hall, who walked by our desks and whispered loudly, "Daniel's coming down." At which point a hush fell over the room, feet were removed from desktops, and disdainful looks were replaced by Stepford-esque smiles. Seconds later Daniel appeared in the doorway, looking surprisingly imposing for a small man with a balding head.

"I want to know who is responsible," he boomed aggressively.

The battery farm of assistants looked up at him with unbridled fear etched across their faces. Even Victoria came out of her office and blinked in the light.

"Well . . . I'm waiting."

"Daniel. Is there a problem?" Victoria asked shakily.

"Some *idiot* put a call from Todd Lyons through to the mailroom on Friday afternoon."

"They did not."

"Yeah, Victoria, they did. And I want to know who is responsible."

"Was he okay?" Victoria looked more ashen than ever. "I mean, did you get him back from the mailroom?"

"He had to hang up. His assistant called me this morning and told me."

"Oh, my God, that's terrible!" Victoria shook her head gravely. I nearly threw up my breakfast.

Todd Lyons was the president of Universal, and *I* had been responsible for his having to speak to someone in the mailroom. To confess or not to confess? Daniel clearly didn't remember me at all from our encounter in Washington. In fact, he didn't so much as look in my direction. And just as I decided that I ought to tell the truth in case there were some way that the FBI could trace the lost Todd Lyons phone call back to me, Scott's office door opened and out he stepped.

"Hey, Daniel."

"Scottie, how's it hangin'?"

"Good man, yeah, good." Scott was furiously wiping his nose. "Hey, you hear about the deal we got for George last week? Fucking awesome, man."

"Yeah, I heard." Daniel made his way toward Scott, and after a bit of backslapping and knuckle punching, the door closed behind them and the color returned to my cheeks. And the assistant pool relaxed with an audible sigh of relief.

"Assholes," Victoria spit, and slammed her door.

Half an hour later, Daniel reappeared, followed closely by Scott.

"Lara?" Scott yelled without looking in Lara's direction.

"Yes?" She stood up, clearly on best behavior for Daniel.

"We're having a party."

"We abso-fucking-lutely are." Daniel nodded at Scott.

"Okay." Lara smiled politely.

"And I want you and . . ." Scott looked blank and clicked his fingers impatiently. "What's his name?"

"Ryan," offered Daniel.

"Thanks." He continued, "I want you and Daniel's assistant, Ryan, to take care of it."

"Great," Lara said perkily, through gritted teeth.

"Not just any party, mind you. This is going to be the party of the fucking millennium," Daniel chimed in. "Two hundred and fifty of the heaviest hitters in town. I want them all. I want food that they'll remember even in the advanced stages of Alzheimer's. I want women to give themselves hernias over what to wear. I want it on V Page but not

People. I want security to pack heat. I want Nicole but not Penelope. I want the most fuck-off Cubans for Jack and his buddies. I only want chicks who would make the cover of *Vogue*."

"Or *Sports Illustrated*," Scott interrupted hastily.

"Exactly. And I want it to be talked about after I'm dead."

"Just leave *that* with me," said Lara dryly.

"It's George's birthday. I want to give him the best party he's ever had. In fact, I tell you what. Let's make a statement here about how much we value George as a client and friend. Let's tell the world how much we love George." Daniel slapped Scott on the back. "Let's do it at my house."

"Genius. Fucking genius." Scott slapped him back. Lara went a deathly shade of white.

"If I do say so myself." Daniel nodded and strode back to the fourth floor with the seal of self-approval. I had been spared. For now at least. I would never transfer Todd Lyons to the mailroom again.

Later I caught Lara splashing cold water on her face in the bathroom, her lips practically blue.

"Have you any idea?" she hyperventilated. "Organizing a party in Daniel's house. With his Picassos and his Warhols and his precious Schnabels. Not to mention his floorboards that were reclaimed from a French railway station. And his bonsai collection that people will pour their margaritas into. And his pool they'll contaminate when they vomit in it. Or, heaven forbid, *swim* in it. It's like I've volunteered myself for lethal injection."

"It can't be that bad." I handed her a paper towel.

"The guy is an anally retentive control freak the likes of which even Dr. Freud could never have envisaged. Somebody once burned popcorn in a kitchen three floors below his office, and he had them fired because the smell upset him. Nobody on his floor is allowed to wear fragrance. Only unscented wash products. The labels on the soft drinks in the fridge have to face out. His girlfriend even has to ask him what she is allowed to wear when she visits Whole Foods."

"Jeez."

"On top of which, I have to organize this with Ryan, Daniel's sycophantic, slimeball assistant. I swear, Elizabeth, his head is so far up Daniel's ass that the guy doesn't need to get his colon checked twice a year like most men his age."

"That's really rough," I sympathized.

"That's not the rough part. Ryan and I have a blood feud. We hate one another's guts, and he's out to trip me up in any way he can possibly think of."

"How come?"

"I had a date with him once. I wouldn't sleep with him, so he came in the next day and told everyone that I was really a guy and I'd had a sex-change operation."

"He did not?" I laughed. Apart from her perfect, pretty face, Lara also had tits that had so patently *not* been inserted through a hole under her armpits.

"People believed him because they wanted to." Lara's eyes were narrow slits. "I tell you, Elizabeth, somebody is going to die over this party."

I walked back to my desk, trying to feel sorry for Lara and empathize with her pain, but I didn't really succeed. I was way too thrilled that I was going to get to go to a Hollywood party. Anything could happen. Jack could take me for a concubine. George could invite me to join him and a few girls in the master bathroom. Nicole could become my best friend.

"There's a message for you," Talitha said as I sat down. Courtney was looking at me out of the corner of her eye.

"Thanks." I pulled the sticky off my screen and read it.

Jake Hudson Called. 1-310-555-2121

"Perfect." I smiled to myself. I put the sticky in my purse, thinking I'd call him when I had some privacy.

"Are you planning to return that call?" Courtney asked.

"Oh, sure, when I get home."

"Why?" They both looked at me as if I'd gone mad.

"I didn't realize we were allowed to make personal calls from the office."

"Personal?" Talitha snickered.

"Jake was the guy I met this weekend."

"Shut up," Courtney said incredulously. "Jake Hudson?"

"Yeah, the Malibu guy. I suppose that must have been his last name.

I gave him my work number. And to be honest, I'm as surprised as you. I imagined I wouldn't hear from him until at least Thursday."

"You made out with Jake Hudson?" Courtney asked.

"Yeah." I shrugged. "Do you know him?" At which point they evaporated into a puddle of mirth.

"You did what?" Lara had appeared from nowhere and was now standing beside my desk. Her hair was still damp where she'd splashed her face, but her lips were no longer blue.

"I fooled around with a guy called Jake Hudson," I said, a little more quietly. There was clearly some problem here. "I'm not quite sure why everyone's so shocked. Who is he? Should I know him?" I was bemused.

"Jake Hudson?" Lara almost spit back at me.

"He was cute," I said sheepishly. But I wasn't going to be too apologetic—he was the best-looking man I'd kissed in my whole life, after all. Lara took in the scene, smug me surrounded by the wildly amused assistants, and rolled her eyes heavenward.

"Yeah, well, in which case, Elizabeth, you're on your own. You obviously didn't listen to a word I said on Friday night, and so I see no point in helping you any further. Good luck."

And with that she marched into Scott's office and slammed the door shut behind her. Leaving me in the doghouse and the dark as to who, even slightly, Jake Hudson was.

"Oh, and by the way"— she stuck her head out again—"*you* can organize the party with Ryan. Since you're clearly so fucking tight with the Hollywood Power 100."

4

How extravagant you are throwing away women like that. Someday they may be scarce.

—Claude Rains as Captain Louis Renault
Casablanca

Jake Hudson, as it turned out, was the president of Motion Pictures at a studio. And not simply any studio. A major motion-picture studio with the highest-performing box office of the year. Six number-one movies. With more Academy Award nominations than you can shake a stick at. He had also dated every single (and married) actress who'd ever graced the pages of *GQ* and rarely went out with a woman whose legs were shorter than forty-four inches. I ought to have been flattered to have kissed his lips, which it now seemed were statistically proven to be the most desirable in Hollywood. Instead I merely felt nauseous.

"Now, let's see," Talitha said thoughtfully as she pulled out a copy of The Agency's client list—a top secret cluster of pastel pink pages stapled together and in alphabetical order that detailed all our female clients. She ran her finger down the page and stopped every so often by the names of almost every major star in town to exclaim, "Oh, yes, he slept with her before she got her trout pout. Oh, and he was engaged to her. And he claimed to be just friends with her, but when the *Enquirer* said that Jake was dating her"—Talitha tapped her finger on the name of another insanely famous, gorgeous, albeit married actress—"then she came in the next day and blubbered on Scott's sofa so I think they were definitely fucking. Oh, and he's slept with supermodels galore. Though usually only the ones with major cosmetics contracts." Talitha put the list back in her drawer.

"Does he ever date normal women?" I asked, wondering if I'd misled Jake Hudson. I was sure that if he had any idea who I was—or, more precisely, who I wasn't—he wouldn't have added me to his tally. Which, as it stood, read like the contents page of the bumper summer issue of *InStyle* magazine. Had I perhaps erroneously led him to believe that my grandfather was Walt Disney? That my dad was president of the United States? That in some way, unfamous though I clearly was, I might actually have mattered in the grand, *Vanity Fair* scheme of things?

Talitha scrunched up her lips and nose and eyes in a way that someone had obviously once told her was cute, and finally proclaimed, "I don't think he's ever done normal. No."

"I see." I decided to let the subject drop.

It was lunchtime, and all the other assistants were in the kitchen down the hallway. Doubtless discussing how I could have fallen for such a libidinous love rat. Or, more likely, how he could have fallen for me. Whose purse nobody could source to the big five: Jacobs, Gucci, Balenciaga, Dior, or Prada in a pinch. Lara had popped out to Saks, and Scott was at lunch.

Talitha, who'd been dying to tell me all about Jake Hudson since my bombshell the previous day, took a spoonful of her soy dessert and continued. "But those are just the women he takes out in public. I guess there's a whole bunch that he only entertains at home. You know, the strippers and . . . well . . . girls like you."

"The ones he picks up off the sidewalk?" I asked grimly.

"Exactly, honey." She smiled sweetly. Obliviously.

"Thanks, Talitha."

I decided not to return Jake Hudson's call just yet. I sort of knew that he had only called to make sure that I was still alive and hadn't enlisted a lawyer to sue his frat-boy hockey team and prevent them from playing down at Venice ever again. And that particular reminder of my distinctly unexceptional status in life could wait. For now I had work to do, as back at my desk I found an e-mail from Ryan entitled "Tasks":

> Your tasks for George's party will be as follows. Please alert me as to the completion of each.

1. Security. At least 25 personnel. Dress code: black, no navy. Suits but no bow ties. Armed but with discretion. I suggest nothing above a KP512. No bull dykes. In fact, no women packing heat. This disturbs Daniel.
2. Beverages. Attempt to get sponsorship. Fax Piper-Heidsieck a guest list and tell them it's going to be covered by *People* magazine.
3. No press.
4. Food. Sushi. But only in The Zone.
5. Music. Norah. Robbie. Christina. Any client who will perform for free.
6. Flowers. White. Unscented. No pollen.
7. Oxygen to be pumped into party. And garden.
8. Cages with live birds. If endangered species are more colorful, then find a way.
9. Dancers from Crazy Girls on La Brea. Though only small-nippled girls. Daniel won't have large nipples in his home.
10. Invitations hand-delivered.

I couldn't imagine exactly what Ryan was doing to help me organize this party, as pretty much everything that constituted hard work was on my list. I also had fifteen scripts to Xerox before the end of the day. But I didn't care. It took my mind off the fact that I was persona non grata with Lara and the laughingstock of The Agency in general after my brush with the notorious Jake Hudson. I decided to begin with the dancers. I pulled out the phone book and found Crazy Girls on La Brea. A man answered.

"Hi, I wonder if you can help me. I'd like to order some dancers, please."

"Sure. For when and how many?"

"Well, it's a week from Saturday. The twenty-seventh. And as to how many? I guess you'd be the expert on that. There are about five hundred guests, so I think maybe . . . oh, I don't know, would you think twelve dancers? Or twenty-four? Do they come by the dozen?"

"They're girls. Not eggs."

"Of course. I'm sorry." This wasn't as easy as I had imagined.

"Will they be required to give personal performances?" he asked as he passed his chewing gum noisily from one cheek to the other.

"Well, I don't know. What does that entail?"

"Will you want them to get naked and grind their ass in anyone's face?"

"I don't think so. No." Though I'd never been to a Hollywood party. I couldn't be sure such things weren't going to happen. "But if they do, we'll happily pay the difference afterward, of course."

"Sure. Well, I'd say you need fifty girls. Enough to be visible but not to get in everyone's face. If you'll pardon the expression."

"Perfect," I said, grateful for the pointers. Now for the awkward part. I wasn't sure exactly how to phrase this, but I went for it.

"And could you make that fifty girls with smallish nipples, if you don't mind?"

"Excuse me?" He sounded as though he'd swallowed his gum. I may just have achieved the unthinkable and actually shocked the manager of Crazy Girls.

"It's just that . . . well, my boss is a huge fan of girls with small nipples, and if you could manage it that's what we'd prefer."

"Did you have a diameter in mind?"

"Oh, I think just not large. Nothing that constitutes large. That would work perfectly."

"You're fucking joking, right?"

"Is that a problem?" I asked tentatively. Hoping not. I didn't want to upset Daniel.

"Well, if you wanna come down here and check them out, you're welcome to. Otherwise you're just gonna have to trust that my girls are the hottest in town, regardless of nipple size. Okay?" He sounded slightly aggressive. I decided to back down at this point.

"I'm sure all your girls are fabulous, and if you could just try to remain within a certain small-nipple ballpark, then I'd be super grateful," I concluded. When I looked up, Lara was walking by my desk. She smirked as she overheard the tail end of my conversation.

"Lara," I called after her.

She stopped and turned around.

"Do you think I could talk to you for a second?"

"Sorry, I don't know anything about nipples." She shrugged and headed back to her desk.

My eyes smarted, and I wished that I had stayed in D.C. I wished I didn't have to show reverence to people who judged women on their nipple size. I wished that Lara were still my friend and that she would tell me how all the men in this town were just high-school losers who abused their power as a way of acting out their issues with the cheerleaders who wouldn't sleep with them back then. But she wasn't my friend anymore. She tucked a large Saks Fifth Avenue bag under her desk and settled down on the phone.

"I need a latte the size of a skyscraper." Scott flew by my desk.

"I see." I stood up and followed him into his office. "Er, Scott. I was just wondering where I might find a latte around here."

"How the fuck should I know?" He was glued to his call sheet.

"Okay. Thanks." I backed out of his office and made my way toward Lara's desk. But she was gazing obdurately ahead at her screen, so I ducked by and whispered to Talitha, "Is there a Starbucks or something around here?"

"There's Coffee Bean across the street." She pointed behind her. "Oh, and hey, if you're going, can you get a soy chai latte for me?"

"Great, you can fetch Mike a double espresso, too," Courtney said. "Please."

"Sure. Soy chai latte and double espresso," I repeated. Mike was Courtney's boss who rarely came out of his office as he was apparently waiting for his course of Rogaine to kick in. When he ventured out, it was usually in a trilby.

"Anybody else want anything from the Coffee Bean?" Talitha called out as I shrugged my jacket on and grabbed my wallet.

"Oh, yeah, grande coffee no sugar," said an agent from an office across the hall who was passing by.

"Decaf green tea and one of those fat-free biscotti," someone else called out. The list, by the time I had written it down on my hand, was long. In fact, it ran to two palms long.

I had to navigate six lanes of oncoming traffic to get across the street to the Coffee Bean, so by the time I arrived, my palms were sweating so much that it was a struggle to read my shopping list. As I stepped into the cool shade of the shop, I tried to remember who wanted what. Green tea was Courtney, right? When I looked up, I saw a group of six people—two guys and four girls—all about my age, in identical clothing to mine, in the corner, sipping lattes in silence, until a cell phone began to vibrate on the table in front of them. They all looked at it for a second or two, and finally one of them, a guy, picked it up.

"Hello?" he inquired nervously. Then what sounded like a muffled explosion issued from the earpiece of the phone. He moved it away from his ear with a look of pain on his face. "Okay. We're coming," he told the person on the other end of the phone. And with that the group rose to their feet in silence and one by one filed past me, leaving a table strewn with shredded napkins, half-full coffee cups, and a one-dollar tip.

When the door had closed behind them, I looked around and saw that the coffee shop was empty. Except for a cute guy behind the counter who was looking at me in anticipation.

"What can I get you?" he asked.

"Oh, er . . . well, I'd like . . ." And I reeled off my list of requests. Positive that most of them were wrong but suddenly much more concerned as to how much this little haul was going to cost me.

"That'll be twenty-eight dollars," he said. I blinked at the guy and began to count the dollars out of my wallet. Shit.

"Do you accept credit cards?" I asked hopefully.

"Sure." He took my AmEx, which I figured might just prove flexible enough for eight hot drinks.

"You work at The Agency?" he asked as he ran my card.

"Yeah." I nodded, nervously watching the till for hissing or spitting noises as it choked out my card.

"New, then, huh?"

"Something like that."

"Figured." He nodded intelligently.

"What does that mean?"

"Well, you looked at those guys who were in here a minute ago like they were Martians. But really they're *just like you.*" He opened his eyes wide as though narrating a horror movie.

"They're new, too?" I asked.

"They're poor abused assistants." He handed me the slip to sign. "They come in here once or twice a week. They work for Mad Max."

"Mad Max?" I hadn't a clue what he was talking about.

"Max Fischer. Head of Fischer Films. Huge production company. Their building's next door to The Agency. He has six assistants, and sometimes, when he's done throwing things at them, after the last Rolodex leaves his desk and there's nothing left to hurl, he'll fire them all."

"You're kidding?" I watched as he expertly packed my entire food budget for the next week into a cardboard egg box–type thing.

"No. It happens about once or twice a week, like I said. They'll come in here, and sometimes a couple of them will by crying. Or bruised. Once one of them was bleeding from her right temple, so we had to mop her up." He didn't look as though he were lying, so I decided to sip my own latte and hear him out. "And they'll sit there for about forty minutes until the phone rings and Max says 'Get the fuck back in here.' Usually with a few more 'fucks' thrown in for good measure. And the rest . . . well, you saw for yourself."

"Why don't they go and complain to Human Resources?" I was aghast, and slightly disbelieving.

"'Cause they want to keep their jobs." He laughed.

"Why would anyone put up with such abuse?" I asked innocently.

That's when he looked at me and smiled. "I'm Jason Blum. And you, I noticed from your credit card, must be Elizabeth." He held out his hand and shook mine.

"Good to meet you." I put the receipt between my teeth and picked up the tray of drinks with the other hand. "Thanks."

"I'm a writer, director, and all-around good guy. If I do say so myself." He swung over the other side of the counter and held the door open for me. He had short, wheat-colored hair and wide green eyes, and he laughed louder than anyone I'd ever heard before, which gave him a warm, open air. "See you around."

"Thanks," I said as I was swept out onto the street, somewhat dazed.

Back at my desk, as I scrubbed the ink from my hand and left ear (go figure) with a Kleenex, I was hit by a wave of schadenfreude. Somehow, knowing that there were other people in this business who were as unhappy as I was made me feel a little better. And even though I got every single one of the coffee orders wrong and everyone looked at me as though I was the biggest lame-ass who ever touched down at LAX, I was feeling optimistic. I was a bright girl, wasn't I? Everyone used to say so. I scored very respectably in my SATs. My school report cards said that I made friends easily, and I'd certainly impressed Congressman Edmunds enough for him to hire me on a top security part of his campaign. I couldn't be such a sorry loser that I couldn't handle the job as, let's face it, *second* assistant to someone in the entertainment industry (for which read Ministry of Fun, Senior VP Mickey Mouse), could I?

I got back to work on the list Ryan had sent. I'd dealt with the live girls, now how about the live birds? I called a man in Sacramento who owned an aviary and did a little deal on some birds of paradise and parrots. He assured me that they weren't going to kill one another. He'd also offered me hummingbirds, but common sense told me that letting the smallest bird in the world loose at a party of Hollywood heavy hitters would mean it was only a matter of time before someone inserted one into an orifice they shouldn't or snorted one up along with their line of cocaine. Daniel had decided that the theme of the party was supposed to be "Jungle Madness." I saw it as my responsibility to provide the jungle part. Hoping that the madness would happen all on its own.

Next I got to work on the sponsorship deal. I made a huge mistake to begin with by telling Piper-Heidsieck and then Veuve Clicquot that there would be no press allowed. I then tried to lie to Tanqueray and told them that I was almost certain that there would be press, but when the woman got pushy and asked me to sign a document testifying to this, I lost my nerve. But I did manage to pull off a coup with Jose Cuervo tequila, who promised me as much as my guests could drink. Who could argue with that? We could have margaritas and . . . well, margaritas. And of course slammers and shots and maybe even girls with guns. Or was that horribly nineties? Who cared—we could bring it back. As soon as anyone saw George with a pretty girl on his arm and a tequila gun on his tonsils, they'd all be dying to follow suit. All I had to do now was ensure that the invitations were hand-delivered. I pulled down the document with the guest list and began to fill in courier forms. Though when I reached about the hundred fiftieth, a shadow fell over me. I looked up and saw a man who I could only assume from Lara's description yesterday was Ryan.

"Elizabeth?" he asked tersely.

"Hi."

"I'm Ryan. I just had a call from Cuervos, and they said you'd agreed to let them supply drinks for the party."

"Yeah, as much as we can drink." I nodded proudly.

"It's not a frat party." He narrowed his already narrow eyes and glared at me. Lara was right—the guy was practically oozing slime. He looked like a weasel, and you just knew that he'd be mean to fat girls in bars. He was that type.

"I'm well aware of that." I tried to keep my cool. Think bigger picture, Elizabeth, think bigger picture. Which was what I'd begun to tell myself when I felt the tears prick at the inside corners of my eyes.

"And you were aware, I suppose, that the liquor they are so generously offering to provide us with is Jose Cuervo tequila?"

"Yes, yes, I was." I even managed a small yet confident smile.

"Do you know nothing about life, Elizabeth?" He moved really, really close to my face. I could smell last night's garlic on his breath. I inched back in my seat.

"I beg your pardon?"

"Well, I guess you don't." He looked at my hair as though he'd been asked to floss his teeth with it. Then at my clothes. I dug my admittedly untidy nails into my palms. "Because even the most clueless douche bag from Idaho would have known that these people don't drink anything but Patrón Silver tequila."

"Patrón Silver?"

"Yes, you silly little girl. Even people from Sherman Oaks know that." And with that he spun on the heel of his overpolished shoe and strutted cockily out of my office.

I looked around to see whether anyone had overheard. There was really only so much public humiliation a girl could take in the space of eleven days, and I think that I had reached my limit. Naturally everyone was silent, and they all seemed intent on figuring out the precise punctuation of their e-mails, but no fingers tapped on keyboards, all telephone conversations had been mysteriously halted, and Courtney and Talitha were chewing on their lips as if their sides would split with laughter if they stopped. I didn't know whether to yell or cry. But before I could succumb to one or the other, Talitha fractured the silence.

"He's right. I once had a couple of margaritas at Bar Marmont made with some low-rent tequila and barfed all over this guy's business card." She nodded sagely. "While he was still holding it."

"Well, it beats shitting on his shoes," said the mail guy, who was passing with his trolley. And everyone laughed. Except me.

5

She looks familiar, but, dearie, these blondes all bleach alike.

—Esther Howard as Mrs. Kraft
Born to Kill

"Elizabeth, we've spoken on the phone. I'm Cameron." I looked up and saw a bright, white, light-gleaming woman and assumed that I was experiencing a divine visitation. Which ought not to have surprised me, because I had been praying an unprecedented amount since I'd joined The Agency. Usually along the lines of:

"Please, God, do not let Daniel Rosen find out that it was me who spilled Wite-Out on the calfskin sofa in the lobby and then tried to wipe it off with a copy of the *Hollywood Reporter.*"

Or:

"Please, God, make Scott Wagner take so much cocaine that he has a nosebleed for the rest of the week and has to stay home. Because even though it's a job that a chimpanzee could perform, I still have not learned how to program his video player and last night recorded *Will & Grace* instead of the Knicks game."

But in spite of my prayers, it wasn't a visitation, it was a movie star. And her teeth shone as brightly as any I'd ever seen. And her golden hair hung about her shoulders more goldenly than even Goldie Hawn's in *Private Benjamin.* Oh, yes, Cameron was a movie star. And as well as blinding me with her light, she seemed to be asking me a question.

"I'm sorry, would you mind repeating that?" I asked with a slight frown.

"I said, would you mind if I waited here and hung out with you until Scott arrives back from lunch? It's just I get a little weirded out waiting in reception." She leaned in and whispered, "I always think Daniel Rosen's going to come by any minute, and he scares the shit out of me."

"Of course not. Of course you can wait here." I scuttled to my feet in such a hurry that my chair overbalanced and ended up on the floor. "I mean, where exactly did you want to *hang out*?"

"Oh, I'll just sit here." She perched on the corner of my desk and pulled a copy of *Allure* out of her purse. "What are you going to wear to the party at Daniel's, by the way? I was thinking hot pink. I'm kinda sick of those dresses of no color. You know what I mean?"

"Pink sounds perfect," I agreed. "If you like, I can organize it so that the cocktails match your dress. Just let me know." I was such a creep. So desperate for friends that I was offering to theme a party around someone's dress.

"So are you taking a date?" she asked as she sipped from the can of Diet Coke that had been sitting on my desk since this morning.

"I don't think that I'm allowed," I confided. "Actually, I'll be kind of on duty."

"Oh, I see. God, well, that'll make it more interesting for you. At least when someone boring tries to talk to you, it'll be easy to pretend you have to whip a waiter's ass or something. So do you have a boyfriend?"

"Actually, no. I'm pretty new in town. And I've been kind of busy." Christ, I had no idea how important boyfriends were in Hollywood. It seemed that having a man to share a pizza with on a Friday night completely validated your existence, your beauty, your choice of gym, and your general interestingness in a way that it never would have done in D.C. I made a mental note not to be too scarred by the Jake Hudson experience and find myself one soon.

"Shame." Cameron, quite understandably, seemed a little over her conversation with me. I didn't have a boyfriend, I was deferential to the point of creepiness, and I kept trying to check out the label on her pants, because if I looked halfway as good in them as she did, I was going to buy them no matter what they cost. I plucked up the courage to be casual-friendly.

"I love your pants. Where did you get them?"

"Oh, I dunno. What does my label say?" She stuck her butt across my desk, and I carefully looked. This time my prayer went:

"Please, God, do not let me extract the label from her pants in any way that will suggest that my interest is in anything more than what brand they are. Or I will die."

"Oh, whaddaya know? Kmart." I laughed too gaily, relieved not to have been arrested for being a pervert.

"Oh, hey, that's cool." She giggled and slid off my desk. "And here he is. The handsomest agent in Hollywood!" And she leaped up like a Labrador, or a golden retriever maybe, as Scott walked along the corridor.

"Cam, baby!" He grinned widely as she hugged him tight. "Come on over here. I've been missin' you."

"You have not. I hear you've been bopping . . ." And she whispered the woman's name in his ear. Scott actually looked a little shocked. Whomever she thought he'd been bopping, Cameron was correct. Lara, who had just walked back into the room, gave Cameron a polite hug before Scott led her away to his room.

"So let's talk business, baby. You gonna bring home that Academy Award for me this year, you gorgeous bitch?" Scott laughed as he closed the door in Lara's face.

"So did you call Jake back yet?" Courtney asked in a faux-casual manner as she swung backward on her chair and checked her newly bleached teeth in a compact mirror.

"No, I didn't," I said calmly. "And to tell you the truth, I don't think I will."

"Jeez, what? You think maybe by your not calling him back, he'll just want you even more?" she asked sarcastically.

"No, I'm just not especially interested."

"You've changed your tune." She snapped her mirror shut.

"I thought he was great. Before I realized what a complete slut he was." I laughed, trying to sound as though I didn't care, when really I had thought of little other than how, short of becoming Julia Roberts, I was ever going to get Jake Hudson to fall in love with me. Shortly after which I officially gave up. "Besides, I'm having enough trouble figuring out how to work the phones around here. I'll leave dating until I'm competent enough to call guys back."

I knew that Courtney was thinking what a stuck-up bitch I was, but then she'd think that no matter what I said or did. I smiled at her as warmly as I could and then got back to my work.

But no sooner had I put my head down than Cameron came bounding out of Scott's office.

"Okay, honey. See you Saturday. Is it a pool party? 'Cause if it is I better call around to the Beehive and get my bush waxed."

"Can I come to the Beehive, too?" Scott slapped Cameron's ass, and Lara looked disgusted.

"Oh, and hey, I love your new assistant." Cameron came over and kissed me good-bye. "See you at the party." Then, as she was about to kiss Lara good-bye, too, she did a double take. "Is your hair virgin?" she asked me.

God, I wondered, what was it with everyone around here? They were obsessed with sex. And hair. I must have looked puzzled.

"Virgin. Have you never had your hair colored?" she asked as she took a lock and gazed at it.

"No, actually. I mean, not really. I once used a plum-colored mousse when I was sixteen, but it was a disaster and my scalp turned pink so—"

"Oh, honey, that is *so* exciting." She was flapping her arms in glee.

"It is?" I asked. Thinking that she was going to say it was the most beautiful, natural color she'd ever seen and that L'Oréal might want to copy it for a new shade. Bumblefuck Mouse, perhaps.

"Oh, my God, yes. Billy is going to die for your hair! He loves virgin hair. You have to go to him and say I sent you. This is wild. You'll look amazing at the party once he works his magic. Tell him Cam thinks honey blond, to make your eyes stand out." Cameron winked at me and began scrawling Billy's number on my notepad.

"Okay, kids, gotta bounce. See you Saturday." With that she was gone. Ladies and Gentlemen, Cameron has left the building.

"Elizabeth, I have to do a run to the Coffee Bean for Scott's three o'clock." Lara stopped by my desk and avoided eye contact with me. "Will you come help me carry the stuff back?"

"Sure," I said. "Shall I put the phones on voice mail?"

"Oh, yeah, you do that." She scuffed the toes of her gray suede boots against the carpet as she waited. In fact, if I hadn't known that

Lara was not a creature given to self-doubt or awkwardness, I would have said that she was experiencing both of the above.

I walked in silence next to Lara as we made our way down the corridor and through the atrium. I wished that I had something to say to her, and that if I did, she might actually want to listen. I hated this cold-shouldering. It had been keeping me awake at night, and yesterday, when I'd talked to my mother on the phone, I had almost broken down and admitted how miserable the whole thing was making me. And that I wanted to come home forever. But I hadn't. I was too proud and didn't want my parents to worry.

When we arrived at the Coffee Bean, the first thing I saw was Jason Blum's face. He smiled at me and gave a lower-wattage version of the same to Lara. Which was understandable. She did come over as pretty terrifying.

"Ladies," Jason greeted us.

"Hi." I smiled.

"We'd love . . . well, *I'd* love a cappuccino." Lara turned to me. "Elizabeth?"

"Oh, I didn't know we were getting anything for ourselves. Well, I'll have a soy chai latte," I said. It was my new favorite, and I suspected it was laced with morphine, because it was highly addictive.

"Great, oh, and six black coffees and a latte, too," Lara added. And as Jason got to work, she turned to me, pulled at the gold chain around her neck, and began, "Elizabeth, I'm really sorry."

I was unprepared for this, and the froth on my chai latte caught in my throat. I struggled not to cough my lungs out.

"I was horrible to you about Jake Hudson, and I shouldn't have been. I know you probably made a completely honest mistake, and I overheard what you said to Courtney the Cunt earlier about him. And even if you hadn't made a mistake, I shouldn't have behaved like that. Can you forgive me?" She looked genuinely sheepish. I noticed that Jason was listening intently between blasts of the milk frother.

"Oh, God, of course I can. I know that you were only trying to get out of organizing the party with Ryan," I said. "And I can't really blame you for that."

At which Lara's stony-serious face broke into a smile. I thought she might hug me, but nah, she wasn't that type.

"You're right. He's a jerkwad and a half!" she laughed. "But seriously, I've had experience dating men in the business, and it truly doesn't work. I just thought that I was passing on the benefit of my wisdom."

"Well, thanks. Personally, the only reason I didn't call Jake Hudson back was because if he'd compared me to all the women he's ever dated he'd have reported me to the FTC for not complying with the term 'girlfriend.' You know. Check legs: one set—fabulous. Check eyes: two—the same color as the ocean at dawn. Check clothes: expensive and beautiful. Answers: no, no, no."

"Yeah, right. Check brain: one—fucked up, weird, neurotic, and empty. Answer: no."

Lara and I laughed as Jason handed over our consignment. And as Lara walked out the door holding the drinks, he turned to me and said, sotto voce and without Lara's being able to overhear, "I cannot believe you fell for Jake Hudson. No way." And he looked like he might die of amusement. Not that I cared anymore. Lara and I had made up. I had a friend. I had a friend. I wanted to jump up and down and perform a tribal dance of gratitude. But I didn't. For all sorts of reasons.

When the Saturday of the party dawned, I lifted my head off the pillow and noticed that it wasn't actually dawn yet. It was 4:00 A.M., and my mind was awash with a million and one problems. I was reminded of the million and second problem when I turned over and caught a nostril full of the gentle scent of peroxide on my hair. Oh, God. Yesterday over lunch hour I'd gone to see Billy. Colorist to the stars. That ought to have been the first clarion call of danger. Stars, darling, not assistants. In no copy of *Allure* was he ever described as Billy, colorist to girls who make under $3 million a year. Billy had apparently done me a "rilly, rilly hewge" favor by squeezing me in at less than six months' notice. Billy was Italian and not nearly so excited by my virgin locks as Cameron had generously imagined he might be. He walked around me, lifting sections of my brown hair as though they were radioactive waste. If he'd had a pair of tongs and a rubber glove handy, I'm sure he wouldn't have hesitated to use them.

"Oh, no. This is nurthing. This *does* nurthing." He let my hair fall lankly back down. "We do the Hollywood Honey," he declared finally after scratching his chin. And with that he waltzed off, never to be seen again—well, not by me anyway. I was duly offloaded onto a surly girl with a shaved head who proceeded to cover me in foil, disdain, and bleach.

But lo, eventually I emerged in my new guise, a Hollywood Honey. A little generic for some people's tastes perhaps, but I was thrilled. I was so completely alien in this town that I was prepared to take any route to Belonging. Even at a cost of six hundred dollars. Not including tax and tip, I might add. My hair was writing checks that my lowliness couldn't honor. Though I did help myself to a very-expensive-looking French mint from the cloakroom. And as I walked out of the salon into the magic hour, that time of day that is so loved for its flatteringly pink glow by cinematographers and women over twenty-two alike, I did feel a little bit special. I felt that this was an investment in my career. And my life. Because, let's face it, Bumblefuck Mouse, even if she were six hundred dollars richer than Hollywood Honey, was never going to get anywhere in this town. And now that I was here—now, as the traffic on Beverly was streaking past me, and now, as girls loitered outside the vintage clothing stores and sipped their organic OJ outside King's Road Café—well, now that I was here, I might as well make the most of it. I might as well dive in, sink my teeth in, and bite off more than I could chew. I might as well get the fuck on with it, as Scott might have said in a more conservative moment.

So after I lay there worrying for two and a half hours, the sun finally came up and I hauled myself out of bed. I had been through every party-disaster scenario in my mind. I had poisoned every one of the Hollywood glitterati with bad sushi. The rose petals that I'd ordered to be scattered in Daniel's pool would be red and not white, and the water would look like someone had been murdered in the deep end. The hand-delivered invitations would have been misdelivered, and we'd have a slew of doormen, maids, pool boys, and nannies at the party instead of their fabulous and famous bosses. And while I would have been thrilled to sit on a lounge chair and shoot the breeze with the woman who washed George's underpants, I doubted that Daniel and Scott would share my perverted pleasure.

When I caught sight of my reflection in the fridge door as I went to get the milk for my cereal, I realized that the stress of the past week had taken its toll on my appearance. I looked very *Dawn of the Living Dead*–ish.

Fuck, I thought, what on earth will Jake Hudson think when he sees me? Which wasn't a terribly high-minded, work-oriented, thrusting-young-assistant thing to think, but it was the truth. I picked up my phone and called my new old friend Lara.

"Lara?"

"Who is this?" It was a man's voice. And I suddenly remembered my status as the only sex-free zone in town. Everyone else had gotten some action last night. Except me.

"It's Elizabeth. A friend of Lara's," I replied. Just a bit embarrassed.

The line went dead. I'd call back later when all of last night's dates were back home.

I poured the milk on my cereal and, as it curdled, realized that I couldn't even afford a new carton, let alone the manicure–pedicure–facial wax–salt-scrub massage–new dress–and–blow-out that everyone else seemed to be having for the big night. And that was just some of the agents at The Agency. That didn't even take into account the armpit botox shots that actresses got to ensure that they didn't sweat on a fabulous dress or the collagen they had injected into the soles of their feet so that they could exist more comfortably in their ankle-breaking high heels. But hey, I was just an assistant, right? As Victoria, my mentor who didn't seem to mentor me in anything other than the best place to find organic, twice-pressed prune juice in West Hollywood, had so succinctly put it yesterday.

"Really, I wouldn't waste your money having your hair lightened, Elizabeth," she'd explained sweetly as I tried to escape to my hair appointment. "Or your time. Really, nobody's going to be looking at *you* tomorrow night, are they, now? Not with all those beautiful, interesting women there." And with that she smiled her disgusting, rodent-toothed smile and bade me farewell. Or fare-miserably, as she'd doubtless have preferred.

Two minutes later Lara called back.

"Hi," she said briskly.

"Oh, Lara, I'm so sorry. It didn't occur to me to think that you might have company," I apologized.

"I didn't," she snapped. O-kay then. I moved swiftly on.

"Well, the thing is, I was wondering if maybe you had any tips on what I ought to wear tonight. I mean, obviously I'm going to be on duty, but then I don't want to look like a complete dork, and I was wondering what—"

"Come over at five. We'll figure it out. 185 Rexford. South of Santa Monica." And she hung up. That girl would be head of a studio in no time. She was so efficient.

And not only was she efficient, as I discovered at 5:00 P.M., she was also the owner of a closet so comprehensive that if she wasn't moonlighting as fashion director of *Marie Claire,* then she had to be the secret daughter of Aristotle Onassis. There was serious wealth in that closet. And in the jewelry boxes and the legion of beauty products strewn around the place, which would have made Brigitte Bardot look twenty-five again. As Lara sat on her bed and directed me toward various dresses and wrap tops and cashmere sweaters and pairs of Jimmy Choos, I was longing to ask, How? How come the daughter of a teacher and a doctor's receptionist from Pennsylvania had so much stuff? But Lara was busy reading a book called *The Art of the Novel,* so I didn't interrupt.

"Do you like this outfit?" I asked eventually, and turned to show her what I had cautiously unearthed from her collection.

"Waaay too librarian." She put down her book and stood up. "I know exactly what will work on you."

And quickly she had me in a satin G-string, a dress that wasn't much bigger than the satin G-string, and then a pair of equally obscene, strappy silver heels.

"I cannot leave the house looking like this!" I gasped as I saw my reflection, complete with teased-up new blond locks and a diamond necklace that Lara was fastening behind my neck.

"You look great," she proclaimed.

"I look like a . . ." I hesitated, hoping against hope that Lara's haberdashery wasn't likely to be funded by the wages of sin. "I look like a hooker."

"Enjoy." She smiled and hopped back onto her bed to resume her book, leaving me torn between wondering what my mother would think and what George would think.

6

There are certain shades of limelight that can wreck a girl's complexion.

—Audrey Hepburn as Holly Golightly
Breakfast at Tiffany's

At exactly eight o'clock on the night of the party, the wrought-iron gates that led to Daniel's Shangri-la swung open. A row of Armani-clad security guards stood in formation behind a silk rope at his front door, and an army of valets in tan jackets waited patiently for the first car to roll up the drive. As I assumed my place at the door, guest list in hand, I took a deep breath and reveled in the scent of jasmine, which drifted on the breeze with the subtlety of a chemical-warfare attack. I'd ordered eight hundred plants the previous afternoon when I realized that Manuel Canovas Fleur de Coton candles, delicious though they might smell, were actually a fire hazard. Now I was glad that I'd paid the extra twenty thousand dollars for the jasmine, because maybe it would mask the stench of white fear I was giving off like a rabid skunk. I'd actually contemplated siphoning off a couple of hundred jasmine-bound dollars in case the party was a complete disaster and I had to decamp to Mexico, but despite my experience with the shady congressman, I had sadly never learned the gentle art of embezzling.

I cast one last look behind me at the hundred waitresses in leopard-print minidresses with silver trays and cocktails at the ready. I checked that the Crazy Girls in gold Simba costumes who were dotted around Daniel's house and garden like poorly hidden Easter eggs, each with one standard-issue diamanté-encrusted riding crop, were all in place. Then I fixed my headset on and was about to practice the breathing techniques that I'd overheard Alexa, my yoga-teacher neighbor, explaining to one of her pupils, when a high-pitched buzz pierced my right eardrum and Ryan came through loud and clear.

"Elizabeth. Where the fuck is Tarka?"

I hastily adjusted the volume.

"The guests are supposed to be able to hear drifting music or something, and he's not here. Daniel's freaking."

I looked around frantically for our lost rock star when I was interrupted again. "Okay, he's here. One of the Crazy Girls had him. Oh, and by the way, about the Crazy Girls. Daniel hasn't clicked yet that they're going to take their clothes off, but when they do, you'll be fired. I can't believe that you ordered cheap strippers to come to his party. Didn't you know that the chairman of Universal is a woman? As is the vice chairman of Sony. Not to mention many, many more women who are coming. And you are planning to humiliate them all at Daniel's home by bringing in strippers. Honestly, Elizabeth, I'm shocked."

"What?" I asked with a suddenly dry throat.

"Glad I'm not in your cheap shoes." Ryan laughed evilly into my ear.

"Ryan, wait . . . you told me to order Crazy Girls," I stammered.

"Did I?" Ryan asked. "I must have made a mistake. Oops." Then there was radio silence.

I looked around in a blind panic to see what I could do to stop the strippers stripping, but George had just arrived, guests were on the grounds, and I couldn't escape from the door. What could I do except pray that I still had Ryan's e-mail instructions on my computer in case I was required to explain myself? I pushed the thought to the back of my mind.

"That's some fine ice, baby." Nick, one of the heat-packing bouncers, winked at me as he clocked my courtesy-of-Lara necklace. I looked down, and despite the fact that my face was melting and my hair was wilting and my spirits were evaporating and I was most likely about to lose my job, I immediately felt pretty special thanks to my diamonds. Which were caressing my chest as no man ever had. I thought how impressed Jake Hudson would be when he saw me, or at least how improved I was from our last encounter, with my greasy clumps of hair and dazed expression.

"Thanks. Not mine, of course." I smiled at Nick. "Oh, look, here they come." I pulled a nervous face as the first of the guests poured from the procession of cars that had begun to drift toward the house. I scoured my list for the bigwigs I'd never heard of and smiled politely as I checked them off and ushered them through. The hair, the ice, the chiffon, the haute couture. Never were so many people so plump of lip and blank of expression. It was all I could do to stop myself from elbowing Nick in the ribs with astonishment every time I saw a remarkable *pièce de surgerie cosmétique,* as I discreetly liked to call it.

All this, though, was par for the course. I had anticipated the fabulousness of the guests. What I didn't know about was the foulness of the Uninvited. Not, I hasten to add, the hundreds of people who had begun arriving at Daniel's gate that afternoon with their sandwiches and baseball caps and cameras in hopes of catching a glimpse of an idol or two. Or the women from Mississippi with their sign that read BABES FROM BILOXI BARK TO BANG BEN. No, *their* screams were nothing compared to those of the professional gate-crashers.

I have to point out here that everyone in Hollywood is desperate to be invited to parties—they differ merely in the degree of their desperation. Some well-adjusted folk will only call in a favor from a producer friend if it's a *Charlie's Angels* premiere. Others have a more pathological need to be seen at everything, and their wiles will necessarily be more drastic. They might use the name of someone they know to be on the list to get into a party, while some other desperados might date a marketing girl at Universal to ensure that they can get onto any list at any time. Because wangling an invite is a popular pastime in Los Angeles. They start young, too. A big-time producer in town was once virtually disowned by his daughter because he couldn't get her tickets to a *Harry Potter* premiere. "What's the matter, Dad, got no juice at Warner Brothers?" she said scornfully before faxing the studio head herself. And scoring, I might add.

And now, all of a sudden, I was the girl with the golden list. Initially I hadn't expected my duties as party planner to be quite so extensive, and Ryan was supposed to be sending someone to take over from me, but, for the time being, the tiny bit of power I wielded was beginning to amuse me. Movie stars slipped by without a hitch, and I'd become quite adept at flicking through the alphabetically ordered pages to find those I had never heard of. I was like St. Peter at the gates of heaven. Until, that is, Veronica Byng turned up on the other side of my clipboard.

"What's your name, please?" I hadn't been in my position of power long enough to lose my manners just yet.

"Veronica Byng, with a *y*." I scanned my list diligently. "I'm sorry, madam, but you're not on the list."

"Yes, I am. My assistant RSVP'd."

"Well, madam, maybe she forgot."

"She didn't forget. She doesn't forget anything. Get Daniel Rosen out here now."

"I'm sorry, I can't do that."

"Yes, you can. Use the two mediocre legs God gave you and walk them in that door and get Daniel. Do it now."

"I'm afraid I can't do that. Perhaps if you're such good friends with Mr. Rosen, you can call him on his cell phone," I suggested innocently.

She looked at me with such arctic hatred that I flinched. I couldn't help it. And Miss Veronica Byng very savvily saw the chink in my armor. Her voice began to rise, and I involuntarily took a step back. A good instinct, as she took a swing at me. Her talons missed my left cheek by an eighth of an inch. But her stilettos set her off balance. She teetered dangerously like a house of cards, and down she went. Ass over substantial tit, right over the velvet rope smack on top of me. Luckily for Daniel and unluckily for his lawyers, I broke her fall. Miss Byng would have run up a pretty penny with a lawsuit if she'd so much as broken a nail. Moments later Nick had placed her where she definitely belonged—outside the rope.

By the time I'd brushed myself off and stopped trembling, the crowd waiting to be let in had grown, and a lot of them, despite looking very legitimate, were not on my list. Much as I longed for them to be, because I really didn't want a repeat of the Veronica Byng experience. There were also a slew of people waiting who weren't on my list that I could have sworn I'd actually sent invitations to. It was only then that it dawned on me what a sneaky-ass thing Ryan had done. He'd edited the list. Deleted the names of some of the invited guests in order to create a sense of urgency on the other side of the rope. There should always be people who want to get into your party but can't. It creates buzz and a whiff of exclusivity. Apparently.

Not to mention hundreds of very pissed-off people yelling at me.

"I was invited!"

"I have my invite here!"

"This is fucking stupid!"

"I'm on the list!"

"Get Scott for me!"

"Fuck you, bitch!"

"Esther Hartley," a soft little voice whispered in my right ear, and I scanned my list as I wiped a stray piece of Veronica's saliva from my left breast. I found Esther Hartley. Thank God *somebody's* name was on the list. I glanced up to wave her on, but my eyes only just met the top of her red-sequined dress. I craned my neck and saw that she had the cleavage of a milkmaid, the white-blond ringlets of an ancient goddess of the moon, and a face that was so extraordinarily pretty that for a second I just chewed on my pencil and stared. It was only after I'd developed a crick in my neck that I was able to catch her emerald green eyes and nod for her to go through. It was at precisely that moment I realized that not only did Esther Hartley have enough blessings for an entire race of Honeys, she also had the man of my dreams holding her elbow in a proprietorial way.

There he was. Jake Hudson. He looked even more devastating than I'd remembered. He was wearing black tie and had the air of a young Warren Beatty. He was a man with the evening at his feet. I had a palpitation or two and then smiled up at him. "Jake Hudson." He grinned lazily and sexily at me, and I nodded at him, without checking my list. I smiled back. He smiled at me. I waited for the flash of recognition, the moment when he'd realize it was *me* and kiss me warmly on the cheeks at the very least. I wasn't delusional enough to expect marriage proposals at this juncture. But after the fifth smile I gave him, he frowned in a faintly alarmed way, as though I might be a crazed fan girl, and hurried off with Esther Hartley toward the melee of guests and laughter. He hadn't even recognized me.

I might have collapsed into a miserable heap had one of the waitresses not chosen that moment to walk by with a tray of Malibu Mules. I hastily grabbed one, and before you could say "drunk in charge of a clipboard," I had necked it back and let thirty people who weren't on the list into the party. I was far too fair-minded to leave the masses out. Especially as they were the invited masses. So, as a gesture of defiance to the detestable Ryan, I just kept on letting them in. Until the room and garden behind me began to pulse with life and it began to seem like a party you might want to crash, rather than an opening at a very important but sublimely boring art gallery where you couldn't afford anything.

The combination of crippling disappointment, fear, and vodka began to well and truly kick in at precisely the moment that Lara emerged beside me from the swirling crowd.

"Hasn't that shitty little pumpkinhead sent anyone to replace you yet?"

"Who, Ryan?"

"Of course Ryan," she said.

"Lara, does Ryan have a problem with me?" I asked.

"Ryan has a problem with everyone. He hates without discrimination. But in your case, Daniel hired you, so he probably presumes you're being groomed for success."

"Well, that's bullshit," I said. "Daniel's forgotten me." Clearly I was less than memorable all around. I let in Marilyn Manson, who was never on the list in the first place because he once stole Daniel's girlfriend from him, which—let's face it—is not flattering.

"Ryan's twisted." Lara took the clipboard from me and handed it to Nick. She gave him an imploring smile, and he took over happily. Unsurprising, as she was looking more stunning than I'd ever seen her, and certainly more relaxed. She had a man's tux jacket slung over her porcelain-white shoulders, and her hair looked very *déshabillé, very* fucked in the bushes.

"Who's the lucky man?" I asked, pointing to the jacket.

"You wouldn't want to know." She slipped her arm through mine and led me into the thick of the party. "Oh, and by the way, great party. Scott and Daniel are thrilled."

"No, you're kidding! What about the strippers?" I asked, not wanting to hear the answer.

"Yeah, nice touch." Lara laughed. "When I first saw them taking off their gold costumes, I thought you'd lost your mind hiring them. But when everyone saw how awesome George thought it was and what fun he was having, even Daniel got into it."

"Honestly?" I asked.

"Sure," Lara said.

I was so relieved. This was a death-row pardon, and I couldn't have been happier. I'd deal with Ryan later. My Crazy Girls were tiptoeing around a cigar-wielding Jack and his cronies in their G-strings, not an oversize nipple in sight, and the lush foliage of palm fronds and orchids seemed to be alive with kissing strangers, deals being brokered, and asses being kissed. Hollywood was definitely a jungle. I caught a glimpse of George chatting to a very cute guy with black hair and groovy schoolboy sneakers on—in defiance of the black-tie dress code, I might add.

"Who's that?" I asked Lara as we weaved our way poolside.

"Luke Lloyd!" she yelled, too loud for my comfort. "He's a hottie and actually not a gross-receipt-obsessed moron like most producers."

"Oh, he's a producer." I kissed the idea of him good-bye and began looking for cute waiters. It wasn't that I was afraid to incur Lara's wrath anymore, just that she'd been proved right with her warning about dating industry men. I hated being the talk of the office, and I hated even more turning the next corner and seeing Esther Hartley sitting on Jake's knee. Her long arms were draped around his shoulders, and whatever she was saying was making him laugh. And if I had previously allowed myself to dream that he might one day want to settle down with a sweet, normal girl like me, whose heart was kind and whose feet were on the ground, I changed my mind. Hell, even *I* wouldn't settle down with me if I'd been adored by Esther Hartley and her numinous body.

"Can you believe she has a degree in astrophysics?" Lara nudged me as we went by the delirious couple. Then she realized her mistake and grimaced. "Oh, sorry, honey."

"Not to worry." I shrugged. "I think he's receding in the wrong way. I noticed that when we were in his sports car and the wind was blowing his hair back."

"Like a monk spot?"

"No, more the abused-hedgehog thing, sparse at the front."

"Oh, that's bad. Lucky escape." Lara laughed as we came to a halt by the side of the pool.

"Drink?" Lara handed me a glass of something the color of a swimming pool, and we both sunk into pool chairs.

"Woo hoo, bush action." She pointed to the shrubbery beside me where a Crazy Girl was being led by the hand into the bushes, but I couldn't make out the man doing the leading. A few minutes later, the girl emerged with a slightly dazed but not displeased look on her face and a business card in her hand. But as Lara and I began to laugh, Scott, who had been sitting at a table nearby, beckoned Lara over. I didn't think she'd noticed, as she was looking determinedly in the other direction, but just as I was about to point him out to her, she had gotten up and was striding, drink in hand, to where he was sitting. With a woman I assumed was his wife. Certainly she looked bored and he looked out of it.

I took another hit of my drink and decided to investigate the bush action a little more closely. Besides, I felt quite vulnerable sitting alone with a spare pool chair beside me. It was like advertising in a singles column where any old crazy could come and size up your wares. I stood up and wandered, cocktail in hand, to the greenery, which I'd gotten cheap because it hadn't been sprayed for bugs, something I hoped Daniel never found out.

"You're back, baby. I knew you would be." A big hand clutched at my wrist as I approached the place where the man had disappeared with the Crazy Girl.

"Hey!" I yelled as I was dragged *forward* through the hedge. Which was novel, at least.

"Oh, it's not you." It was dark, and I couldn't see who the man was, but there was an outside chance that it might be Leo or Matthew, who I'd seen line-dancing with a Crazy Girl earlier, so I didn't scream just yet. "Who are you?"

"I'm Elizabeth. Scott's Wagner's assistant."

"Well, Elizabeth, Scott Wagner's assistant, I think you're pretty cute." The man chose that moment to pull out a lighter and glance the flame over his cigar, and in the light I saw that he wasn't even slightly cute. He certainly wasn't Leo. Or Matthew. Which would serve me right for being such a celebrity whore. But just as I was about to dart off, he said, "I'm Bob." I knew that I'd seen his picture on the cover of *Variety* yesterday and that he'd just closed an enormous deal at Paramount and was responsible for at least two three-hundred-plus-grossing films. I'd also read that he was looking for new representation. Which meant that I probably didn't want to slap him while my boss, an agent with a wife and a drug habit to support, was sitting ten feet away.

"Well, Bob," I said instead, "it was nice meeting you, and now I've gotta run. I'm kind of taking care of the party."

"But who's taking care of you?" he said as he puffed on his glowing cigar and the rubbery redness of his drool-drenched lips was illuminated.

"Oh, I can take care of myself." I tried to sound casual, and I might have succeeded. But certainly I wasn't correct, because a second later he had put his thick, sausagey fingers around my waist and his tongue in my mouth.

"I've really got to make sure that everything's going okay," I said, but he couldn't hear me because he was chewing enthusiastically on my lower lip. So instead I gave him a gentle shove in the crotch and ducked back through the bushes to the poolside, where the fairy lights and floodlit swimming pool dazzled me for a moment or two. Then I made a beeline for the house. I didn't wait to find out whether The Agency would be signing him as a new client someday soon.

But as I tried to make my break, shaking from yet another encounter with an aggressive Hollywood habitué, I was stopped in my tracks by Lara.

"You've got to come with me—now," she said, a dead serious look in her eyes. Holy shit, I thought, Bob had made it to Scott before me and told him that I'd attacked him. I was fired for sure. She took hold of my hand and dragged me toward the stairs.

"Lara, I'm really sorry. But I swear that it was sexual harassment. I swear I didn't encourage him," I blurted as we flew by guests, banged into slightly-worn-out-looking waitresses, and what I could have sworn was one of our hottest young actresses kissing the neck of Tommy, one of my fellow assistants at The Agency.

"Just shut up and follow me," Lara said as my wrist began to burn and I nearly broke my ankle tripping up a step.

"It was self-protection. Any lawyer in the land would back me up," I said, though I suspected that this particular case might not make it to court. I'd be bought off with enough money for my plane ticket back to D.C. and told never to darken the door of The Agency again.

"What the fuck are you going on about?" Lara asked as we finally made it to the cool rosewood interior of Daniel's master-suite bathroom.

"Bob." I collapsed on the toilet seat and was about to cry but was too stunned by the décor—the silver mosaic sunken bath, the dark matte floorboards, and the 1920s mirror. "My God, this is the most beautiful bathroom I've ever seen!"

"I know, Daniel has got to be gay. I don't care what Scott says. A man with such great taste does not eat pussy." Lara turned the large, fairy-castle key in the door and bolted us in. "Who's Bob?"

"You mean I'm not in trouble?" I asked, not really wanting to go into detail if I didn't have to. After all, I could still taste the man's aftershave on my lips—I didn't need to remind myself any more than was necessary. The whole thing was disturbing enough to give Wes Craven nightmares.

"What are we doing here, then?" I asked.

"We need to get you out of that dress," Lara said as she ran her fingers through her hair, which was so red it looked on fire in the low-lit bathroom.

"What?" Of course it flashed through my mind that Lara wanted my body, but only for a second, I swear.

"Julia is wearing the same dress. If she sees you in it, she'll leave the party, and Daniel will flip out."

"You've got to be kidding me!" I laughed with relief. "Julia doesn't care if I'm in the same dress. No matter what she wears, she'd look ten times better than me in it. Come on."

"Jesus, Elizabeth, you're so clueless." And then she came over to me and began to unzip the dress. "It's not Julia who'll care, for Christ's sake. Like she'd even notice."

"Well, I don't care." I stood there shivering slightly as the dress slipped to the floor and Lara lit two cigarettes and passed me one.

"It's her stylist, Nadia, who's here with Julia. She's one of the savviest girls in the business, and if she sees you in that dress, she'll either burn holes in it, spill a tray of cocktails in your face, or tell some lie to Julia to get her to leave the party before she's shown up for lack of originality. Now, what should we dress you in?" Lara looked around the bathroom hopefully as I cottoned on to the enormity of the problem.

"I could go home and change?" I offered. "I only live twenty minutes away."

"It's eleven o'clock, Elizabeth," she said, taking a long drag. "Even the best Hollywood parties end at midnight. The executives have to get home to read their specs for breakfast meetings, the actors need to get enough sleep to handle their morning Pilates, and the agents and managers? Well, no one stays at a party for them."

"Can't I just duck out of Nadia's way and stay for the last hour?" I pleaded, not wanting to miss out on a minute of my first Hollywood party. Even the assaults hadn't taken the fairy dust off my thrill at being here.

"Perfect! I knew I'd find something," Lara called out from a huge glass-fronted dresser where she'd been foraging furiously. "Here." She held up a mermaid green piece of silk with lace edging and examined the tag. "La Perla, you're in luck."

"I can't wear that," I said in horror. "First off, it belongs to Daniel's wife. Secondly, it's lingerie."

"Josie will never notice. She's very well medicated. Just put it on."

"But it's underwear!" I wailed.

"No one will ever know. Just try it on." Before I could protest, she had slipped it over my head and was scrutinizing me. "Great. Now, just take your bra off and we're A-okay."

"Lara, I need a bra. I have C-cup breasts. They're not meant to stand up on their own."

"You look hot, come on," she said, and led me back out into the party, grabbing a couple of cocktails on the way and insisting that I drink both before I moved another inch. "Now, you go and have fun." And with that she vanished. Leaving me alone wearing underwear in public.

Fortunately or unfortunately—and there are two points of view here—the slip was a hit. It took another cocktail to unglue me from behind the white pillar at the foot of Daniel's staircase and propel me out toward the pool. I couldn't see anyone that I knew, not even Lara, Scott, or Daniel. But as I looked around, Cameron tapped me on the shoulder.

"I love your dress. It's neat," she said, and I felt myself buckle in the presence of her sheer starriness. Tonight she was not wearing Kmart pants. She had a white rose behind her ear, the promised pink dress, and a friendly smile on her face.

"Thank you," I managed to say as I gazed at her and marveled at just how unequal human beings were created. For that moment I wished that my fairy godmother had ticked the charisma box instead of the brain box. Because how much fun would life be if you were Cameron?

"There's a guy over there who I once kissed but who's way too smart for me. He makes me feel like an intellectual ant. But I'm sure you'd love him," Cameron whispered conspiratorially to me, moving in close. "Great, great kisser, too. Or I wouldn't recommend him," she added, as if she were urging me to try a smoked-salmon canapé.

"Okay, I'll remember that," I told her gratefully. Though I wasn't tall enough to see the guy she was pointing to over the ocean of guests and wouldn't have had the courage to pursue him anyway. "Thanks."

"No problem," Cameron said before being swept away as dizzyingly as she'd arrived.

Our encounter, though, had mysteriously given me the courage to make my way to where a friendly looking group of people was sitting by the adobe pool house. I said hi and attempted to sit down on the floor beside them in an elegant way, but because I was as drunk as a skunk by this point, I thudded down with the grace of a sack of Idaho potatoes.

"Hi, there," I hiccupped, and noticed, too late, that Bob was one of the friendly looking people.

"Must say I prefer this dress much better," he laughed. He had stripped down to his swimming trunks, and the girls around him were all wearing bikinis. Moments later some beautiful young boy movie star whom I didn't recognize sat down on a nearby bench, and the girls dissolved like lumps of sugar, only to resurface at his side. Leaving me alone with Bob.

"So, honey, are you enjoying yourself?"

I was tempted to tell him irritably that at this moment the only thing I *was* enjoying was myself, but when I looked up again, he was smiling in an almost appealing way at me.

"Yeah, I'm having a lovely time," I said.

"As you should be. You're definitely the prettiest girl here." He winked.

"It must be almost midnight." I said, changing the subject, though I was a bit warm from the flattery.

"Actually, it's ten of," he said. "Still a little time for fun before we all hit the hay."

"Oh, I've had so much fun," I said, realizing that it was actually true. That for all the drama and all my shattered Jake Hudson dreams and the like, I suddenly felt part of something. As if I belonged in a small way. Not that I mattered in an important-person-in-town way, just that I had my own niche finally. And I smiled to myself. I was very far from D.C., but it was all okay.

"Let's swim."

In my reverie I hadn't noticed that Bob was standing above me, holding out his hand. But I was relaxed enough to take it, and the water looked delicious, so I allowed him to pull me to my feet, and before I had time to ponder whether this was a sensible career move, I leaped headlong into the pool with Bob.

Moments later, splashing around in the blissful warmth of the water, I was giggling away and Bob watched as I demonstrated my famous underwater handstand.

"You gotta lose the dress, babycakes," he said when I spluttered to the surface with a noseful of chlorine. "It could be dangerous swimming in that thing. Might sink you."

And because I am very stupid and obedient when drunk, I shuffled my billowing dress off my body and wriggled out of it. I drifted toward the deep end, in just my G-string and diamonds, with my breasts bobbing excitedly in the water. And moments later Bob was also bobbing excitedly in the water, right beside me. And I think I must have been affected by the headiness of cocktails and jewels and water and sadness, because after another moment Bob was kissing me. And I didn't mind. Jake had gone home with his living doll, and they were doubtless making beautiful, magical love together right now in his Malibu beach house. And anyway, there was something comforting about the way Bob tasted of cigars and gently stroked the back of my neck. The water lapped against my shoulders, and reality seemed about a million miles away.

It was only a few minutes later, when there was a huge splash in the pool, followed by another and another, that I suddenly realized what I'd done. Everyone had followed my lead, and four of the Crazy Girls were splashing around with untethered boobs in the water, and where the Crazy Girls went, the hopeful boys followed. So the next moment the water was alive with managers and directors and producers in boxer shorts, or disturbingly less. In fact, the whole party seemed to be in the swim. Except for Daniel, who was standing at the edge of the pool above me, having a Howard Hughes moment over the contamination of his beautiful pool and the vile bodies swimming around in it. He was pale with horror, and it was all my fault. Oh, well, I thought pragmatically as I crawled out, dripping diamonds and water and praying that the taxis were still running, Hollywood is a jungle, so I suppose the only way to survive is to throw yourself in at the deep end.

7

The boss doesn't have to give you a reason. That's one of the wonderful things about being the boss.

—Jimmy Stewart as Alfred Kralik
The Shop Around the Corner

By Monday morning my devil-may-care attitude was languishing in a discarded heap on my bedroom floor, along with Lara's silver shoes, my damp G-string, and the tissues I'd used to rub off my eye makeup when I finally made it home from the party. I hadn't even remembered to pick up a goodie bag as I made my getaway from Daniel's. So all I was left with now was a feeling somewhere between self-loathing and dread at facing the consequences of my wanton antics. Dread that intensified with every ramp I bumped over as I made my way into the terrible darkness of The Agency's parking lot. Down and down I went, spiraling into the fourth, fifth, and sixth circles of hell until I found a corner so remote that it was unlikely I'd meet a cockroach, let alone a coworker of any description.

I finally pried myself out of my car, fearful that if I stayed in any longer with the doors shut, one of the Josés would spot me on CCTV and rescue me from what they would presume was my carbon monoxide death. The Josés, by the way, are one of the best things about The Agency. They're two handsome, elderly Mexican guys, one of whom is etiolated like a bolted string bean and the other who comes up to his friend's pelt of chest hair. They're both called José and run the parking lot with the efficiency of a military operation and more cheek than

J.Lo. They had smiled sympathetically at me on my first day and ever since had been kinder to me than any other person in the whole place. Whenever I lost my car, they would point me in the right direction without insinuating that I was an idiot. They once gave me a Rice Crispy treat when I'd had to spend my lunch hour in the Laundromat getting Victoria's gym kit washed. Tall José taught me how to work out the profit margins of a movie one day when there was a backlog of cars trying to leave the building, and they always mysteriously seemed to know when I would be needing my car, even for an emergency prune-juice run, and would have it ready. There was something omniscient about the Josés. This morning, when I finally made it to their booth beside the elevator, they were waiting for me.

"Ah, you made it. But now you have to go back to your car because it's home time," Tall José laughed.

"Maybe she's too poor to join the gym, so she takes her exercise by walking from her car," the other José joined in.

"You're both wrong." I said miserably. "I just needed some time for reflection."

"Ah, you want to borrow my mirror?" I couldn't help but join in their giggles.

"Well, I'm glad you guys think it's funny. Personally, I have more serious matters on my mind."

"Ah, yes, we know," Tall José said gravely. He was often the less cheery of the two.

"What do you know?" I snapped, and probably blushed furiously, too.

"Si te acuestas con niños, te levantas meado." Short José nodded.

"What on earth does that mean?" I shakily pressed the elevator button. Summoning the very thing that would take me irrevocably to face my personal hell.

"If you go to bed with children, you'll get covered in pee," Tall José explained.

"Thanks." I closed my eyes and pondered the meaning of this, but before it sunk in that the Josés must know all about my nearly naked party antics and were undoubtedly offering me some pearl of wisdom, the elevator doors chimed open and I stepped in.

"Morning." A young agent from the Lit Department was standing in the elevator in his charcoal gray suit and slick hair, grinning at me. A little too broadly for my liking. I tried to remember whether he'd been at the party. But most of it was a blur by now. My brilliant subconscious wouldn't allow me access to my memories of Saturday night in case I murdered myself. I steadfastly ignored him and tucked my chin into my neck and looked at my shoes. He got out on the first floor, and I sailed on up to the next one, wondering what on earth was going to greet me when I walked through the double doors to the assistant pool. Would Scott be standing with his hands on his hips waiting to give me my marching orders? Would my disgrace be splashed across the cover of *Variety*? Maybe my belongings would already be packed into a box and my replacement would be changing the font on my beloved white Mac from Times New Roman to Arial while helping herself to my emergency stash of Junior Mints.

But it turned out that the place was eerily the same as usual. The assistants who were already in were tucked behind their desks, sorting mail, booting up their computers, and sucking on Jamba Juice with extra echinacea. I made a beeline for my desk and slunk into my seat before anyone could notice. Though in reality none of the assistants would have heard the news of my lurid encounter in the pool anyway, as none of them had been invited to Daniel's party. The only reason I had gone was that I'd arranged the whole thing in the first place and had to make sure it ran smoothly. I hid my head with shame. If only I hadn't got drunk and overly friendly, I might be able to have some pride in how well the party had gone. Well, until we destroyed the pool, that is.

Still, at least Daniel wasn't waiting for me. There were no e-mails inviting me to discuss my lewd conduct with Human Resources, and Scott didn't seem to be here to fire me. What a relief. I put on my headset as Noah from the mailroom deposited the trades and mail on my desk.

"Thanks." I smiled. He smirked before moving his cart on to Talitha's desk. I opened the mail: the minutes from Friday's staff meeting, the new issue of *Entertainment Weekly* with Nicole on the cover, *Variety* and the *Hollywood Reporter* without a mention of me on the front page, and an in-house envelope that was bulging, probably with a *Charlie's Angels* action figure for Scott to show to Drew. I stuck my hand inside and pulled out what looked suspiciously like my bra from Saturday night. I stuffed it back in quickly and looked around to see whether anyone had noticed. When I was sure that nobody had, I peered down into the envelope and removed the yellow sticky that was attached to it.

You left this at Daniel's house. You clearly need it back.
Best, Ryan

That fucker. I could hear snickers coming from the other desks and assumed that by now there was an e-mail circulating with my breasts on it. I would figure out a way to pay Ryan back for his little stunt on Saturday if it became my life's mission. I contemplated the old favorites, like lacing his coffee with Visine or setting his computer wallpaper to gay porn.

However, my revenge fantasies were interrupted by a call from Lara, who said she wouldn't be in today. She was ill. She was also very abrupt and didn't say anything that reassured me that I was a valued member of The Agency's team. But I told myself not to be paranoid. The poor girl was sick, and my peace of mind wasn't likely to be at the top of her list of priorities.

I decided to get over myself and get on with my work. That was what I was here for, after all. I looked at Scott's schedule and realized that if he didn't appear five minutes ago, he was going to miss the Monday-morning meeting. This was where all the agents got together and discussed what their clients had on the slate, who they could pitch for different movie parts, which directors they wanted to match up to the hottest new script in town, and whether it wasn't time for a movie about Attila the Hun—he hadn't been done for ages, had he? In short, it was vital that every single agent in the building attended and put forward his or her genius ideas. So where was Scott? I called his cell phone, and a woman answered.

"Hello."

"Hi, there. This is Lizzie calling from Scott's office. Is he there, please?" I assumed it was his wife.

"No, he's tied up right now." I heard a burst of laughter, and the phone went dead. I'd heard from Lara that Mia Wagner was a bit psycho, so I wasn't altogether surprised. At ten-fifteen I got a very pissy call from Daniel's third assistant, Katrina, wanting to know where Scott was, because the meeting was about to start. I said that he was at the doctor's and that it was my fault I hadn't let them know.

"Oh, yeah, right," she said. Another dead line. It was going to be one of those days.

By eleven o'clock I began to worry a little. While it was clear that I was not going to be fired after all, if my *boss* got the boot, then I might be out of a job anyway. I had been fielding calls from just about everyone and had run out of all the usual "He was on the line a minute ago, but he got cut off going through a canyon"–type excuses and was feeling desperate. I riffled through Lara's book, but all I could see, apart from a lot of cryptic-looking red triangles on the corner of the pages, which were obviously code for something fascinating, was that Mia Wagner was at Canyon Ranch spa until tomorrow. Fuck, maybe that *wasn't* his wife who'd answered his cell. Maybe he'd OD'd at home or been murdered by a cult. This was California after all. All I knew was that I had to find him, dead or alive, by one o'clock because he had a lunch with Steven at the Four Seasons, and that was nonnegotiable. I knew that last month Scott had gone out of his way to get invited to a bar mitzvah where Steven was, and then he'd had to be very oleaginous to secure this lunch. There was no way on earth, if he was alive or sentient, that he would miss it.

I picked up yet another call and armed myself with excuses.

"Scott Wagner's office."

"Lara?"

"No, this is Elizabeth," I said with forced cheeriness.

"Where the fuck is Lara?"

"Who is this, please?" The man sounded breathless and a bit psychopathic.

"It's me. Scott, for Chrissake."

"Thank God for that." I couldn't conceal my relief.

"I need to be picked up."

"Okay. Where are you?"

"The Milk Maid, South Fairfax!" he barked. "Someone stole my car, and I have this fucking lunch with Steven. So get it done now. And for fuck's sake don't mention this to anyone!"

"Sure," I said efficiently, but he'd already hung up. I grabbed my keys and the Thomas Guide out of the drawer and hurried, as casually as possible, to the elevator.

When I finally pulled up outside 398 South Fairfax, I wondered if I'd gotten the address right. This whole time I'd assumed that The

Milk Maid was an organic restaurant and that Scott had been having a breakfast meeting and been unlucky enough to have his car stolen. But there wasn't a strawberry smoothie or healthy raisin muffin in sight at this joint. This was a sleazy motel. Probably built in the late seventies. It was one of those drive-by pit stops where you have to check the sheets for pubic hairs and worry all night long that somebody, maybe even the manager, is going to rob you. What on earth was Scott doing here? I parked in the lot, made certain to lock my doors, and followed the half-blinking neon sign to reception.

"Hi, I'm looking for Scott Wagner's room." I took a careful look around. "I think."

"Room ninety-one. Second on the left. Tell him he owes me for two nights 'cause it's after eleven," the skanky young guy on the desk spit. I nodded and practically ran down the sticky brown carpet toward Room 91.

I knocked tentatively on the dirt-ingrained door. "Scott. It's me."

"What?" The door opened a crack, and there was Scott. Not, I have to say, looking über-thrilled to see me.

"Are you okay?" I asked as I edged my way out of the corridor and into the dimly lit hellhole of a room.

"What are *you* doing here?"

"You called me. Said you wanted to be picked up." I wondered if he'd finally crossed the line from recreational drug user into incomprehensible weirdo junkie.

"Where's the car?"

"Down there." I pointed out the window at my Honda, looking very vulnerable in the parking lot below. Scott seemed really spun out.

"I asked for a car. A Mercedes. A limo. I meant to send a driver."

"And here I am." Fake cheery thing again.

"Did you bring any clothes?" I noticed then that he was wearing a very small, balding white towel.

"Clothes? No. Was I supposed to?" Jesus, the least I expected was a little gratitude. I'd stuck my neck out for him all morning, made myself look even more moronic than I really was as an assistant, and come all this way to pick him up. And he was just yelling at me.

"I need something to wear to lunch, for Chrissake. Pants? Socks? Shirt?"

"What happened to yours?" I asked stupidly. I really had to learn when to just *do* and not *ask*.

"Fuck, Lizzie. Not the time for twenty questions. Some bitch stole them. I need something to put on." He paced around the dingy room, which was definitely not the Four Seasons. It smelled of sweat and smoke and every bodily fluid you didn't want to imagine. I held my breath.

"Okay, well I have this Juicy Couture sweatsuit that I just bought, out in the car. But it's meant for girls—"

"Go get it, then. I have a lunch, and I cannot wear a goddamn towel. At least not one from *this* motel!" he yelled, and I darted from the room. Happy to run to the parking lot and refill my lungs.

I was less happy to part with the brown paper bag containing my brand-new Ceylon blue Juicy sweatsuit that I'd bought at a sample sale on Sunday to cheer myself up. I knew that once I gave it to Scott, I'd never see it again. Though, on second thought, I'd never *want* to see it again, as he was clearly going to have to wear it without underwear, and judging by where he'd been sleeping . . . well, I'd have to boil it first. I handed it over and told myself that it was only a material possession and not life or death or anything really important. But it still hurt.

When Scott finally sat down in the passenger seat wearing my snug-fitting prize possession, I could have wept for my loss. That is until I looked at him properly and realized how eye-poppingly ridiculous he looked, and then I nearly howled out loud with laughter. The top was cropped, and he'd zipped it all the way to the neck. The drawstring pants were hanging low so that his hairy stomach was exposed, and the sleeves were about four inches too short. He just looked so un-Scott that, before I could help myself, out slipped a quick giggle.

"Are you laughing at me?" Scott snapped.

I bit my lip and shook my head. "No, of course not," I said stoically.

"You better fucking not be," he said as he sulkily lit up a cigarette without asking if he could smoke in my car. And without opening the window. But as we headed out onto Fairfax toward the Four Seasons, Scott began to stroke the plush velour on his thigh contemplatively.

"I look pretty faggy, huh?" he said with a curl of his lip.

"Just a bit." I gulped back a snicker. With that he began to crack up, and seconds later we were tearing across town in my aging banger, laughing hysterically in the bright, midday sunshine to the sounds of soft rock on the radio.

"I just can't believe it," I said as I wiped a tear from the corner of my eye. "You're going to walk into a restaurant wearing that and take a meeting with Steven S."

"Goddamn right I am," Scott said defiantly. "Those bitches thought they'd screw me over. But I'm not gonna let them win."

"Which bitches?" I asked instinctively, before wondering whether grilling my boss about his sordid private life was a wise move.

"You really wanna know?" he asked earnestly.

"Sure." I shrugged. "I really want to know how you came to be in that den of iniquity at eleven A.M. without a stitch of clothing and a car."

And maybe I shouldn't have asked. But too late now. Scott lit up another cigarette, pushed his seat back for more legroom, and began.

"I was planning to go straight home after the premiere last night. I'd even laid off the sauce and left the party early to get some sleep for this lunch with Steven. Which I have to say I'm fucking proud of scoring. And as I'm driving home, at a stoplight on Doheny, this woman in a black Range Rover starts checking me out. I swear to God, Lizzie, she was hot! No more than twenty-three. Little pigtail things in her hair. And Mia's away and all, and I'm a little turned on from watching a sexy action movie premiere beforehand, and here's this chick in a little white T-shirt with no bra, rubbing her goddamn tits and staring at me. Winking. I mean, what's a guy supposed to do? So I roll down my window and say hi. I figure it can't hurt to be friendly, and then she licks her lips and asks me if I want to follow her to a hotel. I mean, show me the guy who can turn down that, Lizzie, right?

"So I follow her to the Hayloft. And it's not the Bel Air, but fuck it. She seemed to get off on the sleaziness, so who am I to interfere? So I get us a room, and before I can even shut the door, she's taking off my clothes. I mean, she was hot for it. And she's kissing my chest, biting my nipples, and she takes my zipper down with her teeth, and I was bare-assed in a matter of seconds. Then she takes off her top, and I'm trying to touch her really cute little tits, but she wants me to take a pill first. So I pop an X, and we're rocking and rolling. Fooling around. And it's fun.

"Anyway, we party some more, and I'm just about ready to come when suddenly the room starts to spin and the wallpaper's doing the tango. But she's still on the bed and kissing me, and it feels kinda nice when she ties me to the bed, so I let her do whatever the hell it is she wants to do. And I'm just spacing. But the next thing I know, she's putting on her clothes and she's talking on her cell phone to someone, and eventually I just fall asleep tripping my balls off.

"Then, when I woke up this morning, I had no fucking clue where I was, but I managed to untie myself—and guess what? She stole everything. My Porsche, my keys, my wallet, my watch, my phone. Even my clothes. The whole fucking lot. Which is when I realize that she set it all up. She left this nicely typed little note on the bed in an envelope and all, telling me—

> 'Dear Mr. Wagner,
> You may remember that some weeks ago you had the good fortune to leave a party in Laurel Canyon with my good friend Grace. You took her home, and before having sex with her in your hot tub, you told her that you were an agent and that it would be no problem finding her work. That if she left her card, you'd call. And you promised her representation. But you never called, Mr. Wagner. Which we consider to be the worst kind of bad manners, so we decided to ensure that no aspiring actress ever fell prey to your low-life lies again. We can only hope that the loss of your car, clothes, and wallet reminds you to have more respect for others in the future.
>
> Yours truly,
> An Angel of Justice'

"So apparently this tie-up-an-agent bullshit was them trying to teach me some kind of lesson. Yeah, really fucking useful lesson to learn. Actresses are crazy. Like I needed reminding."

I turned left and pulled into the tree-lined driveway that looped in front of the Four Seasons. The doorman looked at my car with horror.

"Well, I'm glad you're still alive" was all I could say to Scott. And I was. He was like a child who needed an awful lot of looking after, but he was also pretty easygoing for a boss. I knew that I could do much worse, and I didn't want to lose him just yet. Especially not to some harebrained actress with a vendetta and, now, a shining new Porsche.

"Do I look okay?" he asked as he ran his fingers through his matted hair.

"The truth?" I blinked. He looked very far from okay.

"Okay, does my breath smell?" He exhaled on me, and I almost collapsed.

I grabbed my purse and pulled out some TicTacs. "Here, take them all." I handed them over, and he popped a handful in his mouth.

"Thanks, Lizzie-o," he said, and leaned over to kiss my cheek. I tried not to let him see me flinch. "I'll get a ride back with Daniel, but you can get me a rental. Hey, how about the new Mercedes convertible? No, make it a Ferrari. Black. Oh, and call my insurance, too. Say I was rolled."

"You *were* rolled."

"Don't tell them it was chicks."

I watched as Scott stepped out of the car into the midday heat in brightest, cutest Ceylon blue with his short, short, tight, tight pants and crazy hair, and oddly enough I think he pulled it off. The doorman smiled at him like an old friend and opened the door. I'm sure that when he strolled into the dining room, Steven the director hugged him warmly, and I'm sure that as he tugged enthusiastically at his bread roll and talked about passion and commitment to clients, Daniel was proud to have him as a colleague. Because no matter what he did, Scott was cool.

I, on the other hand, was 160 bucks down right now, getting evil stares from the valets, and due back in the office an hour ago to help Victoria out in a strategy meeting. Which basically meant to fetch coffee. But that was a moot point. Coffee fetcher or strategy maker, I was still going to get screamed at. All because I had been doing my job. There's no such thing as justice in the world of the assistant, you see, only hope. And that takes a seat way, way back down the bus from experience every time.

8

He's like an animal. He has an animal's habits. There's even something subhuman about him.

—Vivien Leigh as Blanche Dubois
A Streetcar Named Desire

I picked up my phone, pencil poised. "Hello, The Agency."

"Lizzie?" Usually it was only Scott who called me Lizzie, but this voice did not sound as though it belonged to Scott. Besides which, I could see Scott, who was in his office shooting baskets.

"Elizabeth Miller speaking."

"It's Bob." There was a silence as I filled in the blanks. Bob . . . Redford? Bob . . . De Niro? (Okay, I didn't know them personally, but after a mere forty-eight hours in the film industry, *everyone* knows that these men are Bob and not Robert. It's like a Masonic handshake that distinguishes the doyens of Hollywood from the readers of *People* magazine. Neither party has ever shared a restaurant table with either Bob or Robert, but the former like the world to assume that they do so on a weekly basis.)

"Bob?" I was forced to ask for clarification.

"From the party on Saturday night," he informed me with a low, throaty growl.

"Bob. Bob." I'd been so frantically busy with all the calls and paperwork couriering for Scott's new deal with Steven that it was as though Saturday had never happened. But suddenly it all came flooding back: the taste of cigars, the sausagey fingers.

"Lizzie, honey."

"Can I, er, can I transfer you to Scott?" I asked hopefully. He was, after all, a huge producer. Or so he had told me sixteen times as I wove my fingers through his chest hair in the pool. It was therefore much more likely that he wanted to speak to my boss than to me. Most likely he'd taken the Jake Hudson route of once kissed, forever forgotten where I was concerned.

"How 'bout you and I have dinner on Saturday night?" Obviously not the Jake Hudson route, then.

"Saturday? Dinner?" I coughed a little to buy time, and when I glanced up, Scott was standing above me, looking quizzically. Not going away.

"Who is that?" he was mouthing.

"Bob, would you mind holding the line for just one moment, please?" I put Bob on hold.

"Bob Davies," I told Scott, who had assumed, not unreasonably since this was The Agency and not The Dating Agency, that the call was for him.

"Bob Davies?" Scott asked, a little confused.

"Yeah."

"Isn't he looking for new representation? Holy shit, Lizzie, does he want us to rep him? Man, this is my week! He's just signed a six-picture deal at Warner Brothers. He must have read in the trades about our deal with Steven and wants a piece of the action. Put him through, right now."

"He wants to have dinner with me, actually." I broke the news to Scott, expecting him to either get mad or tell me to conduct my sordid sex life outside the office.

"Fan-fucking-tastic!" Scott high-fived me.

"Yeah, but, Scott, I don't think that—"

"You have got to go. He's hot, Lizzie," Scott informed me excitedly.

"He is not. He's kind of gross and overweight and—"

"I don't mean *hot* hot. I mean hot. Just say the fuck yes." This, clearly, was an order, and though I looked imploringly at my boss, though he was a major junkie who barely knew what day of the week it was, though I had donated my Juicy Couture tracksuit to him, he still expected me to go on a date with Bob. I switched my phone off hold.

"Bob, I'm sorry about that. So you wanted to have lunch on Saturday?" I attempted to make the date a little less horrifying. Though meeting him in daylight hours was not necessarily going to take care of that problem.

"Spago, Saturday at nine. Leave your car at home."

"Well, you see, Bob, the thing is that actually—"

But the line had gone dead. Bob knew that he was a hot, if overweight, number. He also knew that a girl in my position was in no position to say no. Well, certainly not with her boss breathing down her neck. I took my pencil and wrote it in my calendar, hoping that something might happen between now and Saturday that would prevent me from having to go through with this. Hip-replacement surgery or a run-in with the bubonic plague would probably cover it. I crossed my fingers hopefully.

Unfortunately, nothing happened between then and Saturday to alter my ghastly fate. Apart from the fact that I began to have recurring nightmares about turning up at Spago and being shown to my table only to discover that I had a date with a gorilla called Gazza who had escaped from the San Diego Zoo. Without fail I would wake up sweating at the precise moment that Gazza the Gorilla reached across the table and put his hairy-knuckled hand over mine and told me that I had hot titties.

Needless to say, for my date I chose a tidy turtleneck number that would have left even the most eagle-eyed ogler uncertain as to whether I even owned a pair of titties. And pants so enormous and flapping in the wind that I could only be hiding the most gargantuan thighs in town. To cap off my sexless ensemble, I tied my hair back in a curt ponytail and donned a pair of pearl earrings that screamed respectability, not approachability. Good, good. I glanced at my reflection in my car door as I got in and headed to Spago. Not a mixed message in sight.

"Honey, I thought I told you to leave your car at home." Bob stood up and kissed me wetly on the lips as I arrived at the dinner table and ostentatiously jangled my keys down. (I couldn't afford to valet-park until September next year due to the cost of the Hollywood Honey, so was still in possession of my keys.)

"Oh, it's fine." I politely wiped his slobber from my lips and sat down. "I love to drive, and I need all the practice I can get. I'm forever getting lost on the freeway and ending up in South Central," I laughed airily.

"Not to worry. I have a driver. I'll just have him drop you off, and you can collect your car tomorrow." Bob was looking desperately for my breasts despite the needle-in-a-haystack scenario of my clever sweater, and any minute he was going to end up needing a chiropractor.

"I've heard so much about this place. You know, I've never been before." I had resolved to keep this encounter very breezy and professional, if that were possible. If I felt that I was doing this for work, to help out Scott, I'd survive, I had determined.

"Oh, it's not too bad." Bob shrugged dismissively. "Heavy hitters, starfuckers. Such a scene."

I wondered why he'd brought me here if that was the case. But then I hadn't been to enough Hollywood restaurants to learn that everyone always complained about "the scene," the fact that this place was full of industry types, oh, such a pain in the ass, etc., etc. But that was the way the cookie crumbled in this town. You had to dis the industry to prove you belonged. Leaden-eyed ennui was par for the course with the movers and shakers.

"Well, the food looks delicious." I admired a pizza that was being served up to the white-leather-clad peroxide blonde with an orange face at the next table. I began to scan my menu as Bob ordered the wine. "So, Bob, I hear you've just signed a great deal over at Warner Brothers."

"Oh, Christ, let's not talk business. It's Saturday night." Bob knocked back the inch of red wine in his glass and proclaimed it drinkable. "It's just a deal, when all is said and done. Six pictures for the next three years. Minimum budget of a hundred mil per picture. I've bought thirty specs and the options on seven novels, and we'll most likely only do the ones that have major players attached. I love a good movie. I hate that foreign shit. Really, I'd rather eat a fried-okra sandwich than pay to see some art house piece of shit. I'm one of the rare producers in this town who isn't ashamed to say that he's motivated by box office. Man, I love that stuff, I love the figures. I mean, someone's got to pay for my house in the Palisades and the lodge in Sun Valley and I have a G4. Did I mention, Lizzie, that I have a G4? You should totally come and have a trip in it one day. Have you ever been to the Post Ranch? Man, that place is awesome for a romantic weekend away. It's just kinda too far to drive, so I prefer to fly. Though Christ knows there are usually too many dissolute industry types hanging out there, so I usually just stay in my room with the lady in question and hang."

Do you get the picture?

By the time Bob turned to me and asked me what I did at The Agency, I was on my second spoonful of my mint-tea sorbet. Dessert, in other words.

"Me?" I asked, genuinely surprised. Miraculously, Bob hadn't drawn breath for the last hour and a half. And in a feat worthy of the circus, he had simultaneously put away a three-course dinner and a side of stuffed-zucchini-flower tempura.

"Yes, you pretty little thing. What is it that you do over there at the Evil Empire?"

"You mean The Agency?" I corrected him. Though it wasn't the first time I'd heard my workplace called that.

"Oh, don't tell me you're an assistant, or I'll cream my underpants," he groaned.

Okay, I'm not prissy. I am not wildly shockable (let's remember that I was on this date with Bob because I had gotten naked in my boss's pool with the man), but this made me choke up my last mouthful of sorbet.

"Oh, honey, the look on your face is priceless." Bob leered. "You are an assistant, aren't you?"

I nodded hastily and made sure that my car keys were still on the table.

And there I'd been just staring at him as he'd talked away and away, thinking, Okay, well, he's not exactly attractive, and he's a super-self-absorbed pain in the ass, but he's not a bad man. He just looks a little like Shrek. But I was wrong—the man was a monster. There was no denying it.

"You're an assistant, and it has to be said I have a bit of a thing for assistants. And D-whores. Sorry, D-girls." He laughed artificially. "So right now I'm a very happy man, Lizzie."

"I'm so glad," I replied crisply, and took a large sip of my water, in preparation for the drive home. I'd steered as clear of the claret as possible and was quite sober.

"A digestif?" Bob leaned over and, very much in the manner of Gazza the Gorilla, clutched my hand in his clammy palm. "Waiter, two large glasses of calvados, please."

"I actually have to go home soon," I attempted.

"Why don't you go to the bathroom and freshen up while I take care of the check, and then I'll make sure that Alfredo takes you home. After your calvados."

Bob ushered me away from the table, and I gratefully stayed in the bathroom as long as was decently possible. A moment washing my hands was, after all, a moment I didn't have to worry about having to dodge Bob's kisses again. But finally I tore myself away from the comfort of the hand dryer and went to face my fate.

Now, I have not lived my life on a secluded island brought up by Carmelite nuns with only a mute sister for companionship. Neither were my parents overprotective religious zealots who made me read the Old Testament instead of watching televison. In other words, I have not led an especially sheltered existence. So, really, I ought to have known that something was wrong. I should have smelled a rat when I took my first sip of calvados and noticed that it seemed to be fizzy. And I ought to have been even more suspicious when I started behaving like a more loquacious version of Anna Nicole Smith right after I'd taken my first mouthful. But I didn't suspect a thing. I just thought, Oh, look, fizzy calvados. Happy me. How weird. But no weirder than the rest of my life in this crazy place.

"Is that good?" Bob asked as I finally replaced my empty glass on the table.

"That was . . . actually very good." I nodded. And it was. I was feeling a whole lot more relaxed about Bob now. And my ride home. Or not. And the more I looked at Bob, the cuter he seemed. He was clearly one of those men whose looks grew on you, I remember thinking.

"You're so lovely." I smiled across the table at him and took his hand. "You really are."

"Great, well, so are you, honey. And I was thinking, I know a little place nearby where we can go." He stood up and, like a gentleman, eased me into my jacket.

"Oh, goody. Can we dance there?" I asked, my feet suddenly aching for a groove.

"We can do whatever you like there," Bob said. "It's a really chill joint."

"Fan-tastic." I giggled and snuggled up to Bob's shoulder affectionately as we left the restaurant.

As I climbed with Bob into the back of his Lincoln Town Car, I was feeling very free and easy, so I didn't mind a bit when the charming Alfredo drove us to Burbank. Which is not where I live. Neither is it the Standard or White Lotus. Nor is it even Les Deux. All of which would be passable venues for a Shrek-like producer about town to take a date to on a Saturday night after dinner. But no, we were in Burbank. In the Valley. And as we got closer to our destination, as Alfredo put on his blinker to indicate that we were going to pull over and stop, I realized that this was Dimples Supper Club. Not, you understand, that I had ever heard of Dimples Supper Club. I sincerely doubt that anyone apart from the manager and bar staff of Dimples had ever heard of it. It's just that it was in Burbank, it was located in a shiny strip mall, and in flashing lights it promised that most horrible of mistakes, karaoke.

I cannot sing. I cannot hold a tune, in neither a paper bag nor a supermarket trolley. But that particular evening, karaoke seemed to me to be the best idea anyone had ever had in the history of good ideas.

"Bob, this is awesome!" I practically sprinted from the smooth, cool leather seats of the car and into Dimples. And as Bob handed over the twenty-buck entrance fee to the cashier, I was already wiggling my hips to "It's Raining Men," which was being sung by an accountant from Long Beach and was pulsing through the darkness and tinsel.

"I'm glad you like it." Bob smiled.

I tried to take his hand and drag him toward the shabby but sparkling stage. But he seemed to have a purse with him.

"Put your purse down and come dance with me," I demanded shrilly.

But instead Bob put his purse down and then began to take something out of it.

"What are you doing? I want to dance." I waved my arms about a bit and moved to the music. "Do you think I can take my turn on the karaoke next?"

"I'm sure you can, baby. But first let me set up my little piece of equipment here. I'd hate to miss your moment of glory," Bob said calmly.

"You're going to take a photo?" I asked as I looked down at the camera he seemed to be assembling.

"Oh, it's just a little digital home movie. For fun."

"Okay. Well, just hurry up." I sailed off onto the dance floor and began to get very into some wordless anthem. Which was highly uncharacteristic behavior for me. I do not dance voluntarily. I have never been to Ibiza, and, most significantly, as I've already mentioned, I cannot sing.

But for some reason, which would become horribly clear to me later, I didn't let any of this stop me from getting up onto the stage at Dimples some three minutes later and belting out "I Don't Want No Scrub" by TLC. It was the most appalling rendition of that cool song that anyone, anywhere, ever, has heard in their lives. And this is not a case of me being modest when really I have the voice of a nightingale or Aretha Franklin. For I do not.

After my moment of glory, after I had fondled Big Bob on the dance floor a little, after I'd cozied up to him in the back of his Town Car while he made a phone call on the way home, Alfredo dropped us off at the afore- and oft-mentioned house in the Palisades. Which I had to admit was pretty spectacular. But nothing I hadn't seen a hundred times on *Lifestyles of the Rich and Famous.* Bob brought me a glass of wine, and I aimlessly looked at his paintings and the framed photographs of him with Bill Clinton (every home in Hollywood, it seemed, had one) and with Barbra Streisand and Nicole and George. There was also a white Steinway piano in the corner of the room overlooking the Olympic-size swimming pool.

"Do you play?" I asked as I leaned over the instrument and tapped out my schoolgirl "Greensleeves."

"Oh, yeah, I play." Bob sidled up to me and began kissing my neck from behind.

"No, I meant the piano, silly." I laughed and shrugged him off. I still felt quite restless and was lost without music. "I know, let's dance."

"Here?" Bob asked, obviously a little exhausted by me by this stage.

"Sure," I giggled. I went over to his NASA-like music center and tried to fathom out some music. When I finally had Fifty Cent blasting out, I turned around and saw that Bob was asleep on the sofa, a whiskey in his hand and a trickle of saliva trailing down his chin. I turned the music down in order not to wake him and wondered what to do next. I tried to shove him in the ribs, but he didn't stir. I wasn't about to dance alone, and I was sober enough to understand that I didn't want to still be here in the morning. So I set about looking for the phone number of a taxi company.

In fact, with all the manic energy I had, I practically turned Bob's house upside down looking for a number. I just ought to have called 411, but I had been brought up to believe that that was lazy and wasteful, so I valiantly sought the White Pages in order to save Bob forty cents. I looked in the kitchen, the hallway, the living room, and then I found his home office. But there was no White Pages there either, just a few scripts, a fax machine that had the weekly BO charts spewing from it, and a mountain of videocassettes—teasers for all of Bob's crappy movies—but no taxi number.

By the time I found my way to the bedroom, I had abandoned any hope of finding the damned thing and decided to just pick up the bedside phone and call 411. Bob could probably afford it, I guessed. I dropped down onto his maid-made, luxuriously blanketed bed and ordered the taxi that would get me the hell out of here before Bob woke and came to find me. Which I was not looking forward to. As I waited for the cab to arrive, I flicked on MTV at low volume (lest the lord and master should wake up) on the vast television set at the foot of the bed. (Do you really think that Hollywood Man can get turned on by just the woman he's with? Of course not. He's an inveterate multitasker and can happily give or receive oral sex while enjoying the highlights of a football game or an old Rolling Stones video on VH-1.) And that's when I saw his video collection and realized that not only was Bob a famous producer, he was also a not-so-famous director. And his hits included positively low-budget pieces of art such as:

Elaine (Fox Searchlight) sings "I'm No Angel," June 2000
Jennifer (CAA) sings "Dangerously in Love," December 2003
Janie (Dreamworks) sings "Big Spender," April 1997

I scanned down the towering, chronologically arranged collection of videos until I saw a couple of names that I recognized.

Talitha (The Agency) sings "It Ain't Over Till It's Over," June 2001.
Courtney (The Agency) sings "Hit Me Baby One More Time," August 2001

I didn't know whether to laugh or throw up. Whether to run or slot one of the videos into the machine and watch. Instead I sat and stared at the titles in horror, imagining the copy of

> Lizzie (The Agency) sings "I Don't Want No Scrub," April 2004

which was sitting in Bob's camera case in the other room. But just as I was about to remove my shoes and sneak in to retrieve it, there was a ring at the doorbell. I flew, faster than a bat out of hell, toward the front door, to prevent my cabdriver from ringing again and waking Bob. If he hadn't already.

"Hello," I whispered as I opened the door. "I'll be right with you. I just have to get my purse."

"Hi, I'm Naomi." Standing at the door was a pretty girl about my age in a pair of knee-high boots and a short black coat.

"Oh, hi," I said, very happy that I was to have a woman driver.

"Shall I come in?" she asked.

"Sure, step inside. I won't be a minute." I tore back down the corridor and into the living room, where Bob was thankfully still snoring loudly. I looked around for his black camera case, which I felt sure must be here somewhere.

"Do you want me to go into the bedroom or something, then?"

I turned around and saw that Naomi had followed me and was taking off her coat to reveal a small red dress with cutout bits.

"I'm sorry?" I asked.

"Well, I could just go on through and get comfortable, while you find whatever it is you're looking for," she said and licked her lips at me. I blinked once or twice.

"You're not my taxi driver?"

"No, honey. I'm not your taxi driver."

"Oh," I said. "Are you a friend of Bob's?"

"I'm whoever's friend you want me to be," Naomi said, pushing her long, wavy black hair over her shoulder and stepping toward me. "But I think that Bob asked me here to be with you."

"He did?" My voice didn't sound like my own.

Naomi was standing very close to me and put her hand on my

shoulder. "You're very pretty. Why don't we just go on through, and he can join us when he wakes up." Naomi had clearly been here before and knew her way to the bedroom, because before I could protest, she had me by the hand and was leading the way.

"Right, thanks," I said. "The only thing is, Naomi, that with Bob being asleep . . . well, whatever it was that you wanted me to do . . . well . . ."

"Sshhhhhhh," Naomi said. She may have been my age, but she clearly had a lot more confidence than I did, because she turned around, put her hand on the back of my neck, and kissed me on the lips. I'd never tasted another woman's lipstick before—it was odd, really—but just as she slipped her tongue into my mouth, there was another buzz of the doorbell.

"Oh, that'll be for me," I said as I pulled away from Naomi. "I have to go." I ran back into the other room, where Bob was doing a very fine beached-whale impression, and thankfully spotted the camera case under a table. I pulled it out, ripped open the Velcro, and extracted the tape from the camera,

"You're going?" Naomi stood in the doorway watching me.

"Yeah, sorry, no offense or anything. It's just that my cab's here."

"So what about me?" she asked with a shrug. It was then that I realized that she'd need to be paid. I looked at Bob, gelatinously sprawled over the sofa making grunting sounds, and remembered that I'd seen him put his wallet into his left trouser pocket. I gestured to Naomi to be quiet as I tiptoed closer to Bob, reached one shaking hand into his pocket—which, let me tell you, is as near as I ever wanted to get to the unthinkable—and with more skill than Fagin, I picked Bob's pocket. I handed Naomi her money, plus a very generous tip, and we shared a cab back to Venice. Leaving Bob oblivious to the fact that he'd just slept through one of the best nights he'd never had.

Further inquiries at the office on Monday morning verified that yes, if I'd bothered to ask a single assistant, she could have told me that this was Bob's specialty—dinner at Spago followed by a swift hit of X slipped into the nightcap (I told you, I never dance sober, and I especially never sing. And even though I'm a sweet girl, I'm not enormously affectionate and tactile with unattractive strangers, so there had to be a chemically induced reason for my behavior), and then a Night of Karaoke Shame captured for posterity on camcorder, followed by a spot of girl-on-girl action. Thank God I escaped and got the tape, is all I can think, because even though Bob's video collection featured more D-girls and assistants than Fred Segal on a Saturday afternoon, I would without a shadow of a doubt have gotten the Academy Award for Worst Dressed and Most Tuneless. And no matter how nice Naomi was and how much we laughed at Bob on the ride home, not to mention how ghastly he and his kind were, I hadn't quite given up on the boys yet.

9

What's the going price on integrity this week?

—Orson Welles as Jonathan Lute
I'll Never Forget What's 'Is Name

After Bob, I swore off dating. There was really no other choice. I clearly wasn't equipped with the emotional or physical armor that one needed to be romantically successful in Hollywood. And while I was sure that there must be a book that I could read about the subject or a seminar that I could go to and learn "How to Find the Love of Your Life in a Town of Sleazoids," perhaps along the lines of Robert McKee's legendary screenwriting course, I didn't have the time right now. I was inundated with a pile of scripts that Victoria had given to me for coverage, I had at least 750,000 lunches to organize for Scott, and since Lara had an assignment to hand in for her online novel-writing class, I also had to cover all her phone calls and coffee runs. In fact, my elbows had become as permanent a fixture on the counter of the Coffee Bean as the jar of three-dollar brownies and the tips cup.

"The usual, honey?" Jason would say as I walked in his shop looking once again as though I'd just spent a relaxing half hour in the electric chair.

"Yes, please." I'd prop my chin up on my hands and gaze at the speckled Formica in the hopes that it would enlighten me as to just what, exactly, I was doing here. In this town where all my paper cuts and spilling guts and sleepless nights worrying whether I'd remembered to tell Scott that his hottest young director's new movie was going to come in $76 million over budget as of week two of a sixteen-week shoot in NYC. (A city where you couldn't shoot yourself in the foot for less than $3 million per day, by the way.) Because if I hadn't remembered to tell Scott, I'd find myself standing in his office the next morning being promised all sorts of new orifices, to be torn lovingly by hand by my charming boss.

This morning as I walked into the Coffee Bean, I noticed that The Assistants were back. Max Fischer's assistants, to be precise. They were huddled in a crumpled heap around a corner table—all six of them—their faces bloodless and their expressions pained. I tried not to look at them—it was too miserable a sight—and made instead for Jason, who was, as usual, standing behind the counter. But actually Jason looked almost as bad as I felt, and not much better than The Assistants. He had dark circles under his eyes that were beyond poetic, and he'd just burned his fingers on the espresso machine.

"Was it a late night?" I asked as I assumed my customary position at the counter.

"An hour of sleep before I had to be in here at six."

"Wow, was she hot?" I smiled, pleased that someone had a love life. Even though the idea of Jason with a girlfriend wasn't entirely pleasing to me. It wasn't that I had a crush on him, exactly. Just that I felt at ease with him, and knowing that there was this sweet, funny guy out there whom I might one day see outside of the Coffee Bean, even if only as a friend, was a comforting thought.

"No such luck. I was up finishing my screenplay."

"You're a writer?" I asked, feeling suddenly guilty that I'd known Jason for almost a month and I'd never seen him as anything other than a professional milk frother. That was how self-absorbed I'd become. I used to be the kind of girl who knew the names of the kids of the man who installed new software on our office computers in D.C. What was happening to me?

"And director. It's my first screenplay. And now that it's written, the hard work begins." He ran his singed finger under the cold tap.

"That's great, Jason," I said.

"You can read it if you like. I'm looking for a producer."

"Well, sure. I mean, I have a whole heap of stuff to read this weekend, but I'm sure that I can get around to it soon, and then I can help to come up with a list of producers that you could send it to. Not that I'm an expert—I mean, I only know what I overhear in meetings, but—"

"I meant for *you* to produce. You do want to produce, don't you? You're a smart girl. I assume you're not planning on being an assistant forever?"

"Well, yes. No. I mean . . . I have no idea," I said. Realizing at that moment that I really didn't have any idea. My dreams for *Crime and Punishment* had never gotten much further than the gown I was planning to wear to the Academy Awards and whether I should borrow my jewels from Harry Winston or Bulgari. Whether I wanted to produce, direct, or turn it into a porn version of the thing had frankly never occurred to me. Which went to show how passionately committed I was to my new career.

"Elizabeth, you're hilarious." Jason gave his first smile of the day.

And though I was glad to have been instrumental in cheering him up I was disturbed by the fact that I appeared to be up the proverbial creek without either a paddle or a game plan. Did I want to produce? I had no clue. I furrowed my brow and looked back at the Formica hopefully.

"Tell you what, I'll give you a copy right now. Then, if you get time before the big read over the weekend, I can attach you as producer before it's snapped up by Spielberg. Okay?"

Jason grinned, but I knew from the look in his eyes that his deal with Spielberg was as carefully dreamed up as my pale blue chiffon, floor-length, boatneck, low-back, embroidered-waistband Alexander McQueen dress for the Oscars. The only difference was that Jason had a real chance of achieving his dream. He was doing something about it. I, on the other hand, was just a human conveyor belt for coffee and phone messages who was going nowhere fast because she had no more profound destination in mind.

"Okay, I'd love to take a look," I said as Jason wrested his magnum opus from his backpack. "My sister's coming into town sometime this week, so I may not be able to get to it right away, but I promise to look at it as soon as I can."

"Cool." He handed over the script and gave me my chai latte for free. "You can be as honest as you like. But just to give you a heads-up, I think that I can probably make it on digital, using non-SAG actors, and we can definitely shoot some of it illegally in New York if we don't have the financing."

"Wow, you really know what you want!" I said to Jason, who had switched from coffee frother to underground-director mode in the blink of an eye.

"Of course I do. I've wanted to make this movie since I was fourteen years old. I've made seven shorts on a similar theme, I wrote my first draft in film school, and I've been revising it ever since. And every night I go to bed and see the scenes in my head, every frame."

"I'd love to read it" was all I could say. Before inanely adding, "Thanks for the latte."

Then I turned to go. But just before I reached the door, it smashed open and a small man with red hair and a beard came tearing through it. I instinctively took a step back to avoid him,

"I knew I'd find you in here, you bunch of hand-holding crybabies!" he screamed when he spotted The Assistants cowering in the corner. "What the fuck are you doing here?" They all looked up in terror.

"You fired us," said one of the guys in a quiet, quivering voice.

"I fire you every fucking day! It doesn't mean that you get to come and drink coffee! Who's answering my phones?" He stood there and bared his teeth at them from behind his angry little beard. "Who's typing my letters? Who's running my fucking company, hey? Answer me that."

But The Assistants didn't answer. They were dumbfounded. After a few paralyzing moments of silence, Max Fischer, one of the most powerful men in Hollywood, picked up a cup of coffee from the table that his young assistants were gathered around and hurled it at the wall. They all turned and watched, with splashes on their faces, as the remainder of it dripped down the orange wall.

"Get back to the office now, you bunch of whining pussies! Or you're all fired!" Max Fischer said, this time in a low, treacherous voice. Then he left as quickly and dramatically as he'd arrived. He was followed by all six of his assistants, who trailed after him like lambs to the slaughter. When I turned around to see Jason, he already had a mop in his hand and was setting about clearing up the mess.

"Hollywood." He shrugged. "Don't ya love it?"

I shook my head and hurried out the door. Actually no, sometimes I didn't love it.

As I walked out of the Coffee Bean into the warm afternoon, I was horror-struck by what I'd just witnessed. Also, I suddenly really didn't know what I was doing here. Jason did, that was for sure, and probably each one of those assistants had a very good reason for putting up with that abuse, too. They undoubtedly had dreams and ambitions and would endure anything to get to where they wanted to be. But I wasn't sure that I knew even slightly why I was here. Elizabeth Miller, producer. It didn't sound right. Neither did any of the variations: senior VP, director of development, president of production, manager, or agent. And as for second assistant? Well, it just wasn't me. I really didn't have the drive, I realized. I suddenly didn't know what I was doing in this town, where I had no discernible talent for anything that meant shit to anybody. Sure, I'd picked up a working knowledge of the industry, but then so had the guy who sliced bagels in my local deli. I also missed feeling as though I could make a difference to somebody else's life. If somebody got better health care because of a comment I made in a meeting or if just one child got into college, then my job would be useful. But that was never ever going to happen in this town. And being surrounded by people who cared so passionately about entertainment and the movies that they were willing to put up with just about anything only made it all the harder to hide from myself what a wrong turn I'd made in coming here.

And so as I crossed the street back to The Agency, careful not to jaywalk with my tray of politically incorrect, capitalist-culture coffees, I decided that it was time to do something that had been weighing on my mind for a couple of weeks now. I think I had what is popularly known as an epiphany, which usually involves great swathes of light flashing across the heavens and holy choirs belting out hallelujahs, though it felt much more as if someone was shaking me by the collar and telling me that I was stupefyingly slow not to have realized this before: It was time to write up my résumé and call it quits in Hollywood. Which was decision enough to lift my spirits and make me practically skip back into the lobby, much to the bemusement of the terminally morose receptionists. I'd apply for any and every job going in Washington: I'd make coffee (no change there, then), I'd be a research assistant (just one word but also a world away from the dreaded second assistant), I'd cover somebody's maternity leave—whatever it took I'd make it up to the world of politics and forge ahead as if Hollywood had never happened.

When I arrived buoyantly back at my desk, Scott had already gone to lunch. Lara was at work on her assignment with a pair of Virgin Atlantic Upper Class earplugs in, and there was a note on my screen saying that my sister had finally called. I'd been waiting impatiently for her call for days now, and when I saw Courtney's mean scribble on the Post-it, my spirits went positively stratospheric.

I dialed the number by her name. "Melissa?"

"Elizabeth? Oh, my God, how are you?"

"I'm great. How are you?"

This continued for at least two minutes before either of us could begin a sensible conversation. I hadn't actually spoken to my sister in four months. Not because we were too busy for one another or because she had married my high-school sweetheart and we were no longer close, but because she'd been in Sierra Leone on a peacekeeping mission with the UN.

"So you're home? You're safe? You're back?" I could hardly believe it. When I'd said good-bye to her in February, I had been convinced that I'd never see her again. And pretty quickly I had to get used to the idea that something terrible might happen to her while she was away. And that if it did, it would be because it was what she wanted. To help others, with her own life a secondary concern to her. Since that day my entire family had operated on the premise that no news is good news. We simply lived for the occasional e-mails she sent from some African schoolroom.

"Not only am I back, I'm in town," she announced, full of life.

"You're in D.C.?" I asked.

"No, you total idiot, I'm in Los Angeles!" She laughed. "Which is culture shockola, let me tell you."

"You're in L.A.?" I repeated incredulously until she finally managed to get through to me the fact that she was in town for one night on a layover and was planning on sharing my bed, the contents of my fridge, and a bottle of red wine with me tonight. Which suddenly made my life worth living. When I hung up, I realized that all the glamorous dates in the world couldn't beat a night at home with my wonderful little sister. And I immediately began to plow through my work with the ease of a seasoned careerphile. In fact, that afternoon anyone who didn't know me might have been mistakenly led to believe that I actually liked being a second assistant.

And as I breezed through the minutes for the Monday meeting and chased up a $13 million check for my least favorite action hero's last movie, I was even in the mood for a down moment with a couple of the other assistants.

"What do you think?" Talitha asked me when I walked back in the room after picking up a parcel from the front desk.

"About what?" I dropped the package straight onto Scott's desk without opening it, as it was marked UBER-PRIVATE in pink felt-tip pen and didn't appear to be either ticking or leaking anthrax.

"About my eggs."

"Your eggs?" I swiveled my chair to face Talitha, who was flanked by a disapproving Courtney. "What about them?"

"I'm going to sell them."

And it did occur to me for a split second that she might keep a hen in her apartment at El Royale, but deep down I knew that she didn't mean that kind of egg. Sadly.

"You are?" I braced myself.

"Yeah, there was an ad in the *Hollywood Reporter* for egg donors. I heard from this girl over at New Line that you can get ten grand if you're blond and have a college education." Talitha was wearing a lime green poncho and somehow managed not to look like a giant vegetable. She flicked a long tendril of hair back and smiled enthusiastically.

"Seriously?" I broke open a bottle of Evian and poured myself a glass. "Typical of my parents to palm me off with low-rent brunette genes. But how do you think you'd feel knowing that there was one of your babies out there? When you didn't even have kids yourself yet?"

"It's an egg, Elizabeth. Not a baby," Talitha informed me. "And I was also on the state volleyball team, which I'm guessing would make my eggs even more valuable, don't you?"

"Well, what do they do to you when they take your eggs?" I asked, suddenly not as hungry for my tuna salad sandwich as I had been two minutes ago.

"Give you some hormone pills for a month and then harvest them. Personally I can't think of an easier way to make ten thousand dollars. I've got an appointment on Tuesday for an interview with the clinic.

Which is just a formality. I was thinking maybe I'd buy myself the pink Marni purse that Drew Barrymore has and go to Maui for a week on vacation. The guys there are supposed to be absolutely gorgeous. Michelle at Fox Searchlight met one called Storm."

"Well, as long as you're selling your eggs for a good cause," Courtney said sarcastically, but Talitha didn't notice.

Being around Talitha always made me think of the adage that the best thing a woman can be in life is a beautiful fool. How blissful must that state be? I always thought far too much about everything. Being smart was very overrated, I'd begun to believe.

"I know, and some poor childless woman gets to have a lovely blond child who's athletic and smart." Talitha smiled. And all was perfect with her world. Which was more than could be said for mine, because something about the idea of selling your eggs to buy a Marni purse like Drew Barrymore's, as pretty as the pink may be, as soft as the leather felt, made me unutterably depressed.

"I heard that it's not tax-deductible, though," Courtney added as she blithely smoothed her hair behind her ear. "Which you may want to factor into your decision."

"Really?" Talitha looked a little surprised, but not despondent. "In that case I'll just ask for more money. Because I'm also five-nine. And height is such an asset in life, right?

"Hey, Elizabeth, I know. Why don't you come with me?"

"Me?" I asked. "Well, I guess I'm all out of blond genes, and . . . well, I'm not sure that I'd be that comfortable with the procedures and all."

"Oh, don't be silly. There are probably a lot of women out there who don't mind at all what their babies look like. They're really into having intelligent children, so you'd be perfect. I mean, your eggs may not be worth quite as much as mine, but you could definitely use a new wardrobe, so the money would be really useful." She flashed her Laura Mercier pink-glossed lips at me. "And it'd be much funner if we went together. Don't you think?"

"I guess it might be more fun," I said, trying to absorb all her insults at once. "I'll think about it and let you know. Thanks, Talitha."

Thankfully, or so it seemed for a split second at least, Victoria chose that moment to appear in her office doorway, yell my name as though I were her Irish wolfhound, and summon me into her black hole.

"Elizabeth," she said sourly, "take a seat." I perched, as was my wont, on the knife edge of a chair.

"Thanks," I said, so quietly that I could have been a mime. For, truth be told, I was terrified of Victoria. Since that first day when she'd so generously invited me to be mentored by her, she had used me as a slave. Or, as Lara had so indelicately put it, "It's like the white version of *Roots,* honey." Victoria had an uncanny way of knowing when Scott was out of the office, which was most of the time, given that he had major ADD and couldn't sit still behind his desk for more than half an hour without losing his mind or getting out of it. Consequently Lara and I had an unofficial policy of getting him out and about as much as possible—visiting movie sets was a firm favorite, since he loved to hang with the actors and directors and shoot the shit. Brunches, teas, and cocktails filled the voids between breakfasts, lunches, dinners, and premieres. Marketing meetings at Dreamworks were a good diversion, because the offices there were done in a western theme and he always came back with a John Wayne swagger. And a trip on a Gulfstream to Vegas or Santa Barbara or Mexico never failed to make his eyes light up.

So as Scott was mostly taken care of, Victoria made it her business to make sure that my idle hands weren't being used for the devil's work. (Just the devil's spawn's work.) And when I should have been typing up Scott's letters, updating phone lists, Xeroxing scripts for him, and generally being what I was paid to be, his second assistant, instead I was commandeered by Victoria. Who, though she had an assistant of her own, enjoyed the power trip of ensuring that I was at her disposal. At first I'd been grateful for the extra work she'd put my way, because it had felt as if I might be learning something. I'd read scripts and write coverage that she could then use to decide whether a project was worth her while. If I thought the script was good, she'd go on and read it herself before she recommended it to her clients. If it wasn't, then she'd just have me write a rejection letter. I was a useful filtering process. Certainly I didn't get that kind of experience working for Scott, because if there was a script to be read, Lara did it or he sent it out to a professional reader. Even when there were more scripts than I could carry home in one L.L. Bean monogrammed tote I didn't complain, even to myself in my head.

And neither did I mind the occasional hunting around town for a Barbie doll or two. I was an assistant, so that's what I tried to do—

make life easier for those I was assisting. Which was necessarily a broad and at times bizarre brief. But after my second week, when she'd asked me to dust out her trophy cabinets and have all the dolls' outfits dry-cleaned, then yelled hysterically at me when it wasn't same-day service, I began to feel that I was being taken advantage of. And that Victoria might not be entirely sane. Since then her schizophrenic bouts of praising me one moment and then moaning about my worthlessness the next had begun to get me down a bit. Especially as they usually came within the same fifteen-minute period.

"Well, Elizabeth. Correct me if I'm wrong here, but I'm sensing a lack of commitment on your part."

"I see." I took a deep breath and braced myself. Not praise this time, then.

"Do you want to make it in this business or not? Or is this just a little vacation from politics for you?"

"Not at all, no," I said unconvincingly. Which wasn't surprising, since I was lying through my teeth. But hey, actually I wasn't lying. This was no vacation, it was a one-way ticket to hell on a tour bus with a broken toilet and a drunk driver.

"I read the coverage that you did for me last weekend, and frankly, it was sloppy. There were four commas missing. Do you think I have time to waste mentoring somebody who doesn't give a damn?" She peered at me over her drink. Prune juice was out, aloe vera was in.

"I'm sorry, Victoria, but I—"

"No excuses. You may think that as an agent you'll never need to do coverage or understand the intricacies of the story, but to be the best around here you have to get a grasp of the entire business. Do you understand?"

"Yes. That makes complete sense," I mumbled, not adding that the top 10 percent of power players in this town most likely thought that a comma was what happened if you got hit by a truck.

"So all I really want to know, Elizabeth, is whether this is a commitment that you're up to taking on?"

Oh, God, now she was beginning to scare me. Did her long dark hair and shape-shifting ways mean that she was actually a witch? That she knew that I was planning to leave? Was I completely busted?

"Commitment . . . well . . ."

"Let me tell you a thing or two about commitment." She leaned forward and rested her chin on her bony hands. "Are you happy at The Agency, Elizabeth?"

"Yes," I lied.

"Well, aren't you the lucky one?" She gave me a foul smile and then the benefit of her wisdom: "I've worked here for fifteen years, and I've hated every minute of it. I have been passed over so many times they don't even consider me anymore. I watch these stupid, arrogant dicks walk in here and make partner before they're out of diapers. Cocksure know-it-alls who've never seen a movie made."

It occurred to me at this point that she hadn't been taking her antidepressants. But what could I do?

"I was married, you know. I was married to a surgeon. He loved me and wanted to have kids with me, but every time I got pregnant, it just wasn't the right time. You see, there's never a right time in this town. Not when you know that if you left to give birth, one of your male colleagues would look after your clients and slowly but surely steal them, until the only thing you had to come back to was an empty office and a pink slip. But, you see, now I want a baby, I can afford a baby, my clients are loyal. Only . . ." She took a sip of the aloe vera juice. "I don't have a husband anymore. And my gynecologist says that I only have a fifteen percent chance of getting pregnant."

I looked at her and was about to sympathize. To feel compassionate for her fate when her only crime had been to be a successful woman. Or something like that. But just as I was about to say my piece, she beat me to it.

"I haven't seen a single spark of initiative from you, young lady. Your coverage is shoddy, your telephone manner distinctly graceless, and you seem to be remarkably lacking in talent of any kind." Which was rich given that she had quoted verbatim at least four of the comments from my script coverage in the Monday meeting yesterday. And I ought to have known—I was there taking the minutes. "So I think you should go and reevaluate your position here. Don't you?" And with that she smiled her Evil Dead smile.

That was my cue to leave. Which I just about managed to do without tripping over a single piece of office furniture despite the tears rushing into the corners of my eyes.

"Oh, God, Elizabeth, don't mind her. She's a cunt on wheels," Lara said, and threw me her packet of Virgin Upper Class tissues as I stumbled across the floor with my head down.

"But she's right," I said, furiously swiping my tears away with my knuckles. "I'm not good enough. I'm not cut out for this job. I'm useless."

"Oh, yeah, and she's been the president of The Agency for the past five years." Lara rolled her eyes sarcastically. "Elizabeth, she only has the three clients she does because they actually mistakenly believe she's a carpet muncher, and so they see it as a political principle to be represented by a dyke. It's a cachet thing. She hates herself. That's why she attacked you. You've got to get over it."

"I'm not sure I can," I said. "I spent my entire weekend working on that coverage. I read sixteen scripts. I didn't see the sky once on Sunday—I just sat in my apartment and read. It was the best I could do, and it wasn't good enough."

"Christ, Elizabeth, you're not getting this, are you? The woman's insane. Fucking Shakespeare couldn't submit coverage that would live up to her standards. Get the fuck over it."

And I realized that Lara was probably right. In her abrasive but well-intentioned way. Though she was really starting to remind me of Scott in the way she spoke, which I guess happened if you worked for someone for so long.

"I'm over it," I said as I stuffed the tissues into my purse, stole a wedge of expensive cream Conqueror writing paper from the stationery closet, and wondered whether my little sister would be okay sleeping on the sofa tonight or whether she would want to share my bed, like the old days. And with that thought wiping Victoria from my mind, I logged off my computer and headed home. A whole half hour early, but frankly, who gave a damn? Not me.

When I arrived back at my apartment, Melissa was already waiting for me in the hallway outside my door. She was sitting on a vast khaki backpack reading a Christopher Hitchens book with a can of fair-trade orange soda beside her.

"Melissa, oh, my God!" I ran toward her, my script bag slapping my thigh, and she stood up and threw open her arms.

"Lizzie! How great to see you!"

We hugged for so long that I forgot where my arms ended and hers began. It had been ages since I'd hugged a person that I loved, and I couldn't bear to let go.

"Shall we go inside?" Melissa laughed, and we disentangled ourselves, and I wrested my keys from the bottom of my purse. "You look so different." She actually appeared a little shocked as she took in my new appearance.

"Oh, the hair." I laughed unsurely.

"Everything." She spun me around so she could check me out properly. "You look so slick, so chic, so . . . so L.A., I guess."

I was privately pleased by Melissa's assessment, even though I suspected that she didn't mean it to be quite the compliment I took it for.

"And you look gorgeous," I said, and slung one arm over her shoulder as I turned my key in the door. "Mel, you have no idea how excited I am to see you!"

We dumped Melissa's backpack by the door, and she declined my offer of a shower.

"Oh, I'm completely used to going for days without showering," she said as she checked out my apartment and poked her head out my window. "Besides, it's a total waste of water to shower all the time. People in the West use water way too liberally. It kills me."

"You're right," I said, and hastily turned off the faucet I'd just left running over the strainer of tomatoes in the sink.

"So have you volunteered yet?" She came and stood in the kitchen doorway as I prepared dinner. "There is so much poverty out here in L.A. It's shocking. So much good that you can do—in fact, I kind of envy you. A real project to sink your teeth into." She looked at me with wide-eyed expectation.

"No, I mean I'm going to. I was thinking of becoming a Big Sister, but I haven't gotten around to it yet. You know, you owe it to these kids to be totally committed, so until I'm really settled in my job and know whether I'm even going to stay in town, I'm not sure I should."

"Good point." Melissa nodded.

I sighed at my narrow escape and tried not to think of needy poor kids with imploring eyes.

"So tell me about Sierra Leone," I said later, as I poured red wine to the very top of Melissa's glass and tucked in to the pasta I'd undercooked in my enthusiasm to feed her. We were sitting up on the roof of my apartment building, the sun was setting pink and apricot over the ocean, and for the first time in days, I felt at peace. At peace with my decision to leave my job and at peace with my sister beside me. She was so energetic, so inspiring, that I couldn't help but feel that there was a whole world out there that I could be of use in. Why was I wasting away here?

"Oh, God, where do I begin?" She laughed and raised her glass before she took a sip. "Well, it was incredible. Truly incredible. Terrible, too, you have to understand, Lizzie. But it was the most amazing thing I've ever done in my life."

"More amazing than the time we ran away and slept in the park for a night?" I said jokingly, wanting to prove that we were still sisters who were bonded by love and life experience. But as she smiled and continued to tell me about her time away, about her brushes with death, about her sleeping rough with soldiers camped just feet away from her, about the atrocities she'd witnessed, I realized that what she had been through made her a very different person from the girl who'd gone away in February.

It also made her a very, very different person from me. The Hollywood assistant. The girl who'd spent months losing sleep over a call sheet, fretting as to whether she'd ever get invited to a premiere, someone who made it her daily business to marvel over Joel Schumacher's amazing profit-making ability. And it showed. Melissa looked incredible. I don't mean in that hair-color and skinnier-than-usual way—I mean really beautiful. She emanated passion for what she did. She was animated, she spoke confidently and with conviction about the social climate in Africa, she was vocal in her opinions on the U.S. government and the United Nations. She told me about political events and theories that I'd never encountered before. She looked like every heroine from history, with her hair longer and wilder than usual, her face and arms tanned, in her worn, scruffy jeans and frayed white T-shirt. And, most important, with a light in her eye. She was sort of burnished and golden. I was envious.

And when we were back downstairs later, when the air was still and the crickets were humming in the trees outside, when I went to the fridge to pull out the ice cream and caught my usual glimpse of myself in the door, I barely recognized the girl with the light hair, drab black pants and shirt, and the mean streak of red lipstick I'd added in a desperate bid for glamour. I looked bland, generic, uninteresting, and most of all sad. I had nothing much to say for myself. I had no convictions. Only that I hated Victoria almost more than I hated the dictatorships of Africa. Which I realized was pathetic. I just couldn't help it.

"Melissa, do you think that there'd be any vacancies at the UN if I were to apply?" I asked as I came back to the table and pulled the top off the Chunky Monkey tub.

"Why, do you know someone who wants a job?" she said as she took her spoon and dug in with a look of wonder on her face. "Jeez, it's been a while since I attacked a pint of ice cream."

"Well, me, actually." I tried to sound nonchalant, but my misery ebbed out of me.

"Oh, my God, Lizzie. Poor you" was all my little sister had to say to show she understood. "I was wondering how you were surviving," she said, now that she was able to be truthful. "I mean, your job sounds so horribly vapid. It's not you. All those award ceremonies and self-congratulatory pricks making movies that corrupt society. I mean, how do you square the violence your profession purveys with your own sense of morality?" she asked.

"Oh, well, it's not *so* bad," I said, just slightly shocked at her lambasting of Hollywood. I mean, it wasn't the Red Cross, but it wasn't a fascist regime either. "I think the violence is quite important in that it's a representation of the society we live in, sadly. And a lot of people in the business give tons of money to charity. There are benefits almost every night of the week. And some of the people I work with are very real, very compassionate in their own way. It's just that . . ." I thought hard for a moment. "It's just that I can't seem to find my niche. I was always so happy in D.C., and I haven't really settled in here. So I thought maybe I ought to go back to what I know. That's all," I said, a tad defensively.

"Well, I'll see what I can do. I have lunch tomorrow with this guy who's pretty powerful in Washington political circles, and I'll definitely ask him."

"Thanks," I said, remembering the paper that I'd stolen from the office. And then remembering Victoria's twisted face during our meeting today. "Wanna help me with my résumé?"

10

I believe, I believe. It's silly, but I believe.

—Natalie Wood as Susan Walker
Miracle on 34th Street

The next morning, bleary-eyed from staying up until two, I dropped seventeen envelopes into my purse. Each contained a copy of my résumé along with a letter to a senator or someone similar, whose names and addresses Melissa and I had found online. Each letter pleaded for employment and dedicated only half a sentence to the hiccup that was my Hollywood career.

"Thanks, sweetheart. You were a total rock star." I hugged my sister as I dropped her off outside the Beverly Center, where she was planning on joining a protest against mistreatment of asylum seekers before lunch.

"Well, I just hope it goes okay," she said, slinging her backpack over her shoulder. "I'll call you when I get into D.C. And good luck with the jobs."

"Thanks. I'll probably need it."

She stood outside my car window and smiled at me like a latter-day Joan of Arc. "You'll be great. You're so cut out for a career in politics. This superficial bullshit doesn't suit you. Remember when you attached yourself with your bicycle chain to the garden tree when you were little cause they were going to cut it down because it had Dutch elm disease? Well, that was the sister I know and love. The sister who inspired me. D.C. needs you."

"You're sweet, Mel. See you soon." I waved and tried not to laugh at her earnestness as I pulled out into the stationary morning rush-hour traffic on La Cienega. In my rearview mirror, I watched my sister stumble along the sidewalk in the same clothes she had worn yesterday, with a backpack twice her body weight over her shoulders.

When I arrived at the office, I realized that if I wanted to go and have my usual chai latte, I'd have to read Jason's script first. There was no way I wanted to show my face until I'd done so. Jason was one of the few people I felt were really decent in this town, and I knew that he'd be dying to have some feedback from me . . . well, from anyone, actually, so I pulled the copy of his script out of my bag and got into it while all the other assistants were perusing the latest analysis of box-office activity in *Variety.* Which there was really no point in my doing anymore, given that I would probably be leaving soon. Either with Victoria's Charles David boot up my ass or to pursue a career where my coworkers wouldn't be as likely to trade their eggs for pink purses and consider me a mutant because of my natural brown hair.

And for the rest of the morning, every spare moment I had, I read a few more pages. And a few more. It was actually really compelling. Which was a pleasant surprise, because the rule was that whenever someone you knew gave you a script to read, it would invariably be horrible. But this made me want to read on. And when Scott finally left for lunch, I pulled it out of my bottom drawer and settled down to finish the third act. Victoria had gone to Sedona for a couple of days to consult a shaman, and Lara was still ensconced in her novel-writing course and had her earplugs wedged in as usual, so I breezed through to the end of the story with no interruptions.

Jason's screenplay was called *Sex Addicts in Love,* and it was about a kid from New Jersey who wanted to lose his virginity, so wound up going to Sex Addicts Anonymous meetings to get laid. I thought from the title that it was going to be an *American Pie* kind of deal, but actually the story was much more sensitively portrayed, and Dan, the main character, was one of the most sympathetic leads I'd ever read. And even though I had only a month of script-reading experience under my belt, thanks to the colossal workload that Victoria had unleashed on me, I definitely knew my onions. This would make a great movie, I thought excitedly. Really, truly great. I could see it—the deprived home life, his Harvard career, his friends, his tragic mother, his porn-obsessed stepfather, and his remote real father. It was low budget, but with a great up-and-coming young actor in the lead. It was gritty, but with humor. It made you laugh and cry, and this was honestly the first screenplay I'd read that I could see working like magic on the big screen. And it was written by Jason Blum. The coffee frother. The guy across the road. Who wanted me to produce it. Which of course wasn't going to happen, because I was D.C.-bound. But maybe if I helped him put it in the hands of the right person before I left, he'd invite me to the premiere. Good for Jason. I grinned as I picked up the script and my purse so I could finally go and have my latte and tell him the good news.

But the second that I stood up for my dash across to the Coffee Bean, the phone began ringing off the hook. And stupid me made the fatal mistake of answering it. Which I needn't have, because the general rule in Hollywood was that once your boss had valet-parked at the restaurant of choice for his lunch, the office shut down and everything went to voice mail. But the persistent ringing was driving me crazy.

"Scott Wagner's office," I said impatiently.

"Scott," a woman sniffed.

"No, this is Lizzie. Scott's actually at lunch right now."

"You need to find him for me." More sniffing and possibly even something that could be classified as a whimper.

"Who's speaking, please?"

"Jennifer." Oh, God, one of Scott's biggest clients. Who often rang in tears from Saks to tell us that she couldn't get the Balenciaga Lariat bag in white. And it was my job to take her as seriously as she took herself. "Brett's insisting on shooting me in profile. And it specifically says in my contract that I don't do profile. I've tried to explain to him, but he just yells and calls me names."

"Jennifer, please try not to worry too much. I'm going to try to get a hold of Scott. Where can you be reached?"

"I'm in my trailer. And I'm not answering the door. *Go away!*" she yelled at some unsuspecting person in the background, so hard my eardrum began to fizz. "He's trying to ruin my career because I wouldn't sleep with him. I know he is. I've always hated my nose from the side. And I won't show it to anyone."

"Okay. Well, don't worry. Just sit tight, and I'll have Scott call you."

"Well, he better hurry, because I refuse to accept this abuse for much longer. It's damaging to my inner child. I'm going to call my driver and have him take me home if Scott isn't here in a minute."

I hung up and reached for the other line, which was also ringing frantically. To be honest, I couldn't believe that Lara's earplugs, even if they were Upper Class, could be quite as soundproof as she made them seem. It was one thing to ignore a ringing phone because it was lunchtime, but when the thing was practically vibrating off the desk, it had to be quite urgent, I figured.

I grabbed the handset. "Yes, hello."

"If you don't get this fucking whore out of her trailer and onto my set in the next ten minutes, I'm going to sue her scrawny, overexposed ass."

"Brett?" I took a wild guess.

"I've had it up to here with her prima donna ways, and I'm fucking sick of it. I never wanted that frigid, over-the-hill cunt in the first place, but the studio made me. And now she's ruining my movie. So get her the fuck out of there. Do you hear me, Scott?"

Actually, Scott probably *could* hear him. Even though he was at the Ivy right now and probably three Bloody Marys to the wind.

"Sorry, Brett, this is Lizzie, Scott's assistant. I'm trying to reach him at lunch right now. We'll get back to you." But before I could finish, the line hummed monotonously. Okay. Righto. Well, here we go again.

Scott's cell phone was going straight to voice mail. He'd switched it off. He was at his table in the Ivy snacking on crab cakes, and he didn't give a shit that right now, over at the Paramount lot, some dark things were about to go down. Sadly, not Jennifer, though, or we probably wouldn't have this problem in the first place, I thought with all the cynicism of a seasoned industryite.

"Scott, it's Lizzie. I'm really sorry to disturb you at lunch, but I need to speak to you urgently. I've programmed my number into your phone as Lizzie, Elizabeth, and Assistant Number Two. So you can call any of those and reach me. Thanks."

I grabbed my car keys and thrust my cell phone into my purse.

"If anyone needs me, I've gone down to Paramount. There's some kind of fracas on the set with Jennifer and Brett." But I might as well have talked to myself as I hurried out the door. The only response was from a winsome Talitha, who mumbled something about Fracas being Gwyneth Paltrow's favorite perfume.

I tapped my foot impatiently on the accelerator as one of the Josés moved a Mercedes that was blocking my exit from the parking garage. The way I saw it, I had about five minutes to get to Paramount and talk Jennifer out of her trailer, or she'd get fired and so would The Agency. Whose fault it would clearly be, in her eyes, that she'd had to endure such torment at the hands of Brett. Because an agent was supposed to be a friend, mother, scapegoat, lover, baby-sitter, and acolyte. And a medieval knight where applicable, too. Charging full tilt to her side to defend her honor. Or side profile. The thing was, most of the time the agent was at lunch or a premiere. Or, in Scott's case, stoned. So his responsibilities were mine. His Porsche was not, I noticed as a blue haze began to drift from under the hood of the Honda. I ignored it and hoped it would go away.

As Tall José maneuvered the Merc into a new space, Short José chatted calmly to me through the open window.

"Going somewhere nice?" he asked, oblivious to my panic.

"Paramount lot. How long do you think it'll take me to get there?" I asked.

"You mean the secret fast route? Or the slow, heavy-traffic, long way?" He grinned slyly and smoothed his jet-black hair down.

"Oh, my God, José, you know a shortcut?" I asked needlessly as he began to jot down some cryptic instructions for me. "I love you, José, you know that don't you?"

"A falta de hombres Buenos, a mi padre hicieron alcalde." He nodded as he handed over my lifeline.

"'Since there were no good men, they made my father mayor'?" I asked, scraping the bottom of my schoolgirl-Spanish barrel.

"Go now," he said as I smiled at him and sped off into the bright sunlight of the day with a screech of breaks and a coughing engine.

I drove down Melrose and deeper into Hollywood in search of the famous Paramount gates. I'd never seen them before in real life, but I had spotted them at the beginning of a hundred movies, so I vaguely knew what I was looking for. But between watching my clock and wondering whether Jennifer would have hurled herself histrionically into the back of her car and left already, and also watching my cell phone to see whether Scott had called and following José's directions, which were taking me through many a luxe-y neighborhood, I didn't have much time to appreciate the fact that I was about to set foot for the first time on the hallowed earth of a legendary Hollywood studio.

And I certainly didn't stop to marvel that these would have been the very streets that Lucille Ball and Greta Garbo and Tom Cruise had driven along on their way to work. Because right now I simply had a visual of Scott's tonsils flaring at me if I didn't prevent Jennifer from committing professional suicide. The reputation of The Agency was at stake. Scott's reputation was at stake. And perhaps most important, as I was planning to drop my seventeen letters into a mailbox at some point today, I didn't want my reason for leaving this position to be the fact that I was fired faster than a bullet from a gun. So I dried my damp palms off on my black skirt, held tight onto the steering wheel, and bore down on the speed bumps like a veteran stuntman.

Until finally my phone rang. Great, Scott at last. I eased off the pedal and answered it.

"Lizzie, it's me." But it wasn't the me I was hoping for. It was Melissa.

"Hi, babe," I said, turning down the radio.

"I'm in a bit of trouble, Lizzie," she announced.

"What kind of trouble?" I braced myself.

"I've been arrested. I was on the march for asylum seekers, and I sort of chained myself to some railings."

"I see. Are you okay? Do I need to come and bail you out or something? Do you want me to tell Mom and Dad? Do you need a lawyer?" I could always be counted on to be practical in a crisis, something I should have put on my résumé but had forgotten.

"No, I'm fine," she reassured me airily. "All I really wanted was to tell you to watch the evening news on CNN, because they're going to interview me about the human-rights abuses against asylum seekers. And if you could send out an e-mail circular to people letting them know, then it'll spread the word. Isn't it fantastic?" She sounded as high as a kite.

"I guess. I mean, will they take you to court? You have been arrested, sweetheart," I said, unable to help myself from playing the older-sister role.

"Not at all. I'm in a cell now, and this is my one phone call, but I'll be out at six and on the air at seven, so be sure to tune in," she said. And obviously her quarter ran out, because the line went dead.

At that precise second, I realized just how different Melissa and I actually were. I had always thought that we were cut from the same cloth in terms of our principles: that we both worried about trees, prisoners of conscience, dolphins, and poor women who got stoned to death for adultery. But while I did genuinely care and maybe I had once inspired my little sister with my militant childhood tendencies, I honestly couldn't pretend that I cared as much as Melissa did. I would not have given up my lunch and liberty and reputation as a blameless citizen of the United States of America by tying myself to a railing and getting arrested. CNN or no CNN. I would sign a petition, I would forward an e-mail to a hundred people, and I would join the ranks of a peaceful protest. But I was not the kind of girl to go and risk my life in either Sierra Leone or the Beverly Center. It just wasn't my cup of tea anymore. It may have been when I was younger, but not now. It all seemed too idealistic, too naïve. I was sure that if Scott or any of the Hollywood honchos had driven by Melissa's protest this morning, they'd simply have cursed her for fucking up the traffic flow. They wouldn't have cared if she was marching for world peace or to stop inhumane treatment of guinea pigs—she would have no impact on their lives. Which made her noble deeds pointless, really. They only served to make her feel good about herself and feel like she belonged. Which I had to admit would be a great feeling. I just knew that it wouldn't work like that for me anymore. I was looking for something else. Though I had no idea what. I glanced back down at my map and hit the gas again. If José's calculations were right, I was just about at the Paramount lot.

When I finally pulled up at the visitor's booth, I realized that the majestic marble gates were in fact concrete and that the security guard was not going to let me through without a reenactment of the Spanish Inquisition.

"No one called in a drive-on, Miss. I can't let you in."

"It's an emergency. I'm needed on the set of *Wedding Massacre,*" I pleaded, glancing at the exit booth on the other side of the entrance to make sure that one of the sleek vehicles pouring under the barrier didn't contain Jennifer. Which action only served to make me look even shiftier and more like a deranged stalker or fundamentalist Muslim than I already did, with my knockoff Chanel sunglasses and smoking car.

"Why don't you call Brett, the director?" I said hopefully. "And tell him that I'm Scott Wagner's assistant and that I've come to lure Jennifer out of her trailer. I know that he'll corroborate my story. Truly."

"Hold on, and I'll speak to the production manager," he said, helpfully enough. Unfortunately, the security guard had probably last exercised his sense of urgency around the same time that Gloria Swanson rocked up here to film *Sunset Boulevard* in 1950, so I was forced to sit and sweat in my car until he finally came back with a proud grin and a pass for me to stick on my car.

"They're at Sound Stage Nineteen," he said, handing me a map and failing to point out that the studio lot was sixty-two acres in size.

One hour, two golf carts, three security guards, and five blisters on my feet later, I made it to Sound Stage 19. But the place was deserted. Except for two pretty girls—who looked like makeup artists, judging by the colorful dashes of greasepaint on the backs of their hands—who were eating sushi on the steps of a Winnebago.

"Hi, I'm looking for Jennifer's trailer," I wheezed when they looked up quizzically at me.

"Jennifer's. Oh, I think it's the one with the wind chimes outside, right?" one of the girls asked the other, who nodded into her yellowtail in a vague way.

"Thanks." I hurried toward the trailer she'd pointed out, which was positioned at the end of a New York City street set, straining to hear Jennifer's crying or yelling, anything that might indicate that I wasn't *too late*. But the place seemed spookily deserted. And though I'd never been to a movie set before, I imagined there ought to be a few more people around gripping and gaffering and directing, if things were going according to plan.

"Oh, shit," I mumbled as I limped along with bleeding feet. "Where is everyone?"

"Hey," a male voice called out behind me. "You looking for someone?"

I turned and saw a man in a baseball cap and scruffy gray T-shirt perched alone on the steps of a mock brownstone eating his lunch.

"Er, not exactly. Well, yes, I suppose I am, but it's okay, 'cause I think I know where I'm going because . . . well . . . I have a map," I finished with a flourish and a wave of the crumpled yellow piece of paper in my hand.

"Okay. Only you looked kind of lost." He shrugged and speared a piece of tuna in the salade niçoise that he was balancing on his kneecap. Then he pushed back his baseball cap, and his brown eyes sort of smiled at me when he added, "But if you're not lost, then that's just great," in what I gleaned was a southern accent.

"Well, actually, I was looking for the set of *Wedding Massacre.* It's this movie that's supposed to be shooting here. Terrible title, huh?" I answered his smiling-eye thing with what I thought was a cute joke.

"Horrible," he agreed. "Well, I think that they're over there. At least, that's where I last heard screams coming from. Then there was an almighty bang, and it's been dead quiet ever since." He shrugged nonchalantly.

"Oh, no! Oh, shit! You're not serious?" I began walking backward, stumbling to make it to the scene of the catastrophe. Could Jennifer and Brett really have killed one another in some deranged moment? Two of Scott's biggest clients.

Then the guy winked at me and popped a cherry tomato in his mouth.

"Oh, right, yeah, ha, ha. Great joke," I said and darted toward the trailers without looking back.

When I eventually found myself outside the door to the trailer with the wind chimes, I stood on the latticed aluminum step at the bottom and held my breath for a second before I knocked. Then I hammered in as positive a manner as I could manage.

"Hello?" I called out nervously when there was no reply. And this time I turned the handle on the door and very slowly and cautiously pushed it open.

"Hey, guys, look, it's Lizzie," I heard from the darkness as I put my head inside and let my eyes adjust. It was a man's voice. As usual in this town, when the obvious was uttered, it was usually by a man. "Come on in, honey." And there in front of me, like the Waltons gathered cozily around their kitchen table, sat Scott, Jennifer, and Brett playing Jenga.

"Oh, I'm really sorry to disturb you all. Only I thought that there was a problem, and—"

But Scott stopped me in my tracks before I could ruin all the hard work he'd clearly had to do to repair the rift between director and actress. "We are having the greatest hang, Lizzie. Just a little downtime before everyone gets back to work this afternoon. Do you play Jenga?"

"Jenga?" I asked, wondering why in hell's name he couldn't have let me know he was here instead of having me rush all over town having a nervous breakdown while my poor sister sat in a lonely jail cell. But relieved all the same that good relations seemed to be very much restored. Indeed, to the point where Brett had one hand up the back of Jennifer's shirt and the other was removing a wooden stick from the Jenga tower. "No, I don't play Jenga," I lied. "I actually get the shakes really badly, so I'm just gonna head on back to the office." I took a couple of steps into the doorway, hoping for a swift getaway to my desk, where I'd be sure to add diplomacy to my résumé as my greatest skill.

"Hey, look out," I heard in my right ear as I felt two hands come to rest on my waist. I spun around, and there, behind me again, was the guy in the baseball cap from the steps.

"Oh," I said, surprised that he'd come straight into Jennifer's trailer without knocking.

"Luke, come in, man!" Scott yelled from the banquette.

"I'm not staying. Just wanted to make sure that this young lady found her way here okay." He stood and looked at me closely.

"Oh, you've met Lizzie," Scott said. "Yeah, she's my second assistant. Hey, Lizzie, meet Luke Lloyd. He's the producer of *Wedding Massacre*." The producer? He can only have been thirty-five years old, and though he looked like he might well be a runner, this was a young industry, and it wasn't unusual for someone of that age to run an entire studio, let alone produce a movie.

"Oh, God, no," I said under my breath. But Luke Lloyd heard me, even above the clatter of wooden blocks and yells as the Jenga tower came crashing down behind us.

"Yeah, and you know, I was thinking that maybe the title doesn't quite work. I was thinking that while it is what it is, it also lacks . . . I don't know . . . maybe a little subtlety, you know?" Luke said this aloud to the trailer, but he looked very intently into my eyes while he said it. And I could just make out the pale brown freckles on the bridge of his nose.

"It's a hit, man. Trust me," Scott bellowed. "Do not change a thing."

"Lizzie?" Luke Lloyd said, and I could do nothing other than contemplate his long dark eyelashes and my own suicide.

"It's probably a grower," I said as I tried to leave the room without further humiliation. "In fact, I like it better already. *Wedding Massacre.* Yup, it has a kind of raw, edgy quality. You're right, it is what it is." I finally made it past Luke Lloyd and down the steps of the trailer, leaving Scott, Jennifer, and Brett noisily rebuilding the Jenga tower. And Luke Lloyd looking down at me.

"See y'around, Lizzie." He grinned and pulled off his cap, revealing a ruffled crop of black hair. It was only then that I recognized him as the producer I'd worked hard not to have a crush on at Daniel's party. The one who had been talking to George and who I'd convinced myself was a supermodel-dating, sports-car-loving, dissolute bastard.

"Yeah. See you around," I managed as I fled back toward the welcoming streets of New York, in a mad hurry to avoid trouble.

But as I walked past the brownstones that had housed every fictitious city dweller from Jerry Seinfeld to Holly Golightly, I began to drink in the strange magic of the place. This deserted movie set, with its hollow walls, doors leading to nowhere, and nonexistent rooms, was just waiting to have romance, life, and adventure imposed upon it. Because Hollywood is, after all, what you make of it. And as I sat down on the step and watched as shooting resumed on *Wedding Massacre,* with Brett behind the camera, with Jennifer acting her heart and lungs out in a screaming scene, with Scott and Luke watching with folded arms and nodding approval, I realized that in a way I did belong here. I loved the fantasy, the make-believe. And even my old egalitarian soul was satisfied by the fact that in this town anyone could make it. From the gas-pump attendants of myth to the yoga teacher in the apartment next door. Nobody was immune to the spell.

Also, the episode with Melissa's arrest this afternoon had made me realize that I certainly didn't belong in politics any longer. There was already too much water under the bridge. Passing through the gates of Paramount had been like crossing over into another world, leaving my past behind. Here I was among the ghosts of Hollywood. Probably sitting in the same place where Audrey Hepburn sang "Moon River." I had to carry on: I loved Jason's screenplay, and I wanted a chance to produce it. I loved that there would always be the vast screen of painted blue sky with puffy white clouds above the parking lot, no matter whether it was pouring rain. I loved that my hair was a little blonder and brighter than real. And as I watched, I definitely liked the fact that Luke Lloyd existed in this world. Even though I would never be with him. He was handsome, warm, and, yes, probably horribly dissolute, but he smiled at me the way the man of my dreams was always supposed to, and I could happily pretend. Even though his southern accent might have been as fake as his concern for my whereabouts had been, it didn't matter, because he looked the part.

And in a certain light, *I* looked the part, I imagined, as I walked back toward the parking lot. I wasn't in the starring role, I didn't climb into a shimmering car, and I didn't have an invite to the big premiere tonight, but I was just starting out. I was excited and hopeful, and I figured that since I was here, I might as well give it my best shot. Just as long as that shot wasn't a side profile, because, for what it's worth, Jennifer and I have one thing in common—we both hate our noses from the side. Especially the left, in my case.

When I drove back out of the gates of Paramount toward the Santa Monica Freeway and home, I remembered José's proverb: *Since there are no good men, they made my father mayor.* And I realized what it meant. In a town like this, where in the immortal words of William Goldman, "nobody knows anything," I might, just might, have a hope at success. I might be able to take on Jason's screenplay, help him produce it, and actually be part of the process. Certainly I thought that *Sex Addicts in Love* was one of the most incredible pieces of writing I'd ever read—barring *Crime and Punishment,* of course. I could see every moment of it in my mind's eye. And I knew instinctively that it would make a remarkable movie. And when it came to making a dream into a reality, if José was to be believed, then I, Elizabeth Miller, had just as good a chance as anyone else.

11

I know that I'm full of hate and anger and frustration and I know that it's going to take all the gold and silver and diamonds in the world to cure me.

—Caroll Baker as Sylvia West
Sylvia

I had been thinking about bronzing products for the past half hour. Powders, lotions, sprays, shimmering liquids, big puffs that are ready to dust. In fact, I had become preoccupied by any and every method of glowing golden without seeing daylight. This was because I had been in a windowless, fluorescent-lit cell for hours now, and I knew that when I emerged, I would be tinged with the kind of unearthly pallor that would send other people clamoring for garlic and holy water and stakes to drive through my heart. I tried to remember if there were any vampire movies slated to be shot in the next few months, because if there were, I might just get myself along to an audition. Or at least if I couldn't star, I could cash in on the inevitable vogue for translucent women when the picture came out. The likes of me and Nicole Kidman would be envied and copied. She perhaps more than me.

Copied. Copied. How many copies? Sixteen. I tapped onto the LCD screen. I was in the photocopy closet, in case I hadn't mentioned. And it was starting to feel as if I had been born here and in all probability would die here. I'd lost any notion of a childhood, an apartment in a cheap but pleasant part of Venice, my coworkers somewhere along the corridor talking on the phones, making sense. I wasn't part of anything anymore, except the surging rise and fall of the machine's noise, which even if you've only ever had to copy one document in your life, will be indelibly Xeroxed onto your brain in the same way as the document you duplicated.

Click. Flash of light. Click. Flutter. As the warm, inky copy lands in its chute.

And let's face it, Xeroxing is not the easy task it pretends to be. People assume that even the village idiot could copy a screenplay sixteen times over. Well, maybe, but I don't find it so simple. In a matter of hours, I'd lost pages, put the sheets in the wrong order, cut my wrist (Freudian, I'm prepared to admit), run out of paper, ink, toner, patience, and now, it seemed, my last shard of sanity, too. I had just begun singing a Céline Dion song that I didn't know I knew, when the deadweight of the fire door, which had been segregating me from the rest of the human race, burst open to reveal a panting Talitha.

"Thank God you're here! We've been looking everywhere for you." Her cheeks were pink, without the helping hand of François Nars for once, and she looked stricken.

"Why? What's happened?" I pushed the stop button so I could hear her doomy news. This scenario, by the way, is exactly what I'd spent my time in the Xerox closet anticipating. It's part of copy-closet paranoia syndrome. You imagine all sorts of angry-boss, job-loss, deathly, terrorist, military-coup-type things happening beyond the closet. Back in the vicinity of your desk. And today, it seemed, something had actually happened. My paranoia had not been in vain.

"It's Mia Wagner," Talitha said, with a bulging look.

"Oh, my God, what?"

"Mia Wagner." She nodded frantically.

"Scott's wife. I know. What about her? What's happened?"

"She's in reception." Talitha waited for my response. I waited for her to continue. Had Mia brought her Uzi? I wondered. Were we talking hostage situation? Epileptic fit on the marble? But apparently not. The bad news, it transpired, was that Mia Wagner was in reception. Period.

"And that's it?" I asked, relieved, as I calmly shuffled my papers into a neat bundle and lacerated a cuticle at the same time.

"Elizabeth, Mia Wagner is in reception. Don't you understand?"

"No, I don't think I do. My boss's wife is waiting for him. Oh, God!" I stopped and came to my senses suddenly. "He's not in his office screwing that cute lawyer, is he? I know he had a meeting with her earlier, but he ought to be at Warner Brothers by now . . ."

"No, Scott's not screwing anyone. Well, not in his office. But Mia Wagner is a total nightmare. You have to come now. I refuse to deal with her. So does Courtney."

"Okay, okay, I'm coming." I gathered up my scripts. "Where's Lara?"

"*Lara* won't deal with Mia," Talitha said to me. As though *I* were the dumb one.

"Why not?" I asked as I shuffled along the corridor back to our office carrying a cardboard box overflowing with scripts.

"Oh, Elizabeth, get with the program." She shook her head incredulously and marched ahead, leaving me to pull in my shoulders at the last moment to stop from being knocked unconscious by the doors that swung wildly in her wake.

"Right. I see." But I didn't. And when I got back to my desk, I dropped the box on the floor with such a resounding thud that even Courtney looked my way.

"She's on her way up," Courtney said. "I suggest you go straight on in to Scott's office. Just deal with her in there. He's over at Warner Brothers, so he won't be back for the rest of the day."

"Yeah, just don't keep her out here. It's too upsetting," Talitha agreed.

"Will someone tell me what's so terrible about Mia Wagner?" I said as I got up from the floor where I'd been closing shut the box of photocopied scripts.

"Yes, why doesn't someone tell her what's so terrible about Mia Wagner?"

There, in front of me, was a petite, pretty redhead who didn't look as if she would say boo to a goose. But she'd just asked a difficult question, and nobody was going to answer. Over to me.

"You're Mia. Hi, I'm Elizabeth, Scott's new second assistant." I thrust out my hand and smiled.

"Elizabeth." She shook my hand but didn't return the smile. Instead she vacuumed me with her gaze. Every out-of-place eyelash, every button on my shirt, the scuffs on my shoes, the fact that I'd recycled my skirt from the dry-cleaning pile at home—nothing escaped Mia Wagner.

"So what can I do to help you?" I asked hastily before she could notice that I was a frumpy suburbanite who had no business being in Hollywood in the first place.

"It's my birthday next week, and I need to make sure that my husband buys me something that I love," she said. And for a moment I had to think hard to remember who her husband might be. Because this immaculate, well-spoken, and brittle creature had about as much in common with my crumpled heap of a boss as she did with . . . well, me, I suppose.

Mia Wagner was wearing a red Louis Vuitton bouclé shift dress, and her hair was Pre-Raphaelite in color but post–Jennifer Aniston in style. Her arms were porcelain white and honed to perfection with something ladylike like Pilates, not a bulging muscle or shiver of flesh in sight. And while she couldn't have been a minute older than thirty-two, she was timeless and ageless in an almost spooky way—she would always have been described as elegant but, I imagined, never as sexy. Except in a strict sort of way, which some men go for. And I wished that she wouldn't look at me like that. I wanted to reassure her that I wasn't sleeping with her husband, because that was clearly what was on her mind. But then again, if Immaculate Mia was his type, she ought to be able to tell that I would hardly cut it, even in the poor-substitute department.

"Shall we go into Scott's office, where we can discuss this in private?" I suggested, remembering what the girls had said about getting her out of the way. But judging by how everyone was staring, I'd have thought they'd prefer it if we stayed, so they could watch. I wondered what they were waiting for. A tantrum? A gymnastics routine? A lightning change into Wonder Woman? I suppose whatever it was that made Mia a nightmare would be revealed in good time. Lucky me.

"No," she said. "I thought we'd go out and choose something together."

"Oh, well, Scott's not in the office this afternoon," I explained. "But I'm sure he's got your gift all taken care of. You needn't worry." I made a mental note to order a devastatingly tasteful bunch of flowers and have them sent to his house, just in case he did forget.

"I didn't mean my lame fuck of a husband," she said disdainfully. "I meant you."

"Oh, you want *me* to come shopping with you? Now?" I asked, stalling for time and hoping that Lara would appear and save me.

"I don't have all day." She glanced at her discreetly diamond-framed Patek Philippe watch and looked at me as if I were a lame fuck, too. "So why don't you get your purse, and we can go?"

"Well, I really ought to clear it with Lara." I tried to be polite. "She's the other assistant, and it might be better if she were the one to go shopping with you because . . ." At this point Courtney and Talitha practically ducked under their desks with looks of astonished incredulity on their faces. Clearly they expected stilettos at dawn at the mention of Lara's name. Thanks, guys, for telling me that there was a little *froideur* between Mrs. Wagner and Mr. Wagner's assistant, I thought.

"I know who Lara is," she spit venomously. "Which is why I'm asking *you*. Now, please, would you just come with me? The valet is probably smoking a cigarette in my car as we speak."

"Okay, right, well, of course. I'll just put the phones on voice mail," I said reluctantly, and followed her invisible bottom and the military click of her heels along the corridor to the parking garage.

"So I'm going for something with resale value," she said as she zooshed up the air-con and eased into fourth gear. And if I hadn't felt a little apprehensive at being hijacked by my boss's terrifying wife, I might actually have enjoyed the fact that I was driving away from my office in a navy blue BMW sport with the most exquisite pale calf-leather interior, by a woman who actually had on driving gloves. We drove along Wilshire past Saks Fifth Avenue and Kate Mantalini's, through the lanes of graceless SUVs, and I felt as though I'd just stepped into a fashion spread. Everything in Mia Wagner's world was beautiful. Right down to the Puccini aria that was drifting at a perfect volume from her stereo.

"Resale value?" I asked uncertainly.

"If they're gifts, then he can't get them back. So the more expensive the better. Jewels and art work best."

"I'm sure Scott would never ask for gifts back," I said, defending Scott's generosity. One thing he wasn't was cheap.

"In the event of a divorce," she informed me. "It's my little insurance policy."

"Oh, I see." I tried to sound worldly, as if I knew all about divorce laws in the state of California. Which I figured I soon would anyway.

"So let's start at Butterfields, why don't we?" She turned and gave me the merest flicker of a thawing smile. "Oh, God, Elizabeth, you probably think I'm terrible, don't you?" she asked as she pulled up in front of the auction house. "But I wasn't always like this. That's why I'm so determined to get as much as I can out of this marriage. Because if money can't buy happiness, it can certainly offer a little compensation for abject misery."

"I've never been to Butterfields before." I didn't really want to get into this right now. "Were you looking for a painting or a sculpture?"

"I was thinking of a Dalí or a Miró. Maybe not Miró. I'm a little concerned that Spanish surrealists are overinflated in the market right now. I wouldn't want anything that would lose value," she said as we handed the keys over to the valet and made our way into the building. "But then again, who cares? It's not my money that I'm throwing away."

Actually, it transpired that Mia Wagner wasn't just a fickle little fashionhead with a fondness for pretty things. And as we wandered among the paintings on sale, me gasping and Mia taking notes in a tan Smythson ledger, I realized that she was a very smart woman. Certainly, way smarter than her poor, probably about to be poor, husband.

"I haven't always been a cunt," she said matter-of-factly. Clearly exhibiting the one trait that she and Scott had in common, a good grasp of Anglo-Saxon. "When I first met Scott, we had fun together. I was working at the Gagosian in New York, and he came to a private viewing with David Bowie and some movie star whose name I can't remember. And I tried to explain to him why Damien Hirst wasn't just about dead sheep. He tried to get me back to the Mercer where he was staying, and he was so insanely charming that I went. Even though my boyfriend was at the same party."

"That sounds like Scott," I said. "The charm offensive."

"'Offensive' being the operative word," she said, quickly remembering that we were here to screw her husband for a few million dollars, not sing his praises. "Anyway, we had an amazing courtship, and it was all very fancy with romantic breaks in Bora Bora and weekends in Rome, and it's not as if I was a stranger to all that flash. I'd dated men before who had way more money and glamour than Scott. But he made it all fun. We'd be in Harry's Bar in Venice, and we'd be dying laughing. Or we'd be smooching beside a fire in Aspen, and he was the sweetest, most giving, most considerate man in the world." She jotted down the reference number of a Mondrian in her book. "But I didn't realize that that's what Scott does. He gives. He is the gift that keeps on giving. Only now he gives to everyone else. He gives to every stray actress who crosses his path, he gives to Daniel Rosen—who isn't fit to lick his boots—he gives to the valets, the busboys, the directors. And he gives to women. He can't resist women. The ones in Range Rovers at the traffic light who roll him for his car—"

"He told you about that?" I was stunned. I'd planned on having that particular secret nailed up with me inside my coffin.

"Of course he didn't tell me. We don't really speak anymore." She turned to me and shrugged. "I have him followed. Every meeting, every premiere, every trip to the gym. And incidentally, you might want to cancel the gym membership for him, because he hasn't been in ten months. He has alternate forms of exercise nowadays."

"I see," I said. Not really wanting to be party to quite so much information about Scott, but having little choice.

"Anyway, the thing is that Scott has time for everyone except me. So between them and the drugs and the never knowing when to quit partying . . . well, it's not exactly a marriage." She gave a long, hard stare at a Dufy and then moved closer to examine the frame.

"Have you thought about couples therapy?" I know, I know, lame. But it was all I could think of to say.

"Well, if it's a toss-up between the opening of an envelope at Mann's Chinese Theatre or two hours with a shrink, guess who wins?" she said bitterly. "Scott doesn't want to save our marriage any more than he wants to quit pushing that white shit up his nose. So it's really just a matter of time before I call my lawyer."

"But if you loved him once, and he clearly loved you . . . well, isn't that a good enough reason to try just one more time?"

She looked at me exactly as I suspected she might: as if I had been dropped from a spacecraft.

"I know, I'm too romantic for my own good, but I like Scott, and I don't know you, but I think you're probably amazingly good for him, and it seems such a shame." I don't know why I was being so outspoken for the first time in my life. But I suppose it was because I did like Mia. For all her outrageously amoral ways, she was a smart and funny woman, and, as she said, she hadn't always been like this, so underneath she was probably as kind and considerate as Scott was. Underneath.

"Oh, we're beyond salvation, honey," she said, and patted me cheerfully on the back. "I caught him screwing the dog walker last week. Which was the final nail in the coffin. She was incredibly trustworthy, and I had to fire her. So now the dog suffers. I realized that I'd never be able to have children with Scott. And so, really, our relationship's over. It's just a question of getting what I can while I can. Because, frankly, after four years of marriage to a man who is incapable of picking up a single item of clothing from the floor and who's in denial about the fact that he's addicted to everything from sex to Excedrin PM, I feel I'm entitled."

"Well, when you put it that way . . ." I said, careful to remain professionally unopinionated.

"Now, as far as I'm concerned, this is all second-rate art." Mia closed her book decisively. "There's not a single piece for over a million dollars, and I think I'd prefer something more fun for my birthday. Let's go to Harry Winston's."

Let's go to Harry Winston's.

Now, I'm not especially jewel-oriented, and I don't know my carats from a hole in the ground, but show me the woman who can resist that particular battle cry. Not me, that's for sure. And soon enough all thought of betrayal of Scott and loyalties and professional etiquette was hurled to the curb as I took my seat in Mia's dream machine. Since I'd given up dating in this town, I suspected that living vicariously through Mia for just one afternoon was as close as I was ever going to get to being a Hollywood wife. So I determined to enjoy myself—even though back at my desk there were sixteen scripts without brads that needed distributing, more unreturned phone calls than Lara had Cosabella G-strings, plus I still needed to visit Jason over at the Coffee Bean and talk with him about *Sex Addicts in Love.* So much for my blossoming new career as a Hollywood player. I'd had my head turned at the first glimmer of distraction.

In the car Mia took calls from at least four girlfriends. And though I pretended not to hear, it was impossible not to elicit that they were variously Jen (who was married to Brad), Courtney (who clearly wasn't an assistant at The Agency), Sarah Jessica (there is only one), and Julia (go figure). She was planning a smallish lunch party at her place on Saturday, and they should all come and absolutely did not need to bring anything. No, not even a bottle of rosé. All right? It was just going to be an informal little something out on the veranda, and maybe they'd have a swim afterward. Perfect, lovely. Can't wait. Kind of thing.

And when she'd finished on the phone, Mia turned off her Puccini and put on some Missy Elliott and sang along: "Can you pay my bills? Let me know if you will cuz a chick gotta live . . ."

And live she did. And I was going along for the ride. For the next two hours, Mia and I were the best of friends. She may have been a ruthless opponent in the divorce arena, but she was a lot of fun in the plush environs of a diamond emporium.

"Do you know that Harry Winston was the last person to own the Hope diamond?" she whispered as we walked from the bathwater-warm air of Rodeo Drive through the doors of the store. The cool air gave me goose bumps, and I rubbed my arms as I followed Mia, who had made a shameless beeline for the larger glass cases containing what I was about to learn were Important Pieces. These were the jewels with names, histories, and the kind of price tags that Mia was looking for. And it soon became clear that this wasn't the first time Scott's credit card had taken a hit in here.

"Mrs. Wagner. So lovely to see you. And looking so well." A man in a charcoal gray suit smiled in an oleaginous way at Mia and bowed and scraped his way to find us a glass of champagne each. This was definitely the life, I thought as I stopped worrying about being busted for fraud by the security guard on account of my twenty-dollar Canal Street Cartier rip-off watch and instead began to lose myself in a world where the purchase of million-dollar gems is just another Wednesday afternoon activity, to be scheduled in between lunch at Indochine and a sacrocranial at home in the master suite at 4:00 P.M.

"How about this one?" Mia pointed to a yellow diamond solitaire pendant surrounded by pavé diamonds. Or so I was told. I wouldn't have known a pavé diamond if it had shaken hands with me and introduced itself. The man handed us our glasses of champagne and opened the cabinet for her.

"It's a splendid piece," he said, and placed it around her tiny little neck. I wondered for a moment whether she might fall flat on her face with the weight of it. I swear, it was the most obscenely large boulder of a thing I'd ever laid eyes on.

"The yellow makes me look a little sallow, don't you think?" Mia turned to me. What was I supposed to say? I hadn't a clue about jewels, and, more important, I didn't know the vernacular. Was it like buying a pair of shoes? Should I ask if she had anything to match it?

"What will you wear it with?" I ventured after a large gulp of champagne. Because she was waiting for me to say something, and nothing was rushing to mind.

"I hardly think that's a consideration." The man was looking at me as though I'd crawled from under a stone. Presumably your average granite rock and not the Krupp diamond.

I don't think he really could comprehend just who I might be. Clearly I wasn't Mia's best friend, who would have been one of the usual clientele who hadn't washed her own hair since her divorce in '97 and was clad in that unmistakably stealth-wealth, quiet-cashmere way. But then equally I wasn't the illegal maid. So he could neither bring himself to agree with me nor be blatantly rude to me. We, the underlings, those who could only afford to look, reached an accommodation by simply ignoring one another.

"You hate it," Mia said neurotically, and quickly had the yellow pendant removed from her neck. "What about emeralds? Much better with my hair anyway," she decided as a pair of emerald earrings found their way to her lobes and hung there as large as robin's eggs.

"Those are special," I pronounced, finding my jewel-buying vocabulary at last. "The clean lines work well with your eyes." Whatever that meant. But it was enough to persuade Mia to pass them over to me so she could see them *à la distance,* as Holly Golightly might have said.

"Here, you try them. I can't tell whether they're in proportion." So I did. I lifted my hair and fastened the dazzling green creations in place. They felt heavy but brushed the skin on my neck enticingly. I turned to look in the mirror, and there, attached to my earlobes, were a couple of gems that probably cost more than my parents' home. How was that for a sense of proportion?

"Oh, they're amazing," I said in a hushed tone as I turned to show Mia. And they *were* amazing. I felt like Elizabeth Taylor. Just off to take a dip in the pool at Cap Ferrat in my tiara, darlings, I wanted to say with a tinkling laugh.

"A bit on the grotesque side," Mia pronounced, disturbing me and Richard Burton on a yacht in Capri.

"Me?" I asked, shaken from my reverie. But she didn't answer.

She had already moved on to an altogether new shopping opportunity, the vintage piece. Woo-hoo, I thought as I wondered whether anyone would miss a pretty little ruby I'd spied sitting out on a counter in a velvet box, which obviously wasn't going to go to any home as happy and loving as the one I would be able to give it. I resisted the urge and shuffled over to where Mia was bent over a warm glass case, looking grave.

"This piece is very intricate. From 1925, the pendant is emerald with coral, onyx, natural pearl, and a diamond necklace," the man said, his eyes alive with the scent of an imminent sale. Mia was a little restless by now, and this was a pretty staggering creation, if I did say so myself. "And I think it's a very youthful piece. It has a vibrancy to it." Wham, bam, thank you, ma'am. Sold on account of the reference to youth to the lady who spends four hundred dollars a month on eye cream even though she's barely on the other side of thirty. It's amazing how young the young start to worry about getting old these days.

"I'll take it," Mia said. "I love it." And that, I realized, was the only time she'd expressed approval the whole time we'd been in here. Was this a part of being rich? Seeming unhappy with everything? Even though I suspected that inside she was leaping up and down with the same glee that I would have been experiencing if I were about to buy myself a spectacularly beautiful piece of American history. Made in the twenties for an heiress who'd probably danced on a lawn at midnight with F. Scott Fitzgerald. How could she not be delighted?

"I bet you'll go home and put it on with your pajamas and just bounce around on the bed laughing," I said, and the minute it flew out of my mouth, I realized how wildly unsophisticated it sounded. How even though it had never really crossed my mind to seek out a rich man, I was never likely to attract one anyway. Women like Mia didn't get to be women like Mia by being excitable about things. That was their one great talent. That was the reason rich men were attracted to them. They seemed unimpressable. A challenge as lofty and icy as

Everest. Sure, they might manage a thank-you if you bought them a small but perfectly formed Caribbean island for Christmas, but generally their faces were as hard as the diamonds that they mistook for affection.

"Oh, I don't think I'll ever wear it," Mia said as we got back into her car and headed for The Agency. "It's actually kind of vulgar, I think. But I happen to know that there's a 'Jewelry of the Twentieth Century' exhibit planned at MOMA later this year, so it'll appreciate brilliantly."

And when I glanced at her from the corner of my eye, I noticed that she did look older than she was. Her lips were drawn meanly into her face, and she was scowling at the road ahead.

"So if you'll just get Scott's credit card and call the store when you get back to the office, they can have it delivered to me by Friday," she said, as if I were . . . well, her husband's second assistant, I suppose.

"Of course," I promised. "I've had a really interesting afternoon, by the way. Thanks for bringing me along."

"What?" She checked her lipstick in her rearview mirror. "Oh, yeah, right. Sure."

"You can just drop me off by the front entrance if you prefer. It'll save you having to make a right turn," I said, indicating a place she could pull up outside The Agency.

"Great. I'll do that. Well, thanks, Elizabeth. And would you mind just giving me a call when you've paid for it? Just to let me know."

"Of course." I nodded and opened the car door.

"Oh, and, hey, why don't you come over on Saturday?" She suddenly turned and smiled at me, and I felt flattered. Cool, Saturday with Mia and her friends. I could certainly think of less interesting things to do. Though it was going to require a little more maxing on the maxed cards, but who cared?

"Saturday?" I said perkily. "That sounds fine. What time?"

"About eleven." She kept her engine running.

"Right," I said. "I'll be there."

"Great." The traffic on the street was honking behind her, waiting for her to move off. "Bye, Elizabeth. See you Saturday. Oh, and try not to be late."

With which she gave the finger to the car behind her and pulled out into the middle lane without putting on her blinker. Well, I thought as

I walked back toward the monolithic marble structure of The Agency, Mia Wagner may not have been the most natural choice of new friend for me, and certainly I wasn't the most obvious pal for her. But that was the beautiful thing about friendships, wasn't it? They were often so unexpected.

12

It's the story of my life. I always get the fuzzy end of the lollipop.

—Marilyn Monroe as Sugar Kane
Some Like It Hot

It was almost the weekend. Well, it was Wednesday. And one of our most prestigious actors had disappeared.

"Get Tony on for me," Scott called out from his office as I barreled into work a hair later than nine o'clock. I'd set off at seven-thirty feeling as daisylike as it's possible to feel when your neighbor has kept you awake until two with what sounded like a very invigorating Ashtanga workout. Consisting of so many thumps and thuds that it would send domestic-violence sirens ringing in your brain if you didn't know that your neighbor was in fact practicing *non*violence in a Zen Buddhist fashion. An unfortunate ten decibels louder than a plate-hurling couple.

Then there had been the traffic. The traffic would in theory be the perfect moment of my day to insert that said Zen Buddhism that Alexa had told me about briefly on the landing when we collided with our garbage bags last week. But as hard as I tried to relax the muscles in my pelvic floor and think of the lotus flower of my Anaharta chakra, I simply wanted to pee and scream expletives at the bitch in the BMW with the personalized license plate who'd just cut me off on the inside lane. And as calm as I endeavored to be, "Fuck you, Tami 69, with your stupid hair!" flew out of my mouth with a damned sight more alacrity than

"Om." I was clearly going to have to take my foul mouth and my soul to Hollyway Cleaners the next time Victoria sent me out with a selection of her funereal garments.

But then, who could blame me for the proliferation of "fucks" (miserably, only the verbal sort) in my life. It was all Scott's fault.

"Did you get Tony for me? I need to speak to him yesterday, for fuck's sake." Scott again. This time over the din of Linkin Park, which was his new favorite way to unwind.

"I'm on it," I said as I tapped out Tony's number with one hand and tugged off my jacket with my teeth and the other hand. But Tony's cell phone was going straight to voice mail. I raided my Rolodex and found his home number. I hated calling clients at home, especially actors, who were often very protective of their personal space. Sometimes to the point of lunacy.

"Hi, I'm not here. Leave a message." Tony was the most charmless man you'd ever want to sleep with in your entire life. But you did want to sleep with him. At least if you saw him at a multiplex near you. And particularly in an Academy Award–nominated role that involved the wearing of demonic leather. Possibly not, though, if you'd encountered him in the bathroom of a Dublin pub with his fist hovering above an intrepid paparazzo's jaw. Though I'm sure there would have been plenty of takers for that, too. Tony was the dictionary definition of devastatingly attractive. With the emphasis on devastation.

I noticed his mother's phone number scrawled in red ink on the card—*Tony's Ma,* it said and listed an Irish phone number. I wondered whether I'd be brave enough to call it. I wasn't.

"Scott, I've left messages at both his numbers, but no reply. All we can do is wait till he gets back to us." I got up from my desk and put my head around Scott's office door. Not having the lungs of Pavarotti, I would have gone unheard over the rap metal otherwise.

"Have you tried his mother?" He was irritatingly on the ball for a man who routinely massacred sixteen billion, never-to-be-recovered brain cells.

"His mother?" I acted as though I hadn't laid eyes on the red scrawl fifty seconds ago. "Well, that's an idea. I'll see if I can find her number and give it a try."

"This is urgent, Lizzie!" he bellowed as his fist crashed to his desk and the vibrations rearranged his pencil pots and caused his mouse to leap defenselessly in the air. David Sklansky's *Theory of Poker* crashed to the floor. Scott's latest crush was Texas Hold 'Em. Based in Costa Rica. Played online. Anywhere. And his mood could be made or broken depending on how he'd fared in the latest tournament.

"Fuck you, faggot asshole from Indianapolis with your three homo kings!" he yelled.

"Oh, hi there. I was wondering if I could speak to Tony please." An Irish woman had answered the phone.

"Who's this?" she snapped. Tony's ma, I was presuming.

"This is Elizabeth Miller, I'm from The Agency in Los Angeles. We represent Tony, and his agent, Scott Wagner, would love to speak to him if possible. Is this Tony's mother?" This in my best PR voice. Which always skyrockets through those octaves when I'm "doing polite." As if I'm talking to a small animal.

"Who I am is none of your business. And I know what The Agency is, you bloody fool," she said and I could hear a chorus of approval in the background. Then Tony's ma announced to the clacking company, who I imagined were similarly beady women lacing the edges of a kitchen table in Galway, nursing sugary cups of tea, "She thinks we don't have a bloody clue because we don't live in Los Angeles." "Los Angeles" spoken in a singsong taunt of a way. More clacking and some hissing from the doily of women. I could see where Tony got his courteous nature.

"I'm sorry to disturb you. And if Tony's not there, well . . ."

"Who said he's not here?"

"Oh, then, if he is, that's great. If you could put him on. Or if he's unavailable right now, ask him to call Scott Wagner." The irritating thing was that I know that I would have gotten exactly what I wanted on the spot from Tony's ma if I'd just spit, "Okay, listen here, you old cow. It's in your fat-ass son's interests if he speaks to his agent, because even though he's one of the most talented actors who ever suffered to show his face on the silver screen, he's also well on his way to the last-chance saloon in terms of being hired, because he has issues with aggression and bloating and women and doing as he's asked by perfectly nice, reasonable people. And to tell you the truth, nobody in this town likes him. And if you're in any doubt as to what I mean, look up Mickey Rourke in your *Hello!* magazine this week. Oh, he's not there? Could that be because nobody gives a shit anymore? Well, Tony's Ma. I rest my case." Naturally, I resisted the urge.

"He's *not* here. Since you're wondering," she said belligerently. Well, yes, actually I was wondering, which is why I called you in the first place.

"Okay, well, thanks for your trouble. Sorry to disturb you. Good-bye." I was about to hang up.

"But maybe I know where he is," she taunted me, with a muffled bleat from the receiver.

"I see."

"But I don't know as I can say."

"Right."

"Although I could tell you if I were so inclined." Somebody had obviously once told Tony's ma that knowledge is power, and she'd taken it very much to heart.

"I'd be incredibly grateful if you would tell me. As would Scott Wagner, who very much wants to speak with his client." I was getting formal. In a bid to prevent myself from getting foul.

"He's on a diet."

"That's great news," I said, a little too readily. Tony had a Brando-esque love of junk food, and after finishing a sexy epic, he'd hit the squeeze-cheese and burgers with indecent gusto. So in between movies, the only thing that looked heroic about him was his jowls.

"Watermelon diet," she announced. "And you should see the state of my downstairs toilet."

"Is he there now?"

"He left on Monday for somewhere hot. The watermelon, it was affecting his brain. As well as his bowels. But he wouldn't stop. I begged him, 'For the sake of your dead father, Tony, will you stop it with the watermelon?' I said. But he wouldn't stop. So he went somewhere hot where the melons were more readily available and fresher than you can get in the Co-op."

"And you don't know where that was, by any chance."

"I'm not at liberty to say to the likes of you."

"Okay, well, thank you for your time. Good-bye."

I put my head in my hands and wanted to scream. I had failed. For all that huffing and puffing with Tony's ma, I still didn't have a clue where he was. I seemed to have Pol Pot's talent for diplomacy. Thus I was about as likely to get Tony on the phone as I was to be adopted by his loving mother.

"So?" Scott yelled in a pause between what I suppose could loosely be termed songs.

"Right, well . . ." I said as I stood up and made my way to his office doorway. "It seems that Tony's gone on a watermelon diet. Lost his mind, and now he's on holiday somewhere hot."

"So put him through." Scott kicked off from his place beside the window and propelled himself on his office chair over to his desk in one push. He was so fantastically adroit on that chair that he could have picked up a gold at the Paralympics. Had he been disabled. He went to pick up the phone.

"Ah, no. You see, I didn't actually speak to him." I screwed up my face in anticipation of the onslaught.

"Why the fuck not? He has the most expensive movie of the year starting Monday in Mexico, and I haven't spoken to him in three weeks. Where the fuck is he?"

"Maybe he's in Mexico already," I said with lightning optimism. "It's hot there, right?"

"Yes, Lizzie, it's hot there."

"And they have watermelons. Plenty of them."

"What the fuck's with the watermelons?" Scott couldn't sustain his concentration on this topic of conversation any longer, and his eyes had flashed to the screen, where a new hand was being dealt in poker.

Thank the Lord for ADD, I thought as I prepared to sneak away.

"Don't. Go. Anywhere." Scott yelled, looking at his poker hand but talking to me.

"Scott, I don't see what more we can do. I've left messages with his mother, at his home, and on his cell phone. He'll get in touch when he's ready."

"Call Interpol."

"I'm sorry?"

"He's a missing person. Right?"

"Scott," I said pleadingly.

"Am I a fucking genius or what?" He lost his poker hand but was so thrilled with his brilliant idea that he didn't care. "See? Rehab had to be good for something. They tell you to use all available resources. Well, what's Interpol if it's not an available resource?" He grinned and flashed his poster-child-for-Beverly-Hills-dentistry smile. "Go get 'em, Lizzie."

I did one more Scott-you-can't-be-serious look, but it simply bounced off the glare of Brite-Smile whiteness like the sun off a mirror.

"Er, yes, hello. Could I please speak to someone in Missing Persons?" I couldn't bear it. I felt like seven kinds of idiot. On rye. But I had to do it. It was what I was paid for, apparently. Thank God they couldn't see me, was all the consolation I had. Even now I can't quite bear to reveal the full details of my embarrassment. Suffice it to say that what the girls in my office heard went something like this:

"I'd like to report someone missing, please . . . No, I don't think I need to speak to the human-trafficking department. This is more . . . well, do you have someone who deals with celebrities? Not specifically. I see. Well then, just plain old Missing Persons would be great. Thanks . . . Hello, I wonder if you can help me. An actor has gone missing, and we were hoping that you might be able to shed a little light on his whereabouts . . . No, I'm not next of kin, I'm actually the second assistant of his Hollywood agent . . . Highly unusual? I understand. He's been missing for, oh, a few days . . . Kidnapped? Well, he's very high profile, so it could be an option. But unlikely . . . No, there's been no demand for a ransom. It's just that he's supposed to begin work on a movie called"—I reached for my grid, the list of every movie shooting in Hollywood at the moment and every one scheduled to shoot someday, finance permitting—"right, yes, well, it's called *Acts of God,* and it's due to start in Mexico on Monday and . . . well, he's the lead, so a lot's resting on him . . . Suspicious? Well, I think if you factor in the watermelon diet that has allegedly made him a little mentally unbalanced, then we could be talking something definitely strange. You see, I spoke to his mother in Ireland and . . . terrorism? No, I don't think so. Though, if your Terrorism Department has a good reputation for finding people, then it'd be great if they could just . . . well, you know, put out a few feelers . . . Yes, I fully understand that Interpol is a serious agency whose objective is to combat international crime. I'm terribly sorry. Yes. It won't happen again . . . Time-wasting? Irresponsible? Yes. I'm aware of that. Yes. Sorry. Thank you."

Quite suddenly it had become *only* Wednesday. The weekend seemed like the hot shower waiting for me at the end of a very grueling army assault course on a freezing December day. But with someone firing a machine gun at me as I clambered over nets as high as a house, it was looking unlikely that I'd ever see the soap.

"And are they gonna get onto it?" Scott came out of his office and leaned over my desk, still glowing from the victory of his great idea.

"Scott, they're Interpol. They support and assist all organizations, authorities, and services whose mission it is to prevent or combat international crime. They don't deal with actors on watermelon diets."

"Millions of dollars are at stake. Did you tell them that?"

"I don't think they really cared too much about that," I explained, still red-faced and dying from my telling-off by the man on the phone.

"Then what in hell's name do we pay our taxes for?" Scott got mad. "I mean, have you any idea how much the IRS skims off my salary? And if you multiply that by everyone in this building, then I think we have a fucking great case for getting back on the phone to Interpol and telling them that we have paid for the right to have them find our actor and they can suck my left nut if they think that—"

"Scott, give it a break, huh?" Lara said, without looking up from her screen.

"Huh? Oh, yeah, right. Okay." Instantly his anger went into remission, and Scott ran an apologetic hand through his hair and weaved his way back to his office. Would that have worked if it had come from me? I wondered. I sincerely doubted it. Lara definitely had something that I didn't.

When Saturday came, I laid my outfit out on my bed like a new persona. Mia's lunch party was going to provide me with an entrée into being someone who had a life in Los Angeles outside the Coffee Bean and her office. And it shimmered before me like a very appealing mirage on the horizon. For while I wasn't exactly a home-alone-every-night-with-a-frozen-dinner recluse, neither were my fridge magnets buckling under the weight of a hundred (or even three) party invites. I also liked the idea of having an answering machine that boasted an occasional message. I liked the idea of putting on my heels instead of my pajamas some nights when I got home from work. Because even though until now I'd probably been too busy and bewildered to notice it, I think I'd been feeling lonely lately.

I could tell I was lonely by the way I no longer considered a bottle of nail polish and a tub of ice cream the most exciting companions a girl could have on a Friday night. And while experimenting with Nigella Lawson's recipe for ham in Coca-Cola was a very worthy way of winding down after a Sunday of script reading, it was a bit too poignant for words to have to throw the ham away on Tuesday because there was nobody to eat it all before it turned green. Now, I'm a self-sufficient girl, and I do know the difference between alone and lonely, but I felt that I had been crossing into the barren, deserty landscape of the latter recently, and I really ought to take action. Here was my chance. Lunch with new people. Not that I wanted to make friends with The Stars, by the way. As far as they were concerned, I was going to consider myself very lucky if I didn't pour red wine on their pants or spit corn in their eye when I asked them to pass the mineral water. Their friendship was a very distant shore, and I had no intention of drowning myself in a bid to reach it. But I hoped that Mia had invited a few more nonfamous friends who might want to grab a coffee with me at Who's on Third sometime, if all went well.

So when I arrived at Scott and Mia's, I was full of the joys. Eleven o'clock on the dot. I pulled up into their drive and tried to park my car unobtrusively beneath a tree. Somewhere that wouldn't scare Scott when he saw it. Their house was beautiful in a typically Beverly Hills way and quite simply perfect, not a leaf or pebble out of place. It was a miniature château looming up amid the palm trees, with sprinklers casting rainbows all over the lawns, armed security guards lurking in the bushes waiting to shoot you (or so the little white sign on the gate claimed), and even roses twirling up the porch and walls in an almost too-fairy-tale-to-be-true manner. I tucked my car keys into my purse, headed for the arch of the oak front door, knocked the golden lion's head, and twisted my sarong back into place as I waited.

I had presumed that Mia had invited me earlier than the other guests because she wanted a little moral support when chopping lettuce or something. Perhaps she wanted to make sure I thought the tarragon dressing was delicious enough or that pale lemon vintage lace napkins weren't too obvious.

"Elizabeth, fantastic! Come in." Mia answered the door in her off-duty-BH-housewife attire of Seven Jeans, flip-flops, and a tank top. Her hair dangled in burnished schoolgirl braids over her shoulders, but at the same time there was absolutely nothing casual about her look. Mia's casualness was all business.

"Hi, am I a bit late?" I asked, for want of something to say, as my watch ticked over to two minutes past eleven.

"A bit, but that's fine." She smiled, and I stepped into her hallway. "Now, I'm sure you're highly responsible, but there are a few things that I ought to tell you before you take her out."

"Right." I nodded, but I didn't have a clue what she was talking about.

"Come this way." Mia led me into the cool, oak-paneled darkness of the hallway, to the bottom of the wooden staircase, which I'm sure had been the backdrop to a few of Mia's Scarlett O'Hara moments.

"Oh, this is lovely," I said as I glanced around, while trying not to appear too fascinated by the schizophrenic—sorry, *eclectic*—blend of Brueghels, Picassos, and Buddhas. The Biedermeier dressers side by side with the wind chimes and Navajo dream catchers, which might as well have come from an ethnic store in Venice Beach. Because for all Mia's impeccable taste, she was unable to resist that peculiarly Californian habit of hedging your bets with the afterlife. A little Buddhism with some Kabala classes thrown in. Appease the American Indian spirits and then make a foray into Roman Catholic icons just in case someone up there really is watching. As if heaven's a party and you're pitching hard for an invite.

"Now, where is she?" Mia put her head through the kitchen door. The next moment she yelled "Anastasia!" with such gale force that I almost had to clutch the banister like the nannies in *Mary Poppins* holding on to the railings, to stop from being blown away. "Ah, here she is."

And with that an Afghan hound the size of a small pony, with exactly the same shade of hair as Jayne Mansfield, trotted up to Mia and sat down.

"Oh, she's . . . an Afghan," I said in a saccharine voice. Because even though I was usually able to convince myself that my filthy lies were just diplomacy by another name and survival by yet another, I still couldn't find it in my conscience to say that this dog was anything other than what she was: an Afghan. With the most ghoulish long blond hair and freakish appearance I'd encountered since my dinner at Spago. A place where every other diner had looked a little like Anastasia. Who may have been a very sweet-natured dog, but there was simply something about that half-dog, half-slut look that gave me the creeps.

"She certainly is an Afghan, aren't you, my darling?" Mia said without moving a muscle to touch her dog. For which I could hardly blame her. It would have been like running your fingers through another woman's hair. "Now, Lizzie, I thought you could take Scott's other car, because I don't want hairs on my seats. She needs at least forty minutes of CV workout, and don't forget the warm-up and cool-down. And when you come back, if you could just leave her with the housekeeper, that'd be great. I'm having a lunch party, and . . . well"—she cast that eye over me again—"the girls won't really want to be disturbed." And with that she snapped a leash onto Anastasia's Hermès collar, handed me a set of car keys, and sort of smiled. Well, it could have been a smile, in an alternate universe where surgeons hadn't discovered that botulism injections were an effective way of inhibiting displays of humanity. In this world it simply looked like an unfortunate twitch.

I hid the great crush of disappointment and humiliation behind a smile and took Anastasia's leash. Of course Mia hadn't invited me to lunch. It was my dumb-ass fault for not realizing how implausible a concept this would have been in the first place. Why on earth would anyone sit me between two of the finest actresses of their time and imagine that I had anything of any interest to say? What witticisms could I lend to their lunch? What wisdoms might I have imparted that made me worth my fillet of organic salmon in watercress sauce? I resumed my place at the bottom of the social ladder and led Anastasia, who in all reality was probably the rung above me, to the car.

Scott's *other* car was a baby blue and silver 1969 convertible Mustang. And as I cruised down Sunset with Anastasia next to me, the pair of us could easily have been mistaken by the man in the car behind for a couple of babes with luscious, long blond locks. Until he drew up next to us at the light and realized that one of us was an impostor from D.C. and the other was a dog. Oh, and did I mention, a dog with a death wish? Although clearly Anastasia had no interest in dying alone and kept trying to take me with her in her bids to escape the car and prostrate herself beneath the wheels of oncoming trucks. The only thing I knew for sure was that her funeral would have had much better flowers than mine.

"Anastasia, stop it, darling." I tried to mimic Mia's verbal patterns, but to no avail. So instead I grabbed her leash and employed a little brute force. Which was even less successful. She just kept turning and snarling at me in a pissed-off way. And by the time we hit the next set of lights, the darling dog and I were entwined in leather like a pair of amateur sadomasochists.

"Okay, for fuck's sake, sit the fuck down, won't you?" I yelled at the top of my voice, much to the amusement of the guy on the motorcycle next to me. But amazingly enough, it worked. Clearly I hadn't been mimicking the correct speech patterns before. I suspected that "darling" wasn't a word much heard in the Wagner household.

And bless her, she was so quiet for the rest of the ride that I almost began to think of her as a sister. A fellow Hollywood Honey. Which was perhaps a reflection of how much I was yearning for a friend right now, particularly after I'd been so ruthlessly snubbed by Mia and Co. From potential friend to dog walker in one easy step. Or perhaps my fondness for Anastasia could simply have been the delirium that is said to follow a near-death experience. Either way, I decided to show Anastasia that while Courtney Love–style outbursts were not appreciated, similarly sweetness and obedience would be rewarded. I reached into my purse and retrieved a few of Anastasia's organic vegetarian dog biscuits, which Mia had slipped me just before I left. On the strict proviso that she must have only one on account of her figure, of course. Well, after the sixth biscuit, she was like a little purring kitten. Only with gross hair. But after the seventh she began to get a little too close for comfort. And by the time we pulled up in the dog park, she was practically sitting on my lap. It took an enormous amount of strength and a few more "fucks" to get her off my knee and out onto the sandy parking lot.

I'd never owned a dog before, so I had no idea what happened at a dog park. I'd imagined that the place would be empty, stinky, and creepy, with maybe a lone pervert sitting on a bench. But then I was underestimating Los Angeles. The dog park was in fact heavenly. First off, it was so crammed with people that I could barely find a place to park Scott's Mustang. And second, this was no slab of dirt. There was a perfectly manicured lawn planted with the latest in haute perennials, a box with plastic bags at every tree, and two water fountains, one at dog level and the other at owner level, at each end of the park. And perhaps more significantly, the place was the most highly functional pickup joint I'd ever been to. And for all those picky Angelenos, it boasted the double whammy of being healthier than sleazy bars and less dubious than Internet dating.

But even here in Freaksville, the Prancing Princess and I must have looked quite a sight as we made our way through the cedar gates into the dog park. Because, in an ironic twist of fate, I was for once dressed as if I could actually walk into Tiffany's and purchase something other than just a heart key ring. I looked the part. For which, read clean hair that I'd gone to great lengths to sleeken, toenails that could have advertised Chanel rather than a paint on fungicide, and pretty kitten heels. Sadly I was dressed for the wrong part. I was kitted out for *Roman Holiday,* and they were obviously all starring in a Tarantino movie here at the dog park. Everyone except me was resplendent in that subghetto-fabulous, low-key-label look that consists of tummy-baring track pants, fab-ab tight little T-shirts, and an array of incognito hats bearing the legend of a movie. From *Charlie's Angels* to *Easy Rider,* this headgear acts as a barometer of cool among the *un*famous. Celebrities needed no such endorsement. Just shades.

I slipped Anastasia off the leash, and instead of delicately sniffing the ground as I'd expected a pampered pooch to do, she fled like a racehorse at the start of the Kentucky Derby. I attempted to catch her tail and drag her back before she could inflict damage, but my heels kept sinking into the grass. So I went to call her but suddenly felt horribly self-conscious at having to bellow such a pretentious name out loud among these hipsters, whose dogs were all bound to be called Killer and Elvis and Bling.

"Hey, doggy, come back!" I tried. Nada. Similarly, there was no response to Stash, Stasi, Sacha, or even Anna. Eventually I gave up and decided that liberating her was a kind thing and that not much harm was likely to come to her in this canine idyll.

As most of the benches were taken by the sharpest lawyers and hottest soap stars, I found myself a patch of grass and settled down with a pile of scripts. I'd wrested them from the trunk of my car when I realized that I wasn't going to be spending my afternoon sipping chardonnay with nice new people after all. I took off my kitten heels and opened a script that Victoria had urged upon me yesterday as we waited for the valets to bring around our cars. But though I read the first page six times, I found it totally impossible to concentrate. The sheer volume of talent here in the dog park was remarkable. And I don't just mean talent like The Agency talent. (Although there were enough actors here with their bichons frisés to shoot a remake of a Cecil B. DeMille epic—there was Hugh throwing a Frisbee for a bounding chocolate Labrador, Gisele on her cell phone with her teacup Yorkie, and a producer I'd seen on the front page of *Entertainment Weekly* only yesterday. And that was just for starters.) But what I really meant were the beautiful-single-people type of talent. And probably a few taken people, too, hot for some action. All scooping and scoping at the same time. Who'd have thought that such close proximity to dog poo could have made for such a sexy atmosphere? But it did. Erogenous zones, erogenous zones everywhere, and not a moment to waste. I put down my script and basked in the virility of it all. If I couldn't touch for fear of reprisals and certain heartbreak, I could surely look with impunity.

However, clearly some god of retribution had other ideas, as no sooner had I tenderly cast my eyes upon a whippet-walking actor in a hooded sweatshirt than a very high-pitched, aggressive bark breached the peace. And from the bushes flew Anastasia with what appeared to be a small mammal in her mouth. Oh, hell, I thought, then immediately decided to pretend I didn't know her. I buried my head in a script and ignored the cacophony of shrieks.

"It's Lilibet!" screamed a woman. "I know it!"

"No it's not, it's a Chihuahua," a man proclaimed.

"Is it dead?"

"No, it's twitching."

"It's Lilibet!"

"Is that blood dripping from the dog's mouth?"

"No, it's the poor thing's intestines."

"Oh, God, I'm gonna vom."

I stared hard at a comma and ignored the chorus of disapproval until some busybody saw fit to ask, "Whose dog is it anyway?"

At which point I contemplated scurrying back to the car and cowering until they'd all gone home. They were like a lynch mob, and if they found out that the bloodthirsty hound with innocent entrails hanging from her incisors was with me : . . well, I was screwed. So I read on. But as I turned my page, not daring to look up, I noticed that the crowd had fallen silent and there was a curious rasping noise in my left ear. I turned around, and in the same instant Anastasia dropped a headless squirrel out of her jaws and onto my script. I screamed and jumped a foot in the air, but when I regained my breath, instead of sympathy for my ordeal and my blood-splattered feet, all I was met with were evil glares.

"It's only a squirrel," I said, for the benefit of Lilibet's owner, who was probably even now calling her attorney.

"*Only* a squirrel?" a woman with a humorless brown ponytail exclaimed. "How would you like it if *you* were the squirrel?"

"I didn't mean only a squirrel," I said as I backed away from Anastasia, who looked like a fucked-up Hitchcock blonde with blood on her lips.

"She probably feeds the dog hormones," someone else said.

"Poor little squirrel."

"Look, I'm really sorry, everyone. But she's not really my dog, and—"

"Jesus, she can't even take responsibility for her actions," quipped a man with a bad nose job.

I stood next to Anastasia, feeling like an inappropriately dressed pariah with my head bent.

"Okay, guys, show's over." From out of nowhere stepped the guy from the movie set. Who was also the guy from the party who'd been talking to George. "We'll take care of the squirrel, and you can all get on with walking your dogs," he said authoritatively in what I had to concede was probably a genuine southern accent. I watched in astonishment as the livid dog walkers dispersed into a miasma of disgruntled tuts.

"I don't know what to say." I looked at the producer of *Wedding Massacre* as Guinevere might have looked at Lancelot if he hadn't been a misogynistic, warmongering pig. "But I think you just saved my life."

"Hardly, sweetheart," he said, and bent to wipe some of the blood from Anastasia's chops with his handkerchief. "And what was all that about, hey, Anastasia?"

"You know her?" I asked.

"Oh, yeah, she and I go back a long way. She likes to lick my dog's balls." Cue a very Churchillian-looking bulldog who waddled toward us without a care in the world. "This is Rocky."

"Nice to meet you, Rocky," I said, and bent to pat him. Just to prove that I wasn't the evil charm when it came to animals. "Do they know one another from the dog park?" I asked.

"No, I'm a friend of Scott's. I go over there sometimes, and Rocky and Anastasia make out." He grinned and knelt beside Rocky, whose stomach he began to jiggle. Okay, cool your jets, baby, I told myself as I found my hand involuntarily checking my hair and my chest performing a greeting ceremony all its own. This is a friend of Scott's. He is not for you. He is not for you. He is not for you. "We've met before, in case you didn't remember." God, why couldn't he go away and stop being so charming? And handsome. Well, offbeat-sexy handsome, lopsided handsome, not dog-walking, male-model handsome. Thank the Lord. Or not thank the Lord. In fact, curse the Lord for putting temptation in my way like this. I was a mess.

"I do remember." I nodded. "I'm Scott's second assistant."

"With rug-burned knees, huh?" He raised his eyebrows good-humoredly and looked down at my grazed kneecaps.

"That would be thanks to the Evil Princess here," I said. "Not what you were thinking at all."

"Oh, really. And you know what I was thinking, do you?" More lopsided shit. Damn him.

"No, but I know that in all probability you're a dissolute entertainment-industry type with a penchant for actresses, cigars, and the bigger better deal."

"Oh, so you *are* psychic." He looked a bit stung.

"I'm sorry." I patted his dog because I couldn't pat him. "But I'm still a little shaky from the squirrel episode, I guess."

"No, shaky's fine. Though, for the record, I can't stand cigars."

"I'm Elizabeth Miller. And I apologize."

"Luke Lloyd." He held out his hand, and we shook, with the dogs looking on like a still from *The Great Adventure*. "So will you and the princess be here again next week?"

"I hope not." I rolled my eyes. "I mean, not with her anyway. And without her would be a bit pointless, I guess, so, well . . . I'm not sure."

"I'll take that as a gentle brush-off," he said, and winked at me. "Nice meeting you, Elizabeth Miller." With which he and Rocky made off for the water fountain without once looking back.

"Damn him," I said to Anastasia as we made our way back to the car. "Why does he have to be *one of them*? Why can't he be a normal person like me?" The kind who talks to herself and abuses virtual strangers because they're sexy.

13

It should take you exactly four seconds to cross from here to that door. I'll give you two.

—Audrey Hepburn as Holly Golightly
Breakfast at Tiffany's

"Elizabeth, I need to see you in my office." Scott marched by my desk without looking in my direction.

I glanced over at Lara, hoping she might be able to shed some light on the matter, but she looked as puzzled as I did.

"Maybe you forgot to renew his Lakers season ticket," she suggested.

"No. Did that last week."

"Huh, no clue then, sorry." She gave a blank shrug. I got up and began my saunter into Scott's office to find out exactly which variety of trouble I was in today. There were about fifteen different sorts, ranging from the amusing faux pas to the unforgivable fuckup. Being castigated for the latter was no fun at all, but thankfully I hadn't had one for at least a month now, and my conscience was pretty clear in terms of dumb things I'd done lately. So I took a quick swig of my Diet Coke before I turned myself in to face the music.

"I said I need to see you in my office." Scott had actually walked over to his office door and was standing there looking either exceptionally hungover or deeply serious. I couldn't quite ascertain which. Lara and I exchanged uneasy glances. I got the feeling this wasn't just routine abuse.

"Immediately, please." He turned and headed back toward his desk.

It was the "please" that gave it away. I had never heard him use that word before. And at once a chasm opened up in my stomach, and my legs began to buckle.

"Could you shut the door, Lizzie?" he said as I took one last look behind me at the office. Nobody but Lara had noticed what was going on, because for once Scott wasn't raging at us like Don Quixote tilting at windmills. I nodded silently and sat down when Scott gestured to the purple suede armchair opposite his desk. I'd never seen his office from this angle before. Usually I was perched on the arm of his sofa or had my feet up on the coffee table as we all watched a teaser or a great moment in baseball or Christina Aguilera's underwear in her latest video. Or I was standing in front of his desk desperately trying to lure him away from a phone call or a computer game for long enough to etch his squiggle on the bottom of a letter. How I wished for some of that levity now. But it was nowhere to be found. Instead of the playroom of an overgrown teenager, before me was suddenly the office of one of the most powerful men in Hollywood. And I was in trouble.

"Listen, Lizzie, I hate doing this shit." He had been sitting, but he was clearly uncomfortable inside, as though ants were crawling under the surface of his skin. And for once that wasn't the cocaine. He stood up and paced around to the front of his desk. Then leaned back against it, a couple of feet in front of me. He folded his arms and looked thoughtful. "Daniel wants me to fire you." I couldn't have been more shocked if he'd kicked the chair from under me.

"Right," I said. He looked at me, and I bit down hard on my lip to stop myself from bursting into involuntary tears. "Why?" I wasn't sure if I'd said this aloud. But I guess I must have because Scott began to run his hand repeatedly through his hair.

"You fucked up," he said. Well, at least some things never changed around here.

"How, exactly?" I had been so certain that I'd been sailing along. And just a week ago, when I'd been dusting down my résumé, it had been *my* call to leave this place. This hellhole. This job that I suddenly loved.

Scott cracked his knuckles, and I shivered. "Last week when we finally found Tony in Tucson, you were supposed to book him on a flight to Los Angeles so that we could get him to Mexico for principal photography on Monday morning."

"Which I did. I had the tickets FedExed to his suite. I got the confirmation, he signed for it. I checked." I still hadn't learned that they don't want to hear your defense. They've already made up their minds. You just have to take the beating and apologize. But I was certain that I couldn't possibly have screwed up that particular task. In fact, I knew I hadn't.

"Hold on a second." Scott's expression was unreadable, and my insides felt as though they'd been whizzed through a blender. "He got on the flight. That wasn't the problem. The problem started when you booked him in cattle class. Jesus, Lizzie, the guy is six foot three and hasn't flown coach since his first movie deal. It's in his goddamn contract."

I put my head in my hands and winced. "Oh, God, Scott. I had no idea. I'm so sorry."

"Oh, baby, that wasn't even the start of the problems." Scott closed his eyes in disbelief. "Where was his flight going, Lizzie?"

"Well, Los Angeles. With a connecting flight through Las Vegas."

"Exactly. You booked him on a flight to Las Vegas."

"You said that I ought to get cheap flights because his next movie was art house and wouldn't gross enough to buy a Pizza Hut delivery. So I booked them through Expedia."

"Elizabeth, don't you know by now that most of what comes out of my mouth is bullshit? Even *I* don't believe what I say. If you didn't know, you should have asked someone."

What I wanted to say was that there was nobody to ask. Lara was gone three days a week writing her magnum opus, Scott was constantly in some Disneyland of the mind, and most of the time I just felt like Stevie Wonder cruising down the PCH behind the wheel of a Ferrari.

"If the transfer was a problem, I could write him a letter apologizing," I volunteered. I knew that this whole mess wasn't a great scenario, but it was hardly a sackable offense. It was a flight, wasn't it? The principle was right.

"The transfer wasn't the problem. The problem is that Tony's addicted to gambling. In 2001 he lost every last cent he made. And trust me, I know, because I made his deals. And we're talking thirty million here. Everyone knows that Tony is addicted to the dice—it was on the cover of *Time, Newsweek, Entertainment Weekly.*"

At this point I think I became extremely pale.

"Where was your head, Lizzie?"

"I had no idea." Because at the time it was happening, I was doing an internship at the White House. You know, that place where real stuff happens, other than self-inflicted ruin by the likes of megalomaniacal, dictatorial gambling-addicted actors who are rapidly hurtling toward the tragic "but then" curve in the story of their lives. . . .

"Thing is, Tony now earns three times what he did back in 2001. And he's been missing in Vegas for three days. And I didn't even know until the fucking producer called me this morning and tore me a new asshole."

"I can go get him, Scott. I promise. I'll leave for Vegas now. I'll buy my own ticket." They were, after all, only seventy-nine bucks on Expedia. "I'll find him, and I'll deliver him to Mexico for his call time on Monday. I swear." I was beginning to sound faintly hysterical now. My voice kept cracking, and the tears were flagrantly disregarding my attempts to keep them at bay.

"Okay, calm down. Unfortunately I'd have preferred to handle this quietly in this office. Only Daniel's sister happened to be at a conference in the Bellagio, and she spotted Tony at a craps table and called Daniel right away. He wigged out. Which for once is understandable, considering that back in 2001 he and I had to sign for every withdrawal Tony made for eighteen months. Which caused serious sleepless nights for him and some major narcotic numbing for me."

"Scott, please don't fire me. I like this job. I love it." And suddenly I really did. "I'll do anything."

"No you won't, Lizzie. And that's what I like about you." His face relaxed for the first time this morning. I contemplated the prospect of not seeing Scott's face again. And though I never thought I'd be sad to see that day, the thought chilled me to the bone. And I didn't want to wake up and come anywhere else but here in the mornings. I loved getting in my Honda. I loved feeling part of the hum of Los Angeles life as I sat on the freeway in traffic with the radio for company. I loved the Josés, who were like surrogate uncles to me with their unfathomable wisdom.

But before I could lose myself in *Elizabeth Miller's Hollywood Career: A Retrospective,* the phone rang and Lara's voice drifted reassuringly over the speakerphone. "It's Big Jack," she said. "He says it's urgent."

"Put him through." Scott picked up the phone immediately. "So what you got for me, man?" I tuned out, thinking that Big Jack was probably his dealer. I wondered if Lara had his phone number so that I could score a little narcotic numbing for myself later. When I was unemployed on my sofa. Because I was going to need it.

I wondered what it would be like to walk out of the assistant pool for the last time. If I were fired, I very much doubted that I'd have the will to find another job in Hollywood. What I didn't realize then was that there was a unique concept in operation in Hollywood known as "failing upward." Which basically meant that if you get fired and have the cojones to apply for a job above your station, you'll probably be hired on the first interview. Because somehow the stench of failure disappears as fast as a Roman profile in Hollywood. People are allowed to reinvent themselves every day of the week. Which makes it a very forgiving town, but a scary place to meet friends or lovers.

Scott put the phone back in the cradle. He showed no emotion, but his hand was tapping rhythmically on his desk.

"It's your lucky day, Lizzie. Big Jack has found Tony, and he's put him on a flight to Puerto Vallarta." Scott looked like a little boy who'd just hooped a goldfish.

"Who's Big Jack?" I asked, wondering if I was supposed to be glad in that Spirit of Communism, "for the good of The Agency even though they're just about to fire your ass" way. Or glad because this meant that I was off the hook.

"He's a PI my wife uses to spy on me. Best in the business." Guilt must have been plastered all over my face, because his lips formed a slow smile. "Oh, so you knew about that, did you?"

"Mia mentioned it when she took me shopping for her birthday present."

"And I guess I have you to thank for the fact that I can't afford to buy a new pair of pants for myself from the Gap right now."

"Sorry," I said. As I decided that Elton John was definitely wrong. Far from being the hardest word, "sorry" was about the only one in my vocabulary today. Not that it was doing me much good.

"For Christ's sake, Lizzie, will you cut out the hangdog thing?" he said, suddenly brightening up and going back to his seat. Well, at least one of us could afford to smile. Even if that somebody purported not to be able to afford Gap pants.

Scott sat at his desk and couldn't resist a shuffle of his mouse. I recognized the telltale click-click-click of the Texas Hold 'Em cards being dealt out from cyberspace.

"Right, so do you want me to pack my things up now, or would you prefer it if I worked my two weeks' notice?" I asked as I watched him.

"Didn't I make myself clear?"

Well, no, Scott, you didn't.

He tore his eyes away from his screen and looked at me with probably a good deal less consideration than Pontius Pilate gave to Jesus. In fact, with possibly less consideration than most people give to brushing their teeth when they're drunk. But for Scott it was significant. He paused a moment, found himself unable to resist one lightning glance at the cards, then looked me in the eye.

"The thing is that Lara really likes you, and she happens to be a requirement in my life. Without her I cannot seem to function. Plus, she's so goddamn difficult to please. She hates all my second assistants apart from you, so even though Daniel wants you fired, you're *my* assistant and *I'm* gonna make the final call."

"Okay." I still didn't know exactly where this was heading. But a girl can hope. And hold her breath until she turns blue. Praying that she's not upstaged by three spades, one of which is an ace.

"So I'm going to tell Daniel to go fuck himself." He pointed a finger at me. "You think you can handle staying?"

"Oh, my God, yes! I mean, I don't want you to go out on a limb for me, but—"

"Actually, I kind of like the idea of telling him to fuck himself right now. So you're in luck. Now, get your ass out of my office. By the way, I need you to get Tony's producer on the line, and before you hand him to me, you need to explain what happened. Make yourself seem unbelievably incompetent. Then I'll get on and tell him how fabulous I am for fixing it."

"Yes, sir." I wanted to kiss him. "And thanks, Scott." I made do with a meaningful look, which was still too much for him. He waved me out of his office and looked embarrassed.

"What in hell's name?" Lara whispered to me when I sat back at my desk, my face streaked in that hackneyed mascara-and-tears combo so beloved by cheap soap operas. Courtney was practically giving herself whiplash trying to listen. Obviously the office door's being closed on an occasion when Scott wasn't in there alone with a honey caused her bloodhound nose to sniff out trouble.

"I sent Tony to Vegas on a layover," I said.

Lara got the picture at once and grimaced in pain. "Ah, sheet," she said.

"But Big Jack found him, and he's bringing him home. Daniel wanted me fired, but because of you Scott's going to refuse."

"Because of me?" She looked genuinely surprised. "Because of me how?"

"Apparently he thinks you'd want me to stay, and your opinion matters because you're a requirement in his life and he can't function without you or something," I said as I pulled a packet of Advil from my top drawer and popped a couple.

"Really?" Lara's demeanor completely changed for one fleeting moment. Her eyelashes lowered, and she smiled softly. It occurred to me that she really never got any validation from Scott. And as she probably was human, she liked it when it came. "Well, I should hope so, given how much of my time and energy I've devoted to his sorry ass in the last two years." And suddenly, fuzzy was yesterday's news. Lara slipped her headset back on and was about to get back to her novel. With one last thought.

"Listen, I know I haven't been around much, and I'm not planning on being around much in the future. But if there's ever a question, a dilemma, or a matter of protocol that you're not sure about—call me."

"Thanks, Lara, that's really good of you," I said, the tears coming again. Out of relief and faith in the unprecedented bucketfuls of the milk of human kindness that had been shown to me by Lara and Scott in the last ten minutes.

"If you got fired, it would really set me back on the book," she added.

Afterward I made the call and convinced the director that I was a twit, thus making Scott seem like a superhero. It was only later, though, that I realized I'd inadvertently earned The Agency a mint. And here's how: Just prior to making *Acts of God* in Mexico, Tony had decided that he was going to become the people's actor. He was only in it for the art from now on. He was going to grow a beard and do three movies back to back with budgets of under $3 million. And, much to his management's horror, he was going to work for SAG scale. (That's the Screen Actors Guild union minimum, which is a side-splittingly laughable $678 per day, apparently.) However, thanks to the little detour that I organized for him and the ensuing seventy-two hours he got to spend in Vegas, Tony blew more money than you or I would know how to spend in several very comfortable lifetimes. But with a large Irish family to keep in potatoes and a livery of bodyguards that would have made Joseph Stalin look paranoid, he needed the cashola. Enough to drop his art-house affectations and replace them with two sequels and an action movie. Which little chess move on my part netted The Agency a cool $11.5 million profit. If only my bosses would have believed that I was Machiavellian instead of simply useless.

With Scott back in his box for the moment, I was free to dash over to the Coffee Bean and have a meeting with Jason. The shock of almost being fired had instilled in me a renewed love of my position at The Agency. So like the man plucked from a fatal train crash with just a bump on the head, I was determined to achieve all the things I had dreamed of from now on. Which also meant helping Jason to make his movie.

"Coffee?" I leaned in and asked Lara, so that nobody else could hear and demand the usual litany of beverages that would have meant that Jason was too busy with his frother to listen to me.

"I'd love a raspberry iced tea," Lara mouthed back.

"Coming up." I stole away from my desk, my wallet hidden in my hand and a hasty trip to the bathroom to splash my face with cold water planned. Any fool could see that I'd been crying, and I wasn't keen for word to get around The Agency that I'd been spared the boot not because I was indispensable but because Lara's Rolodex happened to contain the cell-phone numbers of every doctor in the state who would hand out prescription medication like Halloween candy. And as every good assistant knew, her Rolo was her bond. If she left, it went with her. So the way I saw it, Scott was in no position to risk Lara's wrath. Which meant that I kept my job. But as I passed Ryan in the corridor and he stared savagely at my bludgeoned bullfrog features and fistful of Kleenex, I feared that it was too late to hope that news of my death-row reprieve wouldn't spread quicker than his grin.

. . .

"Hey, Lizzie!" Jason lit up as I walked in the door of the empty coffee shop. And suddenly I didn't feel quite so bad. Outside the marble, Pollock-lined walls of what today masqueraded as the Ministry of Fear, I was once again a sentient human being with a voice and opinions on all manner of things, from Justin Timberlake to genetically modified crops. I was also able to breathe the air without fear that it contained poisoned spores pumped out through the air-conditioning by Ryan. Spores that would react only with my DNA and nobody else's in The Agency, but spores that would leave me with the IQ of Talitha. But without the looks. Jesus, and I'd just accused Tony of being paranoid.

"Hi." I gave Jason a hug. Which was a new thing between us, but not altogether unpleasant. I hadn't had a hug since my sister was here. And that wasn't the same. Maybe it's a daddy thing, maybe it's a subsexual need, but sometimes you just want a man's arms around you. Big, smothering, crushing biceps that make your shoulders hunch and your lips squish together like your face is trapped in an elevator door. And it felt lovely being crunched like a bug by Jason.

"How've you been? I thought about sending out a search party but figured you just didn't like my script, thought I was a pervert, and defected to Starbucks."

"Never," I said as he released me. "In fact"—I savored the moment because I knew it would be sweet for him—"I love your screenplay to pieces, and I'd be honored if you'd let me come on board as a producer." I grinned excitedly at him.

"You're kidding?" Jason surveyed my face for a glaze of dishonesty. "You're not kidding."

"I'm serious. I think it's incredible. The story, the characters, the payoffs, the structure's tight, it could easily be done for under five million, and you're a genius."

"Holy shit! You even sound like a producer!" Jason laughed and picked me up and spun me around. Well, he tried. I was a little unwieldy, so he kind of plonked me back down and punched me amiably instead.

"Yeah, well, I don't work for the hottest talent agency in Los Angeles for nothing." I shrugged. "Clearly all the time I thought that I was just a beneath-contempt subordinate who couldn't patch through a phone call if her Christmas bonus depended on it, I was imbibing industry know-how by osmosis."

"Junior Scott Rudin," he said. "Wanna latte, and we can discuss it?"

"Actually, I'd love a latte. And a raspberry iced tea, but I have to get back and make amends for the most monumental fuckup since *Cutthroat Island.*"

"Lizzie, you get fired every day. How bad can it be?" He got to work on my drinks.

"This was an order from on high. Daniel Rosen wanted my head on a plate."

"So how come you're still here?"

"Death-row reprieve from Scott. Well, actually Lara. Anyway, it's a long story and I *am* still here, but . . . well, I want to get on with your movie, Jason. I like it, and I realize that my career needs to be based on something other than being liked by Lara."

"Ah, the fickle world of the Hollywood talent agent. Well, I'm not sorry if it means that you're on board with *Sex Addicts.*"

"I really am. So maybe we can get together over the weekend and discuss it. I mean, what I just said was only my abbreviated coverage. I have a lot more to say."

"And I bet you can talk when you want to, can't you?" he teased.

"I have been known to get a little carried away in my time. But nothing that a slap across the cheek can't take care of." I picked up the drinks.

"Okay, how about Sunday morning?"

"Sounds great," I said, grateful for having what could be deemed by the desperate as a plan for my weekend.

"We could go hiking," he offered.

"Hiking?"

If I had been successful in one thing since I'd arrived in this town, it was in hiding how supremely unfit I was. With twice the determination that it would have taken to complete a triathlon, I had managed not to join a gym, not to put so much as a toe inside a Pilates studio, not to try out for the ladies' basketball team in my building. And certainly not to indulge in that most disgustingly wholesome of Californian activities—hiking. God, the mere thought of it made me want to take to my sofa, sew myself to a cushion, and stay there for the next seventeen years. Because not only did I not have the mental commitment to hike, I also lacked both the oatmealy socks and the cardiovascular equipment. Granted I had lungs and a heart. I just wasn't sure how they'd like being put to work.

Equally, my clothes and hair may have changed since I made Hollywood my home, but underneath those Petit Bateau T-shirts and Joie combats was still a girl who worked in politics. In D.C. I had existed on heroin-strength black coffee, the occasional protein bar, and turkey subs snatched on the run, and the only exercise I had was racing to a meeting or shuffling around at a cold bus stop on my way in to work. Besides which, hikers had hair the color of wheat, freckles, and shiny-apple faces. I simply wasn't the hearty, hiking type.

"Sounds good. What time?" From what twisted, deep-down place did that come? I wondered as I made my way back to the office and prayed for flooding in Fryman Canyon on Sunday morning. At 7:00 A.M.

14

We all go a little mad sometimes. Haven't you?

—Anthony Perkins as Norman Bates
Psycho

I could hear the phone ringing from the other side of the door. It was a determined ring that said "It's your mother, and I will not leave a message." My answering machine clicked on as I dropped the keys on the floor in my haste to make it. But after the beep a frosty click could be heard in my apartment, and three seconds later the phone began to ring again. I undid the two locks that were the originals from when the apartment had been built back in 1923. I hadn't thought to put in a new one, and neither had any of the other girls in my building. Most of us owned nothing valuable enough to steal, and if it was sex the intruders were after, we'd probably be too tired. Apart from the preternaturally energetic Alexa, and then her pelvic floor was tighter than a nutcracker and would doubtless leave any offender wishing he'd stuck to Internet porn.

I opened the door and lunged for the phone. I still harbored some vestigial hope that it might be Jake Hudson every time it rang. But of course it was always my mother.

"Elizabeth? Is that you?" Why did she ask that whenever she called? What other female did she think would be answering the phone of her single daughter who lived alone in Los Angeles?

"Yes, Mom. Of course it's me. How are you?"

I flicked my shoes off across the length of the room and headed for the refrigerator. Oh, great, it was grocery-shopping night, when I got to throw out all the vegetables I'd optimistically filled my basket with last week. The fennel that I was going to bake. The butternut squash I was going to cut in half and scrape and fill with butter and sprinkle with brown sugar and then put in the oven for forty-five minutes. The same fennel and butternut squash that were now significantly shrunken and malevolently staring out from their shelf, determined to make me feel guilty because, as well as proving me wasteful and lazy, they'd also like to remind me that I'd eaten pizza six out of seven nights when I claimed not to be able to afford it.

"I'm okay, honey," my mother said unconvincingly. I settled on cereal for supper and tossed the healthy dead stuff in the trash. "Apart from the fact that I had a fall the other day. Those dogs will be the death of me."

"You fell? Why didn't you tell me? What happened?"

I hated it when she did this. She never told me when something serious happened until it was too late. Then I felt horribly guilty for weeks afterward that I hadn't been in touch more often. Of course, my brother, Tim, was there to take her to the hospital, and Melissa was there to nurse her back to health. It was just lousy Elizabeth who was nowhere to be found. As usual.

"Well, honey, you're so busy all that way out in California, and I don't like to bother you with such silly little things. Besides, you have enough to worry about, like earthquakes, forest fires, and race riots."

Well, I hadn't until this moment, but better add them to my list of things to keep me awake in the frail, suicide hour before dawn.

"I'm never too busy to speak to you, Mom." I sloshed some dubious milk onto my cereal and rinsed off a spoon. "So what happened?"

"I took the dogs for a walk, and they went after a rabbit, and I'd stupidly wrapped both leashes around my right wrist, and they took off and lifted me off my feet. Dragging me halfway across a field by my arm. But I'm okay. I'm just black and blue, and we have your father's annual black-tie fund-raiser for Save the Dolphins on Saturday, and I look like I've been through a meat grinder."

"Jesus, Mom, you should have called me right away."

"Well, I didn't want to bother you, and I'm fine. But it got me thinking of you, sweetheart. I hate it that you're so alone out there in Los

Angeles. It gives me sleepless nights. What if you get sick or hurt yourself? Who's going to take care of you?"

"Mom, they have doctors in Los Angeles. And if I'm really sick, then *you* can just come and take care of me."

This was not the answer she was looking for.

"So have you met any nice men recently?" She sounded admirably casual, but we both knew that this was the point of the call. Finally.

"No, Mom. I don't think there *are* any nice men in Los Angeles. There is one who seems nice on the surface. But I know that after one date he'd turn from Dr. Jekyll into Mr. Hyde. Or cause me more heartache, rejection, and disappointment than I think I can bear at the moment." Oh, God, I wanted to kick myself. Too much information for one worried, devoted, bruised mother.

"Elizabeth, I think you need to come home right away. We'll pay for your plane ticket, and you can stay here with Dad and me until you find a job. I heard that young senator from South Carolina is looking for a new team to spearhead his reelection campaign, and he's even green, darling." I glanced at my overflowing garbage bin, which displayed the myriad colors of red cans, brown bottles, blue papers—all glaringly in need of division and recycling. Like cooking my vegetables, this would never happen. I turned my back on the distinctly ungreen trash and focused on my mother.

"Mom, it's not really that bad. It'll all be much better when I have a few close girlfriends here and I won't have to use you as a sounding board for my problems. Which aren't even real problems, they're just natural blips when you move thousands of miles from home to a strange city and a new job."

"Well, all the more reason to come home. You've never had problems making friends before. Clearly there's something wrong with Los Angeles. And have you spoken to Tim?"

Tim, my perfect older brother, was a lawyer for Doctors Without Borders. He'd recently been tapped for a place on a war-crimes tribunal in Africa.

"No, Mom. We keep on missing one another. I'll call him Sunday."

"He's told us secretly that he's going to propose to Daphne. But let him tell you for himself. Of course Dad and I are over the moon." Oh, great. I didn't think that it was possible for my perfect brother to get any more perfect, but he'd topped himself. He'd met Daphne six months ago on Capitol Hill. She'd started a nonprofit organization that raised money to turn the worst public schools in D.C. over to the private sector. Apparently it was having amazing results. She was also pretty, stylish, and really cool. I was happy for him. And I thought it might just take the pressure off me for a moment. But instead it had the opposite effect.

"Why can't you find a nice man, Lizzie? I don't understand. You haven't had a boyfriend since Patrick, and that was your last year at college. I'm starting to wonder if you have commitment issues, darling. Perhaps that's why you didn't stick with politics either. Your dad and I were thinking that maybe you should talk to somebody about it."

"Like Tim?"

"Perhaps a professional."

"A shrink?" I asked, faintly horrified. My family's intimacy, though fantastically supportive and loving, could also feel a bit interfering at times. To say the least. I took a deep breath to prevent myself from yelling at my mother. Which wouldn't have been productive and would just have confirmed their theories that I would benefit from a dose of therapy. "Mom, I don't have commitment issues. I had the occasional boyfriend at the White House—you just never met them. And the job with Congressman Edmunds finished through no fault of mine."

"No need to be so prickly, darling. It was just a thought. Some say it's a by-product of being the middle child. There's nothing to be ashamed of."

I had to get her off the phone or I'd say something that I regretted.

"Oh, Mom, what do you know? There's somebody at the door. I think it must be my neighbor, Alexa. She said she might come by and have some supper with me. Talk soon. Give my love to everyone." I ignored her irritated whimperings and hung up. Sorry, Mom, love you but can't be dealing.

The next morning, with the fingers of my left hand hovering between a Cinnabon and my lips, I began sorting through the mail. I separated it as efficiently as I could, and the piles that resulted—one for me, one for Lara, one for Scott—were of mind-bending neatness. It was the day of my new leaf, and it was still too early to have made a single mistake (that I knew of), so I was feeling exhilarated by how good a day I could have. I was even more excited to discover that my mail pile, rather than just being full of the usual out-of-date circulars and requests for photographs of Cameron, contained a very smart manila envelope. And for once the contents were actually interesting, too. Not woo-hoo interesting, but definitely up my *Strasse* in this new efficient mode.

I'd been approved for the company health plan and now had my own Blue Cross card with my name on it and "The Agency" written underneath. I petted the soft plastic. This meant that I could go to the dentist and have my teeth cleaned, and maybe I'd even find a nice dentist who would agree to bleach them, too. Also, Courtney had said that if I went to see a dermatologist, they'd give me facials and I'd only have to pay my fifteen dollars copay. Apparently the medical profession in Los Angeles was very willing to stretch the boundaries of acceptable coverage to help out the young and the struggling. So now that I was one of them, I needed the teeth and skin to make it in this town.

I began leafing through the booklet looking at all the things that were and weren't covered. I could have in-home care, but not a private room. I was allowed to check in to a rehabilitation clinic for drug and alcohol abuse, but I was only covered for a thirty-day stay. Which probably ruled out heroin but left a window for oxycodone addiction. I was also entitled to sixteen visits to a mental-health-care provider. Which sounded free to me. I licked the Cinnabon off my fingers slowly and pondered what my mom had said. Maybe I did need to see a shrink. Maybe there *was* a reason that I didn't have a boyfriend and the rest of the world did. I mean, it wasn't as though there was any stigma attached to your going to a shrink in this town. In fact, quite the opposite. Everyone probably wondered what weirdness I was in denial about that I didn't discuss my issues in an open way in a leathery environment on a weekly basis. They probably thought that I was a seething black cloud of neuroses and passive-aggressive tendencies. Or perhaps that I was egomaniacal for even thinking so much about myself. That was the trouble with psychotherapy: You were damned if you did and damned if you didn't.

"Help!" I said out loud.

Then I began to think about the little Freud that I knew. He believed that there was no such thing as an accident. I hadn't just accidentally asked for help. And there was no such thing as a joke. I hadn't jokingly asked for help either. I actually wanted it.

By the afternoon I had canvassed various people on their head-shrinkage of choice in a bid to find a suitable person to care for what I was by now convinced was my fragile mental state. Talitha swore by Dr. Amanda, who gave her revolutionary advice about relationships. But not so revolutionary that Talitha's life stopped seeming to everyone in the office like a confusing, busy episode of *Sex and the City.* Still, Dr. Amanda scored high on the patience factor. She must have had to listen week in and week out to detailed conversations about the creative executive at Buena Vista whom Talitha had slept with the weekend before and who hadn't called. Even though he'd been to Harvard, had a wealthy family in San Francisco with a second home in Napa, and, if all went according to plan, he'd be a senior VP within the next tax year. Well, at least Dr. Amanda got paid to listen to Talitha. Which was more than could be said for most of us in the office, who couldn't kick her out after an hour. I crossed Dr. Amanda off the list because I didn't want to risk being in the same room when her poor brain exploded.

I glanced at Courtney, who was sitting at her desk with a sour-lemon look on her face as she doubtless dispatched some bitchy quip to IFILMpro about Mike's wife or his hair-regrowth situation. IFILMpro is a chat forum where movie-industry professionals anonymously assassinate their coworkers, bosses, and movie stars online. I think it was for discussing business matters, too, but that wouldn't have appealed to Courtney; her bloodlust could only be satisfied by eviscerating people. So it was no use looking to Courtney for a possible shrink—she didn't have emotions to talk about. She was a gossipmongering automaton who spent every spare hour working out how best to appear busy and indispensable to Mike. I wished I could be more like her and not think about annoying things like the meaning of life or human relations.

I wondered whether Lara's shrink might be good. He was apparently an old-school Jungian who unlocked the archetypes in her dreams and enabled her creativity to flow. I wasn't sure that I had any creativity, though, and he was bound to have a beard, and they always gross me out and leave me obsessing about the scraps of lunch that must be left behind in them. So the Jungian doctor was consigned to the garbage can of fate, too. I could always go see one of Scott's litany of shrinks. I had all their numbers, because I had to make the appointments. But, talking to Lara, it seemed that they were mostly addiction specialists—and clearly not very good ones.

I eventually hit on the idea of asking the most fantastically well-adjusted person I could think of who their shrink was. Which made complete sense, really, I mean, you were hardly going to ask somebody with a really bad skinny-cigar nose job who her plastic surgeon was, were you? It should be the same with your mind. I looked around my office. Hmm, no shining examples of mental health here. I scanned my phone list and found no joy there either. I did a mental X ray of the building, but the sanest and nicest people I could think of were the Josés, and I suspected that their health-care policies might not stretch to sitting in an Eames chair once a week and wondering whether their mothers' guacamole had been good enough. And I'm not making light of this either. I once knew a guy who went to Smith who had huge resentment issues with his parents because they hadn't introduced him to pasta until he was twelve years old. He thought it had made him socially disadvantaged.

Did the fact that lack of sanity seemed to exist in direct proportion to the number of visits to shrinks in my workplace mean that I ought not to risk a visit? I wondered as I bundled up my health pack and eased my new Blue Cross card into my wallet. Of course not. I ought to at least give myself the chance to discover whether I was a fuckup or not. And it could be fun. Like reading your horoscope. Or doing online quizzes about what your choice of colored balls tells you about your mood.

I turned on my iMac and logged on to the Blue Cross Web site. Eventually I found a doctor whose picture I liked the look of. Her name was Dr. Shirley Vance, and her eyes were understanding and insightful. I had decided on a woman because I couldn't imagine discussing sex with a man. Not that there was any sex to discuss, but I remained optimistic that my situation might change, particularly if the therapy was a success and I became as open as one of the doors of perception. Or something.

I waited until lunchtime, when Scott was safely deposited at Ca'Brea with Jennifer and Brett, who, since the day of tantrums on the set of *Wedding Massacre,* had become the hottest couple in town. They were planning on buying Madonna's old house in the Hills just as soon as her divorce came through and his soap-actress girlfriend of six years moved out. The office was deserted, and I dialed the shrink's number.

"Dr. Vance speaking," she said, answering her own phone with perky efficiency.

"Hi, Dr. Vance. My name's Elizabeth Miller, and I got your number through Blue Cross. I was wondering if I could schedule a . . . session?" I think that's what they were called. It was more like an aromatherapy massage than a root canal, I figured—or hoped—so it wouldn't be an appointment, but a session. Right?

"Well, Elizabeth, I have a free hour every Tuesday from seven to eight. Would that work for you?"

"That sounds great. But I'm only covered for sixteen sessions, so I hope that won't leave you high and dry if I turn out to be okay after sixteen."

"That's just fine, Elizabeth. We'll start with one session and see how we go. Okay?"

She sounded so understanding and reassuring, something that you just didn't encounter in this town. I wondered if that's why so many people went to therapy here. It was a replacement for family, friends, and lovers who would want to be in your life longer than a movie shoot.

"So what I'd like you to do for me, Elizabeth, is to write a list before you come and see me tonight of the reasons you think you need therapy."

"Okay, sure. I'll try." Hell, nobody told me you actually needed a reason. I thought it was like taking up Rollerblading, just something you did when you moved to California. "But how long does it need to be?"

"This isn't a test. Just write down what you feel is important. See you at seven."

I sat and chewed my pen for a bit longer and wondered why I was voluntarily giving over my evening to tell a complete stranger my flaws. Apart from the fact that the latest season of *Six Feet Under* had just finished and I had nothing much else lined up.

Then Talitha came back in, carrying a Star Books bag and a smile as wide as Carbon Canyon.

"Hey." She dropped down onto her chair and addressed anyone who'd listen. "I just met the most amazing guy in the bookstore. We're going riding in Santa Barbara this weekend."

"Wow, that was fast," I remarked.

"Well, what's to lose?" She pulled a bunch of CDs and magazines from her bag and began flicking through them. "The way I see it, I'm old enough to know what I like and young enough to still take a chance."

"Great philosophy," I said as I realized that it was two-fifteen, so I took the phones off voice mail.

"Yeah, isn't it? My shrink told me that. And I've gotten lucky more times since I started taking her advice than I even do when I wear my Victoria's Secret Miracle Bra. Which is saying something."

"I imagine it is," I said, thinking that, if nothing else, Dr. Shirley Vance might give me dating tips and stop me from having to be seen with *Men Are from Mars* on my bookshelf.

"Yeah, nothing to lose but your life," Courtney chimed in when she got back from the watercooler. "I mean, are you completely sure he's not an ax murderer?"

"Christ, Courtney, he likes horses. When was the last time you heard of a guy who likes horses being an ax murderer?" she asked with inimitable and unassailable Talitha logic.

"Guess I didn't," Courtney had to admit. "Does he have a friend?"

As almost everyone had now trickled back into the office and the afternoon had begun in earnest, I decided I'd leave my list for later. I took a pen and jotted down the messages.

"Scott, my man." It was Tony. "Filming's all under way, you'll be relieved to know, and the director isn't such a shit-for-brains as I thought he might be. I'm trying the Atkins diet like you told me, but I have to say, man, it makes yer stink something awful. Anyway, let us know about that thirty-three-million offer for the next *X-Men* movie."

The second message was from Ryan, who wanted to schedule a meeting with Daniel and Scott, and then one from Katherine Watson's assistant. Katherine was the superagent in charge of the Literary Department here at The Agency, who, truth be told, I had a bit of a schoolgirl crush on. I'd often just gaze at her in meetings, and if I got into the same elevator with her, I'd step out feeling a bit light-headed. And I don't think that I was alone. I had never heard a bad word said about her by anyone, and literally every time I went to Reception to pick up a package, there was always a huge bunch of lilies or antique roses or a Tiffany bag with her name on it waiting to be collected. Katherine was thirty-six, with the body of a cheerleader, three angelic children, and a dreamboat of a French commercial-director husband. She spoke four languages, was fluent in baseball, and was about fifteen times prettier than any actress we represented. And while it wasn't odd that her assistant was confirming a meeting with Scott, it was strange that it was outside the office, for breakfast at the Hotel Bel-Air, and there was no record of it in the diary.

"Hey, Lara. Did you book Scott and Katherine in for breakfast?" I asked Lara when she came in a couple of minutes later.

"No. Why?"

"It's just that it's not in the diary and it's at the Bel-Air. Kinda far from the office and a bit odd . . . don't you think?" I scrawled it into the diary anyway.

"Why is it odd?" she snapped, and looked too closely at me for comfort.

"Well, I suppose it's not really. It's just that . . . well, maybe they're having an—"

"An affair?" She narrowed her eyes.

"I didn't say that. It's just strange. That's all." I shrugged, wishing I hadn't said anything. Lara leaned back in her chair and began tapping out an e-mail. "Hey, Lizzie. Wanna come to a party with me next Saturday night?" she asked without looking up. "A friend of mine in Silver Lake is having a Halloween party. I'll pick you up."

"I'd love to," I said, as my head flooded with excitement. She was a funny girl, Lara. She looked like she wanted to stick pins in your eyes one minute and then invited you to a party the next. Still, Silver Lake? Groovy people? For that I didn't mind a few pins in the eyes.

Seconds later Scott breezed into the office with the full force of a twister over Oklahoma.

"Hey, ladies," he said, hands out waiting for call sheets and responses.

"Hey, Scott." I was still in class-creep mode, which was admittedly annoying but a necessary evil I felt since the recent Tony debacle.

"Lara?" Scott said, when he received the same pins-in-the-eyes treatment as I had from her. The only difference being that she didn't invite him to a party seconds later. Instead she resolutely ignored him. "Hey, Lara," Scott said, trying to see if she had her earplugs in.

"Screw you, Scott." She looked at him fleetingly and then continued tapping on her keyboard.

"Wassup?" He appeared genuinely stung when she said this. But she didn't answer. Scott began to look awkward. Then spotted me sitting there staring and pulled himself together. "I'm in my office if anyone needs me," he said, stating the obvious and ambling too casually toward his desk, where he sat and picked his fingernails for the next half hour until he headed off for a strategy meeting in one of the conference rooms.

With Scott gone for an hour and Lara hammering out her novel in a fashion not dissimilar to a pneumatic drill, I decided that I'd get to work on my list for Dr. Vance. Why did I think I needed to see a psychologist? I took a sip of my green tea, picked a peanut out of a biscotti, and began.

REASONS I NEED THERAPY

1. I have perfectly good vegetables in the fridge but display a perverse unwillingness to either cook or eat them. Perhaps I don't believe I'm worthy of vitamin-enriched and delicious food. Subclinical need to malnourish myself by preferring pizza? Early-stage eating disorder? Or latent self-loathing?
2. Not confronting the very real dangers in life that face me, such as race riots, earthquakes, and forest fires. Instead preoccupied with unfounded fears, such as what Victoria might do to me if I accidentally behead one of her Barbie dolls.
3. I switched majors twice in college. Then switched career path from politics to entertainment. Have also switched cereal brands four times since I arrived in L.A. Commitment issues?
4. I have had several lovers but not many serious boyfriends. Used to consider myself a product of my generation, but no longer sure. Perhaps I choose the wrong men on purpose? Perhaps just ugly?
5. Prefer working for unpredictable boss with no discernible value system in company where schadenfreude is a group activity of choice to working for sweet, green representative from Virginia who has team BBQs on Sunday afternoons. Why???
6. No longer recycle.

I wondered if Dr. Shirley Vance would provide me with a veritable pharmacy of medication for my maladies or simply declare me a lesbian. I didn't really mind what she did, to be honest. I'd try anything for an orgasm these days. I looked up from my computer for what felt like the first time all afternoon and realized that it was six forty-five already and I had to get to her office in rush-hour traffic.

"Lara, I've got to run. I have an appointment with my shrink at seven," I said as I raced out the door. And when I looked back to check that I'd turned off my computer, I swear I saw untold relief written on everyone's face. They must have wondered what kind of freak I was, not having a therapist this whole time. Maybe they were a little leery of me for that. Hurray, I thought as I ran out. I'm one of them!

I parked in the garage and sprinted into the elevator, pressing the button for the fourteenth floor. I found Suite 1402 and went into the waiting room. I was depressed already, and I hadn't even made it into her office. It was something about the stained industrial carpet and the wall of buzzers listing thirteen different doctors. I walked hesitantly over and found DR. VANCE written in block letters with a green fountain pen. I buzzed her name and waited by the speaker in the wall for a response. Nothing came, and I buzzed a second time, more assertively.

Then a netherworldly response came through the wall: "Elizabeth, please take a seat, and I'll come get you in a second." Then she was gone.

I sat down on a ripped leather-look chair that stuck uncomfortably to the backs of my thighs and stared at the Styrofoam ceiling tiles that you used to throw pencils at in school. I contemplated making a run for it while I still had the chance. But just as I was about to pick up my purse and case the exit, a pair of long, trousered legs walked in the door and sat down opposite me. It looked like Jake Hudson. I pulled my hair over my face and peered up through it surreptitiously. It *was* Jake Hudson. And, Jesus, I know I should have had weightier matters on my mind, but he was just so doable.

He pulled out his cell phone. "Hey, man. Heard from my lawyer that you kicked some ass on that deal. Well, I'm glad, because he's as dumb as a lug nut." Jake had stood up and begun to pace around the room as if he owned it. "Goddamn right. I've offered him seventeen-five, so let him tell me that he doesn't do action now. He can kiss my ass." And he laughed throatily and stopped by a mirror and watched himself talk.

"Elizabeth Miller." The late Dr. Vance chose that moment to appear in the doorway and summon me.

I scuttled to my feet, looking all the time at my shoes, then shuffled toward her. Thankfully, I don't think that Jake Hudson noticed a thing. Not me. Not that I was the girl he'd kissed on his deck. Not the fact that I was visiting a shrink. Only that his right eyebrow might be a little higher than his left, and, far from disliking this, he felt it gave him the air of Sean Connery.

"Nice to meet you. Why don't you come into my office."

I followed her down the corridor and thought how similar she looked to my mother from behind. I could just see her at home watching PBS in sheepskin slippers. Her office was cozy and unassuming, and she motioned to the sofa in the corner.

"Take a seat. Now, did you write your list?" she asked.

I produced my crumpled piece of paper and passed it to her like a sixth-grader handing in her homework. She smiled knowingly as she read my effort. I knew that she could see right through me. Probably even read my mind from the way I was blinking. I could contain myself no longer.

"My parents think I have commitment issues," I blurted out. There was a long and terrible silence. I could have gone on to fill it with a whole list of other things or some tears of relief at finally being able to express myself. But as I was about to take a breath, she preempted me.

"Well, what do *you* think, Elizabeth?"

"I don't know. That's why I'm here."

"I see." She nodded in an understanding way.

I realized then why people did this. Why they came to share their problems. It felt so good to be able to be honest. Such a relief. I began to sink back into the sofa and relax, ready to have all my broken and misshapen bits fixed.

"Well, I think that by simply showing up here today, you proved your parents wrong. But that doesn't mean that you haven't struggled with this issue in one of your past lives," she said quietly.

I wasn't sure that I had heard her correctly, so I continued. "Well, I just want to make sure that my not having a boyfriend isn't symptomatic of a greater problem," I said.

"It very well might be," she said. "Now, I hope you don't mind if I consult my friends." I looked toward the door, wondering if I had agreed to donate my therapy session to medical science in an unwitting moment. But there was nobody in the doorway. And neither did she pick up the phone.

"I don't quite understand," I said, shifting forward a little on the sofa. I was no longer quite so supremely relaxed as I had been.

"Vivianne would like to ask you a question," she said.

"Right."

"So what would you like to ask her, Vivianne?" she said, though there was still nobody here. "Oh, Tom, you have an observation, too. Well, I'm afraid you're just going to have to wait your turn."

I looked around to see if there was a glass wall behind which might be a panel of people fascinated by me, but there didn't appear to be. "Excuse me, but who are you talking to?" I eventually asked.

Dr. Vance smiled reassuringly. "Oh, I'm sorry, Lizzie. You don't mind being called Lizzie, do you? Or is it just your father and your boss who call you Lizzie?" I looked askance at her. "You see, I hear voices. They've been with me from childhood, and they're very *au fait* with past lives, and they're also very intuitive about my clients." She was smiling. "And they're telling me that your current unwillingness to settle down is simply due to the fact that you were a man in almost all your past lives."

"I was what?" I sat bolt upright.

"I know. Amazing, isn't it? And quite unusual. But it does happen. And in your case it's left you with habitual commitment anxiety, because you're programmed, as a man is, to sow your wild oats. Nothing to worry about, and you'll settle down in a few years' time." She smiled warmly. But it was too late for me.

"Dr. Vance, I think I have to go. I'm sorry," I said.

"Oh, dear." She smiled patiently. "It's perfectly usual to feel that our sessions are a little crowded at first. You'll get used to it in time. I assure you."

I wanted to sprint from the room. My first therapy session was giving me the willies—quite literally, as I'd apparently been a man most of the time—and now I had a crick in my neck because I had sat up on the sofa so quickly. I wondered if my remaining fifteen sessions of psychotherapy could be transferred to an osteopath instead. Or whether I could just cash them in for a voucher at Barneys.

"And they're also telling me that you're in pretty good mental shape, Elizabeth. You just need a little fine-tuning."

"Really?" I liked the sound of that. A few afternoons on the couch and I might be the emotional equivalent of a Ferrari, slick and able to navigate all life's bends and forks in the road with ease and style. And really, who better to help one on life's path but those who'd already been and gone and done it? Dead People. "Okay, then, sounds fine." I reshuffled back onto the couch and got comfortable. "And these voices, can they tell me where I'm most likely to meet Mr. Right? Or do they have some sort of code of ethics that prevents that?"

15

I don't mind if you don't like my manners. I don't like them myself. They're pretty bad. I grieve over them on long winter evenings.

—Humphrey Bogart as Philip Marlowe
The Big Sleep

Making my way to the laundry room in the basement always gave me the creeps. You took the elevator down twelve levels to the dank cellar and then walked a long corridor with locked metal doors on all sides and blinking rows of fluorescent lights. I was always certain the superintendent was going to pop out of the furnace room at any minute, having just fed a delinquent rent payer into the burning inferno. Perhaps this was my greatest fear because *I* was perpetually on the verge of being that delinquent rent payer. The whole scenario was sheer neurosis, though, as our super was a stoned old hippie who was too busy trying to see the universe in a leaky tap to care about my financial woes. I scurried down the hall, my laundry basket in my arms, and pulled the door tightly shut behind me, finally relaxing into the reassuring detergent warmth of the quarter-fed Laundromat.

I pulled out my change and fed it to the hungry machine. Per usual, stuffing so much into the machine that I had to throw my entire body against it to get it shut. I was busy pouring in my fabric softener when the door opened. No one had ever joined me in the laundry room before, and it took me a moment to get up the courage to overcome the looming, ax-wielding shadows in my mind and turn around. I assumed that any self-respecting person sent their laundry out or had their own personal machine in their apartment, the height of luxury. But I was wrong. There stood Alexa, my yoga neighbor, in pale blue Nuala, very intently filling four washing machines with what seemed like a lifetime of laundry. She caught me looking, so I waved hesitantly.

"Hi, I'm Elizabeth. I live next door."

Alexa smiled in a very relaxed way. "I know you. You're my quiet neighbor. Nice to see you again. Hope your head got better after that nasty hockey-puck bash."

"Oh, it did. Thanks. And thanks for the Neosporin." I smiled. I had assumed she was a cow because she was so stupidly pretty and flirty, but she just seemed really sweet, actually.

I was about to head back up to my apartment, very certain in the knowledge that my few Banana Republic items were safe from potential thieves. Even *I* didn't want my wardrobe—so I was certain that nobody else would. But Alexa stopped me with an inquisitive look.

"Hey, Elizabeth, did you ever meet my friend Noel? Tall, dark, handsome. Studio executive at Fox? He does private sessions here on Tuesday at nine?" she asked. I didn't even have to cast my mind back. I knew exactly who she was talking about.

"Yeah, I do remember seeing him. I think I met him while I was taking the garbage out."

"Well, what do you remember about him?" What I very vividly remembered was that I'd had three enormous bags of garbage, a box from my new toaster, and my keys in my mouth. Noel had run smack into me as he came out of Alexa's door, causing my bags to drop and half my garbage to be cast all over the hallway. Unbeknownst to me, my keys got lost in the four-day-old Chinese takeout containers, and in my haste to clear it all up, I threw the keys down the garbage chute. Noel, who'd been the cause of all my problems, hadn't even had the decency to stop and help me pick things up. He hadn't even grumbled an apology. Instead he'd looked at me with a smirk on his lips, stepped over the garbage (and me) with distaste, and yelled for someone to hold the elevator.

All of which resulted in my being locked out of my apartment and having to wait for the super to get home. Only to learn that he had no spare keys and that a locksmith after hours would cost me four hundred dollars. So as I had rent and credit-card bills to pay and didn't feel overjoyed at the prospect of forking out more cash for a couple of bits of metal, I spent three hours digging through the building's garbage until I found my keys in an empty jar of peanut butter. In other words, Noel had left a very distinct impression on me.

"Why, is there a problem?" I asked now. I didn't want to admit that I'd spent an entire evening wishing him under a bus if perhaps she was about to tell me that that was where he'd ended up.

"He's been suffering from a rather overinflated ego since he was promoted to senior vice president. I was just wondering if you noticed anything?"

"Like what?" I asked cautiously. I didn't want to damn her friend yet, in case she spent the next year meditating on my demise.

"Like, was he bad in any way?"

"Well, to be totally honest, he was one of the biggest assholes I've ever met. And that's saying a lot, considering I work at an agency." I launched into the entire story of the garbage and my keys while Alexa listened patiently.

"I'm so sorry, Elizabeth. You should have told me. I would have made him pay for a locksmith. But thank you so much for your honesty. I was looking for exactly that kind of input."

"You're welcome. I hope it helps," I said. I was about to walk out of the laundry room when Alexa stopped me again.

"What are you doing tomorrow night?" My God, I was making friends left and right!

"Nothing, really."

"Would you come to Noel's intervention?"

"Oh, God. I'm so sorry. I feel really guilty now. I didn't know he had a drink or drug problem. I'd never have been so rude about him if I had."

"You have nothing to apologize for, Elizabeth. Ever."

"Sorry. A habit I picked up at the new job."

"You're doing it again." She smiled kindly at me "Noel isn't an addict. He's just an asshole. It's an asshole intervention. Basically, since he got this new job, his ego has been flattening mankind. His wife is thinking about leaving him, his sister won't speak to him, and his best friend is advertising in the personal columns for a new one."

"Oh, no," I said. But I wasn't surprised. Noel really looked like a cock.

"And then I had to give up teaching him because his energy was so twisted. It was making me sick. The bottom line is he needs an intervention or he's going to be left alone, disappointed, and broken."

I wanted to laugh. Was she kidding? I looked into her earnest, soft brown eyes and realized that she was deadly serious. "How does it work?"

"Well, he's brought unaware into a mutually supportive group of friends and family, and then we go around in a circle and tell it like it is. Either he gets help and finds his old self again or we turn our backs on him. It's a very serious and intense process."

I imagined a roomful of earnest people with twisted energy and a furious, egomaniacal executive. To be honest, it was just a bit too much like work for me.

"Alexa, I don't think I really know him well enough to be there. It sounds incredibly personal."

But Alexa was busy writing an address and time on the back of her butter yellow business card. "I promise you it's not. We have an entire spectrum of people coming. It's important to have those that are less involved, too, because they're also the people who his horrible behavior affects on a daily basis. Even the mailman's coming, and we really need you and your story, Elizabeth. Please?"

Well, I figured that I had nothing better to do, so it might be uncharitable not to. Plus, I might meet some new people, which would make my mother happy. "Sure. I'll come over after work. Is there a dress code?" I felt it was safer to ask.

"Not really, but maybe something spiritual or colorful. Orange is a healing color. And we don't want him to feel like it's his funeral. Also, we're ordering in from Mr. Chow, so is there anything you don't like?"

God, what heaven! I was definitely there.

"I love everything. I'm looking forward to it. Well, you know, I'm looking forward to helping. See you tomorrow." I waved and practically pranced down the hall, wondering whether I should have mentioned that I was very, very partial to sweet-and-sour prawn balls.

I turned left off Laurel Canyon and wended my way up narrow streets that used to be hippie hideaways and now were worth not a penny less than $1.5 million for a three-bedroom ranch house. Unfortunately,

$1.5 mil didn't seem to include anywhere to park. Plus, you couldn't walk anywhere from your house without ending up roadkill, and since only one car could fit up the narrow road at a time, there were endless traffic jams. Still, the area was one of the closest and most accessible canyons to Hollywood. Which was obviously fun for some.

I followed Alexa's directions and continued my ascent. In L.A., the more successful you became, the higher up you lived. So obviously Noel had done quite well for himself, because my wheezing Honda was still climbing, albeit reluctantly, ten minutes later. I finally found number 106 and parked my car at the bottom of the long row of gorgeous machines that were there to witness Noel's de-assholing. I had a sneaking suspicion that quite a few people there were just longing to bitch at Noel with impunity. And if his family had sold tickets, even more people might have come. I suspected that some pretty evil things might emerge in the name of healing, and I'd spent the majority of the day contemplating leaving a message on Alexa's cell phone canceling. But the lure of Mr. Chow was too much for a girl to resist. I'd never be able to get a table there, let alone afford to eat there in real life, so this was my perfect taste of that famously fabulous restaurant.

Unless, of course, I went on a date with Bob, and that was out of the question. Bob was still in pursuit and had actually called me at the office today asking if I'd go to some gallery opening with him. I was shocked into silence, because I had no idea Los Angeles had galleries and I couldn't figure out how Bob could make something as innocent and public as an art opening sound quite as perverted as he had. Not wishing to risk another date, in case he had installed cameras in the bathroom and was planning a feature film, I sweetly declined. But he'd called back, and I'd hung up on him, since Victoria was standing over me waiting to yell. The scary part was that he seemed to get off on my putting the phone down on him, which made him a very tricky character to lose. Perhaps someone would organize an asshole intervention for Bob, but I was pretty certain he was too far gone and that too few people would care.

I walked up the gravel path lined with perfectly trimmed and watered box hedges, and looked for the doorbell. But Noel's house was minimalist chic gone mad, so I couldn't find one. The architect seemed to have taken an ugly ranch house and covered the walls with gray concrete, enlarged the windows, and replaced what was probably a pitched, tar-shingled roof with beautiful copper panels. The polished slate stairs leading to a stark, handleless door gave the entire house the appearance of a very unfriendly Zen garden. Finding no doorbell or knocker in sight, I eventually just banged on the white, wooden expanse with my fist and offered a prayer to Buddha that getting out would be easier than getting in, just in case I needed to make a dash for it.

I waited for someone to answer the piece of wood. Seconds later Alexa opened the wood and threw her arms around me in a fantastic bear hug.

"Elizabeth, I'm so glad you made it."

There were no frills here, like a hallway, so we were immediately in the imposing white space of Noel's living room, where a crowd of twenty-odd people were eating a fully catered meal of dumplings and lettuce cups.

"Everybody, this is Elizabeth," Alexa announced. "She told me the trash story." There were looks of concerned empathy from the guests and a few oohs and ahs.

"Has Noel arrived?" I was suddenly frightened of seeing him. His hatred for me was inevitable, and unfortunately he wasn't drunk or on drugs and so would remember this entire evening with perfect clarity for the rest of his life. I decided that maybe I should quickly bolt down a bit of Chinese, and then I could slip out in the commotion of his arrival. I walked over to the food and started filling my plate. A man dressed in some type of religious garb came over and started piling strictly vegetarian options onto his plate, while I stared at his robes trying to figure out what order he was with. They were a deep purplish red and looked similar to what the pope might wear, but he had no collar and no cap.

"Isn't the feng shui just glorious in this house?" he said. Not the pope, then.

"I don't know much about feng shui, but I certainly felt very peaceful when I knocked on the door," I said. Which wasn't strictly true, but then neither was it the fault of the décor. It was due more to the fact that I was possibly about to take my seat for a potentially life-ruining ceremony.

"You're very astute. I'm Lee, Noel's feng shui consultant. I went with him to every house he considered buying and either gave it the thumbs-up or -down. This one was glorious, though. But there were a few crucial defects we had to fix before he even moved a shoe box in."

"Wow, that's quite a job. What did you have to do to this house? It seems just perfect."

He laughed and rolled his eyes in mock horror. "You have no idea, Elizabeth. This interior designer had just done it up and was trying to sell it as is. At a premium, I may add. The walls were a deep wine red, and there wasn't a single water feature."

"What's wrong with red? I thought it was good luck in China?" I asked timidly, hoping this wasn't blasphemy.

"Not in the bedroom, darling. It kills the will. You know what I mean. Takes the lead out of the pencil."

I certainly understood what he was driving at. "That's no good. But why water, then?"

"Money. Flowing water promotes the influx of cash. The last guy who owned the house went bankrupt. Before Noel moved in, I added the fountain in the front and this magnificent piece of design in the dining room."

He beckoned me to follow, and I walked into the next room. Noel had taken a section of the roof off and replaced it with a piece of clear plate glass. Under it he'd built a restaurant booth with banquettes that seemed to meet the heavens. One of the banquette walls had been replaced by another piece of glass with a flowing waterfall effect that you could actually lean against while you ate your pizza—but I guessed that anything as commonplace as pizza never crossed the holy threshold of this temple. I sat down at the table and leaned back looking at the sky—which was admittedly a little smoggy, but who's keeping tabs?—and listened to the tinkle of water flowing all around me. I felt like I was in an aquarium. True genius. Though Noel was an asshole, he had really good taste, and for a moment I really wanted to be him.

"You are really and truly amazing," I told Lee. "I'm dead broke, but one of these days I won't be, and I'd love to hold on to your card so I can track you down."

Lee smiled knowingly, without a hint of mockery. He knew how quickly people rose in this business, and he wasn't going to look a nag in the mouth, because it just might turn out to be a gift horse. "Call me anytime, sweetcheeks. Maybe if I have a minute, I'll do a consultation for you on the house." He laughed. Out of kindness, so did I.

"That's funny. Thanks, Lee." And I was about to give him a little bow or something but was interrupted by a small brunette, Noel's wife, Sandy, who was hurrying around the room like a wasp in a jar trying to get everyone seated. "Quick, everyone, sit in a circle—Noel's home."

Everyone dived for chairs, and I decided to perch on a sofa arm, away from the ominous-looking leather library chair they'd chosen as Noel's seat. I didn't want to be in the line of fire if he decided to lash out at someone.

We sat in expectant silence as we heard the key turn in the lock. Sandy went over to the door and greeted him. Oh, God, this was like watching the dentist scene in *Marathon Man*—always even more painful because you knew it was coming.

"Hi, babes. I'm exhausted. I thought you had your knitting circle tonight. This fuck cut me off when I was driving home, and I—" Noel walked through the door, tossed his leather Gucci briefcase on a bench-cum-morgue-slab, then sidestepped his wife without kissing her. Presumably, on an ordinary night, he would have charged on in and asked what was for dinner, but this evening he stopped dead in his tracks when he saw the group of people looking expectantly up at him from his sunken living room.

"Are you having a party?" He looked bewildered and confused.

"No, baby, it's an intervention. For you. You've changed, and no one likes who you've changed into."

Noel assessed the room, and for a moment looked positively shaken. Like a newborn colt unable to understand the evil world he'd been born into. But then, almost as if a door had slammed, he put on his mental armor and sneered.

"This is bullshit. I'm out of here." He turned to go, but his best friend from college, the president of his fraternity, stood up.

"Noel. I think you need to stay and hear everyone out. You may not agree, and that's your choice, but everyone here loves and cares about you and has taken the time to be here for you. So just sit down and listen."

Noel laughed and shook his head in disbelief. "Fine, whatever. But can we make it quick? Because I have two new drafts to read, and I'm supposed to green-light these movies tomorrow. And talking about emotional shit with a bunch of earnest do-gooders isn't going to get my work done for me, is it, now?"

The crowd smiled with satisfaction, feeling that he'd just given them the affirmation that they needed to prove he was an asshole. Sandy led him forward, and he sat down in the library chair, which had clearly been drafted in from a friend's home—because it looked much more humane than the concrete plinth that poor Sandy had to sit on.

"Okay. Assassinate my character." He leaned back and looked bored. If he'd had bubble gum, he'd have popped it in our faces like a defiant teenager.

Noel's sister stood up, then sat down. "I haven't spoken to you in four weeks. We used to speak every day."

"I'm sorry, Samantha, I've been busy. I thought I returned your calls."

"Well, your secretary did return them, but I didn't call you back, and you didn't even notice that I wasn't talking to you."

"Jesus, Sam. I'm busy, and if you're mad at me, just tell me. What are you so cross about?"

"I have an entire list, but the straw that broke the camel's back was the Bambi hunt. How *could* you?" Samantha, who was strikingly similar in appearance to Noel, looked crushed.

Noel started to laugh but realized he might face a firing squad if he continued. "Come on, Sam. It was a little innocent fun, and nobody got hurt."

"Would anyone like me to clarify what a Bambi hunt is, by the way?" Sam looked around the riveted gathering. A few people nodded so she proceeded. "It's where men get together in the forest to hunt down naked women and shoot them with paint balls."

"I've heard about it on TV," Lee said, then hastily added, "it sounded immoral."

Noel rolled his eyes. "Hell, one of the girls made twenty-five hundred bucks because she didn't get shot." The audience remained unsympathetic.

"Noel, you were shooting at women with a gun as they ran through the forest naked. How is that all right?" wailed Samantha.

"They had sneakers on, and they could have worn goggles and a helmet. I heard the guide offer it. Anyway, it was an innocent way of letting off some steam. Us guys lead stressful lives. The Bambis didn't mind. We all had beers together afterward."

"You were hunting naked women. Does that not seem a bit twisted to you, Noel? Are you such a misogynist? You have a wife and a sister.

A wife who made her objection clear before you went, and you ignored her. You're disgusting."

"Hey, hey, it was only paint."

"Noel, you used to be a Democrat. You marched for gun control. What happened to you?"

Wow. This was really intense. A little garbage in the hallway was nothing compared to this. It was the most entertaining thing I'd witnessed for a long time. Maybe I should pitch a show called *Intervention* to NBC. This was live drama unfolding right before your eyes, with family, loved ones, and virtual strangers participating. And Bambi hunting? I'd never heard of that one before. I'd have to look into how you get hired, just in case I was ever really strapped for cash. I had a high pain threshold and could run fast, so I'd probably be really good at it. I snickered at the idea. Out loud, unfortunately. Slowly the whole room turned in my direction.

Noel looked over at me, annoyed. "Who the fuck is that, anyway?"

"See, Noel, you're hostile and abusive to a completely innocent girl. That's Elizabeth, and you were a total asshole to her." Alexa stepped in with this ringing endorsement. Oh, shit, my stupid giggles had put me on the spot. "Elizabeth, would you like to share your experience with us?"

Now I'd have to speak. Everyone was waiting for me. I seemed to have lost my voice.

"To clarify things . . ." I cleared my throat, swallowing what felt to be a bolder blocking my windpipe. Then I looked at Noel's hairline—I couldn't bring myself to look him in the eyes. "You ran into me outside Alexa's apartment. You knocked me over, and all my trash went everywhere, and you walked on without stopping, looking, or even apologizing, like I didn't exist."

Alexa picked up where I'd left off and elaborated on my story. "We're trying to show you a variety of examples of how you've changed. You used to be gallant, a gentleman, a boy who was brought up well, with manners and respect for others."

Oddly, Noel had gone very silent. He looked penetratingly at me, seeming to remember the incident, and, even more than shooting naked girls in the woods, this odd testimony seemed to shame him. He turned toward me and looked me in the eye. "Elizabeth, I know that I was an asshole to you. I should have stopped and helped you pick up that trash. I'm sorry." He looked like a smashed piñata.

"No big deal. You're forgiven."

The onslaught continued, but I felt that I'd been witness to enough and to watch any more was a bit like Bambi hunting—far too easy. So I whispered my good-byes in Alexa's ear and slipped out unnoticed while Noel's mom was having a go at him for showing up late to his grandfather's funeral, then taking a phone call in church while his uncle was breaking down in tears at the pulpit. As I closed the door quietly behind me, I realized that Noel sounded like he was worth saving. He hadn't always been an asshole. He'd just morphed into a stranger, like an X-Man mutant. Maybe I'd helped a little bit, and maybe someday, if *I* turned into the archetypal Hollywood asshole, I'd have enough cool people and loyal friends and family to intervene on my behalf. One could always hope.

The next morning I woke up with a start. My doorbell was ringing. Irritatingly, by the time I found this out, I'd already launched my clock across the room like a rocket, so I had no idea what time it was. I trudged to the door in my pajamas and opened it. Alexa was standing on the other side with a yoga mat in each hand. One blue and one purple. She was wearing white hot pants and a wife-beater T-shirt.

"Good morning, Lizzie. I thought I'd give you a little free yoga instruction. It's very important to repay a kindness with a kindness. And it occurred to me that you might need it."

I rubbed my eyes and yawned. What I really needed was an extra hour of sleep.

"What time is it?" I was trying to open my eyes, but they seemed cemented shut by some mysterious fairy dust.

"Six-thirty. I thought we could do an hour three times a week before you go to work. It's really no problem for me, since this is when I do my own workout, and I don't mind guiding you for a few weeks. Then you can just follow my lead. Anyway, you said you were too poor to join a gym, and this is much better for you."

Alexa marched into my apartment and spread out the mats. Then she sat in the lotus position on her mat and closed her eyes. I looked on. Couldn't I just watch?

"Babe, you need to go and put on something comfortable, something with stretch." She opened her eyes. "Do you own any Lycra?" I shook my head sleepily. "Then your pajamas will do just perfectly," she said, so I reluctantly sat down and crossed my legs.

"This is a perfect apartment for yoga, Lizzie, nice open spaces," Alexa said as she demonstrated a mudra—which was apparently what I was supposed to do with my fingers while I was sitting.

"My boss has his own personal mudra that he uses every day," I laughed, flipping Alexa the finger in demonstration. She didn't seem to appreciate my joke, so I stopped smiling, did as I was told, and followed her lead. I was wise to behave, because the amount of pain that it caused me simply to sit in a cross-legged position suggested that I might need all the guru I could lay hands on for quite some time.

I arrived in the office at eight-thirty on the dot. I'd even had enough energy to read one of Victoria's scripts over my chai latte in the Coffee Bean. I had a sense of overall well-being and practically skipped over to Scott's office to put his mail on his desk. Nobody else was in yet, but I noticed that the door was already a tiny bit ajar. Usually the cleaners locked it and either myself or Lara unlocked it. I pushed it open slowly, thinking perhaps Scott had spent the night there after a battle with Mia. I wasn't prepared when I saw a dark head fumbling behind the desk. My immediate reaction was horror, thinking I'd caught Scott in the act with one of his extramarital dalliances, but when I cleared my throat discreetly, the head popped up like a jack-in-the-box. It was Ryan. I was so shocked I just stared dumbly as he bolted past me, almost knocking me over in an attempt to exit.

"You stupid cow!" he spit. "You're never on time." Then he was gone.

I wandered in a daze over to Scott's desk and checked to see if Ryan had left anything behind, like a clue as to what the fuck he'd been doing there. Nothing seemed to be missing, but the papers on Scott's desk had definitely been rifled through, and it looked like someone had been trying to jimmy open his file drawer. Luckily for Scott, he'd asked me to put a serious lock on that specific drawer just two weeks before. He frequently had his stash delivered, in Beverly Hills style, directly to the office by a blond female courier on a motorcycle. I'd never seen it myself, but Lara said the weed came in a vacuum-sealed pouch with the dealer's company logo on a sticker sealing the bag. Scott had needed a secure hiding place for it, so I'd had the locksmith come in and fit a special metal drawer and given Scott the only key.

I went back to my desk and waited with unmitigated excitement for my boss to arrive. I was finally going to get my revenge on Ryan, and I hadn't even had to plot it. There was nothing malicious about reporting what I'd discovered. Actually, I really had no choice in the matter. If I kept it to myself, I'd be betraying my boss's loyalty. I wondered if Ryan had a drug problem. Maybe someone had told him where Scott kept his stash and he was jonesing for a hit. The Agency was like one big party of whisper down the lane, so it wouldn't surprise me. But then why hadn't I heard about Ryan's addiction problems? No one told me anything.

The shit certainly hit the fan when I reported to Scott what I'd walked in on that morning. But Scott didn't respond as I'd expected him to. I was certain that the second the news of Ryan's attempted break-in slipped from my lips, Scott would have raced in a rage from the office and demanded of Daniel that he fire the little weasel thief. But instead Scott smiled and motioned for me to shut the door.

"Lizzie, did you mention to Ryan that you were going to tell me?"

I blinked a few times. This wasn't the reaction I'd been expecting. "No. It wasn't my immediate instinct. But I'm not afraid to admit to him that I turned him in, if that's what you mean."

"Do you think he would ever imagine that you wouldn't tell me? I mean, does he think perhaps that you're in awe of him or afraid of him?" Scott looked graver than I'd ever seen him. I thought hard so as to do his interest in the subject some justice.

"Unfortunately, I think he could easily believe that I'm afraid of him. He's been a jerk to me from day one. He works for Daniel, who hired me in the first place, and he delights in bullying me whenever he has the opportunity. So it's perfectly plausible that I wouldn't tell you in order to gain his favor," I told Scott.

"My guess is, Lizzie, that Ryan won't leave this matter alone. So if he asks whether you told me about this, I want you to tell him that you haven't mentioned it. Not a word. Try to sound genuine. Practice it in the mirror if you have to. I'm not going to say anything to Daniel."

"But shouldn't Daniel know? Maybe Ryan's a thief and is stealing from him, too."

"Lizzie, he's not a thief. That's all you need to know. Okay? What happened this morning was that you arrived at the office at nine and didn't see a thing out of the ordinary."

I shook my head in passive consent and walked out of the office.

I spent the rest of the day nervously jumping at my own shadow. I kept expecting to turn around and find the snake Ryan slithering near my shoulder in an attempt to save his ass. I really had no qualms about lying to Ryan and didn't even need to practice my fibbing skills on this occasion. Though I'd have much preferred it if I could call him up and tell him to get his slimy ass down here because Scott and the LAPD wanted to arrest him for trespassing and attempted theft. That would have given me a much greater sense of well-being than an hour of yoga.

But whatever Scott was up to, I was pretty certain that Ryan would never escape unscathed. What did bother me was the victory grin that I knew would be plastered across his smug face when I told him that I hadn't mentioned a word to Scott. Though it would be a bald-faced lie, he'd never guess that, assuming instead that his intimidation tactics had worked and that his exalted position as Daniel's chief ass licker had prevented me from filling my boss in. He'd immediately see it as a trump card just sitting in his hand. But if I could spin it correctly, I could make it seem like a favor I was doing him, instead of a knee-jerk fear reaction. Then at least I'd get to save face and do my boss's bidding at the same time.

Yes, I said to myself as I washed my hands in the bathroom, that's exactly what I needed to do. I had to go up and see Ryan before he found me and tell him I was saving his ass. Then at least I could forge a momentary truce between us, no matter how false the base, and buy myself a little peace and quiet. And as my mother always said, you catch more flies with honey. But I guess my mother couldn't have envisaged any human being as repellent as Ryan.

As I walked back down the hallway to my office, I pondered exactly what to say to Ryan, and I realized that I'd never really left politics after all. Perhaps I was reliving the Iran-Contra affair, Hollywood style. But then who was Reagan? More important, who was Poindexter, or Ollie North? I chewed on my pen intently and decided that the analysis was best saved for my next meeting with Dr. Vance. What I really needed to do now was escape the office for my lunch break so I could build up my strength before I made the long ride up to Daniel's office and assumed my role in whatever drama I was too unimportant to know that I was involved in.

16

I'm going up and up and up, and nobody's gonna pull me down.

—Lana Turner as Lora Meredith
Imitation of Life

I launched myself from bed on Sunday morning with the speed of a decrepit ocean liner setting sail from harbor. I did not want to hike in Fryman Canyon. I wanted to sleep in my bed.

"Oh, God, no," I moaned through a mouthful of pillow as I buried my face deeper. Should I just call Jason, yell at him for making such an indecent proposal to me in the first place, and arrange to see him at a sensible hour? Yes, that's exactly what I should do. I stuck an exploratory hand out from beneath my sheet and felt for my cell phone on the bedside table next to me. Hello, phone? But it wasn't there. My phone was in my purse, which was on the back of a chair in the kitchen, which was a whole room away. I pulled my hand back in and groaned like a wounded animal.

Eventually guilt got the better of me, and I dragged myself across the floorboards to the bathroom, with my knuckles practically dusting the earth in an early *Homo sapiens* manner. And unlike the girls in the commercials on television, half a bottle of grapefruit shower gel did not do it for me. Neither did standing beneath needles of hot water. What finally woke me up and persuaded me to live another day was that age-old spur, revenge. Or perhaps just residual anger from Friday, which I was obviously still harboring as it had invaded my dreams, infusing them with such violence that I had to check for bruises as I pulled off my pajamas.

As I made an impoverished attempt at dry-skin brushing with a wet washcloth, I remembered the look on Ryan's face when I'd told him my lie. He had smiled in such a smug, supercilious way that I'd longed to smack him and willingly cover my white cuff in his orange makeup. What I thought would be a moment of victory for me, and a temporary truce between us, had been a moment of sheer degradation. Instead of seeing it as an olive branch I was handing him and showing some appreciation like a normal human, he'd seen it only as a feather in his cap. I'd been dying to spill my guts and reveal the Machiavellian plan that I was a pawn in, but then I'd end up losing my job. Scott's instructions had been very clear, and I'd agreed to follow them. If only I'd guessed how ego-bruising it would be to allow Ryan to think he pulled my strings like a master puppeteer. I seethed and longed to ask him if he used Bobbi Brown liquid foundation or preferred Chantecaille Real Skin. I wanted to bust him in the salon on a Saturday morning getting his nails buffed. I wanted to tell everyone that I'd once caught him checking out his own ass approvingly in the elevator mirror. I wanted to discover documentary evidence that proved beyond reasonable doubt that he subscribed to *InStyle* magazine. I wanted to kill him.

In reality, the only way I was ever going to wipe that smile off his face permanently was to rise above my current gutter-level status or get him fired, which for whatever unknown reason wasn't in the immediate cards. My only choice was to soar above him and then look down and pour scorn—since it was unlikely that I'd be able to lay my hands on any boiling tar and feathers. In that moment in the shower, it became clear to me that, in the absence of medieval torture paraphernalia, I was going to have to torment Ryan by signing a deal for *Sex Addicts*. The kind of deal that made headlines. The kind of deal that would see me swiftly elevated from shakily situated second assistant to Scott Wagner to full-fledged producer with an office of my own, a deal at a studio, and Ryan's having to order congratulatory flowers for me from Daniel. Not to mention a proud father-daughter type of relationship with Daniel Rosen who'd want, of course, to schedule lunch, which would cause Ryan to gnash his teeth in the night and then have to spend a fortune on a gum guard.

"Oh, yes." I stepped from the shower and no longer felt like three miles of bad road, even though I realized quickly that I was towelless. I owned only one towel, and it was growing its very own rain forest in the corner. It hadn't been washed since my arrival in L.A., due to the fact that it was white and would have to occupy its very own load. Yet despite this setback, I flicked myself dry with the backs of my hands and felt hope surge within me. "Oh, yes," I repeated. Jason and I were going to make this happen. And if I had to hike for it, then I'd hike for it. If I had to climb Kilimanjaro, then I would. Bring on Everest. I was going to stride my way to success in oatmeal socks if need be.

As I crammed a piece of toast into my mouth, I began to create a collage of Inspirational Hollywood Women. I plucked a bunch of trades from the garbage and found the one I was looking for. Here it was, the *Hollywood Reporter* heralding its "Power 100 Women in Entertainment." I refused to see the fact that it was draped in a slippery banana skin as any kind of portent at all and wiped the cover down with my sleeve. And there, in glorious Technicolor—well, lots of black suits with a pink shirt thrown in for good measure, actually—were eight of the most serious female players in town.

I imagined that when they'd shot this cover, they'd intended for it to be ten women, but two of them were simply too important to show up. When my turn came, I was going to be one of those two no-shows. While the black suits were in the studio, I was going to be on set in Prague, swathed in sheepskin, clutching a Styrofoam cup of Czech coffee and talking budgets with the director of *Crime and Punishment*. Ryan wasn't even going to be able to draw a mustache on me when the copy plopped onto his desk with a thud as heavy as his heart would be when he read my blurb.

As I carefully cut out the pictures of these almighty creatures, almost all of whom mentioned how they juggled three children with running a studio or a broadcasting network, I decided that hiking wouldn't be such a bad string to add to my bow after all. Nearly all the Power Women claimed to do yoga for two hours a day before dawn. Hiking would help fill up the space in the profile that asked for your Balancing Act: *"Oh, I get up at six every morning and go for a five-mile hike in Fryman Canyon. It's so beautiful to see the world at that hour of the day. And besides keeping me fit and de-stressed, it injects some much-needed spirituality into my day."*

But as I daydreamed about sitting in fifth place on the Power

Women List, above the president of entertainment for Fox Broadcasting, I glanced at the clock and realized that I was late. My Success Secret, sadly, was going to have to wait until later. Possibly even until I'd actually achieved some success. Though that might have been like closing the stable door once the horse had bolted. Much better to have your strategy all worked out in advance. I pulled on the only piece of Gore-Tex I owned, which was a navy blue pac-a-mac, and decided to steal someone else's Success Secret in the meantime. But they were all too long to remember, and I didn't have time to jot one down on the back of my hand. So I simply picked Passion. Everyone had Passion somewhere in her Success Secret. And, thankfully, it wasn't going to involve having to enroll at night school.

"Sorry I'm late. Only I had no idea that there'd be traffic in the Hills this time of the morning," I said as I raced up to where Jason was perched on the wooden gate at the bottom of a steep path.

"I should have warned you. The breakfast crowd, the gym crowd, the dog-walking crowd." Jason gave me a brief and friendly hug and didn't seem as pissed off as I'd be if I'd been kept waiting for forty minutes.

"So what happens here, then?" I tried to be perky to make up for it.

"Well, we hike."

"Hike. Right. Well, let's hike away." I said as Jason folded up the *L.A. Times* he'd been reading and stood up.

"Oh, my goodness," I said in a surprised way, and stopped in my tracks as he got to his feet.

"What?" He opened the gate to let me through first, but I didn't move.

"Well, it's nothing. It's just that you're . . . tall."

"I'm actually only five-eleven. But I have on hiking boots." He looked a little embarrassed.

"No, I didn't mean that. I just meant . . ." And I started to wish I'd never opened my mouth. This wasn't a date, it was a business meeting. I didn't want him to think that I did or didn't like his physique, because it wasn't an issue. Only he was blushing a brighter shade of ketchup right now, and I think he was probably worrying that I thought it *could* be a date. Oh, brother. "I just meant that I've never seen your legs before. Well, not properly." Oh, Lizzie, how *could* you?

"Right, well . . ." Poor, poor guy.

"You see, you're always cut off at the waist behind the counter of the coffee shop, and I suppose I have seen all of you like that before, but only in the coffee shop and only for a few seconds at a time, which doesn't really count. And while you may not be exactly tall at five-eleven, you're a darned sight bigger than the two feet I usually see of you."

"I see." He was mortified.

My shoulders sagged despondently under my ugly Gore-Tex. "Jason, I'm sorry. I was just surprised. Good surprised. Not 'Great, I now have a crush on you' surprised, but just pleased for you that you have legs. And a whole body. You see."

And I must have appeared so pathetic that he forced himself to understand. And then he patted me on the back, hard enough to convince me that this *was* a friendly work thing and not a date, and also to make my tongue fly forward in my head and briefly choke me. I wondered if there was any culture in which such misunderstandings might be perceived as an auspicious start to a business relationship. Apart from the backward world of satanism, and that was a cult.

As we walked up a sandy incline so steep that it might as well have been the north face of the Eiger as far as I was concerned, I wanted to tell Jason that I wasn't what he might call fit. I wasn't what anyone might call fit. But I thought better of it because what was undoubtedly called for now was for me to unveil my Success Secret. My stolen and abbreviated Success Secret, I grant you, but I had to salvage our working relationship before it even began.

"It's about Passion," I said as I panted around the bend and saw another hill, several thousand degrees steep, before me.

"Yup." Jason waited without judgment, but perhaps not without a little trepidation, for me to continue.

"Passionate commitment to the project. And the thing is that I love this material," I said, tripping to keep up with him.

"I'm so pleased. I mean, nobody else has read this, Elizabeth. And I'm not entirely sure why I gave it to you in the first place." He looked at me with an earnest crease between his eyes. "But it felt right, and now I'm glad I did, because even though I don't know a lot about your background, I think that the way you've handled that job at The Agency is pretty heroic. I also think it's going to take the same qualities to make a great producer for this movie."

"Cool," I said. I was going to have to bone up on the vernacular used by successful people, too.

"So where do you think we should start?" Jason said as we reached the top of the hill and were rewarded with a breathtaking vista of Hollywood. It occurred to me then that perhaps the term "breathtaking" had been devised by an unfit person such as myself at a moment not dissimilar to this one, perhaps hundreds or even thousands of years ago. As the unfit person climbed as far as he could manage up a hill, he suddenly seized an opportunity to stop and take a breath so he could pretend to be staggered by the beautiful view. Hence "breathtaking view." I couldn't be sure, of course, but with all the oxygen spiraling around my body and affecting my brain, it seemed a very legitimate theory. Anyway, regardless of the origins of the phrase, what lay before us was quite simply stunning. And, of course, an excuse for a pause.

On the one side was the Valley stretching all the way down to the ocean in Malibu. The sky was a milky morning blue, and I shielded my eyes from the sun with my hand. Though they were swathed in mist, I could just make out the low ranch houses that had been confirmed hippie enclaves until the eighties, when the rich and the groovy had moved in and sunk their swimming pools into the ground. On the other side were the Canyons, with what looked like Frank Lloyd Wright houses perched high on promontories. I imagined that 1930s movie stars and famous recluses had once wandered around these white-walled, glass-fronted buildings clutching at martinis and wondering if this was it. You lived in the highest house in Hollywood, and still you just felt farther from God than ever.

"I've got mine picked out," Jason told me as I gazed out at these rarefied abodes. "It's behind that hill. It used to belong to a silent-movie director, and every time he had another child, he added another annex to his house. So the house kind of swirls up the hillside, and it's surrounded by sagebrush. It's kind of run-down, but I once went there to a dinner party and fell in love with it. It has a great fireplace." He pointed back toward Laurel Canyon.

"I think I'd like to live by the ocean," I said, thinking of Jake Hudson's house and the perfect evening I'd spent there. It still stung a little to think about how resoundingly I had been forgotten by Jake. But I couldn't afford the luxury of dwelling on my fractured heart. "So let's get serious about this project," I said, breaking away from the view and turning my attentions to the path ahead.

The air was still fresh, as the sun was barely above the horizon, and beneath our feet the sand had given way to a forest floor covered in splinters of bark, which smelled like the most exclusive bath products available in the little hip stores on Melrose. Well, this was L.A., after all. Even the air came expensively scented.

"The guy who lives across the street from me went to USC, and he said that he can do a budget and owns Movie Magic," I told Jason as we resumed our walk.

"Where does he work? Maybe I know him."

"He washes cars on the Paramount lot and bartends at Jones at night. His name is Peter."

"Great." Jason was nodding in time to his walking. He was also paying attention to what I was saying, which was an experience that I hadn't had for a while. Funnily enough, though, it made me a bit nervous, because when you're surrounded by people who don't listen to a word you say, you begin to wonder if you actually have anything worth sharing with the world. Jason seemed to still be with me, though, so I took a chance and continued.

"But I think that first of all we need to find you representation. We need some financing, even if we're going to go for a really low budget. And if you have an agent or a manager, we can get it out to some of the smaller production companies. What do you think?"

"I think I'd kill to have representation." Jason scuffed his feet into the bark as we walked. "I've tried before—hundreds of times, in fact—but I've always been turned down. So how do we do that?"

"I thought that I could ask some of the junior agents at The Agency," I said. "Slip them the script and see what they think. And just so we're clear: You won't just sell the material; you're determined to direct as well?" I wanted to clarify the point with Jason, knowing that it was going to be easier for my unexercised butt to pass through one of the cracks in the fence we were walking by than to get any financier in his right mind to agree to let a film-school graduate direct his first movie. Especially given that I and said butt were supposed to produce. Which would just make getting a deal even harder. It necessarily followed that the more people you had attached to a movie before it even began, the more cumbersome and expensive it was and, ultimately, the more unlikely it was to be made.

"I won't do it if I can't direct. And I know what you're thinking, but likewise I won't do it if you're not attached as producer. Okay? I'm loyal to a fault."

"Great. But you know that you could just give me an associate-producer credit and ditch me at the first post if you like. Just tell me now," I said, meaning it but secretly hoping that he wouldn't. After all, I already felt as though I were becoming emotionally involved with this project. Typical woman. One date and I was hooked.

"No way. If you're in, you're in. Trust me on that one, Elizabeth." Jason stopped by a water fountain and offered me the first drink. I bent down and took a sip. Naturally it tasted better than Evian. "So when do you think we can get it to an agent?"

"I think it's best to choose carefully," I said, wiping the water from my mouth. "I'll ask around tomorrow and try to figure something out. But I guess we can get this to someone by the end of the week, no problem."

"Cool." Jason bent for his water and I looked down over the Canyon. The sun was higher in the sky, and it was getting hot. I was thinking how nice it would be to head back for some brunch now that we'd had our Sunday-morning hike and I'd survived.

"So I was thinking that we could go over a few notes that I have on the script first," I said. "Now, if you like."

"Perfect." Jason took off his fleece, revealing a seriously sporty T-shirt. "Since I'm warmed up, I'll be a lot more receptive to ideas. Another five miles and I might actually have something to add." He turned and slapped me on the back again. This time I merely heard the hollow sound of my stomach reverberating through my body. Five miles more meant five miles back, too. I took off my Gore-Tex and reconciled myself to the fact that my fantasy of giving him notes over an organic smoothie and huevos rancheros at the Newsroom Café was at least ten miles away.

17

This is the sort of day history tells us is better spent in bed.

—Louis Calhern as Uncle Willie
High Society

Ritalin is not just a drug for hyperactive children, apparently. It's also prescribed for adults who exhibit traits of attention deficit disorder. It helps them to focus. It had certainly been providing Scott with endless hours of fun since his shrink had handed over a monster-size orange vial of the stuff three days ago. Being Scott, though, he had swiftly dispensed with the notion of prescribed dosage. Instead he discovered that while one or two Ritalin did a fine but generally imperceptible job of reigning in his attention, ten or eleven, pulverized between a Yankees paperweight and a piece of clean white paper, then snorted, yielded much more joy and hours more focus.

"Morning, Scott." I put my head around his door when I arrived at the office on Wednesday morning. "I'm going to the Coffee Bean. Can I get you anything?"

"Triple espresso," he said without looking up from his computer.

Frankly, I was amazed by his newfound productivity. He was glued to his screen every minute of every day lately. He was getting in before us all and was still here when we left in the evenings. In fact, I was beginning to wonder if he'd been home at all. There was a faint whiff in the room, and his five o'clock shadow was darkening to a distinct shade of beard.

"Scott, are you okay?" I asked. I took a couple of steps into his office and heard the familiar Texas Hold 'Em shuffle. There was also an array of credit cards scattered across his desk. Presumably to fund his little habit—the poker, that is, not the drugs.

"How's the game going?" I asked.

"Yeah." He tapped his index finger on his mouse and blinked his dry, purple-rimmed eyes at the screen. I retreated out the door and back into the assistant pool.

Courtney and Talitha were at their desks nursing hot drinks and leafing through the trades.

"Has anyone spoken to Lara?" I asked. She had been away since last week and was never contactable during the day. She simply left messages in the dead of night saying that she had strep throat and would be away again tomorrow. But I didn't mind too much, as Scott showed no sign of being pissed about her protracted absence. Plus, since he was doing his Howard Hughes impression and not leaving his four walls, there was barely anything for me to do anyway. Except ward off all comers. Which was actually easy, once you mastered the knack of lying without simultaneously ducking down to avoid the crash of the thunderbolt. I was able to tell a blatant whopper these days without so much as flinching. It made me a far, far more efficient assistant than any secretarial course ever could.

"Ryan saw her last night at Les Deux with some agent from William Morris," Courtney said, loudly enough to disturb Scott's poker reverie.

"Where's my fucking espresso?" he yelled.

"Coming." I started to leave the office. "Do you think that maybe he needs help?" I lowered my voice and moved toward the other girls. For while I'd never ordinarily ask for so much as the time of day from either of them, Lara wasn't around and I was concerned that Scott might be suffering some sort of breakdown.

"Oh, *hello*?" Courtney said in such a patronizing way that it made me want to shove pencils up her nostrils.

"I know he should be in Promises, but do you think it's urgent? Is he going to go into cardiac arrest with all that stuff, or what?" I addressed Talitha instead.

"What's he doing in there?" Talitha stuck her head out from behind her desk and took a peek into Scott's office.

"Playing online poker. I think he's lost a shitload of money," I said.

"And he hasn't slept or eaten in three days?" she asked.

"Well, he must have, mustn't he? I mean, I haven't ordered him in any food and I haven't seen him sleeping, but I'm assuming he must. Right? I mean, he's a man, not a camel."

"He's on Ritalin, honey." Talitha shook her head in a concerned way. "It's speed. It's calming, and it creates concentration like all hell. A speed freak can water a plant for three days. You can bet your left tit that Scottie hasn't moved since Monday morning."

"Oh, my God, that's gross!" I said, my nice-girl, middle-class roots showing through about as clearly as my Bumblefuck Mouse roots were at the moment, given that I was too poor to have a touch-up done. "Won't he get bedsores or something?"

"Well, if he hasn't blown every red cent he has on poker or died before Friday, then yes, I guess he might get bedsores. But I think they're the least of his worries right now."

"Should I call his wife?" I asked, beginning to panic. I looked into Scott's office once again, to check that he hadn't face-planted on his keyboard, but he was still fixated on his screen.

"Oh, yes, baby, give me an ace give me an ace! An ace on the flop, please, sweet Jesus!"

"If she hasn't noticed he's missing, then I'd just assume she doesn't care," Courtney said.

"Then what about his shrink? Should I call his shrink?" I really didn't think that I could just leave him like this any longer.

"Up to you." Talitha lost interest as the cute guy from Accounts walked through the office, and she and Courtney turned fluffy and began talking to him.

I went to the Coffee Bean and caught Jason in the middle of a rush.

"Hey, Lizzie, any news?" he asked over the heads of a line of six people. I moved around to the side of his counter where we wouldn't be heard by half The Agency staffers as they collected their mid-morning pickups.

"I've approached a few of the junior agents, but none of them have bitten yet. I suspect that they'll read it this weekend," I said. I'd actually sent it to six people and was feeling a little disappointed that I hadn't had a single response yet. It had been over a week now, and as I'd cherry-picked them all and approached them individually, I'd hoped they might have been a little sprightlier off the mark. Still, I knew how long it could take to get around to reading a script, so it didn't necessarily mean anything ominous that we hadn't heard back yet. And it was only going to take one person to like the material and we'd be off the starting block.

"Okay, well we'll keep our fingers crossed. Did you want drinks?" he asked as he dropped a pile of waxed-paper cups all over the floor.

"I was hoping for a triple espresso and a little something for me. But I'll wait in line like everyone else. I don't want to create any bad feelings." Which I already seemed to be doing by engaging the coffeemaker in conversation, judging by the looks on some of the customers' faces.

"Might be wise," Jason said, and I shifted to the back of the line and pondered Scott. My task today would be to keep him out of the ER, I figured, so I picked up three cheese-and-bacon ciabattas and two smoothies. He needed nutrients. "But shall we meet later on at my place to go over the latest draft? I'll call you to arrange."

"Sure, sounds perfect," I said. Jason and I had both agreed after our hike that we would read through the script again and see if there were any changes that would make it punchier, more emotionally hard-hitting, or just generally better. I had my notes ready, and, clearly, so did Jason. And I couldn't wait to get down and dirty and work on the script. To really feel that I was flexing my producer's muscles.

I gathered up my emergency supplies and hurried back to the office with renewed enthusiasm. I was on a steep learning curve, and even in my low-grade office chair, I learned more about cutting a deal than I would if I'd gone to Stanford and done an M.B.A. Because one of the great things about Hollywood was that no matter where you worked or what you did for a living, you couldn't avoid becoming competent in the business of moviemaking. Every coffee shop you sat in, you overheard the terms and the deal brokering; in the nail salon, you were as likely to pick up a copy of the *Hollywood Reporter* as a *People* magazine; and the woman in the dry cleaner's stunned me one day by filling me in on the back of Michael Bay's latest studio deal as she separated the skirts from the pants. Learning about the machinations of producing was osmotic, merely a by-product of showing up at work or the hairdresser's. And the extra hours I put into my new career-to-be by watching old movies and reading about production values and struggling through *Venice* magazine only served to make me feel like a bona fide producer already. Which was just as well, because I was terrible at winging it.

"Scott?" I tiptoed my way into his office with my wares. "Are you doing okay?"

"Hmmmm" was the only response I got from him, so I moved in closer to his desk. Strangely enough, at close quarters, he didn't look quite as bad as I had feared. A little partied out perhaps, but actually kind of bright-eyed and full of vitality.

"So what goes on with this game?" I asked, attempting to gauge the extent of his cerebral decline. I stood behind him and looked over his shoulder.

"I'm sitting second out of six hundred in a two-hundred-dollar buy-in tournament. I'm about to go all in on this hand," he said in a reasoned monotone. "Bring it on, mister. I'm gonna whip your ass."

I placed the triple espresso next to Scott, and some internal radar must have told him it was there, because he reached out without looking and downed it in one gulp.

"Oh, yes, baby! Oh, yes! I've tripped fuckin' aces on the fuckin' flop!"

I examined the carnage on his desk, the metallic glint of at least a dozen credit cards (thankfully, the black ones hadn't been ransacked yet), an empty bottle of Jack Daniel's and a half-empty container of Ritalin.

"Are you *supposed* to crush those things?" I asked quietly.

"Holy fuckola!" Scott suddenly leaped up in his chair and high-fived me. Well, he tried to, but I wasn't fast enough, and he just slapped my biceps instead. "Who's your daddy? Who's your daddy?" He crashed back into his seat and spun around a few times. "I just won a thirty-six-thousand-dollar tournament!" he said. "Now, what did you want, Lizzie?"

"I wondered if you were meant to crush your pills up and snort them," I said.

"Oh, right. Well, yeah, actually you are. Thing is that pills that are fun to snort are easy to crush. Pharmacists make it this way to turn us into addicts, so who the fuck am I to argue?" Scott laid his finger on his mouse and exerted the merest pressure. A second later the cards fell—click-click-click on the electronic baize.

"Really?" I said, wondering if I ought to call Daniel or maybe even Katherine Watson, somebody who might be able to enlighten me as to whether this was reasonable behavior. For an addict. I guess at least he'd just won something, so Mia would be happy.

"Oh, yeah. Zoloft and Paxil and lithium are all coated and can't be cut up, but they'd be no kick to sniff anyway. Vicodin and Percocet, on the other hand, are easy to crush and—surprise, surprise—habit-forming. See? It's a conspiracy. I'm just going along with it."

"Scott, will you do me a favor and eat one of these sandwiches I've brought you?"

"Sure thing, baby. Just leave it there, and I'll get to it."

"I'll come back and check on you in ten," I said. But he didn't hear me because he was making a loud protest about his latest opponent.

"Oh, hey, you sucker from Oslo! You seal-eating, fjord-fucking fuck! You have no business being at this table." He kicked his chair away from his desk in frustration, and I dodged out of the way. Then out of his office. He was still very much alive and seemed to be enjoying himself, so I decided to check out and write an overdue e-mail to my sister.

It was Saturday, and, along with every other person in Los Angeles, I had decided to indulge in a little conspicuous consumption. Alexa had knocked on my door with an organic watermelon juice for me just after her 7:00 A.M. student left, and she asked whether I wanted to go to the Beverly Center with her. She had to buy some Australian Bush Essences and also wanted to drop by Old Navy because she'd heard they had some fantastic yoga pants on sale.

"That's a great idea," I agreed as I swept the sleep from my eyes and tried to hide the worst of the holes in my brushed-cotton floral pajamas by sitting down. "I really need to get something to wear to this Halloween party tonight. Though I have no idea what I'm going as, and I can barely afford a Spider-Man mask. Do L.A. people actually get dressed up for these things?"

"Oh, sure, they go all out. You live in a town full of unemployed actors, you're going to see so many people dressed as train-wreck victims that you'll never get on board a train again," Alexa informed me. "I usually go to a pumpkin festival, but I have a retreat tomorrow, so I'm sitting Halloween out this year."

"Shall I drive us?" I offered, obviously not getting many costume tips there.

"Sure," she said as she struck a few impossible poses that I took to be yoga.

"It's nice to have a friend in the building," I said, trying not to sound like Jennifer Jason Leigh in *Single White Female*. "Just to hang out with and do normal stuff." Ha, ha. Like break into your apartment and wear your clothes and steal your boyfriend.

"It sure is." Alexa ran her finger around the rim of her glass and licked off the remains of her pink juice. "I need to stop by Polka Dots and Moonbeams. They've got great vintage—maybe you could go as a fifties housewife?" She smiled and did a few lunges in the direction of the door.

"Good idea. I'll get showered and swing by in about an hour," I said, handing back her glass and praying we'd come up with something a bit sexier when we were out and about. "And thanks so much for the juice."

"Namaste," she said as she left. I had no idea what it meant, but I smiled anyway. I had a friend. An off-hours, let's-go-to-the-Beverly-Center friend. Try stopping me from smiling.

Any tour of duty in the Beverly Center begins at the Rexall Drug Store, where hours can pass in the contemplation of lime green diamanté hair clips and cocoa butter, and the shampoo conundrum can begin to feel as confusing as cracking the mysteries of the human genome. Then there's Star Books, where compulsory paperbacks have to be purchased so that you can feel fully conversant on literary matters, even though your new acquisitions will simply top up your "unread" pile, which has Dickens somewhere at the bottom and the latest Salman Rushdie at the top. Also essential from Star Books are the latest copies of *InStyle, People,* and that other casualty of a too-busy life, the *New Yorker*. Unlike *InStyle,* with its delicious pages of tasteless weddings and red-carpet fiascos, which quickly becomes sun-bleached and waterlogged through excessive attention, the *New Yorker* remains pristine and important-looking on the coffee table until you realize that half the contributors have died and all the plays written up have ended their run.

Then it's on to Old Navy for more brushed-cotton items that will never, ever see the light of a love affair but will get you through dark days with the flu. And somewhere in between you have to find time for your Gap basics, a couple of DVDs, and a trip to Victoria's Secret, where you buy small things in red and lace and, if you're feeling daring, purple—or midnight, as they like to call it. These are things that will never see the light of a love affair either, because you don't have that kind of life. Instead you just read about it in *InStyle*. Get it? Sometimes it feels so complicated it makes even *my* head spin.

After Alexa and I had completed our full-scale assault on the Beverly Center and I'd acquired a dreadfully obvious French maid's outfit out of sheer desperation, we were badly in need of a pit stop to refuel our engines.

"Jamba Juice?" I asked, thinking that extra echinacea in a power shake would be exactly her thing. Oh, how nutritionally retarded I was.

"Sweetie, you don't seriously drink those things?" she asked as we headed back to the car laden with bags.

"Are they bad?" I asked, avoiding her question. Personally, I lived for Jamba Juice. The head freeze was the closest I'd ever gotten to S&M, and I was always overwhelmed with delight whenever I contemplated a Peanut Butter Moo'd or a Mango A Go-Go. Not to mention the whirring of my mental cogs that was set in motion when I had to look up at the sprawling menu on the wall and decide between a Femme Boost or a Vibrant-C Boost. It was like a big waxed cup full of joy and possibilities, and it seemed to embody all that was best about L.A. as far as I was concerned.

"We'll go to Urth," she said, giving me an understanding smile. "They do smoothies, and you can get your vitamins from *real* fruit." Right, so fruit was the only thing that was acceptable when real in this town.

"Okay." I hoisted my bags into the back of the car. "Can we walk, or shall we drive?"

"We'll drive." Alexa was a born-and-bred Angeleno, and though her disposition was as sunny as the weather, her attitude to walking anywhere but on a treadmill or in a Canyon was as frosty as a winter morning in D.C. "Then we'll swing by Polka Dots and Moonbeams and try on a bunch of outfits for your party, if you like."

"I love," I said, and we piled into my Honda and headed for Melrose.

Urth Caffé is possibly one of my favorite places on . . . well, Urth, I suppose. It's an enclave of all that's organic and delicious, and its sunny patio is a show-ground for people who look as wholesome and healthy as low-fat raisin-bran-and-honey muffins. There you see Los Angeles indulging in the hybrid of work and play that it loves the most. Writers sit with pens and notepads and find inspiration in a freshly squeezed orange juice, and in the couple breaking up at the next table; actors peruse scripts while wearing fake eyeglasses to lend them an intellectual hue; producers brunch, and everyone stares at everyone with the unabashed curiosity of tourists in a safari park. This is another idiosyncrasy of L.A. that I'm only just beginning to get used to—everyone totally checks each other out. It could be the hot weather causing the sap to rise and everyone to look for a mate, or maybe it's the population's innate paranoia at not wanting to miss a single thing, in case it's a big thing or, even better, a celebrity, I'm not sure. When you first arrive, it's disconcerting to be so scrutinized, but then it just becomes license to stare at others, which is frankly heaven. And beneath the umbrellas at Urth Caffé, it's open-season people watching.

I fended off a cell-phone-clutching studio executive (I could tell this because of the deafening mentions of his studio, his hectic premiere and star-fucking schedule, and his second-only-to–Brad Pitt salary) with a rapid-fire machine-gun voice and secured a three-foot-square piece of prime West Hollywood real estate of a table, while Alexa stood in line to order our soup and salad.

As I stretched out my pale legs in the sun and pushed aside the left-behind napkins and foam-rimmed coffee cups of the newly departed from our table, I felt a tap on my shoulder.

"Elizabeth, I thought it was you." I hastily re-covered my legs and turned around.

"Hi." I tried to stand up, but my knees crashed into the tabletop and the cups clattered, and so I sat back down and looked up at Luke Lloyd. Who was smiling down on me once again.

"Oh, don't get up," he said. "You alone?"

"No, actually, I'm with a friend," I explained, knowing that I had some serious ground to make up from our last encounter in the dog park, when I'd been useless and rude. Yet my mind was so devoid of anything to say and any words to say it in that I wished for a waiter to spill a latte on him to give me time to think.

"Cool, well, that's nice." He looked around, as if to find my friend and verify my story. "You managed to ditch the bitch, then?"

"Alexa?" I asked, rubbing my bruised knee. "No, she's inside getting soup and salad."

"The dog." He looked quizzically at me, doubtless searching for a sign of life.

"Oh, Anastasia." I nodded. "No, I'm with a yoga teacher today." I hated myself at this point.

"Great. So how's Scott?" He waded on valiantly, my Lancelot.

"Scott? Scott's great. You know, a little too much poker, and he's discovered Ritalin, which has been interesting. But generally Scott's Scott." Did they give out Academy Awards for Most Scintillating Second Assistant? With a crush, I might add. A second assistant with a hopeless, burgeoning crush on a AAA-list producer. He was trying, God bless him, but I wished that he just wouldn't. I wished that he'd just leave me alone with my empty brain so that I could cut out pictures of him from *Entertainment Weekly* looking ruffled and handsome on the set of his latest blockbuster. I wished he'd just go off and do what it is that types like him did in this town and not indulge his stupid southern good manners near me.

And guess what? He did.

"Hey, Lukey." A girl who can't have been more than eighteen years old, with the rangy legs of a foal and one of those broad, apple-biting smiles that can command love from babies and billionaires alike, appeared by his side with the idle countenance of someone who knows that the world will wait for her. And though I hate to sound 138 years old, she had on preshrunk clothes of such microscopic proportions that you'd be forgiven for thinking that there'd been a fire in her apartment building that morning and she'd had to leave in a hurry. Without dressing first.

"Hi, honey." Luke turned and looked at her with delight as she sucked noisily from a cup of orange juice. "Did you find us a table?"

"Yeah, it's, like, in the shade over there." She gestured with her straw.

"Cool. Well, it was good to see you, Elizabeth. Have a good one."

And that was all it took. A slip of jailbait whose gingham panties were peeking out above her denim skirtette to lure him away from me and my endlessly fascinating conversation.

"Who was that?" Alexa returned and dropped her neat bottom into the seat next to me. She handed over my lemonade, into which I automatically dumped four packets of organic brown sugar for comfort.

"Oh, that was Luke Lloyd." I stirred my drink and refused to look behind me. "He's one of those too-handsome, too-successful men who mess with your heart for kicks."

"Cute," she said, and turned her chair so that she could watch him. "Clearly his girlfriend has a daddy complex, though."

"Do you really think that's his girlfriend?" I asked, voicing my darkest concerns. "Isn't she a little young for him?"

"Are you kidding? She's perfect. Look at her shoulders, though, very closed. She's holding a lot of her energy in her Muladhara chakra and not releasing it. Which probably means she's a tiger in bed but not able to be open in love."

"I think that's what these boys like," I said, and sank another sugar packet into my glass.

"Only the unenlightened ones," Alexa assured me. "And, really, you don't want to go near them with a ten-foot pole."

The waiter arrived with our salads, and I sneaked a look behind me at the table where Luke was listening intently to whatever tale of pop stars and teen woes his child bride was telling him. I turned back around and scowled, my shopping euphoria dissolving along with the sugar crystals in my lemonade.

"Do you have a little crush?" Alexa asked as she bisected some smoked tofu.

"I think I have an enormous crush. He's so goddamn nice to me that it kills me. I wish he'd stop reaching out," I spit. I hadn't quite realized the weight of my feelings for Luke before, but now there they were in the harsh light of day. I must have looked alarmed, because Alexa reached over and stroked my arm.

"It's okay. We all have feelings, and they're always better out than internalized," she reassured me. "We could go over and talk to him now, if you like."

"Why would we want to do that?" I scowled.

"It's good to tell someone you love them," said Rent-a-Cute-Saying. "You never know, he may feel the same."

"He doesn't, Alexa, trust me." I glanced again at Luke and Lolita.

"Nothing ventured, nothing gained," she said.

"I know. But that statement only applies if you have something to offer. So far I've only come across as a total twit in Luke Lloyd's presence. The first time I met him, I was cavorting in my boss's swimming pool accessorized only by a G-string, someone else's diamond necklace, and a legendarily sleazy producer. The second time I interrupted his lunch and insulted his movie. The third time I was mopping squirrel blood off my shoes in the dog park, and today I established my credentials as a witless bore. So even if I turned into a cross between Miss Orange County and a NASA scientist, I think the rot is so irretrievably established that there's no hope," I said histrionically, pushing my soup to one side. I had lost my appetite.

"Right," said Alexa thoughtfully. "But I still think you should go say good-bye to him."

"Maybe when we leave, I'll wave in his direction," I conceded, but only on professional grounds. I couldn't afford to be too obnoxious to one of Scott's friends.

"Good, go on, then."

"What do you mean? You haven't finished." But then I looked at her plate of smoked tofu salad and noticed that she'd polished it off already. I suppose yoga must be good for the appetite. And there was no way that I was going to eat another bite of mine.

"I'm done. You're done. So go say good-bye," she said.

"We have to get the check first."

"I already paid inside. Remember?" She picked up her purse and smiled. "It's a fait accompli, Elizabeth. Now, go on, or I'll march you over."

"Do you have German blood?" I asked, glaring evilly at her.

"Too goddamn right I do. On my mother's side. Now, shoo."

So as Alexa stood watching and monitoring me, I dragged my feet over to where Luke Lloyd was sitting eating ice cream with his adolescent honey. I was so reluctant to go anywhere near him that I might actually have zigzagged toward his table. Less as the crow flies and more as the stoned crow might fly. I finally made it, with a few livid glances back toward Alexa.

"Hey, Luke," I said. But he didn't look up. An LAPD car chose that moment to tear along Melrose with its siren blaring. I cleared my throat to try again. But before I could get the words out, Lolita had spotted me and elbowed Luke in the ribs.

"It's that chick from before," she said as the siren trailed into the distance and allowed her to be heard.

"Oh, hey, Elizabeth." Luke took off his sunglasses and stood up. "Did you want to join us? Did your friend not show up?" he asked, looking genuinely concerned. Clearly he hadn't spent the last twenty minutes staring at me across the crowded café, then. Otherwise he'd have known that my friend had indeed shown up and that we'd been watching him as avidly as a peep-show ever since.

"Yeah, she's over there." I flicked my hand behind me. "But actually, I was just leaving, so I thought I'd come and say good-bye." I avoided his eyes and talked to his shirt, which was white and fraying around the cuffs.

"Ciao, then," Lolita said, and leaned back in her chair in a bored-already way.

"So," Luke said.

"So." I nodded. Glued to the spot.

"So see you around, then."

"Sure thing." I tried to sound casual, but I was racked with awkwardness and didn't really want to move away. His shirt was too compelling. I liked standing three feet away from him. It felt good, and I didn't know when, if ever, I'd see him again. "Bye, then."

"Bye."

"Oh, and, hey, Elizabeth?" he said as I threw a polite smile at Lolita, who had picked up her cell phone in protest at our tedious conversation. "Can I ask your advice on something?"

"Of course," I replied with barely concealed delight. He looked down at Lolita, who was like a ship in full sail as she discussed the new Dior collection, doubtless with a fellow teen who was lounging on a pink marabou bedspread in another part of town while a rock star sucked her pretty toes. Then, when he was confident that she wasn't listening, he moved closer to me.

"I just wondered whether . . ."

Go on, go on, ask me for a date. I'm not proud. I don't mind whether you blatantly two-time me. I don't mind whether I'm just your Wednesday movie-theater date and she's your Saturday night out at Nobu. I have a crush on you, and it's not going away, so just ask.

"Yes?" I nuzzled closer to Luke, close enough to smell his sun-warm, shower-fresh hair.

"Well, I was wondering what your favorite shoe shop in L.A. was?" he said as Lolita laughed like a blocked drain into her cell phone.

"My favorite shoe shop?" I repeated, never dreaming that his illicit words could sound so sweet. "Well, I think it's probably Jimmy Choo," I told him. I'd never actually been in, and I certainly didn't own a pair, but every time I drove past the shimmering storefront on Cañon, my heart skipped a beat. Behind that plate glass, magical things happened. Of that I had no doubt. "They're so incredibly gorgeous."

"Great," he said. "It's Scarlett's birthday next week, and I haven't a clue what to get her."

"Scarlett?" I was in the dark for only a split second before the lurid fluorescent light of truth dawned. Scarlett was Lolita. It was her birthday, and he was going to buy her a pair of Jimmy Choos. "Oh, sure, Scarlett." I covered my tracks more expertly than a world-class jewel thief. "Well, she's going to love them. She really will."

"You've been incredibly helpful, Elizabeth, thanks. I meant to ask my assistant, but I was a little . . ."

"Ashamed?" I nodded sympathetically.

"Ashamed?" Luke frowned.

"Understandably," I added.

"Understandably ashamed to ask my assistant which shoes to buy for Scarlett?" He was puzzled.

"Well, *I'm* pretty open-minded, but I can completely sympathize with why you wouldn't want your assistant to know. I mean, it doesn't look great in a professional environment, really, does it?" I had said before I could stop myself.

"What doesn't?" Luke was now looking a little concerned. "I'm not following you."

"Well, Scarlett. She's young."

"She's eighteen," he said matter-of-factly. God, he was even more unconscionable than I'd imagined.

"Right, well, I hope she likes her Jimmy Choos. And I'll see you around." I lifted my purse higher onto my shoulder and was about to leave when he caught my arm.

"Elizabeth, am I missing something here?" he asked me very directly and with his hand still lightly holding my wrist.

"God, no! I mean, of course not. It's none of my business who you date. And she's over the age of consent, so what's to be mad about?" I said, wondering how this surreal ordeal had actually begun and simply wishing that it would end and I hadn't become embroiled in a debate about underage girls and shoe shops with the only man in the world I actually wanted to hold hands with. Apart from the obvious Clooney-

and-company list. Then I remembered that it was all Alexa's fault. And that she was probably melting in the sun waiting for me. I had to get out of here.

"You thought that Scarlett was my date?" All of a sudden the concern was rinsed off Luke's face and replaced with a look of sheer delight. At the same moment, Scarlett jumped off the line with Merry Toes and caught what Luke had just said.

"She thought that I was your date?" Scarlett snorted contemptuously.

"You did not?" Luke was unable to wipe the grin from his face.

"Oh, that's hilarious," Scarlett added without so much as raising a smile.

"She's not your girlfriend, then?" I was now camouflaged perfectly against the bright pink terra-cotta patio, and I could feel the embarrassment flooding my face.

"Scarlett's my half sister," Luke said, and gave me a friendly, forgiving pat. Which was enormously generous of him, since I'd just insinuated that he was practically a pedophile. But it didn't serve to make me feel any better.

"Well, that's great news. For you," I said. "And I'm really sorry. My mistake. See you around. Sometime." And then I did what I was becoming all too good at—I left Luke Lloyd looking astonished and possibly even a little alarmed that girls like me weren't receiving the drugs they needed to function in society. Then I went home with Alexa and cut out a picture of him at a benefit from the *Hollywood Reporter* and slipped it into my diary, where it remained unlooked at, because every time I so much as thought about Luke Lloyd from that moment forward, I had to sing at the top of my lungs to drown out the horrible memory of that afternoon.

18

When you're in love with a married man, you shouldn't wear mascara.

—Shirley MacLaine as Fran Kubelik
The Apartment

I picked at my fishnet stockings and contemplated my feather duster as I sat enveloped in the plush gunmetal gray suede seats of Lara's Range Rover. I felt a certain dread about the evening that lay before me. It was Halloween, and I was wearing a French maid's costume. Lara was smoking like someone on death row and playing some suicidal anthem by Linkin Park, and much as I wanted to get out and make friends and have fun like you're supposed to in your twenties, I didn't exactly have a great feeling about tonight. My sense of unease wasn't helped by Lara's death-wish driving. She had mounted several curbs, skipped numerous red lights, tried her hardest to kill a coyote that had been ambling across the street, and was now driving with one arm—interestingly, not her cigarette arm—out the window. She was distracted to the point of being catatonic, and so I also knew that once we arrived at the party, I'd be lucky to get an introduction to the host before she swanned off in a blue haze and left me looking like a gatecrasher. Still, an invitation's an invitation, and I wasn't ungrateful—simply nervous.

I started to realize that Lara's excessive headbanging while she drove down Santa Monica was more like flagellation than fun. She had dark circles under her eyes and more makeup than was required even for her risen-from-the-dead, recapitated Marie Antoinette costume. When the song ended, I turned down the volume for a brief second.

"Lara, are you okay?"

She didn't even look at me when she answered, which was just as well, given how bad her driving was when she was supposedly concentrating. "Of course I'm okay, why?"

I shouldn't have bothered asking. Though Lara and I seemed to be making new inroads to friendship, there still seemed to be a barrier as long as the Great Wall of China between us.

"No reason, you just look a little tired."

Lara shrugged her shoulders noncommittally. "I've been trying to get my novel done, and it's doing my head in a bit. I think I really need to just let off some steam. Go a bit crazy. Thanks for coming with me tonight, Elizabeth. I really needed the company."

"Anytime," I said, and meant it as we pulled up to a beautiful Spanish hacienda that seemed to go on for a lifetime. Apparently the party venue had been changed due to the enthusiastic RSVP list. The house was nestled just below Runyon Canyon. We parked the car and walked through the open gates, with the requisite men in black checking the guest list. This was apparently *the* Halloween party to be at this year. It was supposed to be harder to get into than Trey Parker's—so no pressure to be cool, then. I gulped nervously.

We climbed up the steps toward the door, with Lara practically pushing me from behind. I was struck deaf and dumb by the magnificent excess of it all. It was like being in a haunted house without ever having paid the dollar or passed through the curtain. Steam was rising from the front lawn, making an eerie fog formation at the door, and the sound of wind whistling was coming from every direction. Gravestones of the current heads of studios were littered across the lawn, and I was certain I saw something skeletal move in the distance behind the willow tree. Lara looked annoyed as she pulled a bit of cobweb from her Marie Antoinette wig.

"A bit over the top. For fuck's sake," she snarled as the door creaked open.

"Come on, don't you think it's great?" By the death look she delivered, I assumed that the answer was no.

The door swung open, and I looked around hoping to meet and

thank our host for having us, but it seemed the door had opened on its own accord. I shivered slightly as we entered the cavernous hallway. Though the house was almost completely devoid of furniture, with faux cobwebs dangling from every surface, it struck me that it felt less like a haunted house and more like a living, breathing mausoleum to long-gone Hollywood glamour. Every element of the house was gigantic, starting with the slabs of sandstone that covered the foyer floor leading up to the *Sunset Boulevard* staircase. I did consider for a moment what might be buried beneath those enormous pieces of rock.

"Lara, whose house is this?"

"I have no idea, but it's amazing. I think it was Bette Davis's house, or maybe Myrna Loy. One of the guys is a set decorator, and I think he just finished escrow last week."

I learned later from an in-the-know guest that no one had lived here for years and that they were going to gut the entire place and restore it to its original beauty. But at the moment it was perfect for a Halloween party, and the addition of six-by-eight-foot waxworks of naked cadavers in various stages of dissection that hung from the wall made me shuffle closer to Lara. I could hear voices coming from somewhere in the distance, but the lights were so low and the black draping so heavy I couldn't really discern the direction. I felt something touch my ankle, and then a head came flying out of the pitch black, stopping an inch from my face. I screamed so loud that I could have given Janet Leigh a serious run for her money in the casting of *Psycho*. It was a severed head dripping with fake blood. It bobbed in front of me, and I heard laughter coming from down the hall. Maybe Hollywood wasn't the best place to attend a Halloween party. They took it a bit seriously for my liking. I glanced over at Lara and had a brief moment of concern. She was no longer to my left but was clutching me around the waist like a little girl.

"Lara, are you okay?"

She looked up at the bobbing head and blinked her big eyes in wonderment. "God, it looks so real! Sick, twisted makeup artists must have been at this all day." She let go of me and stood up laughing at herself. "Jesus, am I on edge or what?"

I was tempted to agree with her but just smiled instead as she straightened her wig. The wig was sensational. A good two feet high with a birdcage built in. The red guillotine mark across her neck and her alabaster skin were finished off with eighteenth-century garb borrowed from a costume-designer friend. In the dark corridor, Lara looked hauntingly ghostly, immeasurably cool, and amazingly sad.

When we finally made it, with lunch still in our stomachs, to the back of the house, the party was in full swing. Pink champagne was cascading down ice sculptures, and perfectly catered hors d'oeuvres, mostly in the shape of severed fingers, were being carried around by the killer from *Scream*. I snatched up a piggy in the blanket from one of the many hooded figures carrying trays and forgot to say thank you. Much to my surprise, all the guests had gone overboard on their costumes. This wasn't in keeping with the West Coast Casual look that was said to dominate most parties in this town. Ordinarily you couldn't get the L.A. crowd to lose their flip-flops, but tonight that low-key cool seemed to have been cast to the howling Halloween winds as movie stars and hip indie directors who were ordinarily too groovy to dress up were done up as Frankenstein and Dracula, with so much fake blood and so many severed limbs that I started to feel queasy. Clearly it was a cathartic experience for them. I just felt like a low-rent amateur in my French maid's outfit.

Luckily, an hour later, with my feather duster stolen by an overenthusiastic bumblebee and a knight in shining armor's having snagged my fishnets with his chain mail, I was looking more like a cheap Sunset hooker who'd been bashed about. Which was at least a little more horrific in theme. I'd already done a quick tour through the party, hoping to trip over Luke Lloyd, but recognizing my own mother in this crowd would have been a tricky task. Besides which, the people here tonight weren't exactly the glossy Hollywood pack; they were way cooler. But I still had to keep my lip gloss applied and be vigilant, because I just didn't think I could handle another accidental fiasco of a meeting in some public venue; those were starting to really get under my skin. The annoying thing was that he seemed so nice. So genuine. But then I'd just have to keep reminding myself that he was about as genuine as the Incredible Hulk who was serving the tuna sashimi.

As predicted, Lara had introduced me to several people and then been swept away on a tide of greetings and ghouls, leaving me to become involved in a conversation with a makeup artist, who was dressed as Marilyn Monroe after the overdose, about her breast implants. She was extolling the benefits of soybean oil over saline and the new protective coating on the silicone bag. Then, as I surreptitiously glanced at my watch to see whether she could possibly make this treatise last a whole hour, I noticed that she kept fixating on my own cleavage in its Victoria's Secret push-up bra. She clocked my look of concern.

"I'm sorry to stare, but who did your breasts? They're so natural. I mean, look at the gentle curve."

And before I knew it, she had both her hands on my tits and was squeezing them like I was a prize Holstein cow competing at the county fair.

"Donny, come over here and feel these." She smiled reassuringly as her platinum wig slipped a little in all the excitement. "Don't worry, Donny's my husband." Well, that made it all okay, then.

Donny was there in a heartbeat, and his wife took his hand and placed it on my breast. I recognized Donny immediately. Possibly because he was wearing Michael Jackson's clothes but had taken off his creepy rubber postsurgery-Michael mask, so I got to see the real Donny. Who, despite his slightly ravaged skin and failing hairline, was still the undisputed heartthrob of my teen years. He used to be one of those delicate, New Romantic heroes of the eighties, without a chest hair in sight and with every lock on his head gelled as carefully as a Michelangelo sculpture. If I recalled correctly, he'd been a one-hit wonder discovered on *Star Search.* I'd have to call my parents in the morning and see if they could find the signed poster of him that used to hang on my bedroom wall.

"Amazing job." Donny looked and groped, and then his other hand joined in the party. I was frozen to the spot. I didn't want to seem like a prude or too tightly wound, but I soon realized that this was obviously one of their parlor tricks, and if I didn't put an end to this now, after another cocktail I might find myself adding a bit of spice to their conjugal bed. Even though I was all for experience, and when I was fourteen would have traded in my roller skates to have Donny manhandle me and take me home, wiggy Marilyn wife or no wiggy Marilyn wife, I was considerably older now, Donny was considerably less attractive, and I wouldn't have a clue what to do with them anyway, even if I'd wanted to. So I smiled amiably and removed their wandering hands from my breasts.

"Lovely to meet you both." I stood up. "They're real, by the way," I added. Which was mercifully all the shock factor that was required to leave them speechless and give me enough time to escape through the creaking gate to the terraced poolside, where the epicenter of the party suddenly seemed to have shifted.

I stepped out onto the patio and found myself in the middle of a milling crowd staring up toward the roof of the house. They were discussing some crazy girl who was walking on the roof. They were speculating as to whether she was the pièce de résistance in the entertainment or if she was for real. I looked up at the cloudy night sky and saw silhouetted against it an eighteenth-century updo, and even though I hadn't seen Lara in an hour or so, I was pretty sure I recognized that wig even from three stories down.

I turned to the vampire standing next to me. "How long has she been up there?"

"About ten minutes. She keeps yelling something about always having wanted to dive into a pool from a rooftop. I hope her wig's pinned tightly, though."

"Jesus Christ, has anybody gone upstairs to try to get her down?" I said in a panic.

He looked at me like I'd just arrived from Uranus. "*I* didn't give her the drugs. What do you want *me* to do?"

I bolted back into the house and sprinted as fast as I could to the grand staircase. I took three steps at a time until I reached the top floor. There were many doors, so I threw them each wide open as I called out Lara's name, hoping to find the window she'd used to climb onto the roof. Then I realized that there was another staircase leading to the attic. The light was on, and when I reached the top of the stairs, I could see Lara through a small open window, prancing around and laughing in her full skirts on the badly damaged tile roof. It looked precarious from here, and I was still a good twenty yards away. I stopped running and began a calm walk in case I startled her.

"Lara. It's Elizabeth," I called out as gently as I could, and edged toward the window. "Lara, what are you doing up there? Do you mind coming off the roof for a second?"

Lara swung around at such a speed that her left foot slipped. But she righted herself quickly, just as I was about to dive out to catch her.

"Elizabeth, is that you? You've got to come out on the roof. It's so fun. You can see the Hollywood sign—it's amazing!"

"Okay, honey, I'm coming. Just give me a second." I climbed up onto the window ledge and sat with my bottom firmly planted on the inside of the window frame. I smiled bravely at Lara.

"That's right, just come out and join me. My God, we're having some fun tonight. We're going to forget everything and have a fresh beginning. That's why I'm going to jump into that pool down there. A new start, a spiritual rebirth."

I held on and looked down at the pool. It was a speck of shimmering blue in the concrete landscape. I knew all about the lure of a swimming pool at a party, but thankfully mine had just been a subconscious bid for professional suicide. Lara's just might end up as the real thing if she jumped.

"Lara. That's too far. You'll hurt yourself."

"Don't be such a pussy, Elizabeth. You have to live dangerously. Anyway, I've done it before."

"Not from here, you haven't. Can you just come inside for a second? Please. I really want to talk to you about something."

She laughed again recklessly and took a step closer to the mossy slate edge of the roof. I looked frantically into the attic for inspiration. I'd been hoping for a safety net or something polelike that I could reach out and guide her in with. Or even a stray partygoer, perhaps. Naturally, there was no such thing. All that was in the attic were old boxes, books, and furniture. They'd obviously cleaned out the house but never discovered the attic.

"He doesn't care if I live or die anyway."

My attention was drawn back to the roof, where Lara was now peering down intently toward the minuscule rectangle of water.

"Who, Lara?" I needed to get her back in the house before (a) she jumped or (b) someone realized she was serious and called the police. Then it would hit the newspapers and become an absolute fiasco. No one would ever believe that it wasn't sheer misery from working at The Agency.

"My boyfriend. You're so good and moral you'll think I'm evil, Elizabeth, but he's married." She started to cry.

"Lara, why don't you come over here, and we can talk about it?"

Lara laughed scornfully behind her tears. "I don't want to die, Elizabeth. I just wanted to have fun. Forget for a while."

"Well, whether you're planning it or not, if you put so much as a foot wrong out there, you're history," I warned.

She turned sharply to me. "I'm history anyway. See, I'm dressed as Marie Antoinette."

"Okay, time for jokes is up, Lara. Now, please just come in, and we'll talk about your married man."

"I still might do it," she warned with a defiant toss of her head. The wig went tumbling down the slope of the roof, dropping into the pool. A shocked groan drifted up on the chilly evening breeze from the crowd below. And, terrifyingly, at that moment I believed she *might* really do it.

What I needed was a distraction, something to take her mind off whatever she was trying so hard to forget. I glanced into the attic and noticed the books again. They looked like old classics. I swung my legs back inside and went to check out the volumes. I picked one up and brought it closer to the window.

"Wow, Lara! Look at this. It's an old copy of *Anna Karenina*. Oh, my God! Check out the binding. It's so beautiful." I pretended to be entranced and flipped carefully through its delicate, yellowing pages. It was a shot in the dark, but, miraculously, Lara was by my side a moment later.

"Let me see." She sat down on the outside of the window next to me and took the book from me. "It is beautiful," she said as she opened it and read out loud, "'Vengeance is mine, and I will repay,'" from the title page. I breathed a sigh of relief as Lara melted into a veritable swimming pool of tears. I glanced out the window, and, after a moment of vertigo, I saw that the crowd was already dispersing. Thank God for short attention spans. No one would remember it in the morning. Or the ones who did would assume it was just a struggling actress trying to get attention in order to land herself representation or a part in a movie.

Now that she was peaceful again, I reached into the room and dragged out a couple of fur coats that were tumbling from a wooden chest. I wondered whether the real Marilyn might have left one of these behind after a party so many moons ago. I draped one around Lara's shoulders and one around my own.

"So, sweetie, what's really the matter?" I asked Lara.

"Well, I've been going out with this married guy for the last two years. Then I broke up with him yesterday. He's always cheated, even on me, and it hasn't always bothered me, but now I think he might really be into someone else who he works with." She looked distraught. I put my arm around her and led her inside. "Anyway, it just wasn't happening, and it's not who I am. I want more for myself." She collapsed on the dusty wooden floor clutching her book.

Amid hiccupping sobs, Lara explained how she'd met her married man at a nightclub when she was still in graduate school at UCLA. She'd been bartending to make ends meet, and he'd come in and made her laugh. He was a freak, but a charming one, and their affair didn't start for another year.

"I don't know what I'm doing anymore. I'm up and down, colliding between joy and despair. It's miserable. I can barely have fun because I'm so confused."

I untied my maid's apron and handed it to her to use as a Kleenex. "Nothing's wrong with you, Lara. You're just in a difficult situation."

"It's just that whenever I think about living my life without him, I lose all interest in life itself. I know it sounds so stupid and absurdly romantic. I know he's bringing me down. But every time he promises to swear off other women, he stumbles. I just wish life could be different. I wish I could learn to follow my own advice." Then she fixated on her nails and said, "I'm a hypocrite, Elizabeth. He's in the industry."

"He is?" I had a moment of nausea. "His name isn't Luke Lloyd, is it?" I asked.

Lara looked at me quizzically. "The producer of *Wedding Massacre*?"

Shit, I'd seriously blown my cover, but she couldn't be mad at me anymore, not after that revelation. "Yeah. I just met him and . . ."

"He's not married, Lizzie, so even if you did break all the rules and sleep with him, you'd be way ahead of me, babes."

"Oh, it's nothing like that. I just keep seeing him. And he's nice to me and remembers my name. But he's way out of my league."

Lara delivered a swift kick to my shin. Which really hurt. "No one is out of your league, you stupid girl. Elizabeth, you stop traffic. He'd be lucky to so much as stalk a girl as intelligent and sane as you."

"Thanks, Lara." I'd pore over that thought later. "But what are we going to do about your situation? Is there anything I can do to help?"

She shook her head miserably. "I wish. But I guess I'll just keep writing my book. I can put all my pain and heartache into the pages, and maybe this entire mess will have had a purpose."

"Your book's going to be great."

"If I ever finish it. Time to get serious and stop being so damn self-indulgent. I just thought I could come here tonight and have fun, meet another guy who would make me forget him. But every guy that makes a pass at me, I want to kick in the teeth or knee in the balls. They all seem so trivial."

Lara stood up and dusted off her skirt. Her mascara had run down her cheeks and left her with enormous raccoon eyes. I put my hand on her shoulder and stopped her.

"Come here, you've got mascara everywhere." I licked my finger and tried to rub it away but only succeeded at pressing the inky smudges more deeply into her pale skin.

"Oh, it's okay. Just leave it. It'll add to the ghostly effect. Anyway, I think I'm ready to go home. Enough fun for one night." She clutched tightly to her *Anna Karenina*. "Do you think anyone would notice if I took this one?"

"To be honest, I don't think anyone knows this stuff even exists. I'm sure there's a heap more undiscovered treasure up here. Like old love letters from Rudolph Valentino or Greta Garbo." I stuck a hand into a box and was certain something moved. I snatched it back quickly. "Maybe we'd better just go. I'm kind of tired, too."

We stood up and linked arms as we made our way down the stairs and back to the party.

"Yeah, best to stay out of boxes on Halloween in case all the evils of the world fly out," Lara said melodramatically.

"But we'd still have hope," I reminded her. "That was what was left at the bottom of Pandora's box, wasn't it?"

"Oh, yeah, we have to have hope," Lara said as we reached the bottom of the staircase. "Hope is definitely the way forward."

19

The only way you'll ever get me to follow another of your suggestions is to hold a bright object in front of my eyes and twirl it.

—Cary Grant as David Huxley
Bringing Up Baby

Even if Jason Blum hadn't been talented, I would have been fooled into thinking that he was when I entered his apartment for the first time. All the way up the staircase were framed stills from Roger Corman movies. Apparently Corman was a cult B-movie horror director whose credits went on for days and whose eye for talent had ensured that the likes of Francis Ford Coppola, Martin Scorsese, James Cameron, and Jonathan Demme, to name but a few, had all worked for him early in their careers. So as Jason waited for me on his landing in his shapeless gray sweatpants, an even more so Peruvian sweater, and on his feet a pair of woolen slipper-socks, I had to pass by gruesome scenes from *Swamp Women, Bucket of Blood,* and *Attack of the Crab Monsters*.

"Hi, Lizzie," he greeted me, then led me through to his living room, which was similarly a shrine to cinema. There were DVDs, books on Visconti, reels, and piles of obscure moviemaking magazines, and I could be wrong, but I swear the place smelled of popcorn.

"Wow, anyone would think you liked the movies!" I laughed as I dropped my bag on the floor and eased back into one of his red velvet—no surprise there—chairs.

"I guess I'm a geek," Jason said. "Can I fetch you a Coke?"

"Perfect," I said, and pulled some new pens and my copy of the script out of my bag, "This is like doing homework, isn't it?"

Jason reappeared from the kitchen and handed me a can. No such luxuries as a glass around here. Jason was suddenly not the smiley, happy-to-help coffee-shop hand but rather an auteur in the making. His hair was unwashed, and I was just an observer of genius, here for the ride.

"I guess," he said as he sat down on the floor in front of me and began laying out fifty or so index cards, all marked up with the scenes from the script. Clearly it *wasn't* like homework, then. It was far more serious. The expression on Jason's face suggested that we'd just created the H-bomb and now had to think hard as to whether we shared our secret with the world or burned the plans. "So I thought we'd begin by plotting the character arc of his mother. I think her back story is vital to the major expositions in the first act."

"I agree," I said. And I did. I just might have put it a little differently myself.

Several hours later Jason and I collapsed with aching backs, fingers bruised from scribbling, and blurry eyes. I took out my ponytail, which was making me feel like I was being slowly and deliberately scalped. Jason clicked his knuckles one by one and turned on a table lamp beside him. We had been working so intently that we hadn't even noticed that it had grown dark outside.

"I feel like my ass died at about the time of the dinosaurs," I said as I shook out my hair and rubbed my lower back.

"It was great, though. We really nailed some of the major scenes, I think. We cut all those superfluous interstitial moments, and it's much, much tighter. Thanks, Lizzie."

"Not a problem," I said as I stood up to stretch out my legs. "I think we should definitely give the new draft to a few more people. Some new agents. And I'm going to look into financiers. What do you think?"

"That'd be great. Though you're the producer—those decisions are in your hands. I couldn't do any of this without you, Lizzie. You know that, don't you?"

"Oh, I'm just the grunt worker, don't mind me," I said. "The only thing I have been thinking is whether we're a bit heavy-handed with the intensity in the story. There isn't much laughter in here, is there?"

I said, motioning to where the script sat, discarded on the floor. It was something that had been worrying me for a while. Because Jason's work really was an exercise in unrelieved seriousness. Levity was not his forte.

"Why would I want it to be humorous?" he asked, bewildered.

"Because life can be funny."

"It can also be terrible."

"Think of Mike Leigh," I suggested.

"I'm Jason Blum," he said. And I think I knew at that moment that Jason was going to make it. Big. Huge. Enormous success.

I shrugged. "Yeah, maybe you're right. The tone's perfect."

Later, as we ate pizza and talked about the movie and planned our assault on the major talent agencies and purse holders in town, I caught Jason looking for a moment too long at my face. I was tugging a piece of wayward, stretchy cheese off my finger and trying to coax it into my mouth. I didn't let him know that I'd noticed his lingering gaze, but I did wonder whether I would have liked him to kiss me. Or something. It had been so long since I'd had any romantic contact with a man. Well, one that I liked anyway, and Jason was so unlike the usual horrors about town, the Jake Hudsons and Bob Davieses and Scott Wagners, that he made them seem like living, breathing Roger Corman movies all on their own. Definitely he was a little earnest for me, but he was so dedicated and passionate about what he loved that it would have been quite something to have Jason Blum in love with you. Quite a production, I imagined fondly.

"What you were saying about humor, Lizzie." He interrupted my train of thought. "I think it's overrated. Too many real emotions are debased by humor. Too much is lost in the name of enjoyment." He was picking the olives off his pizza and placing them in a tidy little mountain on his plate. It was then that I knew that Jason and I were never going to be. I might be able to get around the gray attire and the hallway strewn with pictures of bloody intestines, but his saturnine streak was too much for me. A total deal breaker.

I was on my way to pledge pretend allegiance to Ryan when I was joined in the elevator by Daniel Rosen. Although he was a slight man and was only in his mid-forties, his demeanor was so redolent of power that I almost dropped to my knees and gave thanks. His airbrushed perfection—the creaseless pink shirt, the weightless drape of his deep navy suit, and his smooth, lightly tanned face—made me think that I could have been looking at him through a Vaselined lens. He was as slick as his house, vintage Rolex, and Aston Martin put together; he smelled elite, if that's possible. He looked at me vaguely and smiled. Foolishly thinking that the nod of the head was recognition, I decided to acknowledge him—big fat mistake. And if I'd had a split second longer to mull it over, I'd have done the sensible thing and gazed down at my shoes until I went cross-eyed and Daniel left me alone in the elevator once more. But I didn't have time to think, and I came from a world where I said hello to fellow dog walkers and old ladies in the street. This was a habit that Hollywood had yet to divest me of entirely.

"Hi, Daniel."

He looked puzzled as he tried to place my face. I was really hoping what sprang to mind wasn't me topless in his pool.

"It's Elizabeth Miller. We met when I worked for Congressman Hutchens in D.C., and you got me my job here at The Agency." Why on earth I'd felt the need to draw attention to myself I had no idea. But it certainly cranked open a can of worms that I could happily have lived without for some time to come.

"Elizabeth. Yes, of course I know you. You work for Scott Wagner, right? How's it going?" He voice was rich and melodious and perfectly pitched to make money and friends.

"Really well. I'm learning a lot. And really enjoying the business." His eyes bored into me as I struggled to remember if I'd spritzed on any perfume this morning that might cause him to go into anaphylactic shock or fire me again. I hadn't forgotten the firing incident—I was just hoping that he had.

"So do you want to be an agent, or are you thinking of heading back into politics? I hear Scott's pretty tough to work for." Well, he was misinformed there. In comparison to the stories I'd heard about Daniel, Scott was a walk in the park.

"Scott's great," I said, not really wanting to get involved in that conversation. Then I had a moment of pure inspiration. I should mention Jason's script to him. Maybe he'd have some advice or even want to help out. After all, I was his protégé in some vague sense of the word, and I wasn't having much luck getting it read by any of the other agents. I deliberately hadn't given it to Scott because he quite simply didn't read, so where was the harm in asking Daniel's advice?

"Very loyal to Scott, are you? That's interesting, if a little misguided." Daniel raised his eyebrow and chuckled.

"Daniel, would it be fair to say that even though you're president of The Agency, you're always on the lookout for promising newcomers?" I asked as the doors slid open on an empty floor. They closed again, and we resumed our climb.

"Of course. The day I stop being interested in talent is the day I retire."

"Well, the thing is, I'm passionate about this script that a friend of mine has written, and I'm trying to help him get it made into a movie. He's also a great director," I added. Though if I were being truthful, Jason's directorial talent had passed me by. I'd seen a couple of his reels, but they'd been very blurry, very incomprehensible, and would have served as a substitute for Ambien in one of my rare bouts of insomnia. But what did I know?

"Sounds great." Daniel nodded with interest. The door to the elevator was opening on his floor, and I had a ten-second window to define how I'd approach my new challenge. If I chickened out, I knew full well that I'd remain a lackey for the rest of my days. Daniel glanced at his watch and put a hand out, gesturing for me to step out before him. I stayed where I was.

"Would you mind taking a look at it? I mean, if you have a spare moment, which I'm sure you don't . . . On second thought, just forget I asked," I backtracked clumsily. Now it was Daniel's cue to swiftly reject me. At least I'd tried to move forward with our film, and I could tell Jason that I'd given it my best shot. What I wasn't prepared for, though, was success—perhaps because I'd seen so little of it thus far in my new career.

Daniel motioned me onto the landing a little more vociferously this time. I stepped out, and he followed me.

"I'd love to. I'll have one of my assistants call to set up a meeting with you, and we can discuss what help you might need. I'm impressed by your determination, Elizabeth."

I couldn't believe my ears. Maybe helping his underlings up the ladder was the key to Daniel's incredible success. Career karma, perhaps. He was proving to be a much greater man than I'd ever imagined. He walked down the hallway toward his office, and before I could get my wits together, the door had closed and I was riding back down the way I'd come—wondering how the headline would read in *Variety* when we got the deal set up. Having completely forgotten about Ryan.

Lara was an unpredictable girl, to say the least, and it was very possible that in the sober light of day she'd regret the new intimacy we'd forged at the Halloween party. I'd left her a message on Sunday checking on her wounded heart but hadn't heard back. I just hoped she hadn't had any other brilliant urges for fun, like swimming in the Pacific after a little MDMA. But pretty soon my traditional Monday-morning funk had given way to a whole new means of having fun—I could worry about Daniel. So as I leafed through the trades, I began to wonder why Daniel had been so swift to set up our meeting in the first place? I stared at the telephone like it might be sprinkled with anthrax. Our meeting was scheduled for today at noon and I was waiting for Ryan or one of Daniel's numerous other assistants to call and confirm our appointment. I started to think how I'd much prefer to be pouring coffee, photocopying, or shopping for Barbie's prom dress rather than risking humiliation in Daniel's office. Maybe I wasn't cut out for this producer thing after all. I was just a delusional dilettante.

"Are you going to answer the phone or not?" Courtney walked by my desk and glared at me.

I picked it up reluctantly and gave her a filthy look—once she'd passed by. "Scott Wagner's office."

"Is this Elizabeth Miller, assistant to Scott Wagner?" The voice was deep and male. Usually clients didn't know my name. And if they did, I knew who they were. Still, it wasn't Ryan. He had a thin, reedy whine.

"Speaking."

"You're sounding good enough to eat this morning. Interested?" Gross. The sheer weight of flashback was heavy enough to practically knock me right off my ergonomic swivel chair onto the carpet. "It's Bob."

"I hadn't guessed."

"I bet you're blushing right now."

"I'm actually in the middle of typing a memo, Bob. Do you need Scott?"

"No. I need you."

With that I hung up. An enormous feeling of liberation flooded my being, but before I could really revel in the unusual sensation, the phone rang again, and, as assistants do, unless they have something better to gossip about, I picked it up. "Scott Wagner's office."

"The beauty of dating assistants is that you always know you can get them on the phone, even when they hang up on you. Why haven't I seen you in the last few months?"

It was Bob again. I decided silence was the most effective defense. Little did I know.

"God, you turn me on. Just thinking of you sitting with those fabulous tits in that office full of people, you're making me har—"

I hung up again.The phone rang again. Where the fuck was Lara? She hadn't called in sick, and beside the obvious irritation at having to fend off Bob alone, I was starting to worry about her. The phone continued to ring. "Scott Wagner's office."

"If you hang up on me again, Elizabeth, I'll call Daniel Rosen and tell him you're a very rude assistant."

"That's blackmail."

Talitha's typing came to an abrupt halt. Apparently that was a word that garnered interest at The Agency. I lowered my voice.

"Bob, I am at work. If I never mentioned it months ago, although I'm certain I did, thank you for taking me to Spago. But it was unconscionable to slip narcotics into my drink and . . . the rest." I could barely catch my breath.

He had absolutely no remorse. "You sound just like Mrs. Jenkins when you get mad. She was my third-grade homeroom teacher. Fuck, I've got a woody. Have dinner with me tonight."

I hung up for the third and last time. I didn't need this abuse. A disgusting pervert was stalking me, and he refused to take no for an answer. What was I supposed to do?

"I do hope that wasn't Bob Davies you just hung up on. He gets one point two million a movie and has the highest net profit in terms of points of any of our other producers," said Courtney with a smile as tight as her scrawny little ass.

"Well, he happens to be calling desiring phone sex, and last time I looked, Courtney, this wasn't a 1-900 number."

"Well, Elizabeth, maybe if you tried to keep your clothes on and not bend over backward to date clients, you and Bob wouldn't be having this misunderstanding."

Touché. I was about to come back with a real zinger, but the phone was ringing incessantly. I knew now that Courtney would clearly be of no help at all in the screening of beastly Bob, and Talitha was on the phone already. I picked up the receiver with a vengeance.

"Bob, leave me alone!" I shouted.

"Well, that's a very professional way to answer the phone, isn't it? I suspected that your limitations were numerous, but I thought you'd at least be able to do *that* correctly."

"Hello, Ryan. How can I help you?" You little toad, bastard, fuckface.

"For no reason that I can understand, Katrina, Daniel's third assistant, set up a meeting for you and Daniel. Apparently you ran into him in the elevator? Awfully well planned for someone like you. You have my admiration." I had known that my meeting with Daniel was going to pique Ryan's curiosity, but I didn't think he'd be so ragingly obvious about it. "So why does Daniel want to see you?" Ryan asked shamelessly.

And I had to admit to myself that it was highly unlikely that he'd grant me a whole meeting simply because I wanted to be a producer. He hadn't even read the material yet. Why, I wondered, was Daniel even remotely interested in a second assistant's pet project? But I had no intention of divulging any of my uncertainty to weaselly Ryan. For once I had the cards, and I still hadn't forgotten about the delivery of my bra via the mailroom.

"I know exactly why he wants to see me, Ryan. And that's a matter between myself and Daniel. Would he still like me in his office at noon?" I could hear Ryan spitting, or perhaps he was breathing into a paper bag.

"Three o'clock, and be on time. He has a three-fifteen." Click.

Oh, well. Even though I was scared to death of Daniel and I suspected that his motivations weren't straight up, at that particular moment I'd have happily faced a pack of rabid dogs just to annoy Ryan.

. . .

"Lara, I have a meeting with Daniel Rosen. Can you cover?" I asked Lara when she finally turned up looking remarkably more cheerful than Saturday night, with nary an apology.

She knitted her brow. "Sure. What's it about?"

"Remember that script I'm trying to produce? I rode the elevator with Daniel and asked him to give me some advice. But I never expected a whole meeting. I didn't even pitch it to him." I shrugged my shoulders cluelessly in response to her now deeply furrowed brow.

"That's random. Watch your back." Lara shifted her focus to her computer and booted it up. Per usual, she wasn't working on anything that had to do with The Agency, or Scott Wagner for that matter. I hoped for her sake that she finished soon, because when Scott or, worse, Human Resources finally got wise to her dearth of work, she wasn't going to be employed for long. I brushed the salt-and-vinegar chips from my skirt, did a quick swipe of my lip gloss, and headed up to meet the big medium-size man.

One was allowed access to Daniel's penthouse only if granted permission. Kind of like a hall pass in high school. Apparently this was a requirement for insurance purposes, as each of the *objets* scattered around his floor was worth more than my yearly salary. When I stepped onto the other side and walked through the closed door, I was launched into the Los Angeles version of Versailles. Which, let me tell you, was possibly even more spectacular than the Sun King himself could have envisaged. Where the rest of the building was decorated in sleek, modern Eames, Daniel, as had been correctly rumored in the dungeons below, had gone for cornicing, intricately carved doors, mirrored walls, and tapestries, marble, chandeliers, and even statuettes.

"Stop ogling and get into his office. He's a very busy man, and he's waiting for you." Ryan appeared from nowhere wearing a livery uniform of knickerbockers and . . . okay, he was wearing black pants and a collared shirt, but it wasn't beyond the realm of possibility when one was confronted with this ridiculous spectacle. I looked at my watch. I was one minute early.

I followed Ryan into Daniel's den. I had been imagining a throne but was disappointed to find only a leather-topped, gilt-edged desk and an enormous roaring fire, which was odd, as it was ninety-two degrees outside. Apparently Daniel had his floor kept eight degrees cooler than the rest of the building so that he could have his fire burning all year round. On a trip to India, Sai Baba had told him that a fire was needed to burn off the negative energy of a very competitive business and hostile adversaries.

Ryan accompanied me into Daniel's office. As was to be expected, Daniel was on the phone, with his Gucci loafers propped on his desk. Today he was wearing casual jeans and a white shirt, and he looked like my most harmless preppy college lecturer. Or rather like a $20 million actor playing the part of my most harmless preppy college lecturer. He smiled welcomingly and motioned for me to take a seat. I sat down in one of the enormous leather chairs and fell backward. Daniel hung up the phone and turned all his perfectly capped teeth to face me.

"Hi, Elizabeth. Thanks for coming up to see me." He winked in an avuncular fashion.

"No problem, thanks for asking me." I was an idiot already.

"Ryan, why doesn't Elizabeth have a drink?"

"Well, I thought she was only staying for a few minutes, and—"

"I don't pay you to think, Ryan. I pay you to do what I tell you to do and to never make judgments as to the importance of my guests. Ask her what she'd like to drink. *Now*."

I was trying at that very moment to *become* the library chair.

"Elizabeth. Would you like a cold beverage?" Ryan was grinding his teeth while desperately attempting to smile. In order to follow through with my latest attempts at producorial assertiveness, I needed to think up a drink that would make Ryan perform back flips. Cocktail names from my college days whizzed through my head—Fuzzy Navel, Alabama Slammer, or, more appropriately, a Slow Screw. But I obviously didn't have the vile edge required.

"A Diet Coke would be fine, Ryan." I could see the wet bar from here. "I can get it myself." I half stood up, but Daniel interrupted.

"Sit down, Elizabeth. That's Ryan's job, not yours. For however long you visit my office. So just relax."

I was obviously a pawn in a rather twisted power play between boss and assistant. No wonder Ryan was such an evil warped toad.

"So, Elizabeth, we met in D.C., right, at a fund-raiser, and you were wearing that very pretty floral dress?" I couldn't believe he remembered. "God is in the details," my mother used to say.

"What a great memory." I smiled.

"A prerequisite in this business," Daniel informed me. "So you can remember who fucked you over in order to screw them back twice as hard when you get the chance." He laughed, and I didn't know whether to laugh or to cry. He wasn't seeming so fuzzy after all. "Are you happy in Los Angeles, Elizabeth? Was my advice to switch from politics to film correct?"

"Well, it's certainly been an education. I thought politicians were hard to keep track of." I was starting to feel more comfortable with Ryan gone from the room.

"Really?" Daniel's face lit up. "I can imagine that Scott's probably a handful. Is he in the office a lot?"

Oh, hell, I'd opened up that door by accident, and now I didn't know how to close it without pissing Daniel off.

"He keeps regular office hours. Just like everyone else, I guess."

"Then why did you say he was hard to keep track of?" Daniel laughed too loudly for it to be funny. He looked like a movie villain glinting with evil intent.

"I meant the business was hard to keep track of. It's constantly changing, and there are so many people involved in every deal." That seemed like an appropriately naïve answer and a good segue into my producing prospects. But Daniel wasn't finished with me.

"I've been a little worried about Scott lately. I ran into his wife, Mia, at a City of Hope fund-raiser, and she seemed at the end of her tether, you know? She sat me down for about twenty minutes and told me how restless Scott was and how maybe he was doing too many drugs. Have you noticed anything, Lizzie? Don't worry, by the way, you can speak freely. It's all in Scott's best interests."

Yeah, right, I wasn't born yesterday, buddy, whipped through my mind, but instead I tried on a concerned, thoughtful look for size. With a whisper of stupidity for good measure. "Hmm," I said. "Well . . ."

As I hammed up my thoughtful consideration Ryan pushed open the oak door of the office with my Diet Coke on a tray. I never thought that I'd be so relieved to see him. He banged the large, frosty glass down on the table in front of me. I was parched but also too paranoid that Ryan had peed in my drink to risk taking a sip.

"Ryan, could you try to be less of an oaf? *Set* the glass down on the table—don't throw it. Would you try that again, please?"

I couldn't believe what I was hearing. Ryan had to pick up the glass and put it in front of me gently. I had a wave of sympathy for him. I felt like I should call in Human Rights Watch, or at the very least the SPCA. This was sheer cruelty. But then perhaps that's why they got along so well. I'd started to notice in this business that like attracted like. I'd never heard a single kind story about Ryan, so perhaps he was a twisted fuck before he ever arrived at The Agency. I just hoped that Victoria hadn't become my mentor because she had thought that we were similar.

Ryan left the room, and I decided to steer the conversation in a direction I was more comfortable with.

"Daniel, this script I've agreed to produce is called *Sex Addicts in Love*. The writer/director, Jason Blum, is incredibly talented. I know we can raise the money if we can just get access to the right people. I've had a budget done, and we could do it for four million."

"Have you talked to Scott about this? Have you shown him the script?" Oh, no, he was insidiously accusing me of disloyalty, and he was right.

"Well, not yet. I just ran into you in the elevator and you were so nice and offered to help and . . ."

Daniel's grin was like a cup of hot chocolate after a sleigh ride. "Elizabeth, relax. I'm not criticizing you. I'm glad you came to me first. I take that as a compliment. Anyway, I *did* hire you, so ultimately you answer to me." Okay, I could breathe easy again.

But could I? What did that last sentence mean? Daniel had tried to fire me once, and Scott had saved me. Who was I ultimately answerable to? It wasn't the kind of thing that HR could tell you.

"So tell me what a typical day is like for you as an assistant." Daniel was getting into his stride.

"It's pretty standard, really, Daniel." I smiled innocently. Well, that would be minus the drugs, women, booze, and Lara missing in action, I suppose. "Our office probably runs just like yours. Scott's at meetings all the time." I began to expand on how busy Scott was trying to sign this new director and chasing his actresses and getting points for Justin on his first film. Then I realized that I was probably getting a little too comfortable. It was so warm and dark in Daniel's office. Like a library in a stately home, and I was being lulled into divulging way too much. Daniel's incessant questioning was subtle, but it always steered back to Scott and the implication that he was incompetent and irresponsible. In short, Daniel had an agenda, and it had nothing to do with me or the script.

"Does he have meetings with Katherine Watson?" I wondered if *he* thought they were having an affair, too. I'd never mentioned the subject again to Lara, but Katherine seemed to be calling Scott a lot these days, and always directly, without her assistant on the line.

"Not that *I've* ever scheduled," I said truthfully.

He glanced at his watch, which seemed to signal the end of our meeting.

"Elizabeth, why don't you leave your script with Ryan, and I'll take a look. It was great seeing you, and I'm really glad we have you at The Agency. I think you'll make a great addition. Let's meet again soon and have another one of these very informative chats. I love to know what's happening at all times with my employees," he said. My grin was plastered to my face like a bug on a windshield.

"Great, Daniel, thanks for your time." Had I been informative? I certainly hadn't intended to be. And did I really have to leave Jason's script with Ryan? I wasn't sure that I wanted to anymore. I pulled the script out of my bag and gazed at it lovingly. Could I really leave it in the hands of Ryan the cannibal? But I guessed that it would cross his path one way or another. "Thanks so much. Again. See you soon."

I walked backward out of the office in ridiculous deference. Thankfully, Ryan wasn't at his desk so I just smiled at Assistants Two, Three, and Four, dropped the script on the friendliest girl's desk, and darted for the stairway. I just couldn't handle running into Ryan in the elevator—my nerves were already too shot.

Before heading back to my office, I raced down to my car to grab the blouse I kept there in case of emergencies. I was positively damp with anxiety after that audience with Daniel. Plus, I needed a few minutes to collect my thoughts. I wondered whether Daniel really did have Scott's best interests at heart, as he claimed to. I knew that Scott had worked under Daniel for years, and he had been the one to promote him exponentially to his current esteemed position. I collected my shirt from the trunk and slammed it shut before making my way back to the elevator. Could I really have been in this business so long already that I could only see a friendly helping hand in a suspicious light? All I did know was that my loyalties were with Scott. Something about all that slithering on the fourth floor just didn't sit well with me. Daniel and Ryan, the organ-grinder and the monkey. All that easy chatter and fake homeliness. It just didn't ring true.

As I was about to press the elevator button, José approached me urgently. "Lizzie: *Donde hay humo, hay calor*." That was an easy one. I'd decided that the Josés were in league to help me bone up on my Spanish. Perhaps so that I'd be better agent material, or maybe so that one day they could marry me off to one of their sons. "'Where there's smoke, there's fire,'" I translated proudly. "I remember that one from eighth grade." The Josés didn't seem overly impressed with my translation. "Be careful, little lizard," one of them said, and then they both scurried off as two guys from the Accounting Department arrived and thrust their valet tickets onto the shelf of the booth.

I hopped into the elevator and made my way back to the sanctuary of my office. And no, the irony of my office's feeling like a haven did not escape me. I pressed the button for the first floor and wondered what it was about the Josés that made me think they had a superhighway into the heart of goings-on at The Agency. *Where there's smoke, there's fire* rattled around my head. Things had been strange at The Agency lately. Ryan in Scott's office, Scott's mystery meetings with Katherine, and then Daniel's sudden interest in *me,* of all people. He hadn't cared a lick about my project in the meeting. It struck me that I couldn't afford to be such an ostrich anymore, or I'd risk appearing disloyal to Scott. I decided to talk to Lara as soon as possible and try to ascertain whether I was just suffering from routine industry paranoia or whether there was genuinely some chicanery afoot. Ought I to give Scott a heads-up on what I'd observed? I suspected so and ditched my plans to change into my clean shirt and hared back to my office.

I arrived out of breath, only to find Lara missing from her desk and Scott's door closed to the world. I had to tell him now, before I lost the nerve, so I went straight to his office and threw open the door dramatically. He didn't have any appointments scheduled, so he was probably just watching a game or a movie. What greeted me was not a usual sight. I blinked a few times in an attempt to identify the clean-shaven, fragrant, gray-suited man at Scott's desk. Between this morning and now, he had transformed himself from a dodgy *Jackass* extra into a sharply attired partner of The Agency. Scott looked up expectantly with a calm smile on his face.

"Do you have a wedding this afternoon?" I asked.

Scott smiled, a bit embarrassed. Then motioned to Katherine, sitting on the sofa to his right. "Lizzie, you know Katherine Watson, head of the Lit Department."

I was even more astonished when I saw that Scott had cleaned himself up for the irresistible Mrs. Watson. It was really sweet in a pathetic sort of way. Thank God I hadn't walked in on anything illicit. They were both fully clothed, and Katherine seemed perfectly in control and a good ten feet away from Scott. I stood there like a bronzed Mercury with my mouth open.

"Lizzie, is there something I can help you with?" Scott prompted me.

"Yeah. I just wanted to talk to you about something." They both looked at me expectantly. "It was kind of private, but it can wait." Now it was Katherine's turn to raise an eyebrow. I turned on my heels to leave, but she stood up quickly, straightening her skirt.

"Lizzie, stay. Please. We're finished here anyway. It was nice meeting you, and, Scott, I'll let you know." Know what? I wondered. Maybe what hotel they'd meet in next. Or if she was planning to leave her perfect husband, or what position she favored, or . . .

"Lizzie, what's up?" Scott stared at me patiently as I struggled to shift my mind back to the subject at hand.

"I just had a meeting with Daniel. I thought it was going to be about this project I'm trying to produce, but . . ."

"What project?" Scott looked surprised. "Why didn't you come to me?"

"Well, it's just this amazing script I'm trying to produce that a friend of mine wrote." I stopped speaking because Scott was looking disconcerted. Or was that hurt in his eyes?

"You had a project that you loved and didn't bring it to me first?" he asked. I looked at him and was flooded with guilt. And regret.

"Scott, really, I didn't mean to . . . it's just that . . ." Then the story spilled from my mouth like a newly discovered geyser, in one serious run-on sentence. "I met Daniel in the elevator, and he asked how I was doing and if I liked working for you, and before I knew what I was saying, I'd told him about the project, and then he asked me to meet with him in his office about it, and I never thought he'd call, but then his assistant called to set up the meeting, and then he asked me questions about you, and I wished the entire time that I'd never even been polite and said hello in the elevator in the first place."

"Okay, Lizzie-o, take a seat," Scott said, and guided me onto his sofa. Then he sat down opposite me in an armchair. "Let's take this from the top. And a little more calmly this time."

"Thank you," I said, and inhaled.

"So you didn't *not* bring me the project because you thought I was shit at my job?" Scott asked.

Oh, God, typical. Why was it that Scott's insecurity was the primary thing to be addressed here when we had much more important things to worry about? Like Daniel. Like subterfuge. Like dark doings.

"Of course not. I think you're brilliant at what you do. I just thought you were too busy, and actors seem to be your thing more than writers. Also, I didn't want to waste your time. You can read the script if you want to. I have it in my desk drawer." I motioned behind me to where my desk was. "Anyway, Scott, you don't read." There, I'd said it. I had to give the guy coverage of coverage. And then he made me read it out to him. Or pitch it if it wasn't action or comedy.

Thankfully, Scott dissolved into laughter. "You're right, I'm totally swamped, and I don't read. But let me know if you need any casting ideas. Now, what did Daniel want to know?"

I proceeded to fill him in on the Daniel grilling. Scott took it all in stride and then asked me only one question.

"Lizzie, are you with me?"

"What, here? Now?" I asked. Was Scott being existential?

"No, I mean you're either with me or against me. Not that there's anything going on. But I just need to know."

"I'm with you, Scott. One hundred percent." It came out before I had a chance to think about the possible ramifications. I had just chained myself to this fantastic lunatic of a man, and now all I could do was hope and pray that he wasn't the *Titanic*.

20

I wish I was going someplace. I wish you were going someplace. We could go together.

—Mary Murphy as Kathie Bleeker
The Wild One

My mother believes that traveling in private airplanes is God's way of telling you that you have too much money. Every time she hears on the news of one crashing, she shakes her head gravely with an I-told-you-so sigh. She's an atheist, too, so I'm not sure where that leaves her theory, but I suspect that statistics probably bear her out. Anyway, I pushed all this to the back of my mind as I wheeled my suitcase full of sweaters and scarves and warm things behind me through the foyer of The Agency one rainy January morning. I had been invited to the Sundance Film Festival with Scott, and since it was the first business trip of my entire life, and my first time in a private plane, I was completely psyched.

Originally Lara was supposed to accompany Scott—to go along and answer his cell phone and make sure he got to meetings on time and go to the movies that he couldn't see because of his busy meet-and-greet and party schedule. But Lara's parents had chosen that weekend to visit from Philadelphia, and so she had to stay in town. Her loss was my gain, and fortunately it happened just when I most needed it. Everyone had told me that the industry basically went into hibernation from Thanksgiving through New Year's, but I hadn't really believed that life could be quite so unequivocally sleepy. Scott hadn't done a single deal throughout December, Lara spent her days out of the office meeting with literary agents, and even Victoria seemed to have people to buy Christmas presents for. So apart from a very busy afternoon when I'd had to try to ascertain whether to send Hanukkah cards or Christmas cards to Scott's clients, basically making sure that those who were supposed to get Baby Jesus in a crib didn't get a menorah card and vice versa, life had been fairly unstimulating.

Not a single agent had responded to *Sex Addicts in Love,* and I had even sent it beyond The Agency doors to people I vaguely knew at CAA, William Morris, and Endeavor. Plus, I had never heard another peep from Daniel about it. In fact, Daniel had been eerily quiet lately. I hadn't seen him and Scott slap each other's backs for as long as I could remember. Even Ryan seemed to have crawled back under his stone. And to make the boringness even more deadly, I had heard from Talitha that my one beacon of romantic light, Luke Lloyd, was on location in Morocco. So I couldn't even gaze at him in the V Pages and wonder who his gorgeous date might have been at this premiere or that dog dance. Instead I envisaged him having an affair with the leading lady of his picture and imagined them secreted away in some Moorish palace feeding one another fresh figs and making love in the hot afternoons.

When close of business finally arrived, I logged off my computer, then dashed over to the Coffee Bean to say au revoir to Jason and pick up a revised draft of *Sex Addicts*. While we hadn't managed to get anyone to read it yet, we were very far from giving up on the project and had spent countless weekends doing read-throughs of the script. I'd overcome my mortification at acting and played the parts of various hookers, mothers, and girlfriends, while Jason had sunk himself into the male roles with the conviction of a seasoned thespian. Whenever our characters were supposed to kiss, we had simply smiled shyly at one another and then skipped to the next scene. Still, though, we remained the unattached stalwarts in one another's lives, even though any sexual chemistry had been laid to rest long ago. We went to weekend matinees together, made roast-chicken suppers at my apartment when one of us was feeling homesick, and though I didn't hike with him ever again, we did sometimes stroll along the beach together. To all intents and purposes, we were a couple. I just never got close enough to feel the scratch of his yak-hair sweaters.

"Have fun, Lizzie," he said as I packed the newly polished manuscript into my bag and made my way toward the door.

"I wish I could put you in my luggage, and then we could run around Sundance together and get some funding for this puppy," I said, patting the bulge of the screenplay in my purse.

"Well, just do what you can." Jason waved me off. "And if you need to take one for the team, then make sure you do."

I shot him an evil stare and then laughed. "Oh, okay, then. I'll do whatever it takes."

Our poor movie did seem to be languishing in the doldrums of late. I'd been told that the spring was going to be the time to sell it, though, and get it up and running, so all hope was not lost. I was more convinced than ever that this was a work of genius, and I'd even come around to appreciating Jason's scratchy directorial efforts, since I'd become a little more educated in cinema through innumerable bleak afternoons watching Elia Kazan and Preston Sturges, not to mention a slew of European films that had previously passed me by as subtitled nightmares for tedious undergraduates. So the deal was that Sundance might just present Jason and me with an opportunity to get *Sex Addicts* off the ground finally, and I was planning to pitch it to anyone who'd listen.

An hour and a half later, Scott and I emerged from our limo at LAX. It was raining, and our driver was holding up a giant umbrella to shield us from the evening downpour. I looked up, and there, in front of us, was my first Gulfstream on the small airstrip. The steps were down, and a pretty flight attendant was standing at the door smiling at us. I was about to go to the trunk of the car to help pull out my luggage, but instead the driver ushered me over to a red carpet that was rolled out on the tarmac leading to the plane. I wanted to laugh, to shove Scott in the rib cage and tell him how insane the carpet was, but he didn't seem to notice. He was on his cell phone to Katherine Watson, talking attorneys in hushed tones. Besides which, where Scott was concerned, the Gulfstream was like catching a Greyhound bus, just without the irritation of having to smell the cheeseburger being munched noisily by the guy across the aisle.

"Welcome aboard our flight today to Salt Lake City." A flight attendant smiled at Scott, who handed her his coat as he continued talking to Katherine.

"We're covered from all angles. I have fifteen lawyers working on the documentation, and even if he wanted to sue our asses, the board will back us up." Scott marched toward the interior of the plane. I followed, smiling at the pilot, the five flight attendants, and the fact that I was about to enter the most exclusive echelon of travel known to man.

"Excuse me, but which one is my seat?" I asked nonchalantly, as though I did this all the time.

"Oh, you can sit anywhere you like on this plane, Miss." The flight attendant smiled, letting me know that she was well aware that this was my first, and probably my last, trip on a private plane.

"Of course." I blushed and looked around the plane. Scott had made his way to one of the seats at the back, like the naughtiest boy in school that he was, and the rest of the seats were free. I slung my purse over my shoulder and made my way to a plush brown sofa beside the window. Then I picked up the matching cashmere blanket and settled myself into the seat. Who cared if the cabin crew thought I was a confirmed coach passenger? I was going to Sundance, it was going to be freezing cold, I was going to be able to wear my favorite Aran sweater for the first time in a year, and I was going to have fun.

I pulled the revised draft of *Sex Addicts* out of my bag and secured my hair in a ponytail. Jason had put my name and address on the front as a contact for anyone who might like it. I only hoped that one of these days someone might actually call me back. I began to read.

INT. HARVARD AUDITORIUM—DAY

JACK stands alone at graduation and watches as his friends file by.

"Lizzie, honey, you got a spare pen?" Scott put his head over the back of my seat.

"Sure thing." I reached down and rummaged for a pen in the depths of my purse, then emerged triumphant. "Here you go."

"Thanks, doll." He ruffled my hair, and before he could pull his hand away, a shadow fell over the pair of us.

"Scottie, my man."

I looked up as Scott disentangled himself from my ponytail and saw the perfect frame of one Jake Hudson.

"Jake!" Scottie greeted him. "Glad you could make it, you dog."

"Yeah, well, you were right. Sundance is always full of hotties, and, hey, we like to scout for new talent, right? Thanks for the ride, buddy."

"Right on." Scott and Jake banged knuckles and laughed in their handsome, uproarious way. The flight attendants practically had orgasms.

Sundance, by the way, is an independent film festival dreamed up by Robert Redford to discover and reward young talent, and every budding film director, writer, and producer in the business makes it their business to be there. So where the young and the hip go, the older and the desperate naturally follow. Hence the proliferation of studio executives and sharky agents who think that they might be able to pick up a groovy sleeper movie on the cheap. They generally regret the trip, though, because the good movies aren't so inexpensive anymore. They also tend to break legs and humiliate themselves on snowboards, which they can't resist because they think that since their emotional life is that of a thirteen-year-old, their sporting prowess will be, too. This is generally not the case.

I could see that Jake had paid a special visit to Prada Sport, and I couldn't quite decide whether rabbit fur around his ski jacket's collar made him look like a god or a geek. Either way I was glad that some of his luster seemed to have worn off a little. Thanks to my Luke Lloyd displacement activity.

"And this is . . . ?" Jake, who was large enough to make the plane feel small, pursed his lips thoughtfully as he looked down on me.

"Lizzie," Scott said, thudding back into his seat.

"Lizzie. I'm Jake." He held out his hand, and I didn't flinch when I looked him in the eye and said, "Pleased to meet you."

And for all he knew, it could have been the first time.

"Do you mind if I sit here?" he said as he dropped onto the sofa opposite me.

"Not at all." I lowered my eyes back down to my page. I actually found it remarkably easy not to shake in his presence these days. I think it was because I'd done so much aversion therapy on myself, along the lines of:

Jake Hudson is a bad man
Jake Hudson is a bad man
Jake Hudson is a bad man

So now my emotional hardwiring was able to see, think, dream about him without any ill effects at all. What I couldn't escape was the fact that he was quite simply the most delectable eye candy you have ever seen, and so I developed a very antisocial squint in my right eye trying to look at him over the top of *Sex Addicts in Love*.

"So you're with Scott," he said, leaning in toward me after about ten minutes, once he'd settled onto his sofa and strapped in. And after he'd finished flirting with the flight attendant.

"Well, no, actually I'm his . . ." I was fully intending to be honest about my status as second slave to Scott, but he interrupted me.

"Darling, we're both well aware that you're not the boy's wife."

"I know that I'm not his wife, but neither am I his—"

"It's fine." He reached over and put a hand on my knee. My naked-but-for-a-few-denier-of-sheer-pantyhose knee. He eased a thumb into one of the grooves. I twitched out of his way. "I understand."

"Great."

I tucked my knees into the brown suede of the sofa and resumed my reading, and, thankfully, a moment later the plane took off. I cast a look behind me outside the window and watched the haze of rain over the ocean as we soared. I felt elated. I was on a private jet, and sitting opposite me was the most attractive man in Hollywood. Who cared if I hated him? I could look, couldn't I? I wondered whether when I was forty I'd look back on this dot on the graph of my life as one of the highest points or whether it would simply be the start of a charmed, successful future. I crossed my fingers for the latter but hoped I'd never become too cynical to appreciate it. Then I remembered that nobody had called back about *Sex Addicts* and that I was a second assistant, so I probably shouldn't get too far ahead of myself.

"Would you like some lobster salad, Miss?" Above me a flight attendant was pushing a trolley of delicious dishes. "Or perhaps a cheese plate?"

"I'd love a lobster salad." I moved my script to one side so that she could put the food down. "Oh, and a cheese plate, too, if that's okay."

"Wine or champagne?"

"Red wine would be lovely." I was planning on eating and then falling asleep for the rest of the flight . . . well, I had been until Himself had appeared. Now I might be afraid to fall asleep for fear of sagging chins and drooling head lolling.

"Oh, I love a girl with an appetite." Jake had settled himself back into his seat with a Scotch on the rocks and was looking at me as if *I* were the lobster salad.

"Got to keep up my strength," I said mindlessly.

"Oh, yes, I'll bet. I hear Scottie can go for hours." He winked. I shivered. Ugh, the idea of having sex with Scott was worse than incest.

"Actually, Scott's my—" I began again, attempting to set the record straight.

"Here's the low-carb meal you ordered, sir." The flight attendant shimmied down the aisle and presented Jake with his plate of lettuce with a flourish.

"Great, thanks." He beamed at her. Not in the least embarrassed about the fact that he was on a diet. Now, don't get me wrong, I'm not exactly prejudiced about men who take care of themselves, but there always strikes me as something wholly unmasculine about a man who's a shameless proponent of Dr. Atkins. Or any regime that suggests he thinks only of looking good. I'd prefer a more corpulent man who has read Proust any day of the week. Except perhaps today. Because despite the low-carb stuff, I was looking at Jake right now and thinking how unutterably fantastic it would be to kiss him, just once.

"So, darling, where are you staying in Sundance?" He devoured a lettuce leaf and gazed intently at me.

"To be honest, I'm not really sure, I guess in a condo—"

"With Scott?"

"Well, probably."

"But you might be able to sneak away, right?" he asked sotto voce as Scott snored loudly on the seat behind us.

"Sneak?" I still wasn't sure whether he was coming on to me or whether he was trying to ascertain whether I'd be available to purchase Marlboro Reds and cook him bacon and eggs in the middle of the night.

"Come on, baby. I think you're gorgeous," he said. And for a second I nearly lost my head. The flight attendant was standing at attention nearby and looking at me as if I were the luckiest girl on earth. "You know you want to." He winked, and déjà vu hit me like a hockey puck on the temple. The guy had kissed me and not remembered me. Come on, Lizzie, that's pretty insulting, I thought. And, strangely, at that very same moment I had a flash of something else, of something that Lara had once said in her inimitably scornful way: *There's no better buzz than fucking the girlfriend of someone more powerful than yourself.* Instantly I realized what Jake's game was. He thought that I was Scott's girlfriend, so he wanted to bed me.

"Actually, I'm not sure that I do want to." I smiled politely and took a mouthful of lobster salad. Oh, that was manna from heaven for him. A refusal. He was like Hannibal Lecter—I swear he made that funny lip-smacking noise. A slow grin crept across his face. "Mile-High Club?" He winked.

"What about it?"

"No, *how* about it?"

"How about not?" I took an overambitious slug of wine and nearly choked, but he didn't notice my bulging look.

"Have you ever tried it?"

"To be honest"—I was fortified by the gallop of the pinot noir cavalry to my head—"I've always thought that fucking in a sink under fluorescent lights with your foot on a toilet was a pretty unsexy notion."

"You've never done it with me, though. And I can arrange for the lights to be dimmed. If you're shy."

"I'm not shy, I'm just not interested. Sorry," I said, and wished that I'd been a little kinder in my rebuff. Not that he deserved my kindness, just that I felt bad. But, clearly, heaven knows no pleasure like a man scorned. Because right now Jake Hudson was in clover. It was obvious that nobody had turned him down since the day he had his braces removed in high school.

"You can't turn me down, Lizzie."

"Hmmm. I suspect that I can. And that you'd rather like it."

"No."

"Oh, yes." I ate my last piece of lobster and reclined into the sofa with a satisfied sigh. "I think you do."

"You're so smart. You have no idea what a turn-on that is and you're beautiful to boot. Please agree to have a date with me."

"Where, in the bathroom?"

"In Los Angeles. How about when we get back? If you're spoken for at Sundance." As he said this, he pulled his navy blue sweater over his head, and it left his hair tousled like the billboard again.

And much as I wanted to keep on saying no, so that he'd keep on wanting me, I just desperately wanted to kiss him again. To feel his thighs beneath his jeans. To taste the whiskey on his breath.

"I'll tell you what," I said, lifting my lashes to meet his eyes with possibly the most perfect timing of my life. (Well, apart from the occasion I'd made the split-second decision to go into a store to buy some Hubba Bubba just as a brick crashed fourteen stories down onto the sidewalk where'd I'd been standing.)

"What?" He leaned forward with a look of undiluted excitement. "Tell me."

"If you can remember my name by the time we get back to Los Angeles, you can take me to dinner."

"I can?"

"Maybe," I said, and flicked the button next to me to dim my reading light. I don't think I'd ever been so cool in my entire life. And I knew that I couldn't keep it up, so I'd have to go to sleep. Well, actually, I couldn't go to sleep, because that would shatter the illusion. So what I really had to do was to spend the next fifty minutes pouting so that I'd look beautiful in repose, and digging my fingernails into my palms in order not to drop off to sleep and ruin everything.

21

Haven't you bothered me enough, you big banana-head?

—Marilyn Monroe as Angela Phinlay
The Asphalt Jungle

"Scott, they've only made up one bed."

Me and my omnipresent wheelie suitcase stopped in our tracks. I examined the blister on my hand. After the driver had dropped us on the doorstep of the Wildflower Mountain Home, where we were staying, I had lugged my suitcase up three levels and around four bedrooms—each with a bare, unfriendly mattress—before I'd found "our" room.

"Wassup?" Scott tossed his bag onto the bed and failed to notice my throbbing palms. Just as he'd failed to notice how my suitcase kept lashing out and beating me up as we made our way through the house—up stairways, through doorways, around tables. Well, if he had noticed, he hadn't thought to intervene.

"Was Lara going to stay here with you, or did she have separate accommodations booked?" I asked as I looked longingly at the plump duvet, which had crunched in a finest-Siberian-goosedown way when Scott's bag had landed on it.

"Lara?" Scott took off his jacket and walked into the bathroom. "Oh, yeah, well, I guess she just forgot to tell them to make up an extra bed or something for her." I watched as he flung his shoes across the en suite bathroom and then leaned over to put the plug into the bathtub. Then he cranked up the taps, and steam began to fill the room. "Hey, you got any woman's shit to put in my bath?"

"Woman's shit?" I was tired, and it was clear that Scott was not about to go all gentlemanly and offer up his luxury quarters to freezing-cold me.

"Bubble bath."

"Somewhere in here." I sat on my suitcase and contemplated whether I should just push it back down the stairs or whether I could be bothered to spare the décor by shuffling down one step at a time, behind the beast, as though it were a rodeo horse.

"Great. I don't use sulfates, though. They dry out your skin. Hasn't got sulfates, has it?" I looked at him incredulously and understood fully why Mia felt entitled to rape his bank account on a daily basis. Hell, I hadn't even spent one night under the same roof as Scott and I felt a twenty-two-carat tantrum coming on.

"You're worried about dry skin?" I asked as he hunted through his bag for his toothbrush.

"It gets itchy when it's dry."

"Doesn't cocaine have the same effect?"

"No, cocaine makes you high."

"I mean, doesn't it make your skin itch? And also doesn't it make you look like shit?" I wanted that bed. So much, it wasn't decent. I had been up since 5:00 A.M. because I'd had to make sure that Scott's Sundance schedule was idiotproof and laminated and that his cell phones were charged, and then I'd had to go to Rexall over my lunch break and buy padlocks for all his drawers and filing cabinets, and then I spent the afternoon erasing all his e-mails because he couldn't do it himself, due to the fact that the ping sound gave him preepileptic sensations. Apparently. Though why he wanted his e-mails deleted and his drawers bolted shut was beyond me. I suspected it was early-stage paranoia, but Lara had seemed to think it was perfectly reasonable when I'd tentatively mentioned how peculiar I thought it was. "Scott's instincts are usually pretty sound" was all she'd said. Then she'd resumed Chapter 19 of her novel.

It was a shame that his manners weren't as sound as his instincts. Because I had to watch as he hummed himself into his steaming bath, complained about my inability to produce sulfate-free products, and then asked me if I'd mind fetching him a whiskey. He'd seen a bottle of Jack in the game room on the first floor when we came in, and there'd probably be ice in the freezer, he guessed. I strapped my suitcase to my hand and heaved it out of Scott's room onto the cold landing, leaving behind the dazzling floor-to-ceiling views of the snowy mountains from his picture window.

"Oh, and, hey, can you get me Lara on the cell phone? There's something I need to ask her."

"Scott, her parents are in town," I yelled back from halfway down the steep stairs where I was hanging on to my bronco case for dear life. "Can't *I* help?" I had visions of Lara's elderly parents imagining that she was a call girl if her "boss" started phoning her in the middle of the night. I know that my mother would jump to that conclusion under the same circumstances.

"No, you can't help. So get her on."

"It's late, Scott."

"Lizzie." That was the warning tone, and I couldn't ignore it.

"Okay, let me just get down the stairs and I'll bring in the phone with the Jack Daniel's, okay?" I took his silence for approval and bumped down the remaining six steps to the second floor, where I'd spied a relatively cozy-looking bedroom, without bed linen but with its own stone fireplace.

As I lay in bed later, wrapped in the blankets that I'd found inside an ottoman, I listened to a distant owl. It had been so long since I'd seen snow, and even longer since I'd been in the countryside, that I actually found it difficult to drop off to sleep without the constant sound of sirens and the backfiring of engines outside. But this was lovely. Except, I realized, for the empty expanse of bed beside me. It was one thing to sleep alone on a close, balmy California night with the sheets kicked off, but it was another entirely to be in a place of such staggeringly beautiful scenery as Park City, with the deer and the elk and mountains and forests and the moon hanging low and heavy in the inky midnight sky, and to be alone. And that night, more than any other in my life, I yearned for someone to fill the space beside me. That said, I didn't yearn enough to make me want to tiptoe up to Scott's room for a snuggle. Or even enough to make me reach for my cell phone and call Jake Hudson, who had slid his card into my hand at the airport as I was about to get into the limo with Scott. So I suppose I wasn't really that desperate at all, I reassured myself as I sank into a dribbling, lolling, unattractive, but heavenly sleep.

The film festival was a blast. At first I'd started out with every intention of seeing every minute of every movie that I was scheduled to see. But with the nod from Scott, I dropped that notion as quickly as a hot potato.

"Lizzie, don't be crazy. You don't have to sit through the whole thing, okay? Unless it's genius and you think we should sign up one of the cast or the director, don't bother." I took that as my cue to relax a little. And certainly I stopped taking my miniature Booklover's Flashlight that I'd picked up in Barnes & Noble into the screenings so that I could see my notepad. At first I'd seemed like the class creep, sitting there trying to make notes, attempting to draw parallels with Spike Jonze or Aronofsky and waiting till the last of the credits had rolled to write down any name I felt deserved honorable mention. But by the second day I'd become blasé and made the executive decision that if the film was good enough, I'd remember it.

On our first day, Scott was awake before me. He came back from his morning run with his beanie hat on, snowflakes in his hair, and his cell phone glued to his head.

"So where's my first meeting?" He stood in my bedroom doorway and didn't seem to notice that I was still dreaming of castles and princes.

"I've written it all down on the laminated sheet I left on the breakfast table last night," I croaked. I was actually quite surprised by Scott's oxymoronic existence. The health-conscious junkie. The hardworking playboy. I think that's another Los Angeles peculiarity. Certainly I came to realize in time that you always knew that you were sharing a house with a producer or an agent because you developed a secondhand brain tumor from his unstinting use of his cell phone. Morning, noon, and night. Also, they were only ever clad in exercise clothes or a white towel with bare chest displayed and they never knowingly conversed with anyone in the same house or in the same time zone. For some reason best known to God.

"Okay. So are you ever going to get up?" Scott said as he stretched out his hamstrings. "I've got a breakfast meeting in town, and unless you get in my car with me, you're going to be stuck here. And I need someone to carry all that shit around for me." That shit being a file that weighed about eight ounces.

"Good thing I've been doing all that weight training at Venice Beach, then, huh?" I said as I sat up in bed and pulled my sheet around me.

"Sure." Scott wasn't paying any attention to me as he hit redial on his phone.

"I'm up. I'm up," I promised, and waited for him to leave the room so that I could clamber naked from my bed.

"Did Lara help you with what you needed, by the way?" I called out as he moved into the hallway to get better reception. When I got her on the phone for him last night, she'd sounded amazingly unperturbed, and possibly even pleased, that her boss was calling her while she was at dinner in Chi Venice with her mom and dad. Obviously they weren't as suspicious and overbearing as my parents.

"Lara?" He clearly got whomever he was calling's voice mail, because he kicked my doorframe. "Yeah, she did help me. She sorted out what I needed."

Scott's first movie screening was in a multiplex where they gave out free popcorn and Coke. Mine was in the unheated library. Unfortunately, it was a really interesting documentary. I say "unfortunately" because I had to sit on the hardest, least ergonomic, most ass-numbing seat in the history of chairs. And I also had to sit next to a hyperscented D-girl from Warner Brothers who was trying to flirt with the guy on the death chair next to her. She kept making intellectual-sounding murmurs and stroking her own knee with more suggestiveness than would have been decent in a Dirk Diggler movie. Let alone the Sundance Library. I wondered what Robert Redford would say if he could see her. The guy she was supposed to be flirting with didn't seem to notice, I think because he'd fallen asleep during the opening sequence, where the Amish teenagers left their community and took to the open road. When Scott and I hooked up later, I told him that he ought to meet with the director, who I thought had a great eye for detail and story. She was also young and apparently cute, so he agreed, and I set up a meeting for tea the next day.

I also wondered whether I'd run into Jake Hudson on my travels. It was pretty much inevitable, I thought as I sat alone in the Bluebird

Café writing up my notes and taking smaller-than-usual bites of my bagel in case he, or anyone else, should walk in and require me to say hello. I read the Sundance Specials in the trades, and I boned up on who was hot, who was buying what, and which stars were in town. If Scott missed a single person or event because I'd failed to alert him, then I'd be in serious trouble.

"Oh, hey, how's it going?"

It was Courtney. She looked like an escapee from *Doctor Zhivago,* with bunny fur draped around her face and her hands tucked into a white muff.

"Courtney, I'd forgotten that you were coming."

Actually, I hadn't, and she'd given me her cell-phone number several times before we left the office and told me that she'd definitely get me into this party that Harvey Weinstein was throwing at his house tonight. But I just knew that it would involve lying and humiliation to get beyond the door, and I wasn't sure that I'd have anything to share with Harvey if I did meet him, so I'd sort of forgotten to call Courtney. Besides which, I saw her every single minute of the day back at The Agency, so three days apart weren't going to wreck our beautiful friendship.

"Yeah, I'm here with Mike." Mike was now doing public again. His hair had grown in beautifully after Rogaine, but he was so thrilled to have it that he insisted on wearing it long, like a bad eighties rocker. Courtney sat down at my table. "Though I have got to say that the talent is so lame this year. All the movies blow."

"All of them?"

"So I hear." She opened my Fresh Samantha juice and helped herself. I wasn't sure if Courtney had ever seen a movie with a budget of less than $60 million anyway, so Sundance was hardly going to float her boat. She was, though, all about the scene. "So Harvey's party is tonight. You want to come?" Courtney had never ever been so friendly to me, and I knew that it was just because she didn't have anyone else to hang with.

"I'm not quite sure what Scott's schedule is and I haven't got an invite. I hear they're like gold dust."

This was actually true. The Sundance party circuit was reputedly even more fearsome than L.A.'s. On my way in from the airport with

Scott last night, our car had driven down Main Street, and I'd gotten a flash of the hellaciousness of it all. There was a private party in every restaurant, and standing outside each one were bouncers and publicists with lists and traffic jams of 4x4 limos, so beloved of celebrities and hot young directors. Scott had told me that no bastard got into any gig worth going to in this place without a bracelet. And that was only the studio parties. The more exclusive ones, like Redford's and the Miramax party, were held in condos or private homes. It would take me at least one Academy Award or a wedding ring from Mr. Weinstein himself to get into either of those parties.

"Scott's going to be there anyway, and I'll get you in. I know the bouncer."

"Okay, sure. Thanks." Well, that seemed to solve that. Even though I didn't especially want to gain entrance through the kitchen window, I knew that there was no getting out of it. And I knew that if I turned up there, I'd run into Scott, who would know that I'd crashed the party. Then I'd seem kind of cheap and unprofessional. But I figured that ultimately he'd be more forgiving of my transgression than Courtney would if I didn't go. "What time?" I surrendered.

"Six-thirty. I'll swing by and pick you up. And I'm so glad that you came instead of Lara. She's always so uptight about this kind of thing. She's afraid that if Daniel catches her gate-crashing, she'll lose her job."

"Is Daniel going to be there?"

"*Everyone's* going to be there," she said, and took an enormous bite of my peanut butter cookie.

Oh, the joys of sharing a house with Scott Wagner! While he was still in town in a meeting with the actor from a movie he'd seen this morning, I was in his bathroom with his products. I had put on an old Fiona Apple CD that I'd found in the living room, drawn a huge tub, and wrapped myself in one of the plush, warm towels from the linen closet. The kind that would never emerge from the washing machines in my basement—even if I lived to be 102 and inherited a fabric-softener fortune. Then I'd run up to his room and become a beauty bulimic. I'd rubbed two types of cleanser on my face, run downstairs and squeezed half of Kiehl's pharmacy into my bath, run back up and exfoliated, or rather grazed myself, with some sea-salt scrub, and then dashed back down, leaving a mist of vertiver in my wake. When Scott came home, I poured him a whiskey, put out a plate of cheese and crackers that I'd picked up at the market between screenings this afternoon, and swapped Fiona Apple for Van Morrison. Not that I wanted him to marry me. I just wanted him to agree to take me to the party so that I didn't have to risk certain mortification on the doorstep if I didn't get in—or being fired again by Daniel if I did.

And of course it worked. Scott was fine with my tagging along, as long as I elbowed him in the ribs occasionally and reminded him of people's names. And though I think that Courtney was pissed at me for getting legal entry to the party, the two of us did hang out together and bonded just a fraction. She had her bouncer friend slide her in, and we met in the main room of Harvey's condo. Courtney and I sipped mulled wine outside on the veranda, and after pointing out every single person in the room, giving each of them an A-, B-, or C-class status, and telling me who they'd slept with and what their particular kinks were, she regaled me with even more tales of Jake Hudson's unsavory dating history. I actually found it hard to believe that I'd ever seen Jake as a charmingly harmless man. But ignorance is bliss, and I hadn't known any better that day that we drove up the PCH, me with my bleeding wound, he with eyes only for my legs. He was phenomenally bright—that went without saying. The guy was the head of a major studio, and no matter how dismissive people were of Jake, he would never have gotten to where he was on just looks and smooth talk alone. He was a brilliant businessman and an irresistible lover. He just happened to be afflicted with satyriasis, which was becoming more apparent with every passing moment.

"I just hope the man-whore uses a condom while he's sharing himself with the whole town," Courtney said as she scoured the room over my shoulder for people to bitch about.

"Well, I guess at least he's honest about having a good time," I said. "Can't do too much harm that way, can it?"

"Oh, yes it can," she spit as she picked a cinnamon stick from her glass. "He really fucked up last summer."

It turned out that one weekend in July, Jake had actually gotten married to some really famous pop star one weekend in Tijuana. Sometime after their third pitcher of margaritas. Courtney barely dipped her voice as she told me the story. In fact, she may even have gotten louder.

"They were both there for some cheesy freebie thrown by one of the studios, and they got totally smashed and fooled around and then went and got married the next day. But the marriage only lasted a weekend. They both got back on Monday morning, and she decided that it'd been a huge mistake and they had to get a divorce. Before anyone found out."

"You're kidding?" I said. "But she's gorgeous. Shouldn't he have stayed married to her just for the kudos? Plus, I read in *People* that she buys cars and boats for her boyfriends all the time."

"No way, she didn't want to be married to someone who wasn't famous. Or a busboy. She only does the two, no middle ground. Plus, she's a total thug." Courtney tossed a cigarette butt over the edge of the balcony where we were standing, and it drifted down into the snow.

"Like how?"

"Oh, she has all these bodyguards and gangster connections. She told him that if he tried to sell his story or get his hands on any of her money, she'd get someone to take him out with a lead pipe and ski mask."

"But she's so sweet. She has such amazing skin." I thought of the videos I'd seen of her on MTV.

"If word ever got out that she'd gotten drunk and got married, it'd have ruined her rep with the preteens. To her it would have been worth breaking his kneecaps for that."

"Poor Jake." I almost felt sorry for him.

"Anyway, it's a total secret, so don't breathe a word," Courtney broadcast to the whole party.

"Don't breathe a word about what?" Jake Hudson appeared beside me holding his drink. Of course he was going to be at this party—he was Mr. Fast Pass. Access All Areas. And, as I was about to find out, when he wanted something—i.e., his friend's girl—he was also Mr. Take No Prisoners.

"Holy shit." Courtney burned her finger on her lighter. She might have acted as if she knew everyone in the room, but the truth was she got all her so-called information from IFILMpro. So in the presence of actual powerful people, she became unsteady on her feet.

"Were you talking about me?" Jake's chest puffed out like a pigeon's.

"Actually, we were discussing a movie we went to see this afternoon," I managed.

"How are you, darling?" Jake moved in and gave me a kiss on the cheek. Courtney could hardly conceal how blown away she was.

"Jake, this is Courtney," I said. "And actually I have to go and talk to Scott, if you'll excuse me."

I was about to edge away from Jake, because really I hadn't a clue what to say to him anymore. I couldn't discuss movie stars, because he's slept with all the women and the men were his best buddies. I couldn't discuss movies, because that was about as interesting as discussing your hemorrhoids. And I was afraid that if I brought up politics, he'd suddenly have a eureka moment and realize that he had been here before. Then he'd lose interest in hunting me down like one of the Vegas Bambis, and, to be honest, I was quite enjoying the pathetic interest he was showing in me, even if only because he couldn't remember that he'd actually paint-balled me before.

"Oh, hey, you don't get away that easily." He reached out for my arm and guided me back to his side. "Scott can come over here."

"No, really, it's fine. I just thought . . ." Shit, now my cover was definitely going to be blown. Scott would reveal that I was his assistant and not his girlfriend, and Jake would go over and flirt with Harvey's wife instead.

"Scott, my buddy. Get the hell over here!" Jake yelled, and Scott slapped the guy he was speaking to on the arm and made his excuses.

"Lizzie has something to say to you," Jake told him.

"She does?" Scott looked confused. He was probably under the impression that he was going to be asked to resolve a scintillating baseball-trivia argument.

"It's actually private," I spluttered.

"Aw, they're in love," Jake said, checking out my cleavage.

"Wassup?" Scott was looking at me expectantly. Thankfully, the room was noisy, and he hadn't heard the news that we were in love.

"Well, I was thinking that . . ." And at that moment I saw a guy behind Scott in a god-awful beige ski turtleneck, and before I could censor myself I added, "That we could go skiing tomorrow. Only I've never been, and I hear it's fun." Dolt.

"Skiing?" Scott pursed his lips, thinking hard. "Sure, why not?" Oh, God, not the response I was hoping for. I'd forgotten that Scott had the soul of a frat boy and would love anything that involved gear and hot showers with the guys afterward.

"Great. Let's all go skiing," Jake added. "I'll come pick you kids up at about seven A.M., and we'll go to Last Chance—it's a great spot up the mountain. You'll love it, Scottie, my man."

"Do you ski, Scott?" I asked, praying that he'd veto anything called Last Chance and insist that we start on the bunny slopes. Somewhere called Soft Landing. Or, even better, that we'd sit in some Alpine theme bar and laugh into our Gluwein as we watched everyone else fall over.

"Sure I do. I went to school in Boulder. So see you in the morning, man," Scott said, and then wandered off. Our three minutes in his company were obviously up.

Jake, on the other hand, had clearly had an empty-bed episode similar to mine last night, because he was determined to take me home. And the more mulled wine I had, the more I wondered if he might actually succeed.

"You see, there really aren't any women you'd want to marry in Los Angeles. I mean, it's okay for a sleazy fling, but you don't meet classy chicks." His drink was swinging precariously between his thumb and his index finger. "And you, Elizabeth, are a classy chick." Luckily for me and my weak will, Courtney chose the moment that Jake began to rest his hand on the wall behind me, hemming me in close to his body, to decide that she had a migraine and that I needed to take her home.

"I'll get you a car," Jake volunteered to Courtney, without taking his eyes off my lips.

"No, I'll take her. I can't leave her alone," I said, ducking under his arm and reappearing at Courtney's side. For once I was really grateful that she was a demanding, jealous bitch. If he said "classy chick" just one more time, I would probably have done something that I'd regret throughout the universe and into perpetuity, as a lawyer might say.

"See you in the morning, then." Jake looked pissed for a second, then he spotted across the room an alternate and very badly dressed means of filling his bed. Leaving me and Courtney to attempt the impossible—find a ride home in a town where you were about as likely to find a free taxi as you were to encounter a Nobel Prize–winner wandering down Main Street singing "Smells Like Teen Spirit."

22

Hearts will never be practical until they can be made unbreakable.

—Frank Morgan as Professor Marvel
The Wizard of Oz

"Would you like me to valet your skis for you, Miss?" A young man in overalls came over to me as I finally made it to the bottom of the slope. I had been suffering for about an hour and a half. Which had been divided equally between forty-five minutes on my butt and forty-five minutes on my knees. With the interstitial moments spent on my face.

"No, I'd like you to burn them, please," I retorted bitterly. He looked alarmed. The cold had obviously numbed his sense of humor.

"Have you finished skiing for the day or not, Miss?"

"I'm not sure yet. I'm just going to get a hot chocolate from the café, and then I'll get back to you." Then I decided to play straight and not torture him any further, poor guy. "Oh, and just for the record, how do you valet skis?"

"We take them from you, clean and wax them, and return them to you tomorrow morning." He gave me a friendly smile—he was back in his comfort zone.

"Wow. Great. I'll get back to you," I said. Then I stuck my poles in the ground and attempted to push off. Only I didn't go anywhere. The snow now appeared to be flat and not the kind that was going to propel me at 160 miles per hour into a killer pine tree. Which was a mixed blessing—for while I was now unlikely to die skiing, I might be stuck here until the spring thaw.

"Er, excuse me," I called after the ski valet. "Would you mind . . . giving me a push?" But he was parking somebody else's skis. I stabbed my poles into the ground behind me once again and thrust my body in a forward direction. To absolutely no avail. "Fuck," I said, and a tiny cloud of breath rose in front of my face. I shuffled to the side and tried to scissor my skis like Scott had shown me this morning on my abbreviated ski course—the course that had pretty much consisted of him saying, "Just avoid trees and people, and if in doubt fall down." And then Jake, whose pearl before swine had been, "Just don't break anything. I've had sex with girls in plaster before, and while it seems like it might be kind of kinky, it's just annoying after a while." If my tear ducts hadn't been frozen, I might have cried.

"You fucked a chick in a cast?" Scott was clearly impressed, and the two of them slipped onto a chairlift together, leaving me floundering like a washed-up trout on a riverbank.

I had made quite a brave go of my time on the slopes, if I do say so myself. I'd shuffled over and shimmied onto the lift and finally made it to the top of the mountain and then tumbled down. And tumbled again. And then repeated the whole chilly, chilling experience. Because, despite Scott's having rented me a very high-tech ski outfit, which was probably designed to keep germ warfare at bay, I still managed to perform such unimaginable maneuvers that I ended up with ice packed around my knees and down my front. Guess at least I'd have hot-to-trot nipples, I had thought.

But now I'd had enough of the activities corner. I had no luck with the scissoring, so I turned back around. I thought of removing my skis, but I was in the middle of a major thoroughfare, which was only marginally less busy than the Santa Monica Freeway, so I didn't think I'd try that.

"You wanted a push?" I turned around, thinking that the ski valet was dashing to my rescue at last.

"I'd love a push," I replied. But it wasn't the ski valet. It was the very same man who seemed to be making a career of getting me out of trouble—Luke Lloyd.

"You," I said accusingly.

"Hey." He smiled and sailed effortlessly around me, stopping smack at the tip of my skis as just the right amount of snow flew up behind him.

"Do you just hang around waiting for me to screw up so that you can rescue me?" I asked. I wasn't sure yet whether I was pleased to see him. Would I have preferred that he were playing Casanova in Morocco with Little Miss Harem Pants, or did I want him to witness my catastrophic ineptitude in yet another arena of life?

"I can leave, if you like." He had on a red ski hat that was less Prada Sport and more festering-in-the-back-of-the-coat-closet. But he looked fine in it. His cheeks were raw-looking, and I knew that if I touched them, they'd burn cold in that frostbitten way.

"Well, now that you're here, I suppose I wouldn't mind a push," I said grudgingly. He was just a little too cocky for me to feel grateful.

"Does that mean I get to put my hand on your bottom?" He smiled.

"Did you just turn into Jake Hudson?"

"Ha, I wish. But if that's your attitude, then I'll just be leaving." He turned deftly as if he were about to ski away. He was joking. I think. He seemed to have a sly, faintly perverse sense of humor that I didn't expect coming from a Hollywood veteran.

"No, I'm sorry. That was a terrible thing to say. I'd love a push. Truly. I *need* a push."

"Do you really think that I'm like Jake Hudson?" He turned his head to look at me, a concerned expression on his face.

"I have no idea what you're like. I don't really know you," I explained. "Listen, could you just give me a shove, please?" I said with a catch of desperation in my voice.

"If I give you a shove, can we continue this conversation in the café?" he asked teasingly.

"Yes, anything you like," I agreed. "Only please be quick because any minute now one of these skiers is going to come flying down that slope and slice me in half like it was logging season."

"Fine." He picked up the pole in his left hand and poked it in my direction. "Hold on tight."

"You're going to pull me?"

"I've been trying to do that for months," he laughed. I blushed and looked at my ski tips. "Here, catch hold."

I did. And Luke Lloyd pulled me slowly and embarrassingly in the direction of the café, like one of the two-year-olds you see on the bunny slopes.

"I think you're deliberately being slow," I said as groups of slick D-girls and young filmmakers shot by us.

"It's not as easy as you think."

"Are you saying I'm heavy?" I was tempted to let go of his pole.

"I'm saying nothing," Luke replied as I followed the back of his navy blue ski jacket. "Look, we're here now." He gave me a final tug, and we landed in front of a bench. He clicked the heels of his skis with his poles and stepped smoothly out onto the snow. Then he made his way to me and stood on my bindings.

"I guess I owe you a thank-you," I said.

"An espresso will do the job." He released me from my sports-equipment hell, and I was free to stumble around in my deadweight boots.

"It's the least I can do," I said as an avalanche of snow tumbled down my trouser leg and onto the ground between us.

"First time skiing?" He upended our skis and arranged them into a small, colorful forest of fiberglass.

"No, I was an Olympian until I lost my nerve."

He took my gloved hand and helped me up the wet wooden steps to the café. "I just wondered what the hell you were doing on a black-diamond run."

"Doing as I was told." We walked to a table and eased ourselves in. Luke took off his jacket and placed it on a radiator next to us. Then he reached out for mine. "Scott and Jake Hudson came up here, and so I had to as well. The joys of being an assistant."

"You're lucky you're alive." He glanced over the menu. "Do you want some lunch while we're here?"

"Sorry, but I'm not sure that the twenty bucks I have in my pocket will stretch that far. My wallet's in my purse, which is in a locker in the ski lodge." I winced. "But maybe we could both get a sandwich."

"Okay, my treat, then." He took in the specials board.

"But you pulled me." I smiled at him, suddenly happy that I was here. And feeling relaxed for the first time since I'd arrived at Sundance. The café was dark and cozy, and the snow down my chest was beginning to melt.

"Exactly. Which means that I have to buy you lunch." He was remarkably cute, even with his hair flattened to his head from his hat and his crazy pink cheeks.

"Here," I said, and reached over to fluff up his hair. "You looked really dorky."

"Gee, thanks," he laughed, and turned to the waitress. "Two espressos, and what're you having?" he asked in that melting southern drawl.

I shrugged. Anything. I'd have whatever was available. "Toasted ham and cheese sandwich," I suggested.

"Great. Two of those," he told the waitress, who jotted it down and walked away.

"So you think I'm cut from the same cloth as Jake Hudson?" he asked, idly moving the salt and pepper shakers around.

"I have no idea, to be honest. I was just lashing out because you always seem to catch me at the most embarrassing moments of my life. In fact, I'm really surprised you weren't there when the elastic went in my underpants on my first day of high school."

"I'm sorry that I wasn't." He raised an eyebrow. "But to set the record straight, I'm nothing like Jake Hudson."

"You're not a dissolute, evil-minded man-whore who shares himself with the whole town, then?" I asked, remembering Courtney's charming summing-up of our mutual friend.

Luke laughed loudly, then looked seriously at me. "You don't think that even slightly, do you?"

"Does it matter what I think?"

"Well, yes, actually, it does," he replied. I was surprised. Even if he was lying.

"I honestly don't know. I've only met you a handful of times, and you've always been sweet. But I haven't really had very positive experiences with men in Los Angeles. We've always had a bit of a clunky time."

"Clunky?"

"Yeah, they've all been into the usual L.A.-boy stuff—strippers, hookers, karaoke, drugs, fast cars," I explained. "All very sexy, but I'm a bit intimidated by that. Boring old me, huh?" I wasn't sure how we'd gotten onto discussing matters of my heart, and I tried to back off. "So have you seen any films you like since you got here?"

"Films?"

"It's a film festival," I informed him.

"Right. So you won't date men in the business?"

"I was very strongly advised not to." Thank heavens for Lara. Not that I'd followed her advice to the letter, exactly.

"Shame."

"Why? Do you think I'm missing out?" Our drinks arrived, and we buried our cold, red noses in the steam.

"I'm not at all like those guys." He took a sip of his espresso and looked at me over the top of the cup.

"Right." I wondered why he thought it would make any difference to me to know this. I thought that maybe he was flirting with me, but compared with sledgehammer come-ons like Jake Hudson's and Bob's, I couldn't really tell. "Well, with all due respect, Luke, you would say that, wouldn't you?" I said.

He nodded sagely. "So how did you get here, Lizzie Miller?"

"On a G4."

"No—here. Hollywood here. Here in your life?"

"Oh, here?" I said, and settled back into the soft cushion on the bench. "Do you really want to know?"

It turned out that he really did want to know. And that, surprisingly, his attention span was much longer than my gnat boss's. Or even Jake Hudson's. Or almost anyone else that I'd ever met, in fact. He wanted to know what my parents did for a living and whether I'd preferred international politics to local and if I thought that the UN should be dissolved and what I liked about my job.

"You really want to be a producer?" he finally asked as I confessed that I had a project I wanted to develop.

"I'm afraid so."

"Oh, yes, you're right to be afraid. In fact, be very afraid."

"It's quite a good project, I think. I mean, as a movie it probably wouldn't make much more than the price of a can of soda, but it's interesting. For indie material."

"So you might be showing your movie here next year?" He smiled encouragingly.

"I suppose I might." What a thought that was. How happy would Jason be?

"I'd love to look at it. The script, that is."

"Oh, it's not really ready to be seen by producers yet. I mean, we don't have representation and all, but—"

"Well, if you wanted to show me . . ." He shrugged, letting me know that the choice was mine.

"I don't really believe in mixing business with pleasure."

"And this thing we're doing here . . . it's pleasure, then?"

"Well . . . I'm not sure, but I'd hate it if you were good enough to save my life for the fifteenth time and then I made you read my script, too—that wouldn't be fair."

"Well, if you decide that this is pleasure, then don't give the script to me. But if it's business, then you must. I don't want to miss out on a potentially great piece of material."

"It's a deal," I said. Hoping that I wouldn't have to show him the script at all. Because at that moment he had his hand up his T-shirt, flapping it around so that it dried before the fire. And . . . well, he looked sexy as all hell. And right now *Sex Addicts* could wait. I wanted this to be purely pleasure.

The ironic thing is, I don't think that my time with Luke Lloyd would have been quite as amazingly pleasurable as it turned out to be if it hadn't been for Jake Hudson. But it just so happened that back on the mountain he had just finished a great run of moguls and then he'd bumped into his pal Bob Redford on the chairlift. Bob had persuaded Jake and Scott to come to a cocktail party he was giving at the institute at six. Naturally, the fact that my boss had arranged to meet me back at the Wildflower Mountain Home at six did not factor anywhere in his memory at this point. And even if it had, it wouldn't have made one speck of difference. Scott and Jake trotted off to the Sundance Institute with their friend Bob and didn't spare me a second thought.

"You really don't have a key?" Luke said as I drummed on the door in vain.

"There was only one, and Scott took it." I peered through the window. The night was drawing in, and my teeth were beginning to chatter, as I still had on my wet ski clothes. "But it's fine. He'll be back soon. Really. You just go, and I'll wait here," I told Luke as I zipped my ski jacket up to my nose and tucked my hands far up inside my sleeves to keep them warm.

"You're insane if you think that I'm leaving you here alone in the dark." He overturned a few rocks by the door to see if a spare key was lurking there. "You'll get eaten by an elk or something." He looked at me as I shivered. "Or die of hypothermia. So just get back into my car, Lizzie."

"I'm fine."

"Get in the car."

"He'll be back soon. I swear." I sat on the step obdurately.

"We're talking about Scott Wagner here. He may not come back for days."

"We're leaving tomorrow evening," I said optimistically. Luke looked at me like I'd just fallen down the stupid tree and hit not only every stupid branch but every stupid squirrel and every stupid leaf on the way.

"Oh, well, in that case I'll leave." He threw his hands in the air. "I'll go back to my luxury hotel room, where there's a bath and a hot tub and a log fire and a clean pair of sweatpants, and I'll just let you sit here until tomorrow evening, then. Okay, Lizzie, been nice knowing you." He walked down the path back toward the car where his driver was waiting patiently.

"Luke?" I called out.

"Yes?" He turned around.

"Do you have sulfate-free bubble bath?" I laughed and got up and ran down the path to where he was standing and looking at me with such complete incomprehension that I might as well have been speaking Chinese.

"You're such an odd duck," he said as he piled me into the back of his car, shaking his head. "Truly."

We drove back to his hotel, the superwinterwonderland Stein Eriksen Lodge, in relative silence, looking out the car window at the aspens and the pines, and every so often one of us would point out a deer or the moon shadows being cast over the blue-white snow on the ground.

"The full moon means weird stuff happens." I turned and glanced at Luke, with his arms stretched out over the back of the seat.

"Oh, well, that explains a lot." He looked at me out of the corner of his eye, and we both cracked up laughing. He put on *Tattoo You* by the Rolling Stones, and we both melted back onto our warm seats.

"You want first bath?" he asked. "'Cause if you do, I can just hang out downstairs in the bar until you're done."

"God, no, it's your room! You go first."

"Actually, it's a suite, so I can watch TV and you can bathe. How's that?"

"You're a gentleman."

"I'm from Kentucky." He turned to me. "I can't help it."

"Well, I'm glad, because I think that if I did have to wait any longer for a bath, my whole body would be one giant Christmas tree." I pulled off my damp glove and showed him the wrinkled tips of my fingers. He took my hand and looked closely at it.

"Is your whole body like that?" he asked.

"I don't know. I haven't looked," I said. "Though I did get a bunch of snow down my front. So the damage could be extensive."

"Yuck." He let go of my hand. "I know just the thing for it," he said as we pulled up outside the hotel.

"You do? What?"

"Wait and see." He got out of the car and held open the door for me. Then he spoke to the driver, and we went inside.

"Good evening, Mr. Lloyd," the concierge said as we clattered into the lobby, looking more like washed-out dishrags rather than chichi clientele. "Will you be dining in the restaurant this evening, sir?"

"I think we'll be having dinner in the room." He turned to me. "If that's okay with the lady?"

"Perfect," I agreed, as it dawned on me for the first time that something might actually be about to happen between me and Luke. Other than dinner and separate baths and sweatpants.

"So what was your genius solution for getting rid of Christmas trees?" I scavenged desperately for something to say. We were in Luke's suite, and he was busy turning on lights and kicking off his boots and readjusting the air-conditioning and closing curtains. I sat down on the edge of the sofa and tugged at my boots. Then I unzipped my jacket. My sweater underneath really was soaking wet, and so were my socks. But I said nothing.

"Oh, that. Sure, wait here," he said, and vanished into another room. "I'll go work on my miracle cure." I heard the sound of running water.

"It's a great suite."

"Yeah, it's nice." He came back into the room. If he'd been Jake Hudson, he would have come back in his boxers. Or nothing. But, thankfully, he wasn't. He was wearing the same T-shirt he'd had on all day, and he'd changed into a pair of sweats. "I'm going to put you out of your misery in a minute," he said, and handed me a cold glass of champagne.

"Good." I took the glass. "Thanks. I think."

"Cheers." He sat down on the chair opposite me and raised his glass. I moved forward and clinked his.

"My savior." I grinned.

"Well, I happen to think you're worth saving, so it works both ways, I guess." He took a sip of his champagne, and I took a mouthful. He sat back in his armchair and looked at me.

Fortunately, he'd dimmed the lights enough for me to be able to pretend that he wasn't giving me meaningful eyes, so I got up and walked toward the picture window. "You have a great view of the mountains."

"I do."

"And the moon," I added, swallowing half my glass in one go. I was terrible at this kind of thing. I wanted to kiss him, but this dance-of-seduction thing was too stressful. I could feel my ulcer beginning to burn in my stomach. He didn't respond. And then I realized that he was behind me.

"What about it?" he asked quietly.

"It's . . . well, it's pretty. Isn't it?" I didn't dare turn around.

"Guess it is." Luke put a hand on my waist, and I did eventually turn to face him. I mean, I had to, right?

And that was that. Va-va-voom. He kissed me.

And then there was the hot tub. Somehow we made our way incredibly slowly from the kiss to the point where we were standing beside the steaming water on his outdoor deck.

"Was this your miracle cure?" I asked.

"I can always get you a bathing suit," he said nervously as the water gurgled at our feet.

"It's fine." I smiled and lifted my sweater over my head. Luke looked relieved and began to take off my wet clothes piece by piece, dropping first my T-shirt, then my extra T-shirt, then my ugly ski pants, and finally my undies onto the wooden floor beside us.

"I didn't have this planned." He looked at me earnestly.

"You could have fooled me." I laughed and kissed him on the mouth. I didn't really care if he had stalked me up the mountain and planned every last detail. I wasn't exactly kicking and screaming.

"Lizzie, are you sure?" He was looking into my face. His uncertainty was almost touching.

"Can we just get in the water and then discuss it?" I said, and dipped my toe into the molten bubbles.

"Of course." He kicked off his sweatpants and climbed in behind me. The water was steaming up around our faces, and we sat back and shared another glass of champagne. He'd left his in the sitting room. I hadn't let go of mine, and he'd filled it up for me as we kissed our way across the room and out here onto the moonlit deck.

"I remember you from Daniel's party. You know that, don't you?" he said as he stroked a wet strand of hair back from my temple.

"No." I was surprised. Really surprised. "Are you sure? I mean, there were a ton of girls there. You probably just saw someone else and thought that it was me."

"I think you were the only girl drunk enough to kiss B-O-B." He curled one corner of his mouth up into a not-quite-amused smile.

"Oh, God. You did see me at Daniel's party."

"You were the only person there who looked like she was really having fun. I liked that."

"I saw you, too," I confessed as I let my toes float to the surface of the tub. "I thought you were cute, and I asked my friend who you were."

"Well, I never." He seemed immeasurably satisfied with this news.

"Oh, not never. I bet that happens to you *all* the time."

"Listen, Lizzie, you think you've got Hollywood sewn up. You assume every guy is a lying, cheating, sleazy asshole."

"In my experience a lot of them are."

"Which makes you narrow-minded." He frowned.

"Which is preferable to being brokenhearted."

"In your book."

"Well, who else's book is there?" God, what had happened to the fun stuff? Where'd the kissing go? Obviously my perfume had worn off.

"Well, in my book I'd prefer it if you gave someone like me a chance. I think you're great. I'll admit I hardly know you, but I like your . . . vibe." Even he had to smile at this point.

I raised my eyebrow with what I hoped was gentle sarcasm. "My vibe?"

"Your energy, your boogie, your thing, your fucking body and mind and the thing that you have going on. Whatever the fuck that might be." He finished up: "I like you, Lizzie."

"You do?" Now I was the one on the back foot. He liked me. "Really?"

"I'd like to take you out when we're back in L.A." He blinked expectantly at me.

"I'd like that."

The next morning I woke up and found myself locked in by Luke Lloyd's arms. Which were clamped around me in a viselike grip. I could feel him breathing on the back of my neck, and one of his knees was lodged between my legs. I didn't move. Not only because I couldn't but also because I didn't want to.

"You're not allowed to go yet," he whispered, and kissed the back of my neck. I sighed contentedly and slipped back into a dream. I hadn't shared a bed with a man for a very long time, and certainly not one I liked as much as this.

Thank heavens it was a gray day and there was no sunlight to make me feel like I ought to be doing anything other than lying here and looking at his fingers clasped across my chest and the carnage of last night strewn across the room—the empty champagne bottle floating in the silver bucket full of melted ice, two pairs of worn-out sweatpants and my discarded boots next to my purse on the floor, a champagne glass on the nightstand beside me. Last night had been about as perfect as it got. I felt so at ease with Luke and yet also so spun out by how great it had been to kiss him. How instant and amazing the chemistry had been between us. And in all honesty the best bit had been that this wasn't just some opportunistic pickup. Luke swore that he had noticed me before. At the party, in the park, at Urth—he'd remembered every detail of our encounters. Which made it oddly and wonderfully real.

I slipped under his arms and writhed out of the bed. I needed the bathroom, and I needed to get to some screenings. Much as I wanted to stay until he woke up and proved himself to be more than just a figment of my fantasy, I also had work to do, and while Scott's patience might stretch to taking me to the Miramax party or being amused at

Jake's chatting me up, if I wasn't there this morning to read out his schedule to him and arrange for his driver to come by, he might revoke his decision to fire me. Or yell at me. Neither of which was desirable.

So I loped—cavewoman style, with my shoulders hunched to make myself less noticeable—into the bathroom and helped myself to all the things I needed to ensure that I wasn't arrested or ostracized when I arrived back in the outside world again.

"You're going, honey?"

"I have to, I'm sorry." I sat gently on the bed next to him and kissed his cheek. It felt oddly intimate and . . . well, just plain odd.

"'Kay, well, I'll see you soon, right? I'll call you. That was fun, right?"

"That was great fun," I said, and planted another kiss on his shoulder for luck. "See you around." And I took one last look at him. His eyes were closed shut, and his black hair was like a wild doormat on the pillow, sticking up and crazy. He had the dark, scratchy beginnings of a beard, and the creased white sheets barely covered his chest, which was a warm golden color, doubtless from Moroccan afternoons by the pool.

"Bye, angel," he said as he opened one sleepy brown eye and looked at me. I resisted the urge to clamber back into bed with him and stood up.

Then I hit the road. I picked up my purse and made my hushed way out across the warm, plushly carpeted room, stopping to pick up a couple of faxes that had been slipped under the door in the night. God, these boys and their faxes, I thought fondly as I reached down for the shiny bits of paper. I'd almost forgotten that Luke was a producer until now. He'd so cleverly dissuaded me from my prejudices that I had begun to think of him as normal.

The header at the top sheet of paper read WEEKEND BOX OFFICE. I glanced at the columns to see what the number-one movie was and how much it had taken in. This was as automatic for me now as scratching an itch. Then I put the pages onto the table beside the door. The WEEKEND BOX OFFICE fax curled up and slid onto the floor. I picked it up and was about to place it back down on top of the other faxes when I noticed a huge heart scrawled on the bottom of the next page. Next to it were enough kisses to give someone lockjaw. And I do firmly believe that if you read something that wasn't meant for your eyes and it upsets you, then you've only gotten what you deserve. But I read the fax anyway.

Darling Luke,
Paris is lonely without you. Shooting in Tuileries today. Thought of you going headlong into the boating lake that time! Won't make it back now until early March. J is insisting on reshooting all my outdoor scenes.

À bientot to you and Rocky
Emanuelle ♥♥♥♥XXXXXXXXXX

"All rightee," I said under my breath and replaced the fax with my shaking hand. I wasn't sure which bit was the worst—that her handwriting was beautiful, that she seemed to speak French, that she was an actress—ergo fantastically pretty—or that the asshole in the bed in the other room had lied quite so consummately last night. I took a deep breath and thought calmly about my options:

A. Go back in and tear the fax into little pieces and let them rain down on him from a great height.
B. Send a reply fax to the impossibly cute Emanuelle and tell her what a coincidence it was that her boyfriend was about to go headlong into a lake today, too!
C. Put it on the bottom of the pile and fall in love with LL anyway in the hopes that she got fat from eating too many baguettes and he decided to dump her.

I moved my purse from one shoulder to the other as I pondered my dilemma miserably. Then, feeling the deadweight of my bag, I remembered that I'd been carrying *Sex Addicts* around for days now. And with that I pulled out the script and a pen and did the only thing that I could do under the circumstances—I scrawled on the front of the script:

I guess that it was just business after all, then! Hope you like the script.
Elizabeth XX

Then I left.

23

It's a perfect night for mystery and horror. The air itself is filled with monsters.

—Elsa Lanchester as Mary Shelley
The Bride of Frankenstein

Banishing my bittersweet memories of Sundance when I returned to Los Angeles had been much easier than I had imagined. For only a day after we got back into the office, Scott had gone on what Lara referred to as a rampage. Apparently this wasn't the first time this had happened. The last rampage had been three years ago, and it had ended with Lara taking a trip to the hospital, where the best plastic surgeon in town had to stitch up an inch-long cut above her eyebrow. It seemed that one Tuesday afternoon, having had enough of Scott's tantrums, indecisiveness, blame, and accusations, Lara had finally hurled the Rolodex at his head—but it had hit him on the shoulder instead. This had left Scott needing years of physical therapy. In fact, I had heard him mention a few times that if it hadn't been for that Rolo, he could have pitched for the Yankees.

Anyway, with his good arm Scott had returned fire with the only thing he could reach—his lucky deck of cards, bought on eBay and signed by Amarillo Slim. The corner of the deck caught Lara right above the eye, and she started to bleed. That put a quick kibosh on the tantrum. Scott's guilt had been so extreme, as had The Agency's concern over a lawsuit, that he'd insisted she take a two-week spa trip to

Canyon Ranch, fully comped by Scott Wagner, and paid leave happily granted by The Agency in return for her signature on a document waiving all rights to sue.

I was secretly plotting what item *I* might throw at Scott that would inflict the least amount of damage on his person but would grant me the maximum amount of spa time. My only concern was that Mia had given him a glass paperweight for Christmas (which I was sure I'd seen at Rexall in the clearance bin), and if he hit me in the head with that, I'd certainly miss out on the revitalizing salt glow and The Agency would be tipping the embalmer.

As Lara and I waited in the kitchen in a bid to avoid flying objects, I'd filled her in on the Sundance episode. Luke Lloyd and all. And instead of being scary and judgmental, she told me that Emanuelle, the French tart he was dating, had a tendency toward violent outbursts and that she would very likely maim Luke before she allowed the relationship to end. That gave me momentary pleasure, but then I started to think how much I actually liked that stupid, infidel's smile of his and how cute he had been when he'd pulled me by the ski poles to the café.

But I hadn't heard a word from Luke since my return, and I was sure that he'd simply chalked the whole thing up to experience. I also hoped that he regretted being found out just as much as I regretted finding him out. The Sundance fallout had taken a surprising turn when Jake Hudson had shockingly remembered my name and had been calling every couple of days. I had continued adamantly on my path of total inaccessibility, and as a result he would occasionally vary his approach—gradually upgrading the offers. First it had been a few phone calls, then an invite to his house for dinner, next an invite to dinner in a public place. Then, when none of those tempting offers worked, he'd sent flowers. I wasn't dumb enough to think that I was the only woman on his call sheet, and I'm sure Jake and his love life could have supported Luna Gardens, who did wonderful things with twigs and exotic flowers, single-handed. But the truth was, I didn't care if half the women in Hollywood received the pretty twigs and lilies that very same day, too—they brightened up my desk and made the entire floor smell delicious for a whole week. So being pursued by Jake wasn't nearly as horrible as being pursued by Bob.

Similarly, the girls in the office were taking great pleasure in my rejection of Jake the Rake. He had smashed so many hearts in this town that he had become required, if twisted, entertainment, and those in the know were taking bets on when he'd call and what he'd offer next. Courtney, who was keeping the book, had even received a phone bet from one of our top actresses, who had fleetingly fooled around with Jake herself once upon a time. But it wasn't as though I was callously stringing him along. The first time he'd called after our Sundance trip, I'd told him in no uncertain terms that he had misunderstood the relationship between Scott and me and that I was only Scott's assistant. Oddly, what I thought would put Jake off for good simply managed to stoke his ardor. I think the gall of a lowly assistant's turning the golden boy down was too much for Jake to bear, and he'd been thrown into a tailspin, wondering whether he was losing his touch.

Needless to say, after a few days of flowers and dinner offers, he upped the ante and invited me to the one thing Lara had told me not to turn down—Jake Hudson's biggest premiere of the year. If not his lifetime. Two studios had joined forces and made one of the highest-budgeted films in history, exceeding $180 million. And apparently they'd gone over budget, which meant the real figures were probably closer to $200 million plus. Though the risk was split with a rival studio, Jake Hudson still had an enormous stake in the success of the film. A star was cast in every bit part, and the premiere was going to be *the* event of the year. Alarmingly, Jake was offering to degrade himself and forgo the arm of a supermodel or movie star to take me as his date. Being high-minded and moral, I immediately agreed to go. Lara assuaged my feelings of hypocrisy by reminding me that it was vital I went in order to prove to myself that I'd overcome my feelings for Luke Lloyd. My only concern had been that I might run into him there, but Lara quickly assured me that he was in France scouting locations for his next film. Yeah, more likely scouting some French actress's underpants. So Jake got the answer he'd been hoping for, and I got a whole new set of insecurities about how difficult it might be to walk down a red carpet and whether I was tall enough and what dress I might wear.

When the day of the big night finally arrived, I was drafted into a meeting at the last minute to take notes and fetch coffee by Victoria, who I was sure was acutely aware of my plans, because every time someone made a move to leave the boardroom, she would splutter on about some bizarre, not-a-cat-in-hell's-chance casting idea that she'd had that would make The Agency millions. The whole sorry meeting had finally finished so late that I had to sprint from the elevator to my car and could have matched Michael Schumacher with the speed at which I took those ramps in the parking garage. But as I pulled up to the exit, I was delayed by Daniel, slowly getting into his Aston Martin. Unable to honk and yell, "Get the fuck out of my way, baldy!" I gave a strained smile in his direction and picked the peeling nail polish off my fingernails. At least that would save my having to do it when I got home.

Tall José was helping Daniel put a few brightly wrapped presents in his trunk when the other José came up to my window.

"How are you doing, Lizard?"

"Oh, hi, José. I'm pretty well. I have this big premiere tonight, and I'm running late as usual. How long does Daniel usually take to get going?"

"He's a deliberate man, Lizard. *Hierba mala nunca muere*." I tried my best to figure it out as José stood staring at Daniel with a steely look I'd never seen before on his gentle face.

"José, I have to admit that I haven't had time to sign up for those Spanish classes I mentioned. Nothing dead? Is that what it means?" I tried to guess, and he patted my arm as he watched Daniel get into his car.

"The devil looks after himself."

"Okay. I'll remember that."

"You better get moving, little Lizard, or you'll be late for your big date." Only when I'd emerged from the garage into the sunshine did I wonder: How did José know I had a date?

I was just sliding into Lara's shoes when the buzzer rang. It was Jake, sounding very much like the man of the moment. He had a slight lilt in his voice, which always made you believe that at any moment he just might break into song. It was a charming characteristic that made people feel at ease with him, but to unsuspecting girls it was like the song of a man siren, as it had been to me just after the hockey puck, before I'd gotten wise.

"Lizzie, it's Jake. I've come to whisk you off." I gave myself one last check in the mirror, then ran down the stairs to find him outside my building, leaning against the black stretch limo looking like the kind of man they don't make anymore. Because despite all the terrible things I thought about Jake, you had to appreciate his style. He let out the best wolf whistle I'd ever heard and opened the door of the limo with an appreciative nod of his head.

"C'mon, darling. Don't want to be late," he called out. Then I had a distinctly joyful *Pretty Woman* moment as I ran toward the car. But my enthusiasm was just slightly dampened when I recalled that Julia Roberts had in fact been playing a prostitute.

"Hop in," Jake said and theatrically held open the door for me. "You look great, by the way."

"Thanks," I said and felt like, well, a movie star, I guess. I ducked under Jake's arm as he stood looking up at my building for a moment too long.

"Everything okay?" I asked as I slid in against the black leather seats in Lara's finest.

"Oh yeah." He got into the car and closed the door. "Everything's cool." I inhaled the reassuring air of luxury. Jake sat on the other side of the seat and grinned at me and off we went.

"So this is fun," I said, suddenly realizing that even though I knew a lot about *him* (all that I'd gleaned that afternoon on his deck for starters; that wasn't even to mention the gossip I'd heard and the articles I'd read), he didn't remember anything about me. So technically we didn't really know each other very well at all.

"It sure is." He stretched his long legs out and smiled languidly. "So Lizzie, what did you do before you came to Hollywood? You did say you'd been here about a year, right?"

"Wow, you remembered," I teased. "I'm impressed."

"Oh, come on," he chided. "So what were you, like a heart surgeon or something smart and sexy?"

"Actually no. I worked in politics," I said before I could engage my brain. Rather stupidly, it hadn't occurred to me for a second that Jake might have recognized my apartment building, then looked at me and suddenly remembered the hockey puck and that we had dallied before. The reason this slipped my mind was that the man had had at least a hundred other clues as to who I was and had not picked up on any of them, so why would this one be any different? Why would he suddenly put two and two together now? Clearly, I had completely lost my own mind, or begun to massively underestimate Jake's mind, because no sooner had those words sailed from my lips than he looked very closely at me and squinted.

"We've met before, haven't we?"

"Sure, I'm Lizzie," I said goofily, thinking that this was just a cuteness of his.

"No, I mean we met before Sundance. Before the plane when you were looking really hot. Right?"

"Ah," I said, finally getting the picture.

"I knew I'd been to that apartment building before," he said, glancing over his shoulder. "Only when we met on the plane. With Scottie. You never mentioned that we'd already met, did you?" Jake actually looked deeply serious. Maybe even mad. Certainly he wasn't smiling anymore. And he'd drawn his legs neatly into the seat.

"I don't think I did mention it, no." I looked up because, well, he was tall, and tried to gauge whether I was truly fucked.

"You should have."

"I'm sorry."

"Sorry?" Jake Hudson frowned at me. His blue eyes were flecked with yellow and surrounded by wonderful, warm creases. His nose belonged to a sculpture and in the magic hour, with the sinking sun behind him, he looked startlingly perfect.

"Yeah, I should have mentioned it. That was rude of me." I lifted Lara's beaded purse onto my lap and prepared myself to have to get out of the car and walk back home with my head hanging down. It served me right for countenancing the office sweepstakes and the betting and for allowing a decent, if fantastically lascivious, man to be used for sport.

"You're fucking kidding, right?"

"What?" I lifted my shamed head and asked as Jake's lips broke open to reveal his miraculous teeth.

"That is so fucking funny. You're the hockey puck chick." He laughed.

"I know," I said, still in a state of shock.

"You were hot. I wondered what had happened to you. I called you, didn't I?"

"I think you did, yes."

"And you never fucking called me back."

"Well, I heard things about you. I mean, I was going to, but then I saw you at a party and you didn't recognize me and . . ."

"This is incredible. You were the hot hockey puck chick. I mean, you are. I love it." Jake laughed loudly and then kissed me on the lips. Obviously, he figured he'd done the groundwork before. "Lizzie the hockey puck chick and me are going on a date to my premiere. You just blew my mind, darling. I love it."

And not once in the entire forty-minute drive to the Universal Amphitheater did he try to grope me. Instead, I filled him in on my Hollywood career so far, which took all of one and a half minutes, and then we chatted the rest of the way about what a nightmare the movie had been to shoot and how the director had been kicked off the project halfway through. Apparently the first AD had taken over with the help of the DP and finished the film with the studio's backing. They'd worked together through the editing process and saved the film. Unfortunately, no one was allowed to divulge this well-known secret as the director had legal rights and the studio could face a lawsuit if it let slip who was really responsible for the final work. As a result, the director would be there tonight smiling at the flashbulbs and taking all the credit for someone else's labors. The more I learned about the movie business the less I felt I knew.

I had never been to the Universal City Walk, let alone to a movie venue of that size, and as the limo pulled up to the back of the arena, I started to feel my heartbeat under my red satin dress. Though I had seen premieres on *E!*, I just wasn't prepared for the sheer magnitude of it all. Not only were there thousands of people waiting outside to get snapshots or merely catch a glimpse of a celebrity, but the noise they were making was almost deafening. A portion of the amphitheater seats (the nosebleeds, of course) had been sold to Joe Public, and the proceeds were being given to the star of the movie's favorite charity. An enormous scoreboard blinking the name of the film and its stars in electric lights and a TV screen built for a stadium were hung high above the crowd for their amusement. The unrecognizable were ushered down the red carpet at top speed, like cattle being led to the slaughterhouse, as the photographers strained to snap the stars.

As we stepped from the limo, Jake put on his game face, and down the red carpet we went. No one was cheering for us, but you never would have guessed it the way he waved to the crowd. The sheer audacity of it impressed me. Also, the way he sidled up to Julia as the bulbs were popping and planted a big one directly on her lips was pretty mind-boggling. But, just like any other girl, she seemed to enjoy it and kissed him back with similar effusiveness. The cameras had a field day—because although Jake wasn't a movie star, he was very much part of the Pretty Posse, a clan of powerful yet cool young execs much beloved of the media. Any one of them could have been the captain of the football team in school or perhaps posed for their college calendar for charity. There were a few women involved, but, like most of the film industry, it was still male-dominated, one big fraternity house. They worked ceaselessly to build each other up and were now having quite a remarkable run, with four or five members firmly placed in pole position at studios, agencies, and production companies. They might not always be the brightest of buttons, but they'd chosen the winning team.

As Jake and Julia were exchanging flirtatious anecdotes, I stood a few feet away, like a coat you keep meaning to take to Goodwill. But I didn't mind—it was all so buzzy. Young girls were screaming, and their faces dissolved into tears when Leo cruised by with a casual wave. I just watched in wonder as the roar exploded anew with the arrival of each actor. Suddenly I was grabbed by the hand and Jake was pulling me along past the fans. Obviously red-carpet time was over, and he had to move on to more serious meet-and-greet.

Once we were inside the amphitheater, the noise of the fans faded to a gentle din. Jake was smiling like the cat who ate the canary.

"God, Elizabeth, it gets me every time. I mean, it's such a rush. I never quite get over it, and it happens a couple of times a month. All those people fucking cheering and screaming, just dying to be me." His eyes were shining as he looked at me. "Doesn't it make you horny?"

Even if I hadn't been speechless, I wouldn't have been able to say anything, because he pushed me against the wall in his euphoria and kissed me. Suddenly, in the exceptionally public environs of the Universal Amphitheater, I was kissing a man who made Heidi Fleiss look like the Virgin Mary. And despite his sweetness when he picked me up and our nice talk on the limo ride, he was still Jake Hudson, so I just wasn't really that into it. I glanced over his shoulder, hoping to find some excuse to escape, but what I found instead was an appalled glare. Luke Lloyd was back from France.

"Hello, Elizabeth." Luke pointedly ignored Jake, who slapped him on the back as he quickly disengaged his tongue from my tonsils and wiped his mouth.

"Luke, buddy! How's the picture going? I can't wait to see the finished product."

"The film is in the can. I just got back from scouting locations for my next project." Luke continued this conversation without once taking his eyes off me.

"Yes. I heard you were very busy in France." I couldn't help but drive the final nail into the coffin of what had been my last hope for true love in Hollywood. Just in case the Jake kiss hadn't done the trick already.

"Cool. Lucky you, those women in France are fierce. Weren't you dating that actress? The really sexy one who was in that sci-fi movie last year? What was her name?"

"Emanuelle," I replied with a sneer as Jake put his hand on my ass.

"Actually, Jake, we've split up. And I would have ended it sooner, but I've just never been a believer in ending relationships over the phone," Luke said grumpily. Not that Jake seemed to notice the lack of humor settling like a black cloud over our friendly banter.

"Yeah, you're right. Always easier not to end them at all. Eventually the gal gets the message." Jake laughed, and Luke winced. "Well, Luke, good seeing you, and for fuck's sake bring me your next project."

Jake hooked his arm casually around my shoulder, and off we went. I longed to look back, but I knew that in order to preserve what little dignity I had left, I needed to tuck myself into Jake and walk the straight line. I held on for dear life in the rushing river of backslaps and handshakes that followed.

"You having some fun, Elizabeth?" Jake whispered in my ear as we walked up to the VIP seats, roped off for those directly involved in the film on strictly an above-the-line capacity.

"It's great fun. Amazing," I assured him as we found our seats. At last a chance to sit down and for the lights to go dark so I could rehash my encounter with Luke Lloyd. I had been so surprised to see him that I'd struggled to make sense of anything he said. My head was just starting to ache when we were accosted by an overenthusiastic publicist heaping praise on Jake's already overinflated ego. She gave Jake an extremely familiar kiss, and for the hundredth time that evening, I thanked God that forewarned was forearmed. Or I'd be in the bathroom by now in tears as my date spread himself very thinly among the womenfolk.

"Jake, sweetie, I made sure I'm sitting next to you," she brayed in an English accent as she tossed back her badly bleached hair.

"Fabulous, darling," Jake said absentmindedly.

She gave me the once-over and immediately dismissed me as unimportant. I knew that she was wondering what my secret was. How had a regular girl like me snagged Jake—and for the most coveted ticket of the year? I longed to be able to tell her that I had something that she didn't—indifference.

Jake slipped off his jacket and placed it in his lap as I looked around at our seat positioning. I quickly realized that we were bang in the middle of the cast row, with everyone in the theater straining to get a look at the key players of the evening. In such a high-tech place as Hollywood, I loved the practically rustic methods used to assign seats. They'd just printed up a few sheets of copy paper with everyone's name on them in boldface and Scotch-taped them to our places. It was the same for Cameron, Ben, Jen, et al. Such equality made my heart soar for a second. I also noticed that the infamous Tony was positioned just a few seats down from me, and I thanked my lucky stars, no pun intended, that he had never actually met me, or there might have been a ruckus.

As the lights went down, I settled into the picture. Which was nothing if not huge, with enormous explosions and great silences and a screen as broad as the Himalayas. Once he'd finished his complimentary popcorn and spun his ice cubes around in the bottom of his Coke cup, Jake leaned over and took my hand. And in the dark I just pretended it was Luke Lloyd, and during the daylight scenes I cast my eyes around the theater to see if I could glimpse the man himself. But before I could even study the backs of heads in the rows before me for tufty black hair, I was distracted by Jake's strangely sporadic squeezing of my hand. At first I thought he was getting amorous, but then, when no amour or even acknowledgment of my presence was displayed, I decided it must have to do with scary or sad or even just plain huge moments in the film. And the squeezes were Jake displaying inadvertent emotion. I observed the pattern.

During an endless monologue by a dying soldier, he grabbed my hand with such ferocity I thought he was having a heart attack. But he wasn't. He was completely absorbed in the movie. Eyes front.

Then, during a breathtaking, sweepingly romantic scene, he began to press my fingers together with rhythmic intensity.

Gun battle. No squeezing.

Landscapes. His squeeze nearly caused my fingers to turn blue and drop off.

Sex scene. Nada.

Finally I came to the conclusion that Jake must really be a country boy at heart. I knew he was from Kansas, but to get excited at fields and cows was almost too sweet for words. My estimation of Jake was starting to rise ever so slightly from the depths of the gutter. After all, Luke Lloyd had never called me, or for that matter sent me flowers, and I had slept with him. Luke was the worst kind of Hollywood male—at least Jake was honest. Luke hid behind morals and ethics, yet he was the biggest liar and sleazebag of them all. But then, just as I was ready to switch allegiances and see the light, Jake's head collapsed onto my shoulder. I thought maybe he'd fallen asleep, but when I looked down at him, he let out a long groan. And not the kind that's inspired by a cheesy joke, sadly. This was a groan of satisfaction. And a loud one, too. Thankfully, it was drowned out by the bombing of Berlin, or the entire theater would have turned to check out the live action.

No, this was the kind of groan a man gives before . . . well, in this case before the badly blond publicist slides her hand out of his pants. I blinked incredulously as Jake turned and smiled broadly at me. The publicist just wiped her hand on the armrest of the theater seat before giving me a curt, victorious smile. Never again would I shake anyone's hand with the same innocent enthusiasm. It was air kissing all the way from now on. The credits started to roll, and the audience rose for a standing ovation. His film was a success, and Jake Hudson's meteoric rise was assured. Just not with me on his arm. And certainly not holding his hand.

As the lights went up, I winked at him and made excuses about escaping to the bathroom. As I launched myself toward the themed buffet, I caught sight of Daniel Rosen pressing the flesh. As I was deliberating whether I could be bothered to go say hello before he saw me and thought I was ignoring him, I felt a light tap on my shoulder. It was Luke Lloyd.

"Hi." He just stood there and stared.

"Hi," I replied, unable to do much better.

"You look beautiful."

"Thanks."

"Why are you here with that guy?" He looked like a little baby who'd just spit out his pacifier.

"Why didn't you tell me about your girlfriend?"

"I wanted to, but . . ."

I knew what came next. The inevitable apology and bullshit excuse that I was so desperate to hear. I wanted to forgive and forget, but my survival instinct took over before I could lay myself bare for more abuse. I put my hands up as a signal for him to stop.

"Never mind, Luke. It doesn't really matter anymore. It's none of my business." He put a hand on my arm, and I moved back a step to break the connection.

"Fine, I understand if you don't want to be with me. But don't be with him. He's scum. Goes through women like boxer shorts. I can't stand to see you ruined by him."

"Ruined? What is this, Luke, the eighteenth century? I can take care of myself."

Luke bit his lip. "I know that much." Then he smiled, and I couldn't help it—I smiled back.

"Well, you said if it wasn't going to be romantic, then it could be professional, and I loved that script you gave me."

I wasn't expecting this. "You what? You're just saying that because you feel guilty."

"No, I'm not. Because in the first place, I have nothing to feel guilty about. I also firmly believe that love is one thing and business is another. Okay? I don't risk fifteen million dollars to say sorry."

"Ever?"

"Never. So when can we meet to talk about the project? I'd love to meet the writer/director guy as well—his work is incredibly powerful. I think he's a real talent. What's his name, Jason Blum?"

"Yes." I nodded enthusiastically. Suddenly Luke raised his hand and waved at someone behind me. I glanced over my shoulder, and there was Daniel Rosen, within spitting distance. Just standing there. I was glad we hadn't been discussing our "romance."

"Hey, Luke. Call me tomorrow. I still want to discuss a few points on Mel's deal," Daniel said. Luke nodded agreement, and then Daniel turned to me. "Hello, Elizabeth, nice to see you out of the office. Have a good evening," he said, then disappeared into the crowd.

Short José had been staring directly at Daniel when he'd mentioned the devil earlier. I turned back to Luke, who gave a shiver in the damp night air.

"That guy gives me the creeps," I said, unable to hold back, per usual.

"Me, too," he agreed with a smile. "So when can I see you? I mean, when can I have a meeting with you?" He was like a dog with a bone. And I couldn't have been happier.

"How about Thursday? Morning, that is. At your office. In daylight." I was a certifiable moron.

"Well, Lizzie, it is usually daylight in the morning."

"Okay, I'll call to arrange it. And now, before you change your mind or I say something horribly rude, I'm going to walk away." I made a move to go.

"Alone?" He stumbled with his words. "I don't . . . mean with me, but not with him . . . right?" He looked so crushed, and I knew that I should tease him for a little bit longer, make him feel I was worthy of pursuit, make him regret the existence of that stupid French tart. But I just couldn't do it.

"No, Luke. I'm going home alone. Jake's not my type. I like honest men." I winked.

"Ouch." He grabbed his heart as I shrugged playfully. "You know, I never lied to you, Lizzie, I just failed to mention something that I knew would never be important in the long run."

"I'll see you Thursday. And don't keep me waiting."

> Hollywood lore: The more powerful you are, the longer you keep people waiting for a meeting.

I turned away, my feet barely touching the ground, and headed off into the crowded street of Universal City Walk to find myself a taxi.

24

How can all these things happen to just one person?

—Cary Grant as David Huxley
Bringing Up Baby

I'd called Luke's assistant the next day and confirmed the meeting at his office on the Universal lot. I had wondered whether we ought to meet in some café in town, which wasn't quite so intimidating. But then I thought that if we did, I might find my mind drifting to romantic possibilities or, even worse, bitter recriminations. At least in his office I wouldn't be tempted to slip a mickey into his coffee and leave him on the sidewalk afterward for people to trip over. Hopefully, in a fluorescent-lit environment, I wouldn't be as likely to cry either, if I was unexpectedly blindsided by a memory of the hot tub or his loving words.

"At the lot is great," I'd told Allison, Luke's assistant, who I hoped would be a homely looking girl who wore glasses for close work. At least then I wouldn't lose the last shred of respect I had for him.

"See you at eleven tomorrow," she'd chimed. "Oh, and will Mr. Blum be joining you?"

"He's going to come in halfway through the meeting to introduce himself to Luke," I told her.

"Great. Look forward to meeting you." She hung up.

I hoped that I came across as such a professional, polite assistant as Allison did when I answered The Agency phones, but I doubted it.

Then again, Allison didn't have to contend with Victoria hovering like a vampire bat behind her every minute of the day, as I had recently. I suspected that Victoria had a new cocktail of hormones, because as well as her usual disorder, which I had diagnosed as a close cousin of Tourette's—whereby she'd stick her head out of the office door and say things like, "I wish everyone at Disney would die"—she had now begun to perform primal screams in her office, too. Sometimes without bothering to close the door.

When I put my head in one day to check that she was okay after one of these episodes, she informed me that it was a technique developed by Arthur Janov for the curing of neuroses and for ridding herself of her primal pain. Which I suppose I ought to have applauded as a proactive foray into self-healing. The trouble was, she was just so bloody loud and difficult to explain to clients on the other end of the phones.

In fact, Victoria's behavior had been so bad recently and her insults so biting that when I'd gone to see Dr. Vance last week I had asked her if it was possible to commit someone to an institution if you weren't the next of kin.

"Of course it is, dear," she said. "You just need to take the person to Cedars Sinai and get them to desk nineteen. It's unmarked for that very purpose. Two doctors will talk to them and make the decision whether to section them under the mental-health act. Very simple."

"Great," I said, much encouraged by this news. I was certain that if Lara and I could lure Victoria there under the pretense of my having broken a thumb or something, we'd definitely score at least a short stay for her in an institution. And, really, that was all we wanted—a vacation from her festering bitterness and freaky ways.

But while the institutionalization of Victoria remained merely the stuff of my daydreams and not reality, I was inevitably going to be a little brusquer and sharper with our clients than sweet Allison was.

"Is Jason in, Alannah?" I asked the pretty Japanese girl behind the counter of the Coffee Bean when I went in to give him the good news and tell him to iron some pants for our meeting. I'd left him a message when I got home from the premiere, screaming the good news about our meeting with Luke Lloyd through the phone. This was what we'd been waiting for. This meeting was the break that Jason had wanted so badly since he'd first seen *Close Encounters of the Third Kind* and fallen in love with cinema when he was a child. And for me it had become my labor of love, too, something that I was more passionate about than I ever had been about anything before, even politics.

"He's not here today. Sorry," Alannah said.

"I thought tomorrow was his day off," I said. "Otherwise I wouldn't have made the meeting for Thursday. I'd assumed he'd be free to come along."

"Oh, he called me and asked me to swap shifts. Said he had something very important to do today." She shrugged.

"Okay, thanks anyway, Alannah."

I left and figured that Jason must be at home boning up on his meeting etiquette, refining his pitch for *Sex Addicts,* coming up with casting ideas. Not that he and I hadn't spent the past few months doing just that, until we were literally word perfect. But I didn't mind. I was glad that he was being so conscientious. Our meeting with Luke could potentially change both our lives, and Jason obviously realized that.

"Okay, Jason, I know that you're there and that you're doing grammar checks on the script and changing the margins so that it looks shorter, but you don't need to. Luke loves it, and we can deal with the minutiae later." I was back at my desk and trying to speak quietly so as not to broadcast my news. I'd told Lara about the *Sex Addicts* meeting, but I still hadn't broken the news to Courtney and Talitha, and certainly not to Victoria. Not that there was any news to break yet, which made it worse. If Jason and I fell at the first hurdle, the delight on the girls' faces would be unmitigated. "Jason, where are you? I just want to confirm with you the meeting with Luke Lloyd on the Universal lot tomorrow. Okay? Call me back."

I put seven drops of Australian Bush Remedy, which Alexa had given me to instill calm, under my tongue and prepared to face my pile of letters.

"Elizabeth, I've got to run now, but I just wanted to wish you luck for tomorrow." Lara leaned over and touched my knee. I looked at her hand with surprise—she was definitely not the most tactile person in the world and had never knowingly patted me before. Still, I was touched. In both senses of the word.

"Thanks," I said. "Do you have a meeting with another literary agent?"

"Not exactly. But I have something really important to do, so I won't be in."

"Okay, well, do you think that I should get a temp in? Otherwise Scott's going to be without both of us," I asked.

"Oh, don't worry, Scott's not going to be here either," Lara said, and she leaned back in her chair with what I can only describe as a beatific smile on her face. "So no need for a temp."

"Okay, fine. I'll put the phones on voice mail tonight when I leave, and I'll come in straight after the meeting. Well, after the debriefing of the meeting with Jason. Which I promise to keep short." I smiled. "By the way, you're looking great. Is it that SK-II moisturizer you bought the other day? 'Cause if it is, I'm going to Saks to see if I can score a sample."

"Thanks." She stroked her cheek lightly. "Could be the SK-II, I guess." Then she looked off into space with a goofy expression on her face. Which made me decide that it must be love, not face cream.

But lest I forgot, this was Lara, so even if she had softened enough to put her hand on my knee, I wasn't about to grill her as to whether the married man had finally come through for her. It would just have been folly.

"Hello, The Agency." I made an effort to be a perkier assistant.

"It's Jason."

"Thank God. Did you get my messages? Where have you been? Isn't it exciting?"

"It's great." The line was crackling. "Well done, you."

"No, well done *us*. We're a team," I laughed. "God, do I sound like a cheerleader?"

"No. I mean, yes. You sound fine." Jason was suddenly sounding very Hollywood, very distracted, and as if he had much better things to do. I guess that was a portent. I smiled. I wondered if I'd develop the same traits when I was a fully-fledged producer.

"Hey, where are you, by the way? You don't sound as though you're in your apartment."

"Oh, no, I'm not I'm . . . I'm out."

"I'll bet you're in Fred Segal men's department buying some suitably directorial-debut shirt, aren't you?"

"Not exactly. But listen, Lizzie, what time did you say that meeting was tomorrow?"

"Eleven A.M. Do you want me to give you a ride? You can always hang out at the lot café or something until it's your time to come in."

"No, it's fine. I'll make my own way there. No problem. Listen, I have to go because I'm on someone else's cell phone, okay?"

"Fine. See you in Luke Lloyd's office, then. God, isn't that weird? The next time I see you, we could be well on our way to getting a deal for the movie," I said, forgetting my secrecy policy.

"Yeah. Gotta jump, Lizzie." And Jason was gone. I put down the phone and took a cautious look around when I realized that the office had been dead quiet except for my verbal spazzing. Thankfully, the girls all seemed to have cleared out. Only Scott was around, and he was lying on his sofa watching a teaser for some teen-o-matic action-chick movie. Which was just about the best conceivable combination when it came to distracting him from the fact that he was paying me to sit on the phone and do deals on my own projects. I vowed to be more discreet in the future. I needed this job. Well, at least until tomorrow anyway.

What a strange thought. Would I, could I, really give up my job if the film looked like it was going to get made? The one truth about movies is that they're never a sure thing. Getting a green light is a pretty good indicator that you may be about to shoot some reel, but there are so many banana skins lying around waiting to trip you up—from a lead actress getting sunburn, to your location of choice turning into a war zone, to foreign financing falling through because some German playboy gambled away his inheritance, to . . . well, just about anything you would care to lose sleep over. They're all legitimate concerns. So, really, no matter what Luke Lloyd said tomorrow, I was never going to give up the day job. Short of, "Here, take this five million dollars and bring me back a movie." Or that other bon mot that I pretended even to myself had not crossed my mind: "I can't live without you. Let's go to my house in the mountains and have babies together." Exactly! Which is why I never thought it in the first place.

The other thing I hadn't really dwelt upon, surprisingly enough, was my fantasy of what life would be like if the movie did ever get made. What my future would entail. I'd been too busy wondering whether the character motivation of Dan was solid enough and whether his arc was as dramatic as it might be to indulge my silly dreams. That was a good thing. New shoes and a couple of weeks in Bali were just not places my mind would go to right now. Besides which, the work seemed to be proving to be its own reward. After a day of learning about budgets from a book I'd bought or looking up line producers and location costs, I was invariably so happy that simply cooking spaghetti made me grin as if I'd fallen in love. Truly, I'd never experienced this feeling of professional fulfillment before—even when I was absorbed in a campaign in Washington, I merely felt stimulated and valued. Now I felt the kind of unbridled delight in this project that I thought could only come from winning the lottery or giving birth. Or having sex in a hot tub with a wonderful man and *not* discovering afterward that he was a cheating liar.

The Universal lot was in the Valley, so on Thursday I set off early. But not so early that I'd get caught up in the morning rush and sit there for hours until my clothes resembled scrunched-up love letters. On the drive I tried to focus on the project and not on what Luke's office might look like. Or what it'd be like to see him again. The other night I'd been caught off guard. Now I had all the time in the world to fixate on the fact that my stomach felt like a tied-up sack of ferrets. I turned on the radio and felt the scorching morning sun on my face as I drove with Elton John on the radio singing about how Daniel was a star and he missed him so much.

I, on the other hand, didn't miss Daniel this morning as I sped along the Ventura Freeway. He still hadn't responded to the script, though I was afraid of what he'd say if he found out that Luke wanted to buy the project. I'm sure I'd be branded a traitor, or even sued. He'd sued an enterprising employee before, apparently. On what grounds, I wasn't sure. Possibly just on the grounds that he had very powerful lawyers. Allegedly, one of the receptionists had written a screenplay and then sold it to Fox for $1.2 million (which is the apocryphal sum that other people's screenplays always seem to sell for. When it's your own or one of your clients', it invariably goes for about $40,000 if you're lucky). Daniel had been livid and completely taken the poor girl to the cleaners after they were able to prove that she'd used The Agency's computers to type up her ticket to a better life.

I wondered whether he'd try to bring a case against Lara, too, if he ever found out about her novel—certainly he'd be entitled to ask for some of her salary back, as she hadn't exactly been the most diligent of employees since inspiration had struck. Then again, I'd like to see him *try* to sue her—she'd probably bite off his nose and then shred it, so that nobody could put it in a bag of frozen peas and have it stitched back on later. Lara was like that when provoked.

"Hi, Allison, I'm Elizabeth Miller," I said as I entered the door of Luke's office. When I say "office," it sounds misleading—for most Hollywood production companies that have studio deals are consigned to a building that is little more than a glorified trailer. They're called bungalows, and if you punched one of the walls, you couldn't guarantee that your fist wouldn't go through it. There are exceptions that prove the rule, of course—Spielberg's company, Amblin, is made of bricks and mortar, even though it's on the lot; most of the Paramount walls can safely be kicked, which they frequently are, apparently; and some companies that have self-financing or are really riding high might rent offices in other parts of town, like Santa Monica or on Melrose, for instance. Often these belong to more style-conscious (frequently gay) producers who have "space" rather than offices and often a water feature, either in the form of a Zen fountain or the Pacific Ocean. Drew Barrymore's company, Flower Films, has a great office nowhere near a studio—with a view that stretches for miles and a meeting room wittily called the War Room, with maps and model planes strewn around. If you have a personality in this business, it's a shame not to show it.

Luke Lloyd, on the other hand, was not gay or an actress. His office was your bog-standard production-company headquarters.

"Hi, Elizabeth. He's on a call right now, but take a seat," Allison said when I introduced myself. Then she pointed me in the direction of a lilac sofa with a fan of magazines before it on a coffee table—*People, Us, Variety,* and *Vanity Fair*. I sat down and whipped up a magazine so that I could look over the top of it and scour the room for details. "Can I get you a Diet Coke or some water, maybe?" Allison, who was not as homely as I had hoped but who *was* sporting a giant engagement ring, asked.

"Oh, I'd love regular Coke if you have it," I replied. Then, when she'd disappeared back to the fridge, I shamelessly checked out all of Luke's movie posters. That was another production-company thing—your walls were always hung with your movie posters. Luke had quite a few that I had never heard of. Most of which seemed to be in the vein of *Wedding Massacre*. Relieved, I noticed that these were interspersed with sufficient arty, indie pictures that didn't prominently feature a man with a machine gun under his arm to restore my faith in my erstwhile crush.

"Here you go." Allison handed me my drink.

"Thanks," I said and began flicking through *People*. I could hear Luke's voice through the paper-thin walls from the other room, and I felt almost faint.

"I just can't move forward with you on those terms, Allen," he was saying calmly. "We renewed the option before it expired, and for you to tell me this now is just a crock of shit. I want my percentage. It's non-negotiable."

Allison tapped away on her keyboard. I trembled. Why did he have to go and sound all powerful like that? It was too annoying. Then, just as I was wondering whether there might be a picture of him and Emanuelle together in his office, Allison's phone beeped and I shot three feet in the air. Well, my stomach did. My body remained deceptively earthbound. I knew the horrible hum of the internal phone-call beep only too well.

"Sure, I'll tell her." Allison put down the phone.

"He says to go right in." She smiled. I wondered if she suspected from my jumpiness that Luke and I had fooled around. Or whether she had a crush on him herself. Well, she had eyes, didn't she, and a brain. How could she not?

"Lizzie." Luke stood up and shook my hand. "Good to see you."

"You, too," I said as he pointed to a beautiful, fraying yellow chair for me to sit in. I guessed this was one of his own chairs.

"So how've you been?" He sat back behind his desk and gave me a sad smile.

"Good, thanks." I tried to be brisk. I could only think of us in his car at Sundance bumping through the snow to the Stones.

"Great." He read my body language (or maybe he read my clothes, which were not dissimilar to the ones I'd worn to Spago with Bob—fleshless, sexless, back-off-buddy garments in not-in-a-million-years hues) and sat forward some in his big executive chair. "So, like I said, I love the project, and I'd like to make you an offer."

"Fantastic." Marriage and babies?

"Naturally, it'd be an indie movie, but I was thinking at the higher end of the scale. Say, ten million dollars, with more factored in if we decide we need to attract more high-profile talent."

"I see."

"It's just that the lead male role is so great that if we could get, say, Ashton Kutcher or Orlando Bloom, then I'd be prepared to pay more. Or at least foreign financiers would. I'm sure."

"And do you think that the actors would be likely to do it for less than their usual payday because the material's so clearly indie?" I asked.

"Perhaps." He was chewing on a pencil and doodling something on a pad. Numbers, not my name, I hazarded a guess. I took the opportunity when his eyelashes were lowered to see if there were any photographs around. No. There were cards and immaculate, expensive invitations to weddings and black-tie functions, and there was a painting behind his desk, which was an oil of a racehorse. Well, he was from Kentucky, I guess. "I could send the material out to some talent and see what we get back. We could begin by packaging it. Or the other way around. I think either could work on this project."

"I've always thought that packaging with talent first would be the way forward. It brings it to life more for investors," I said.

"I agree." We both stopped for a moment and caught each other's eye. It was a second too long. And it was loaded. I broke first.

"I wonder where Jason is. He should be here by now."

"Traffic, maybe," Luke said, and he began jotting numbers down on a pad. "So those are the figures that I'm floating, and I think I can get you a green light, but it would have to be with a bigger back end than up front. Would you both be okay with that?" Luke asked. Which basically meant that we got our money later, if and when the movie was a success, rather than beforehand. I looked at my watch again. No Jason.

"I don't really know. I mean, it sounds fine with me, but strangely enough he and I haven't really discussed what sort of ballpark figures or payment schedule we'd prefer," I said honestly.

"Well, do you want to call him and see if he's nearly here?" Luke asked. I wasn't sure if he wanted to be getting on with other stuff, but I assumed he would be. Being a big producer and all.

"Sure. That'd be great." I stood up walked toward Luke's desk. He handed me the phone, and I dialed Jason's number, which I knew by heart.

"Hi, you've reached Jason Blum. Please leave a message."

"Jason. It's me. Just checking that you're okay and on your way. I'm at Universal now." I handed the phone back to Luke, who had elegantly been pretending to do something online. Without clicking or clunking or typing. There were no photos on his desk either, I noted. "Voice mail. Sorry," I said, suddenly feeling embarrassed. Were we going to have to sit here and twiddle our thumbs until Jason arrived?

Jason never did show, in fact. I sat with Luke for another twenty minutes, and we had a halting conversation about casting and locations, but we both had our eyes on the door the whole time and other things on our minds. And no matter what anyone ever tells you, it's really, really weird sitting in a business meeting with someone who less than a week ago was kissing your nipples. Eventually I made my excuses and left. Having apologized ad nauseam for Jason's no-show. I hammed up the terrible fates that might have befallen him—car accident, emergency tracheotomy, hockey puck to the head, broken-down car in South Central, burning accident involving his pants and an iron—my fears were limitless.

My anger, too, was pretty much *sans frontières*.

"What the fucking hell happened to you?" And various permutations of that same message were left on Jason's home number and cell phone throughout the rest of the day, until both machines suffered the electronic equivalent of cardiac arrest and stopped taking my calls. But by ten o'clock that night, my fury had been replaced by something altogether more terrible—the fear that something bad really had happened to Jason. I had been back to the Coffee Bean, and they were in the dark, too. He hadn't shown up for his shift today, and poor Alannah was still there valiantly holding the fort. I went to his duplex on South Sweetzer and stood on the lawn beside his lemon tree looking up to the windows of his second-story apartment. The place was in pitch darkness. I even threw a few pebbles for good measure.

"Excuse me, have you seen Señor Jason?" I asked Perdita, his seventy-year-old downstairs neighbor who had a crush on him and made him hamburgers and fried ice cream when her husband was out playing chess.

"He left the house this morning at seven-twenty and hasn't been back since. He looked very smart, though. Nice shirt," she said. I feared the worst.

Back at my apartment, I tried to remember if I had met any of Jason's friends or family who might have news of him. But L.A. was as strange in that respect as in so many others—most people were itinerant and had no family to speak of. I knew that Jason was from New York City and that his father was an art dealer and his mother was a schoolteacher, but short of calling my friends at Interpol again, I might as well give up for the night. As to any friends he had . . . well, I knew that he usually hung with a bunch of USC alumni when he wasn't with me, but who they were and where they all lived was about as mysterious to me as why Fellini was considered to be a genius.

"I give up," I told Alexa later when I tapped on her door to see if she wanted to come sit on the roof with me for a homemade margarita before bedtime. "I just can't imagine what on earth could be serious enough to make him miss this meeting. I mean, apart from the very worst of things."

"It's pretty weird, I have to confess." Which, coming from a girl who believes that we live in the third dimension of spirituality and if we all stopped believing in the universe at the same moment it would cease to exist, made me a little nervous.

"I just can't think about it anymore. I even called a few of the local hospitals this afternoon, but it was like getting blood out of a stone trying to find out if he might have been admitted. They're so private. Anyway, I'll go fix those margaritas, and I'll meet you on the roof in a few minutes," I said, and rummaged in my purse for the key to my apartment.

Alexa and I sat for the rest of the night on a couple of her Nepalese prayer mats with salty, limy margaritas in our hands and looked at the lights dotted along the horizon. There were boats out on the sea, the Ferris wheel on the pier was studded with rhinestone brightness, and the breeze from the ocean meant that we had to hug our knees into our chests to keep from getting goose bumps.

"I ought to have been celebrating with him now," I said.

"We can celebrate without him. You still did fantastically well. You've almost got your deal. That's amazing, Elizabeth."

"Thanks. I guess you're right." I lifted my glass and clinked it against hers. "And I'm sure he'll be fine. No news is good news, right? That's what we always used to say when my sister was in Sierra Leone."

"Exactly." Alexa smiled sweetly at me. Then she lay back and looked at the sky. "We'll only go to bed when we've seen a shooting star and wished on it for Jason to be okay."

"Perfect," I said, placing my margarita to one side and lying back on the asphalt.

25

As God is my witness, . . . they're not going to lick me. I'm going to live through this . . . If I have to lie, steal, cheat or kill.

—Vivien Leigh as Scarlett O'Hara
Gone With the Wind

"Elizabeth, I am so sorry," Lara said as I walked into the office, hollow-eyed from a night of insomnia and worry.

"About what?" I said, and felt my knees weaken. She knew something about Jason that I didn't. Oh, my God, I had to sit down before I fainted. The news was bad. I made for my desk, my hands groping in front of me.

"This." Lara handed me a copy of *Variety*. I shot her a puzzled look. "Oh, no, you haven't seen it!" She whipped the copy back out of my hands.

"Seen what?"

"You should sit down." She pulled my chair out for me.

"No way. Tell me what you're talking about." My voice shook with emotion.

"Elizabeth. I'm sorry." She didn't move. Just stood there with *Variety* in her hand and looked at me with horror. I couldn't bear it any longer. I snatched the magazine away and held it before my body with my trembling hands.

Then I let out a scream that was so primal it would have cured my neuroses, Victoria's neuroses, and Woody Allen's all put together. In fact, this was a primal scream of such apocalyptic proportions that it'd be a wonder if anyone in the building ever suffered from a neurotic moment again. Or heard anything again, for that matter.

"He didn't," I said with my eyes narrowed to slits.

"I'm afraid he did." Lara was almost as cut up about the whole thing as I was.

"Fucker."

"Lousy, executive-cock-sucking fucker."

"How could he?"

"More to the point, where is he?" Lara said, and slammed *Variety* down on my desk so that I could see it again, just in case it hadn't been true the first time.

FIRST-TIME SCRIBE BLUM TO HELM
"SEX ADDICTS" FOR REVOLUTION IN $3M DEAL

And, really, what more did I need to know? Apart from the last line, which cheerfully informed me that

Blum is repped by Agency prexy Daniel Rosen.

Talk about raising the dead. Scott's head emerged from behind his door, and he had a thunderous look on his face.

"What in Christ's name is going on here?" he demanded. Lara and I looked at him with such a force field of hatred toward the male species that he simply blinked and retreated like a mole back into the earth.

"I blame Daniel Rosen," Lara said. "That morally bankrupt little fuck should just park his Aston Martin in the garage and inhale deeply."

"Well, I blame Jason. How could he do this? How could he sign with Daniel and then go and land himself a fucking deal at Revolution? He knew that he wasn't going to come to that meeting yesterday. Jesus, he was probably celebrating at the Four Seasons with a bottle of champagne and a cock massage."

"What are you going to do?" Lara asked, her green eyes glinting with menace.

"Set you on them," I said, wishing I could.

"Oh, you don't need to worry about Daniel. He's old news." She looked enigmatically toward Scott's closed office door. "And if he isn't—then I'll make it my mission in life."

I held *Variety* close to my chest, willing the print on the front page to change. I longed for a few words—five, to be exact—to appear hidden deep in the paragraph that Lara and I had overlooked, saying,

Elizabeth Miller attached to produce.

But when I pulled the copy from my chest and examined it closely, nothing had altered. I was still fucked. Mind-numbingly fucked. And this time there was no pleasure in it.

"Oh, and Luke Lloyd called." Speak of the devil.

"Lara, I just can't deal with him at the moment."

"I know, but he said he read *Variety* and was concerned that you might not know yet."

"Was he really concerned?"

"Yeah, Lizzie, he really was. I also think he was bummed that he wasn't going to be making the movie, but you were the first thing he mentioned."

"He must think I'm the biggest moron."

"No. I think he thinks you're too trusting."

"And he would know," I quipped. I couldn't think about Luke Lloyd at the moment. My head was spinning, and I was feeling mildly nauseous.

Lara made me leave the office immediately and had even tried to slip me a hundred-dollar bill from Scott's petty-cash envelope.

"Treat yourself to a massage at the Beverly Hot Springs. It'll take your mind off your misery. These enormous women, with their bathing suits rolled down to their waists and their breasts flapping about, scrub you to within an inch of your life. You can feel all the dead skin just flaking off."

"Good idea, maybe my skin will grow back thicker." I'd pressed the money back into her hand. "I can't take it, Lara. Anyway, I just might decide to drown myself in one of the springs." Besides which, I really needed to keep my job right now, and stealing from my boss was not the best way to go about that. So instead of loping off to drown my sorrows in the hot spring with some grannies and a few naked pop stars, I drove back to my apartment.

A fog had settled over Santa Monica as I drove down San Vicente, unable to see more than a few feet in front of my windshield. I switched on my lights, concerned that with my luck I'd get plowed down by a hit-and-run actress in a four-wheel-drive monstrosity. This had become something of a trend lately, and surely it couldn't be long before it was as fashionable as being skinny enough to have a lollipop head. I finally reached Venice, though for once the sea wasn't visible through the haze. The angry crashing of the waves against the sand had replaced the blue horizon, which usually lifted my spirits no matter what. I guess today I wasn't supposed to be exalted.

I walked down the hallway of my building, barely able to hold my head up. I had been an idiotic fool. It was my own fault. I'd never asked Jason to sign any sort of contract; our agreement had been done on a handshake and a chai latte. We were friends. Or so I'd assumed. Never once had it occurred to me that he'd cut me out of the whole deal without even the courtesy of a phone call. I guess I had nobody to blame but my naïve self. As I approached my apartment door, I saw, on the floor, three dozen long-stemmed roses with a card attached. I took another step, leaned over, and tugged the card off the cellophane wrapping. But before I'd even opened it, I recognized Jason's childish, ugly handwriting.

> Dearest Lizzie,
> I'm so sorry about this entire mix-up. I should have told you sooner, but Daniel didn't tell me he was leaking it to the trades. Please, can we talk about this? I'll be at home waiting for your call all day.
>
> Love,
> Jason

I tore up the note with such venom that I gave myself at least three paper cuts. Then, with aching fingers, I battered those roses around my hallway until the corridor looked as if a twister had roared through a flower show. I scooped up all the pieces and went to find Jason. I wasn't going to accept his stupid apology—how dare he? After I had risked life and limb to give the damned script to Daniel Rosen. He was sorry about the mix-up. Jesus, as far as I was concerned, there was no mix-up. He was a lying skunk of a rat bastard, and I would make him pay. Miraculously, I no longer felt depressed. I felt elated. Energized by the pure desire for vengeance. No. Jason and I weren't going to have a dialogue. *I'd* talk, and then I'd kick his ass. I'd take the roses, or what was left of them, and shove those long stems right up his scrawny little behind. Now, that would give me immense satisfaction—considering they still had the thorns on them. I wondered if he'd paid for them with the $3 million he was getting for selling me out.

When I arrived outside of Jason's, I was still seething. I parked my Honda illegally and marched up the stairs to his doorstep. I banged on the door, and when Jason buzzed it open, I marched up his stairs and threw the pile of ripped-up roses directly in his face.

"Fuck you!" I screamed at the top of my lungs, and then turned around and sprinted down the steps and back to my car. Then I turned around again and climbed back up the stairs two at a time. I wasn't finished yet. Jason was still standing there in shock, with rose petals stuck to his shirt.

"You are a disgrace to the human race. I was your friend, and we were partners. I hope you're happy with your deal, because you've just sold your soul to the devil. And for what? Money. I had a great deal set up for you. It was an honest deal with an amazing producer. I hope they rewrite your script, kick you out of the editing room, and piss on your dream like you have on mine." I spun around on my heels and walked at a dignified pace down the stairs, got in my car, and drove away.

The fight had drained from me like air out of a leaky dinghy. I couldn't make the drive all the way back to Venice, certainly not in my flattened state. Hell, I felt like I couldn't even make the drive to the end of the block. Luckily, nothing in L.A. is far from civilization, and I remembered this dive bar where Jason and I had gone on one of our many script sessions when his apartment was starting to close in on us. I sighed with relief when I saw its pink façade and little striped awning. The word "Taquería" over the entrance made my mouth water for a margarita and an endless supply of guacamole and chips. A much better source of comfort, I thought, than a fat Asian woman ripping the skin from my body in the name of beauty. I valet-parked at the restaurant next door, as I felt I deserved a little spoiling, and swung open the heavy door of El Carmen.

It was still daylight, but you'd never have guessed from the velvety darkness that swallowed me when I walked in the door. Without a single window, it was the type of bar that had looked exactly the same for the past fifty years. Day or night. You could imagine Raymond Chandler knocking back whiskey on one of the many barstools. The bar ran the length of the room, and, hauling myself up onto one of the red vinyl stools, I gazed deliriously at the two-hundred-plus types of tequila. I was home, at least until I could no longer see and had to drive back to Venice risking my life and the life of my trusty car. I handed over my credit card to the bartender and made a swift prayer to any deity who was listening that it wouldn't be rejected like its pathetic owner. I must have looked in need, because the bartender didn't even run it. She just stared at me hard and then poured my tequila sampler. One. Two. Three.

Two minutes and three shots later, I breathed in, taking my first proper hit of oxygen all day. I just had to remember that I hadn't really lost anything real. *Sex Addicts* had been a fantasy. I'd never really believed that Jason and I would pull it off, even though I'd certainly worked as if the whole thing might come true. So I had to stop looking at it like a setback. I was in the same position I was in a week ago, but wiser. And a lot more hostile. That was something, wasn't it? I'd learned that deals—no matter who they were with—had to be realized on paper. And also that Los Angeles, no matter how good the weather, was a dog-eat-dog world. The picket fences didn't make it Kansas.

"Excuse me, Miss, but can I get you another round?" the bartender asked. "Different tequilas this time?"

"Sure, whatever you think." She smiled and poured me a few more.

"Can I buy you one?" I asked her, realizing that getting wasted by myself wasn't all it was cracked up to be. Instead of drowning your sorrows, you just ended up wallowing in them.

"Sure," she said. I pushed her one of my three drinks, and we clinked glasses. "You know, I don't know what you're upset about, but whatever it is will eventually end." Little did she know that was my fear. I didn't want it to end. What was I going to dream about now?

At that moment the door to the bar opened and the light flooded in. I didn't recognize Jason standing there until the door closed behind him. Then I turned away and pouted into my tequila.

"I came looking for you. I saw your car parked on Third Street. I've been in and out of every place on the street," he said nervously. I think he was afraid I might rip the bull's head off the wall and run at him. He wasn't wearing his Peruvian sweater for once. He had on something altogether softer.

"Congratulations" was my best reply after three shots.

"Can I sit down?"

"It's a free country." He sat down next to me as the bartender approached him—with thinly veiled hostility, I was happy to note.

"What do you want?"

"A margarita, please, with Cuervo Gold."

"Cuervo Gold," I mimicked childishly. "Aren't we Mr. Fancy Three-Million-Dollar Director now? Oh, and by the way, I like your sweater. Is it cashmere?"

"Lizzie, I'm sorry. I'm really sorry. I'm torn up about this whole thing."

"Well, then you shouldn't have done it." I took my last shot of tequila and spit it right back out. I didn't really want to get drunk after all. I wanted to pick myself up and start dreaming again. I waved to the bartender.

"Do you by chance have any coffee, maybe, and some tacos?"

"Sure, doll. On the house." She winked at me, and Jason smiled. "For her, but not for you. Prick." Jason withered beneath her gaze.

"See? She doesn't like you either, and I didn't even tell her what a shit you are," I said, staring stonily at the wall ahead.

For the next hour, Jason sat there like a good boy and took the abuse he had coming to him. We had the same conversation, in various guises, about thirty-seven times. The gist ran something along the lines of:

"Listen, Lizzie. How can I make it up to you?"

"Turn back the clock, fuckface."

"If I could, I would," he replied pleadingly.

"Then, you bitch, tell them I'm attached to produce." I was pushing my luck now, but I couldn't help myself.

"I can't. Daniel made me sign the contract yesterday. And when I called him to say I was unsure and I needed to talk to you first, he said it was too late and that if I backed out now, they'd sue me for breach." To give Jason his due, he didn't look much like a man who had just landed himself a $3 million payout. Rather, he looked like he'd run over his own dog.

"He's lying. They won't sue you. I don't think. You cocksucker." Break over. Then we'd start back at the beginning.

Eventually, though, I think that my anger must have bottomed out, because just as I was in the middle of telling him that he was the henchman of Beelzebub himself, I suddenly got the most irksome, ill-timed fit of the giggles. Maybe it was the tequila or perhaps just sheer resignation. But most likely it was that I'd never called anyone a cocksucker before, and it sounded really funny coming out of my mouth.

"Lizzie, thank God you're laughing." He tried to give me a hug, and I shoved him away.

"Don't look so relieved. I still hate your guts. I'm just laughing at myself. For being such a moron and trusting a rat bastard like you."

"Maybe I can just tear up the contract, and then we can set the project up with Luke Lloyd like you'd arranged."

"Too late now, Jason." He relaxed a little on hearing that I was simply able to speak his name.

"What I'm most sorry about was that I wasn't straight with you," he began to explain. "But it happened so fast. After you called me and told me about Luke Lloyd, Daniel Rosen called. He said that you'd given him the script and he knew all about the Luke Lloyd deal but that he had a better offer already lined up."

I turned to Jason, shocked. "But how did Daniel know about the Luke Lloyd deal?"

"I don't know. He just said that he'd spoken to him about it at some premiere."

Then it hit me like a ton of bricks. Daniel had been eavesdropping the night of Jake Hudson's premiere. He'd heard Luke say that he was interested in the project, and then Daniel had run with it, calling all the studios and creating a bidding war on the back of Luke's potential offer to me. It occurred to me then that I was going to struggle to remain working at The Agency anymore. The idea of being under the same roof as Daniel Rosen was unbearable. I might find myself making homemade explosives instead of butternut squash dishes from now on.

"I told him I needed you to come to the pitches, but he said that you'd throw off the buyers and put the whole thing in jeopardy. He said we'd address your position as producer later. But then Revolution made the offer, and it was so much money, Lizzie. They were offering me pay-or-play for my script and my directing services. That was more money than I'd dreamed of making in a lifetime. And more opportunity than I'd ever dared to hope for. Then Daniel dropped the bomb. Telling me that he'd tried his hardest to get them to agree, but they said if you were attached, there was no deal. He asked if you'd signed anything, and I'd told him we hadn't." Jason took a brave sip of my tequila at this point, and I remained silent—he didn't deserve to know that I'd spit in it. "I was weak. And at the moment I really don't like myself very much, but I was sick of mopping up after Max Fischer at the Coffee Bean and sick of trying to be heard. I just couldn't help myself."

That was when I realized that this outcome had been inevitable. I couldn't hate Jason for making the decision that he had. I'd been pursuing this dream for less than a year; he'd been pursuing it for twenty.

"I guess almost anybody in your situation would have done the same thing."

"Not you," he said sulkily.

"Well, I'm an idiot," I reminded him.

"Daniel played me, and I know it."

"Join the gang." I suddenly caught sight of the clock behind the bar. "Shit, it's six o'clock. I have to stop by the office to pick up the weekend read on my way home, so I'd better get a move on." I stood up to go.

"Lizzie, I'm going to make it up to you. I promise you. I'll think of something." And I truly believe he meant it.

"See ya soon," I told him.

"Very soon, I hope," he said plaintively.

I waved and walked out the door nonchalantly. I was getting good at that move, and I'd left him with the check.

26

I've fallen in love! I'm an ordinary woman—I didn't think such violent things could happen to ordinary people.

—Celia Johnson as Laura Jesson
Brief Encounter

At six o'clock I went back to the office to pick up my weekend read, which Victoria would have left on my desk. Now that I was going to be a second assistant for the foreseeable future, I was going to have to work on coverage like everyone else.

"Elizabeth, what are you doing back here?" Lara was at her desk, and the rest of the office was like a graveyard—chairs were tucked in, most of the lights were off, except for the lamp shining on Lara's desk, and the cleaner was in Scott's office tipping out the wastepaper basket and polishing around the phone.

"Just came to collect my things. More's the point, what are you doing here? It's Friday. It's way past your home time." I altered course and made for her desk, where I could perch and tell her all about the roses and Jason's groveling, sniveling apology. "Oh, you're Internet shopping." I looked at her screen, which was patterned with an array of baby garments—tiny cardigans, little sun hats, and a primrose yellow jacket. "Cute, baby shopping. Is this for a godchild?" I asked.

Lara looked up at me, then flicked off her screen. "Elizabeth, do you have time for a drink?"

"Sure. Then I can tell you all about what Jason said when we went to El Carmen and he offered me the moon." I hopped off her desk and picked up my house-size pile of scripts with Victoria's usual arid note paper-clipped to the top.

"Perfect. How about Chateau Marmont?" She flicked off all her switches and stuffed a few bits of paper and a folder into her bottom drawer.

"Sounds good to me," I said, and we walked out of the building toward the parking garage together.

Lara valet-parked up at the Chateau, and I parked on the street a minute down the hill and walked up, because I wasn't going to be getting rich anytime soon. I met back up with her in a quiet corner of the lounge, where she was sunk deep into one of the plush sofas. A guest was sitting at the piano, gently coaxing out a tune while his dog watched him. The other sofas were occupied by couples having affairs and romantic tête-à-têtes over champagne. I turned the other cheek.

"I've ordered us both a martini, is that okay?" she asked as I approached the table.

"Great." I was working on my martini drinking. Truth be told, I found them bitter and unpleasant, but they were an undeniably elegant cocktail, and I'd been determined to learn to drink them for a while now. Just as I'd been determined to learn French and the flute—so one out of three wasn't bad.

"Love is in the air," I said caustically as I sat down on the chair across from Lara and turned to the cooing room of lovers. "I guess at least I should feel inspired. If it wasn't right with Luke, it's because I'm meant for someone else. Or is that me being delusional?"

"Elizabeth, you're going to be fine."

"I hope so." Our martinis arrived, and I lifted mine stoically to my lips. "So I have got to tell you about Jason. I mean, it wasn't exactly the result I was hoping for, and I'm still high and dry because he's got the deal, and I'm not attached to produce, but at least he was contrite—"

"Elizabeth, I have something I want to tell you." Lara was holding a cocktail stick thoughtfully between her beautiful lips.

"Oh," I replied, and took a sip of my martini. I knew that it wasn't going to be good news. I just knew it. It never was good news these days, and she also had a look of vague mortification in her eyes. "Is it bad?" I asked warily.

"It's great news, really. But I feel bad having to tell you," she said, and her shoulders dropped despondently as she sighed out loud.

"Oh, God, just get it over with then," I said, bracing myself. I couldn't even begin to imagine what she was going to tell me. I put down my drink in case I spilled it in shock or felt compelled to throw it at her when she imparted her mixed tidings.

Lara looked directly at me as though conducting a risk assessment on a condemned building she was about to demolish. Then she lowered her eyes and focused her gaze on her red cotton skirt. "I'm pregnant," she said without a frill.

"Wow." I gulped and took a sip of my drink. "That's amazing. I mean, it's great. Isn't it?"

We looked at one another for a moment.

"It is great. And we couldn't be happier." She gave a faint smile.

"The married man?" I asked tentatively. "It's his baby?"

"It is."

"And he's happy, too?"

"He's thrilled, and he's been amazing," she said, her sketch of a smile suddenly blooming into a full-blown, ear-to-ear number. "We went to get the first scan yesterday. He came with me, and it was so exciting. So small and perfect. Of course, he swore that he saw a huge penis, but I think it was just the umbilical cord," she laughed.

"That's great," I said, and gave her a hug. "I'm so happy for you. Both."

"There's something else, though." She managed to shake me off gently with her words.

"I'm sure there is. I mean, it can't be simple being with a married man. But, hey, you said his marriage was rocky anyway, so it can't be *too* bleak." I was delighted now I knew that whatever would follow was not going to affect me in any way. It was about the married man and babies and—

"It's Scott," she said flatly. I swiveled my head and surveyed the room behind me. Just our luck to rock up to the same joint as our boss. But Scott wasn't there.

"Where?" I asked, then it occurred to me what she had meant. He wasn't here at the Chateau. "Oh, you think he'll mind?" I leaned back in my chair, finally relaxing into my drink. "Well, too bad. Scott can't mind. Women get pregnant all the time. It's life. It's your life. Just because you're his assistant doesn't mean you have to live your life to please him. He'll have to learn to be a little less reliant on you from now on. It won't hurt him. I think he's too codependent on you anyway," I said boldly.

"You do?" She looked at me like a goofy teenager in love. And suddenly the penny dropped.

"You're kidding me?" I sat stark upright in my seat. Oh, my God, I was such an *idiot*.

Every single day since I'd arrived at The Agency, I had failed to see what was going on under my nose. Despite the fact, I suddenly realized, that everyone else in the office knew and had openly made references to it and I . . . well, I had been such a thickhead that I hadn't realized. "You've been having an affair with Scott this whole time, and I never noticed," I told Lara.

"There were so many times I wanted to tell you. But you and Mia seemed to get along so well, and we didn't want to take that risk in case you found yourself in an uncomfortable position, with her asking you a bunch of questions. So, well . . ." Her face had flooded with relief. Her little secret was out in the open. But I wasn't done with her yet.

"So you waited until it was impossible *not* to tell me, even though everyone else knew? Even Courtney and Talitha knew, didn't they?"

"I guess they must. I mean, I haven't spoken to them about it, but they make snide remarks all the time, so I figure they found out somehow." She shrugged.

"Lara, I thought you were my friend." I thought back to all the lies she must have woven like a cobweb over my eyes since the day I started. Then it all made sense—the exhaustive wardrobe, the shiny SUV, the spa trips, her ability to make Scott fall into line when nobody else could, their huge fight, after which she'd gone out onto the roof of the party at Halloween and he'd lost his mind on Ritalin. All of which made me feel like a total fool.

"I *am* your friend. And now you know, so we can celebrate, right? And you can come baby-clothes shopping with me, and when I give up work, you can come and meet me for lunch at Il Fornaio."

"Hey, back up a minute, you're giving up work?" I asked. She couldn't leave, could she? Life at The Agency without Lara would be like drinking battery acid on a daily basis.

"Of course I am. I have a novel to write," Lara said mildly. "And someone has to take care of Scooter here." She patted her tummy.

"You're going to become a Beverly Hills soccer mom," I said in horror.

"I know. Isn't it exciting?" Lara said.

"I guess." I sank back into the cushion and felt about as depressed as it was possible to feel. The rug was well and truly gone from under my feet, and I was flat on my ass on the stone cold floor.

Then I caught sight of Lara's beaming face and realized that I had to rally. This was an amazing event in her life, and she wanted me to be happy for her.

"Right, then, no more martinis for you, young lady," I said sternly, moving her half-finished drink out of the way. "I'll order you an orange juice, and we'll discuss what you're going to call Scooter there. Because if you really want me to be your friend, you're not allowed to name it after a baseball or basketball star. Okay?"

"Funny you should say that," Lara touched my arm conspiratorially. "Because only last night Scott tried to convince me that Shaq could be a girl's *or* a boy's name."

"So what about Mia?" I hesitated to ask, but it must have dawned on them between scans and baby naming that Mia would have to find out eventually.

"She's promised him the mother of all divorce battles. She's hired the biggest, meanest lawyer in town."

"Shit, poor Scott," I said, knowing that Mia would sting him for all he was worth. I hoped he'd be able to keep their kid in diapers by the time she was finished.

"Oh, it's fine. She's been having an affair with some crazily rich old guy who used to own a TV network. You should see him—he's had so much work that he looks like he's been reanimated—but at least Mia's been unfaithful, too, and Scott has proof, so she won't get more than half," Lara said cheerfully.

And when I thought about it, I honestly believed that Lara and Scott might not care even if they had no money. I could tell that they were both clearly mad about each other, now that I had enough pieces of the jigsaw to figure it all out—the mooning looks, the filthy fights, the fact that they were still together despite Lara's bitching and Scott's occasional infidelity—it was as plain as the ring that wasn't on Lara's finger.

And she must have read my mind, because she turned to me and said, "We're getting married in Vegas just as soon as the divorce comes through."

"That's great news," I said. "A Vegas wedding, that'll be fun."

"You'll come, won't you?"

"I'd love to. I mean if I'm invited."

"Of course you're invited. You're one of my closest friends." She patted my knee. And even though I didn't exactly feel a sisterly, warm vibe from Lara most of the time, I think she really meant that. Which was both lovely and sad at the same time.

"And the honeymoon?" I skipped on quickly.

"Arizona," Lara proudly informed me.

"Arizona?" I imagined there was some groovy new hotel there, news of which hadn't reached my unhip ears yet.

"Scott's going to the Meadows Rehab Clinic to clean up before the baby's born, and I'm going hiking in the canyons nearby. So we'll both be happy."

"Fantastic," I said dubiously. But then, just because it wasn't *my* idea of a honeymoon . . .

"Oh, Elizabeth. I'm just so happy." Lara said, and knocked back her orange juice. "He's so sweet and sensitive. I can't wait to be married to him."

All of which merely reinforced my theory that there's somebody out there for everyone. Because if a smart, cool, beautiful girl like Lara could want to scrape a wastrel like Scott up off the sidewalk and love him, then maybe even I could meet someone funny and great who I liked.

But then I remembered that I had. And now it was over. I hugged Lara good-bye and scuffed my shoes against the ground as I walked back down the hill to where my car was parked on Sunset.

I tucked my purse under my arm and wandered up the street a short way until I saw a liquor store. I went in and paced around a bit. I wondered whether I should buy a bottle of vodka or something to forget. Maybe if I became a drunk and had to go into rehab, Luke would come to visit me or buy me a basket of muffins. Then I saw my martini reflection in the window of the store. I didn't want sympathy. I wanted Luke Lloyd back. I had to stop drinking—booze made me reckless. I bought a packet of Junior Mints and went home.

. . .

Finally I decided that there was nothing for it but to call him up. But it was so indecently early on Saturday morning that I was afraid that if I left a message on Luke's machine and he saw the time I'd called, he'd never speak to me again. Five A.M. was the hour of stalkers. It was the hour of joggers. It was the hour of breast-feeding mothers. Normal people didn't watch for the pale, encroaching light of dawn. But I couldn't sleep. I'd lain awake for what felt like hours, listening to my gurgling toilet tank, with a feeling of blind terror at the thought that I might never see Luke again. And if I did see him, I'd have to smile and kiss him on the cheek and nothing more.

For not only were we never going to be lovers now, we weren't even going to work together. I couldn't console myself with the prospect of weekly meetings and eating Krispy Kreme doughnuts with him on our movie set in the fall; there would be no dream of us getting drunk at the wrap party and declaring our feelings; there would be no dazzling at our premiere. Nothing, in fact. Apart from what might have been. I felt nauseous at the thought. I really, truly think that I loved him. Of course, not in any profound, eternity-band, for-his-faults-and-all way, but I did think that he was the only man I'd met—ever, really—who I liked so much. Who made me smile even when he was dumb or cross or ridiculous. And for whom I had the hots quite so uncontrollably.

I don't know how long I tormented myself with thoughts of the treacherous twists of the knife of fate that had brought us here. To this place where I liked him and he liked me and, despite the French tart, we wanted to hang out together. But we weren't. Didn't we at least owe it to ourselves to see what it would be like to walk down the street together, to sit in a movie theater, to talk about our childhoods? Even if we only discovered that we didn't work—that he checked out other chicks all the time, that he didn't share his popcorn, and that he'd spent his teen years playing sports instead of listening to *Darklands*—didn't we have to try at least?

But then, what could I do about it? I'd never called a man in my life, and calling a Hollywood Man and suggesting a date was not the safest kindergarten for trainee manhunters.

Men like Luke Lloyd, even if they have the waistline of a hippopotamus, the manners of a chimpanzee, and the sexual predilections of the Marquis de Sade, are never at a loss for a date. Because they have something that every man and woman on the face of the earth wants—they have power. Now, I don't know if it's true that power corrupts and absolute power corrupts absolutely, but I do know from my peregrinations in politics and entertainment that power gets you laid any night of the week and absolute power gets you laid in any animal, vegetable, or mineral fashion you choose. Any night of the week. By anyone you care to shake a business card at. And I don't think that this is just an L.A. thing either. I think it's a universal, harking back to the days when we had more body hair than Bliss Spa could handle, early-primate-type instinct. And it can't easily be overturned one Saturday morning in January.

So instead of calling, I got up and scrubbed my kitchen floor in my nightgown. I had no sensible cleaning products, as I'd never really taken an interest in my kitchen floor before yesterday, when the rot had set into my life, so I used a brilliantly effective recipe of dish detergent and Jolene Crème Bleach. When I finished, I took a toothbrush to the stove and marveled at the filth I'd been cohabiting with. Perhaps if life never improved, I'd become a Clean Person. I'd dedicate myself to pristine baseboards and moth-free closets. I'd perfect the art of dusting, and beeswax would be my friend.

"Screw that." I flung down my greasy toothbrush at nine o'clock, when it became apparent that cleaning and I were just having a meaningless fling, and peeled off my rubber gloves. "Where did I put it?" I wandered through my apartment looking for the taxi receipt on which Luke had carefully printed his cell-phone number.

"Luke, this is Elizabeth Miller," I said as a sleepy voice answered the phone.

"Lizzie." He didn't sound pissed at me for waking him up, which was something.

"I've been thinking." I sat on my windowsill and pressed my forehead against the glass as I looked mindlessly at the palm trees along the promenade.

"Right."

"Are you alone?"

"Yes?"

"Are you sure?"

"Seems that way."

"The French tart?"

"I beg your pardon?"

"Your girlfriend? Is she in France?"

"I don't know where my ex-girlfriend is."

"Good."

"Is that why you called me at . . . nine A.M.?" He sounded bemused.

"Oh, if you're busy or something, then fine. We can talk later. Or not. It's not important," I said as I opened the window and looked down at the concrete path six stories below.

"Lizzie. I'm awake now. I'm sorry if I sounded disinterested. I couldn't be more thrilled that you've called, and I'd love to hear what you have to say."

"You don't sound very sincere."

"Lizzie," he pleaded. My feminine intuition, or perhaps his beleaguered tone, told me that I'd pushed him about as far as he would go. So I backed off a little and jumped down from the window ledge onto my living room floor.

"Well, you know how we were having that whole professional-relationship thing? That I said I didn't want to mix business with pleasure, and so we were working together but not dating?"

"I remember that distinctly, yes."

"Right. Well, the thing is, circumstances have changed now, haven't they?"

"In that we're no longer doing business together?"

"Exactly."

"Lizzie, I think I know where you're going. In fact, I'd be really excited if this was leading where I think it's leading." I could hear him take an exhausted breath. "But would you mind just getting to the point?"

"Sure," I said.

"Thanks so much."

"I've just been fucked by my boss, and I'd prefer it if it were you."

Luke took me to dinner at Gladstone's that night. Which no self-respecting producer would ever usually do. It's a cheesy outdoor lobster-and-seafood restaurant by the beach at Malibu, where everyone sits under heat lamps, gets buttery chins from the crab claws, and knocks back pitchers of low-grade alcohol. Luke was cool with the whole thing, because he liked Gladstone's, and he didn't really have a huge amount of respect for the fact that he was a producer anyway. And I didn't mind going to the secretaries' Saturday-night venue of choice on a date, because . . . well, for one thing I was with him, and for another, no matter how you spun it, I was a secretary.

"So here we are." Luke leaned across the table and handed me a shrimp.

"I know. I'm still in shock." I peeled off the shell. "I was beginning to think that I'd end alone and living in my car on Sunset when I was sixty."

"With gray dreadlocks?"

"And a fetish for collecting Fanta cans." I tried not to dribble dripping butter down my top. "Still, there's no guaranteeing that's not going to happen just because I'm going on a date with you thirty-four years before my potential decline."

"I guess. But there's something you don't know about me," he said, and took a sip of his beer.

"Which is?"

"Which is that once I get a woman, I don't let her go too darned easily."

"You have a dungeon?"

"I have something much cooler."

"I know." I winked at him and we both laughed.

"I'm glad it left an impression on you."

"It scarred me for life." I smiled at him with his baggy white shirt and handsome, suntanned face. "I mean, if it hadn't been quite so memorable, I wouldn't be here. I just couldn't really get you out of my head."

"I wouldn't have let you go," he said, and put his hand over mine on the table. "Even if you hadn't chased me, we'd still be here."

"I didn't chase you, you pig. I asked you to dinner."

"Whatever."

"Big difference, buddy." I shot him a look. He caught my hand and kissed it.

"So the truth of the matter is that for all your protestations about not wanting to date in the business and all, I feel just as strongly about that kind of thing as you do."

"So strongly, in fact, that you dated an actress for three years," I said with as much derision as I could muster for a man who was holding my hand. For a man who I *wanted* to hold my hand.

"She was French."

"So?" I didn't really want to discuss his last relationship with La Tarte on my first date with him, but I suppose we had to get it out of the way.

"It didn't count. She lived somewhere else. She didn't know how to use a StairMaster or that no-fat milk existed. She spoke a different language, for Christ's sake. How could I resist?"

"Wow, you have really tough criteria."

"Would you take me seriously for once, please?"

"I'll try," I said, and curbed my smile.

"You're the first woman I've met in this town who I could ever think about reading the *Sunday Times* with. And you might think that's jumping the gun and it might freak you out, but I want you to know that this does not happen every day."

"That doesn't freak me out," I said.

"You're sure, angel?" He was so southern I wanted to die.

"No, it makes me happy. I'm really happy not to be freaked out by a man in a town where freaks seem to be waiting on every street corner to get me. Because I was starting to think that if I had to kiss one more freak, I might not make it through."

"I really am your savior, then."

"It's possible," I said. "'Cause you know anything's possible in the movies."

27

My! People have a way of coming and going so quickly here!

—Judy Garland as Dorothy Gale
The Wizard of Oz

When I drove into The Agency's parking garage on Monday morning, something had changed. And it wasn't simply me. It wasn't that I had spent the weekend with Luke and we'd lain on the grass in front of the Getty Museum and talked about nothing for hours. And it wasn't that we'd walked along the beach eating ice cream cones or that he'd promised to teach me to ride a bike and I'd bought a copy of *Crime and Punishment* for him in Book Soup. No, what had changed had absolutely nothing to do with the rose-tinted glasses of new love. It had to do with the fact that there was a pack of journalists outside the front door of the building and there was a peculiar atmosphere of foreboding at The Agency.

"José. What's going on?" I asked as I walked toward the elevator where Tall José was waiting.

"Ah, you'll see," he said with a tremendously serious look on his face.

"José, you must know. You were right to warn me about Daniel's being the devil. You've both been right about everything. So what's this all about?"

"We can't say."

"You can't tell me why the press is outside the front door?"

"Lizard, you will find out for yourself soon enough," the other José said, and pressed the button for me. Then he was silent.

"Don't either of you have any words of wisdom for me?" I felt like Alice down the rabbit hole. Everything was suddenly very different. Nobody was doing what they were supposed to do, and even the Josés, the standard-bearers of all that is right, had altered. I wanted my old world back.

"Josés, please say something."

"Lizard, we have nothing left to teach you," Tall José said as he patted my shoulder and guided me into the elevator. A butterfly settled in my stomach as the elevator rose smoothly to my floor. My reflection was the same in the mirror—same murky blond hair, same black skirt and top, same bag overladen with Victoria's weekend reading. But something was different. Something was definitely up.

As I walked across the vast, brilliantly bright expanse of lobby to my corner of the office, the receptionists' phones were ringing off the hook. The beeps sounded like a demented computer game. Like Scott's deleted e-mails gone crazy.

"I'm sorry, we can't comment on that right now" was being repeated like the refrain of a swan song behind their glass counter. I turned to look, but nothing there was really any different: four girls with neat headsets, superstraightened hair, and better makeup than mine. And the cropped-haired, lilting-voiced guy with the camp pout. It all looked absolutely as per usual. It just wasn't. I hurried across the floor in my scuffed black court shoes and headed for my corridor.

Lara wasn't at her desk. Courtney and Talitha weren't there either. I could see through the glass doors of Mike's office that Courtney was sitting with him. And that, shockingly, Talitha seemed to be talking to her boss, Gigi, whose unprecedented presence would have been reason enough to set alarm bells ringing. Clearly, they were both being briefed on something. Scott's door was closed, and I was about to tap on it to see whether he and Lara were having a similar discussion, but then I remembered that their version of congress between boss and assistant would have been more likely to involve debriefing. So I went to my desk again. There was a photocopied sheet of paper on top of my keyboard that read:

> AN OFFICIAL ANNOUNCEMENT WILL BE MADE AT 12:00 REGARDING CURRENT EVENTS WITHIN THE AGENCY. ALL MEMBERS OF STAFF ARE RE-

QUESTED TO MEET IN THE BOARDROOM ON THE 2ND FLOOR PROMPTLY. PLEASE DO NOT COMMUNICATE WITH MEMBERS OF THE PRESS IN THE INTERIM.

I stared at the words and wondered what they could possibly mean. Then Scott's office door opened, and instead of Scott and Lara, three men emerged in navy blue workmen's overalls. Two were carrying Scott's desk, and the other was holding the door open. Scott's Lakers sticker was still there.

"Excuse me?" I ran over to them. "Where are you taking that?"

"Can't say, Miss. Sorry," a red-cheeked man with a Queens accent informed me.

"But that's my boss's desk," I insisted.

"Then you'd better ask *him,*" a string bean with acne chipped in.

"I could just follow you to see where you're going," I told them cockily, but they ignored me. Had Scott been fired? I wondered as I watched another team of men come in and remove his television set. Or were they the marshals? Had Mia bled his bank accounts dry, and these guys were the receivers impounding his property? I wondered if it was part of my job description to stop them as I watched the back of Scott's plasma screen vanish out the door.

I sat down at my desk while I still had one and wondered what in hell's name was going on. I switched on my computer, hoping for e-mail enlightenment, but all that was there were two junk-mail offers to enlarge my penis and one e-mail from Jason. But before I could click on it to open it up, Courtney walked out of Mike's office looking flushed.

"Isn't it wild?" she said as she sat back down at her desk and made no bid to turn on her computer. Or play her flashing messages.

"What's going on?" I hated admitting ignorance to her, but there was no getting around the fact that I appeared to be the only person in the building who didn't know what was happening.

"You mean Scott hasn't told you?" She ought to get a job in a spa giving salt scrubs, she was so practiced at rubbing it into people's wounds.

"Well, no. He hasn't."

"That guy is unbelievable."

"I know," I agreed. "So what *is* going on, Courtney?"

"Hostile takeover," she said smugly.

"What?"

"Hostile takeover." She slumped back, safe in the knowledge that she wasn't going to be doing a scrap of work today. Then she reached into a drawer and pulled out a throat lozenge—oh, yes, because she planned on doing a *lot* of talking.

"So where's Scott? Has Daniel fired him?" I asked, not really understanding what she meant.

"Elizabeth, you're so naïve sometimes."

"Listen, will you just please tell me what's going on? My boss is missing, his first assistant's not here, and his furniture is being removed from the premises."

"It's not being removed from the premises. It's being taken to the fourth floor." She took off her sandal and admired her pedicure. I wanted to throttle her.

"Courtney." I tried the warning tone that Scott and Luke used to such great effect on me.

Weirdly, it seemed to work. She sat up straight, put her sandal back on, and explained, "Katherine Watson and Scott have formed an alliance with the backing of the board to take over The Agency. Daniel has been ousted as president, and there's now a battle royale to lure clients. Daniel's setting up his own management group and wants to take the big names."

I looked at her in disbelief. This meant that I never had to see Daniel Rosen again. I would never have to pass him in the corridors and hiss at him as if I were Othello and he my Iago. Though if I ever crossed his path on the red carpet at the Oscars, I might still be tempted to trip him up or shoot peas at him from afar.

"Scott's president?" I was flabbergasted.

"He and Katherine are copresidents."

"Oh, my God! I had no idea."

"Nobody did. So for once you weren't the only one in the dark." She stared pointedly at Lara as she walked in through the door looking very casual in Joie pants and T-shirt, with her shades on.

"Morning," Lara said, and strolled on by to her station, where she tossed her khaki Marc Jacobs purse and began clearing out her desk.

"Oh, some people don't waste any time," Courtney snapped. "Moving to the fourth floor already, are we?"

"Actually, I'm moving to The Colony." Lara smiled and winked at me. For once Courtney was speechless. "Elizabeth, can you and I have a word in private?" she asked and pointed to Scott's erstwhile office.

"Sure," I said, and we wandered in and leaned against the few sticks of furniture left.

The room had a hollow echo, and shafts of dust flickered in the sunlight. Nothing remained to suggest that Scott had ever been here. I wondered who would move in next. There was obviously going to be an enormous reshuffle.

"You know that I couldn't tell you about this, don't you, Elizabeth?" Lara slipped her sunglasses up onto her head and looked imploringly at me. "I didn't even really know that much about it myself. Just that Scott was really stressed and excited. And he only told me vaguely in the end, because I accused him of having an affair with Katherine Watson when they started going to meetings alone off the premises."

"I suppose I do understand." I shrugged. "But it was a bit hard to bear Courtney's smugness."

"Oh, God, I know. And she's going to be even harder to live with when she finds out that she's being promoted to a junior agent under the new regime." Lara rolled her eyes to the ceiling.

"She is?" Poor unsuspecting clients, was all I could think.

"Scott wants to keep Mike happy and on the same side, so he promised he'd do that for him."

Lara and I looked at one another and both said "Whatever" at the same time.

"Anyway, it's all good, I guess," she laughed.

"Yeah, now when you marry Scott, you're going to be one of the most powerful wives in Hollywood," I told her. But she already knew that.

When Lara left for a busy morning of shopping and a pregnancy yoga class, I idled back to my desk and wondered what was going to happen to me now. Would I still be working for Scott? Would I still be an assistant? I tried not to listen to Talitha and Courtney, who were bitching in the kitchen next door about Lara's new purse and trying to make head or tail of The Colony comment. At least for once I knew something that they didn't. Was *this* how it felt to be important?

No sooner had I sat down than I heard a terrible keening sound from behind me. I turned around when I realized that it was coming from Victoria's office.

"Get your filthy hands off my things!" she was shrieking.

"Sorry, Miss, but I've got orders to pack up all your things and escort you from the premises," a security guard was telling her.

"How dare you?" Victoria yelled, and then she emerged into the main office area with her arms full of Barbies. "How dare you hold my dolls by their hair?"

"Sorry, Miss, I'll be more careful with them. I just have to get them, and you, out of the building," he said. Courtney slid out of the kitchen and materialized beside me.

"Victoria's going with Daniel to set up the management group. She told Scott this morning that she would rather live in her car than work for a no-talent junkie like him."

"Wow, go Victoria!" I said. "I didn't think she had it in her."

"Go Victoria is right," Talitha said as she joined us, and we all three watched in amazement as Victoria exited with her armload of little friends. "And if you touch me or my dolls again, I will murder you!" she said. Then she screamed at the poor, horrified security guard till he backed off.

"Oh, well, good to know that all that primal-screaming practice was useful for something, hey?" Talitha giggled as the door slammed shut behind my banshee of a mentor.

With nothing much else to do other than marvel openmouthed over recent events, I went to my e-mail to see what Jason had sent me. Another creepy apology would do me very nicely. I wasn't noble enough not to want to get my pound of flesh from him. What I read was actually worth much more:

TO: SCOTT WAGNER
CC: ELIZABETH MILLER
FROM: JASON F. BLUM

SUBJECT: REPRESENTATION

Dear Scott:

It was good to meet with you yesterday evening, and I thank you for taking the time to see me at what I know is a critical juncture for you. It was much appreciated.

I simply wanted to confirm my decision to remain with The Agency as a client of yours rather than transfer with Daniel Rosen to another management company. This, as we discussed, is entirely due to my allegiance and respect for your colleague Elizabeth Miller. I have had extensive dealings with her and have found her to be exceptionally inspiring, hardworking, and, in short, extraordinary. To forgo the professional guidance of Elizabeth would, I feel, be detrimental to my career.

Therefore I hope that The Agency will agree to manage my career as a writer and director henceforth.

Yours truly,
Jason Blum

Ha, I thought. Then I was overwhelmed by gratitude toward Jason. I picked up my phone and called his cell.

"This is either my agent Scott Wagner or Elizabeth Miller calling me." He'd obviously programmed The Agency into his phone already, presumably so that he could speak with Daniel, though. "I'd know that number anywhere."

"It's Lizzie." I smiled.

"I knew it was you, darling." Darling? That was new. And very un-Jason.

"Where are you? Are you busy?" I asked, wondering if he was over at Revolution in a creative meeting.

"I'm at this great spa. Shame you have to work, or you could come join me."

"Okay, don't rub it in, buddy," I warned. "I just called to say thank you for sending that e-mail to Scott. It was really good of you."

"Yeah, well, I didn't want to fuck you over and not redeem myself." I could hear rushing water in the background and the strains of a woman's laughter. "'Cause I've seen what happens to people who screw with you."

"What do you mean?"

"I mean, look at Daniel Rosen. He does one tiny deal behind your back, and the Four Horsemen of the Apocalypse come to seek vengeance against him on your behalf." Jason laughed.

"You're so dramatic, Jason." I shook my head and sighed. "But I like it."

"So what's going to happen to you in the shake-up?" Jason asked while multitasking in some indiscernible way. But I knew distraction when I heard it at the other end of the phone.

"I guess nothing. I mean, I'll move to the fourth floor. Scott will be president, and things will carry on pretty much as normal. Don't you think?" I hadn't really had time to assimilate the events of the day, let alone predict what might become of us all. Although Courtney as a junior agent was pretty encouraging—if she got a promotion, then there was always hope for me.

"Are you crazy, Lizzie?" Jason said. "I sent that e-mail to give Scott a heads-up on how great you are. Also he has to appreciate that thanks to you The Agency now has an extra three million dollars' worth of business, and . . . well, I hate to sound conceited, but according to *Entertainment Weekly,* today I am one of the hottest properties in young Hollywood. I am a Spielberg of the future. So he should be grateful to you that he has my business."

"Jason, you are so far up your own ass already." I laughed. "Does it really say that in *Entertainment Weekly,* by the way?"

"Oh, and much more besides. Let me tell you, I am what they call a prestige client. The fact that I went with Scott and not Daniel in this takeover will mean that The Agency is now seen as the hot, in place to be. Others will follow." Jason laughed loudly. I sort of knew that he was telling the truth.

"Okay, well, since you're such a rock star, you better go and make out with a chick in a hot tub or something," I told him. "I'll call you later so you can slum it and say in interviews how you still keep in touch with your old friends and haven't changed a bit."

"Darling, I'll take you to L'Orangerie for the best chocolate soufflé you've ever tasted," he said. "Warm love coming from the West, okay?"

"Okay," I said as Jason hung up. I had a feeling that in the future Jason might become my most amusing friend. Already the scratchy sweaters had gone, he was suddenly cognizant of every sleazy Hollywood phrase and expensive restaurant, and I suspected that he was not multitasking alone in the Jacuzzi. He'd always been sweet and easy to be around, but rich, famous, powerful, successful, Academy Award–nominated Jason was going to be too much fun to miss.

I clicked onto the *Hollywood Reporter* online to see whether there was any breaking news on our takeover. Clearly, the embargo on information was still in effect, because there wasn't a hint anywhere. I knew, though, that it would be huge news in the industry. It was also the sort of piece that *Vanity Fair* would write a feature on one day. They'd make it seem like a den of vipers and then talk about the constellations of stars we managed and whose loyalties had lain where and what carnage of egos had ensued.

I thought back on my part in these historic occurrences. Really, I'd been as clueless about this takeover as I had about so many other things in my time here. Though I suspected that if I were ever in the same situation again, knowing all that I know now, I would be a much more savvy operator. Certainly the likes of Ryan would never be able to get one past me again. Especially if I found him with his head in my boss's filing cabinet. Next time I'd just close it on him. I even felt that I could handle an abusive harpy like Victoria if one ever happened to cross my path in the future. Also, after seeing the merit in *Sex Addicts in Love,* I felt more confident of my ability to spot good material.

I looked at my computer clock—half an hour to go until we all had to report to the boardroom. I was looking forward to seeing Katherine and Scott, the new captains of our ship, deliver their news. I wondered whether Scott would have shaved.

I decided to go and get a Diet Coke from the kitchen. Now that Daniel wasn't here, we could all rebel and fill the fridge with cans of soda whose labels didn't face outward. But as I stood up, my phone rang.

"Lizzie."

"Scott?"

"How you doing down there, Lizzie-o?"

I was flattered that in the midst of what was doubtless chaos, he found time to remember me.

"I'd love it if you could come up here and tune in my plasma for me," he said. I might have known that he wouldn't think to fill in his second assistant—who he wasn't fucking—on developments.

"Sure. I'll be up in a minute. Where are you, exactly?"

"My new office."

I loved how Scott was so instinctively a survivor. He wouldn't have dreamed of saying he was in Daniel's *old* office. That would have been to acknowledge that Daniel had once worked here. But under the new order, Daniel might as well have never existed. You had to be ruthless to get ahead in this Mickey Mouse industry.

"I'll be there," I said, reading between the lines and assuming that it was Daniel's old office. Though I'd be billyclubbed by the thought police for even having that cross my mind.

On my way through the lobby, I caught sight of a diminutive figure with a balding head standing outside with the pack of journalists. At first I wasn't sure if my eyes were deceiving me. It looked like Daniel. I took a slight detour via the vase of flowers on the reception desk so that I could get a better look through the glass doors. And, curiously enough, it *was* Daniel. He was speaking into a boom in front of a TV camera. Talking animatedly. I knew that it would all be a lot of horseshit about amicable partings and wanting to explore new frontiers. Only today he looked smaller and older. I suppose he was just stripped of his power. The suit was the same, and the smooth attitude was the same—he just looked very ordinary. I was overcome with the urge to bounce peanuts off his shiny pate, but, fortunately for him, I was all out of bar snacks, so I went on my merry way to Scott's new floor. The king was dead, long live the king.

As I rode the elevator up, I wondered what Scott had in store for me. Except to get me to tune his plasma, of course. Could Jason be right? Might I be in line for some new challenge at The Agency? I mean, I wasn't expecting anything, but it would be nice to have some sort of recompense for what I'd lost out on when Jason screwed me.

"Lizzie, come in."

As I stepped out of the shining elevator doors onto the fourth floor, Scott was standing in his office down the hall. All Daniel's country-house antiques were gone, and in place of the Stubbs paintings and the red, leather-bound rows of books on the library shelves were a Space Invaders machine, a jukebox, and Scott's multiplex-size entertainment center.

"Whaddayathink?"

"I think it's going to be great," I said truthfully, walking past a row of small glass offices and wondering who'd be filling them. At the other end of the corridor, I noticed Katherine dressed in heavenly shades of caramel arranging an orchid on her desk. Her room was literally deluged with congratulatory bunches of flowers. On the back of her promotion alone, the stock price on lilies must have skyrocketed. I suspected that together these two were going to be a pretty dynamic duo, and I genuinely looked forward to working under them—in some capacity.

"Come on down!" Scott yelled along the hallway. "It's in here. It's kinda fuzzy."

"Don't you have an electrician or someone who can do that for you?" I asked as I approached a bunch of wires hanging out of the back of the screen.

"I don't trust anyone like I trust you," he said as he tested his chair wheels out across the new long-length floor of his office. On parquet flooring. For the thrill of whizzing on his chair across his new office alone, I was sure that Scott's hostile takeover had been worth it.

"Congratulations, by the way," I said as I flicked his aerial until the screen was as clear as day. "I mean, I don't know the full details of the takeover, but the changes all seem to be good."

Scott moved his chair back into its rightful place behind his desk. Then he folded his hands and rested them on the familiar cherry wood in front of him. "Can you close the door, Elizabeth?" he suddenly said as he transformed himself into the head of this insanely powerful Hollywood company. I did as I was told. "Take a seat," he told me.

"Thanks." This felt a bit too reminiscent of my firing episode. I pulled up a chair and sat down.

"See, here's the thing, Elizabeth." He paused momentarily. "Here at The Agency, we really appreciate what you do."

"I'm glad."

"I got Jason Blum's e-mail this morning, and it's because of you that we as a company now have this great opportunity to work with an exciting new director."

"Well . . ." I said modestly, "I'm not sure about that."

"No shit, Sherlock." His voice rang out around the half-furnished room. "You have taste. You have judgment. And in a couple of years' time, we're going to be looking a couple of those Academy Awards in the eye, thanks to your ability to spot a good thing when you see it."

"Oh, Scott, really, I think that may be a little premature," I said. "But thank you." I didn't want to seem ungrateful for his praise.

"Plus, we're going to make a fair amount of cash on Jason Blum's career, I'll bet."

"Well, yes, that's probably true."

"And you know me, Lizzie, I'm a fair guy." He laughed. "Most of the time."

"Well, you haven't hit me with a deck of cards yet, so I'd say that's pretty fair." I shrugged and smiled. Embarrassingly, he didn't laugh at this. He simply continued as if I'd never spoken.

"I'm a fair guy, and I believe in rewarding the loyalty of my employees. Now, *you,* Lizzie"—he pointed at me the way a sports coach might point at his star player—"you are something else. You've put your ass on the line for me. You've been a good friend to Lara, which I know only too well isn't a piece of pie. You've worked hard and brought in new talent. And I don't know how you came to work for me in the first place"—I wasn't going to put my hand up at this point and tell him that it was Daniel's doing—"but I am glad that fate brought you to my door." He paused for a moment. Go, Scottie, I thought breathlessly.

"I'm glad I got the opportunity to work for you, too," I assured him.

"I guess what I really want to say is that I believe in rewarding greatness. So I have an offer to make to you, Lizzie." He sat up in his seat and beamed at me expectantly.

"You do?" My toes were fizzing with anticipation. A million thoughts raced through my mind, but, like swirling snowflakes, none of them settled.

"I do." He leaned forward and looked me in the eye. I sat up straight in preparation for what he had to ask me.

"I also like you, Lizzie. You're a great kid. You have a level head. You're easy on the eye." He winked. That would go down well with Human Resources, I thought.

"Lizzie?"

"Yes, Scott?"

"Lizzie, as you know, there's going to be a vacancy in this office as of today."

"Yes?"

"And I would really, truly love it if you'd agree to come and work for me."

I held my breath and blinked. "Yes?"

"As my first assistant."

ACKNOWLEDGMENTS

We would like to thank some special people who have helped to bring this book into being.

The Blonde, our éminence grise. You are a genius, a loyal friend, and the wildest, greatest girl in the world.

Barney Cordell, with loving thanks—for your poker expertise and all the other things you do so brilliantly.

Emma Parry, who miraculously manages to be Rumpole of the Bailey, Don King, and Mother Hen all at once. We're so happy we found you.

Molly Stern, for your vision, enthusiasm, and generous ministrations.

Jon Levin, who is one of a rare breed—a dedicated agent and a lovely man.

Kamin Mohammadi, for your encouragement and for always laughing in the right places.

Meg Davidson, for your kitchen table, unerring hospitality, and the chats.

Marcie Hartley, for the joy with which you allow us to invade your life every time we descend on L.A.

Jason Blum, our favorite producer and greatest friend, who would never be seen dead in a yak wool sweater. Thanks for all that warm love from the West.

Lloyd Levin, unbeknownst to you a lot of this originated in your den. We promise to replace the Pop Tarts.

Richard Charkin, for the cocktails. We trust the adoption papers are in the mail.

Simon Amies, for your round-the-clock support and encouragement—even when you didn't feel like giving it.

And thanks to all our friends, who put up with the panics and the flakiness with good grace and are always there when we need a margarita.